RAPTOR'S RIDGE

A MAX BLAKE MYSTERY

WILLIAM FLORENCE

WILD**Blue**
PRESS

WildBluePress.com

RAPTOR'S RIDGE published by:

WILDBLUE PRESS
P.O. Box 102440
Denver, Colorado 80250

ISBN 978-1-947290-75-4   Trade Paperback
ISBN 978-1-947290-74-7   eBook

Interior Formatting/Book Cover Design by Elijah Toten
www.totencreative.com

ALSO BY WILLIAM FLORENCE:

The Max Blake Mystery series ...

Misery Ridge
Faraway Ridge
Snowfall Ridge
Emerald Ridge
Emerald Ridge
Melia Ridge
Raven's Ridge

The Max Blake Western series ...

The Killing Trail
Trail of Revenge
Trail to Redemption
Trail to Dead Man's Gulch
Trail from Crooked River

ACKNOWLEDGMENTS

To Bill Kohlmeyer, for lending not only a stately name but also his vast wisdom from more than 30 years of experience on police matters; Michael J. Parker and Michael McClinton, for their superb legal expertise and treasured friendship; Andrew Bone, Bob LeRoy, and Tim Hannan, for their suggestions and advice during the early days when the manuscript was still evolving; Erin F. Lee, Clifford Corn, Alisa Angelakis, and Janel Foster, for their insightful critiques and timely suggestions as the manuscript took shape; Bernie Knab, whose critical early reading produced key revelations; and Steven P. Jackson of WildBlue Press, for his sage advice on the changing nature of the publishing business.

Additional Acknowledgments

- Edgar Allen Poe for a passage from *"The Raven"*
- Bob Nolan for a passage from *"Tumbling Tumbleweeds"*
- Dylan Thomas for a passage from *"A Child's Christmas in Wales"*
- Lewis Carroll for a passage from *"The Walrus and the Carpenter"*
- Gerald Marks and Seymour Simons for a snippet of *"All of Me"*

CAST OF PRIMARY CHARACTERS

RAPTOR'S RIDGE

Dashiell "AJ" Bohn: Timber king, retired multi-billionaire, owner of Raptor's Ridge

Audrey Flowers: Former movie star, AJ Bohn's paramour

Dr. Floyd Strand: Bohn's personal physician

Russell Vineyard: Butler and personal assistant to Bohn

Edward L. "Ned" McClinton: Bohn's personal attorney

Paul Deeker, AKA The Snarl: One of Bohn's bodyguards

Tom Deeker: Brother of Paul Deeker and another bodyguard

Charlie and Francis: Members of the Deeker brothers' goon squad

TOWNIES

Maxwell Blake: Private detective, college professor; former investigative reporter

Caeli Brown: Max's girlfriend

Michael J. Parker: Max Blake's lawyer

Dr. Charles Wilson: State medical examiner

Lawrence Hultz Fuller: County district attorney

Jim Maddaux: Restaurant owner and Max's friend

Todd Wright: Automobile dealership owner and Max's friend

LOCAL LAW ENFORCEMENT

Bill Kohlmeyer: Chief of police

Robert LeRoy: County sheriff

Ken Chichester: State police liaison officer

Lieutenant Patrick McDonough: The police chief's primary aide

Lieutenant Charles V. Downing: City police officer and shakedown mastermind

William "Buzzsaw" Stone: Key member of Downing's shakedown crew

Ron Clarin: Recalcitrant member of Downing's shakedown crew

JOHN DAY PARTICIPANTS

Little Cliff Corn: Chief of police

Betty Sours: Retired high school teacher

Lucas McCoy: Retired high school principal

Lieutenant Timothy J. Petrone: Head of the State Police post in Grant County

Nicholas Drake, AKA Axton Hoyt, *et al*: Serial killer

Monte Simmons: Wilderness guide

Jim Reeves: Horse wrangler

Fred Chancey: local character

RAPTOR'S RIDGE

A MAX BLAKE MYSTERY

PROLOGUE

IN THE FRONT DOOR

FIVE YEARS EARLIER

He first spotted her at the local Safeway store and was smitten.

Absolutely smitten.

He considered the idea and laughed.

Smitten, he thought. *Such an old-fashioned word. But it's exactly right.*

He watched her waltz past the cereal boxes and breakfast snacks and knew – he just *knew* – that she was exactly what he'd been searching for.

And what better way to find a young housewife, he thought, *than to hang out at the local supermarket and ... shop the aisles?*

She was spectacular, he quickly decided, with wavy blonde hair and radiant, sparkling blue eyes that reminded him of the cheerleaders they show on TV during the Saturday afternoon football games – the extraordinarily pretty ones, where the cameras move in close as the girls smile and kick their trim legs high in the air. She had a natural wholesomeness about her that was both eye-catching and alluring – and he knew that he had to have her.

Right now.

The only question was how he would pull it off.

It was true that he'd been thinking about such a moment for weeks, but he didn't want to be impulsive. Impulsive could get you killed – something he'd learned first-hand in Special Ops, when a buddy with a quick temper and a penchant for mayhem and sniffing out trouble didn't make it home.

But he had to have her anyway, after all of that field time and all of the months that he'd spent away from civilization and any semblance of what rational people would call a normal life.

And he knew in that instant – in that single blink of an eye as she unknowingly sashayed past, without so much as a sideways glance – that this was going to be his new life.

My new normal ...

He smiled when he noticed the curves beneath the sweater and her perfect white teeth – *All the better to eat you with, my dear* – and the large wedding ring that she proudly wore on her left hand. Even from a dozen feet away, he could tell that the ring was extravagant, and he thought of it now as his to keep: a trophy of sorts, just like the ones he'd saved from the battlefield.

He had to get to her first, however, which was no easy task. This wasn't Afghanistan or Iraq. He was in a grocery store in suburban north San Diego, and he knew that security cameras and rent-a-cops and Neighborhood Watch associations and common, everyday busybodies could thwart his best tactical efforts if he moved without proper caution.

He decided on a loaf of Italian bread and a tin of coffee and left the store after paying with cash in the express line. He walked swiftly across the parking lot, pulling his ball cap low across his forehead to keep his face shielded from the surveillance cameras that were strategically mounted on light poles. He climbed into the non-descript white panel van that he'd liberated the night before from a used car lot in

Chula Vista, focused his eyes on the storefront, and waited patiently.

She was out of the store eight minutes later with three plastic bags filled with groceries, which she loaded into a sporty green Subaru wagon a couple of lanes over from where he was parked. He started the van and headed toward the exit, which spilled shoppers onto a busy thoroughfare. Urban planning was his friend. All supermarket traffic was forced to exit to the right, and he took that turn and moments later pulled into another parking lot down the street – one that serviced a strip mall with a dozen or more smaller shops – and immediately looped around in a quick half-circle so that the van was ready to again enter the main thoroughfare.

When the Subaru carrying his delectable target passed by, he merged into the passing traffic and tagged along at a discreet distance.

The Subaru turned left at a traffic signal, wound its way through a narrow residential neighborhood, turned left at another major cross street, turned right three blocks later, and eventually passed a sign that welcomed visitors to the Oaks North Golf Club.

Perfect, he thought. *No wonder she looks so ... wholesome.*

When she pulled into the driveway of a rambling one-story ranch home that was painted in moderate earth tones appropriate to the subdivision's codes, he continued past at a slow pace and noted that the sign above the front door read, simply, *The Walkers.*

What could be easier?

He wound his way toward the golf course, pulled into a parking lot, climbed into the back of the van, and decided on a San Diego Gas & Electric uniform from the many selections that he'd left hanging inside flimsy, see-through laundry bags.

The van was in her driveway twelve minutes later, and he pulled a SDG&E ball cap tight on his head. He leaned across the front seat and grabbed the clipboard and cheap plastic pen from the passenger's seat, then left the van and stepped smartly up the concrete walkway with a confident, unhurried stride that belied the jackhammer racing of his pulse.

"Mrs. Walker?" he asked as she opened the front door and looked at him inquiringly.

"That's right," she said. "Can I help you?"

You have no idea ... he thought, maintaining his sincere grin.

"Mrs. Alice Walker?" he asked, this time examining the clipboard in his hand as though it held pertinent information.

"No, Terri Ann Walker," she said, a crease of doubt instantly shading her forehead.

He stared harder at the clipboard, looking momentarily confused, and ran his index finger along imaginary lines, then smiled fleetingly. "Oh, yes, here it is," he said. "Sorry. You are Mrs. Terri Ann Walker, of 17995 Cumana Terrace – that's right, isn't it?"

"Yes, that's me. Is something wrong?"

"I'm afraid there is, ma'am, though there's really no need to panic, I assure you," he said, looking into her eyes once again.

God, she's even better than I thought ...

"I'm Drake Nichols, from the gas company. We've had reports of a leak in the area, and I've been sent to check the neighborhood and make sure we don't have a major problem. I've already seen to a couple of your neighbors' homes" – he waved his free arm to the east, pulling the clipboard closer to his chest – "and wondered if you'd mind if I checked ..."

"No, please – it's fine," she interrupted. "What do you need from me?"

Don't get me started ...

"I just need to check the connection around the side of the house," he said, flashing his best *Everything's-under-control* smile. "But the first stop's always here, at the front door. I didn't want you to see someone poking around and think that I was trying to …"

He paused and grinned shyly, letting her fill in the unfinished thought.

"No, that's not a problem at all," she said. "Go right ahead. The gas meter – is that what you need?"

"Yes, ma'am."

"The meter is on that side of house" – she pointed toward the west – "over there."

"Yes, that's right. Thank you, ma'am," he said. "Better safe than sorry, I always say. I'll let you know if I find a problem, of course."

"Sure," she said. "I'd appreciate that – thank you."

He tugged on the bill of the ball cap, just as they used to do it in the old cowboy movies, and stepped quickly off the porch – *ever the smiling, accommodating professional* – moving quickly around the west side of the house.

No husband home, he thought. *She'd have called him right away when I rang the bell.*

No toys in the yard, either. Better yet.

He spotted the meter, drew up close enough to examine the dials, pulled a cigarette lighter from his pocket and held it next to the metal, as though he were taking a reading, shook his head back and forth – *just in case she's looking through the window* – and then headed back to the front door again, making imaginary notes on the clipboard as he walked.

He rang the bell and stepped in close. She opened the door promptly, a questioning look on her face, and asked, "Is everything all right?"

"I'm afraid not, ma'am. There's a potential problem, I'm sad to say – good thing I caught it when I did." He noted the look of concern that flashed across her face and knew that he had her. "If you'll let me in for just one minute, I'll check to make sure the gas levels are all right before I work on the connection. If they aren't, you'll need to evacuate the house for a few minutes, until everything is …"

"No, of course – come in, please," she said, stepping aside so that he could easily pass. "Should I get out of the house right now, while you check?"

"That's not necessary, Mrs. Walker," he said as he stepped inside, keeping his body between his target and the door. "In fact, I much prefer it this way."

He glanced at his watch – *not quite 1 p.m.* – and smiled again. He figured that he had at least two hours, perhaps three if he wanted to push things.

Plenty of time ...

He abandoned the van three blocks from the ocean, wiping it down to remove any lingering fingerprints before packing the gas company uniform that had so easily disarmed his prey into a paper grocery bag.

As he headed toward a busy business district five blocks away, he began to hum and then silently sang a few lines of an old jazz tune that suddenly ran through his head:

"All of me. Why not take all of me?

Can't you see, I'm no good without you ... "

That made him laugh out loud, and he could hear Louis Armstrong and Billie Holliday and even Willie Nelson, almost as though they were standing next to him at that very moment.

He swerved into an alley two blocks later and dropped the paper bag into an open dumpster. He left the alley for the sidewalk on the main thoroughfare a moment later, still humming happily to himself. It occurred to him that the plan he'd successfully orchestrated that day to capture the attention of the lovely Terri Ann Walker was modestly efficient, given its hasty execution – the thought of the word made him laugh aloud – but it would need some perfecting if he wanted to use it again.

It's all about the details, he thought. *One after another, like rats in the desert – a place for everything and everything in its place.*

He began to run the myriad little niceties of the just-finished encounter through his mind, again and again, as he boarded a city bus that would return him to the flophouse he was renting by the week. He took a seat close to the exit doors and admitted during the evaluation that some things went better than others and that the next time he encountered a woman with such considerable allure, he would be smarter, and he would plan more thoroughly, and he would take fewer chances, and – best of all – he would allow himself more time.

He stuck his hand into his jeans pocket and wrapped his fingers around the large wedding ring that he'd slipped from Mrs. Walker's finger, just before she'd slipped away for good.

On this first day of the hunt, Old Saint Nick, as he sometimes called himself, didn't learn all of the tricks and trademarks that he would use in his future encounters with the Terri Ann Walkers of this world.

But he had to admit that it was a start – a hell of a good start, in fact.

And if it went well …

… there's plenty more where that came from.

Plenty more.

ONE

EUCHRE TOURNAMENTS
AND NO SLEEP

EARLY MONDAY MORNING
FIRST WEEK

The phone rang sometime after 2 a.m.

I was having trouble nodding off anyway after a two-day euchre tournament at the local country club, where I'd placed second and drank enough whiskey to float a small ketch during the forty-eight-hour marathon. Now I was lying in bed, the air hot and muggy, and I kept running the last play of the day – the one that cost me first place – through my mind again and again. I struggled to find a comfortable spot on the sheets, trying for the life of me to forget the hand and the play and the damned tournament altogether.

If only I'd led with the 10 of Clubs, I kept musing.

The mere thought of it would make me groan all over again, and from time to time I'd sneak a peek at the cheap wind-up alarm clock at the side of the bed, cursing aloud when I saw that another fifteen minutes had slipped by and I still just couldn't let it go.

The image of that self-righteous, smug, pompous, preening Connelly kept playing, over and over, in my head. I could picture him in the last few minutes of the marathon, just before he finally broke me. He'd tried to look casual in his cheap Sears and Roebuck suit, even as his eyes darted wildly around the room, broadcasting the triumphant emotions that he couldn't keep in check. It was like a trip back in time, to the marbles tournament in the first grade: his ugly face, his lurid grin, his whoop of success with the last trick.

"No-good bastard," I muttered.

I cursed aloud again and smacked the pillow a couple of times, then tried it from the other side, doing my best to find a comfortable spot that would finally put me out.

I was tempted to get up and grab the bottle of Powers Irish that I kept in the cupboard and have another go at it. Hell, I was desperate enough to climb out of bed and pull together a lecture for one of the classes that I teach as a professor of journalism at the local community college, where I've worked full-time for the past however many years … *too many to count.*

And then the damn telephone started to ring.

I tried to ignore the incessant jingle, figuring that if I gave up on sleep now, it would never come. But the phone keep ringing, and sleep wasn't coming anyway, and I finally leaned across the nightstand, snatched the black handle from its cradle, and barked into the line.

"You have any idea what time it is? This'd better be good."

OK, I'll admit: I was still seething over my failure to lead with the Club, and I was still hopped up on the coffee that I'd gulped to try and stay sharp during the final hours of the euchre marathon. Otherwise, I would've been a bit more polite, if only because I moonlight during my time away from the classroom as a part-time private detective to keep the creditors at bay.

Who else would be calling at this hour but a potential client?

"You Blake?"

The voice was a snarl, as though its owner were somehow angry with me, angry with himself, angry with the world, angry with everyone and everything in it. I didn't recognize it – not with just two words hurled at me – but I took the opening instead of asking the logical question.

"You were expecting the president of GM, maybe?" I said.

"A regular wise guy," The Snarl whispered, deep and throaty this time. Then he added, "The boss wants to see ya. Right now."

"All right, I'll bite," I said. "Who the hell are you, and who in hell is the boss?"

"Don't matter 'bout me," The Snarl shot back. "The boss is AJ Bohn."

I let that sit a moment, then said, "Are we talking about *the* AJ Bohn?"

I tried to sound casual, but I'm certain that my effort fell short, considering the power of the name. It's not every day that some flunky with a snarling voice representing the richest timber baron our city has ever known calls you on the telephone, at any hour, and tells you to haul your ass out of bed to meet with the great man.

"Only one I know about," The Snarl said. "I've sent a car. It'll be outside yer place in five minutes or less. I expect you'll be ready when it arrives."

So here's the deal: In this town, you don't turn down a call from AJ Bohn, even if the actual words of invitation are delivered by a surrogate. I certainly wasn't about to break precedent with a bad idea that, given Bohn's reputation in at least some circles, actually might get me pistol-whipped – or worse.

I'll also admit to being nervous: Bohn's name alone makes people – smart people; thinking people – nervous. And I'll confess that when I get nervous, for whatever reason, I often change from mild-mannered college professor into fast-talking smart-ass, a trait that my sainted mother never seems to appreciate.

But I was ornery enough, given the hour and my recent caffeine and whiskey intake, to play hard to get in an effort to elicit more information, and I feigned a long yawn and waited.

I could hear The Snarl breathing on the other end of the line, and I also could sense that he was growing impatient. He apparently wasn't used to dealing with people who didn't jump and scrape when he pulled out his boss's name, like a derringer drawn from a vest pocket, and hurled it across the telephone wires.

"Hey, Blake: You still there?" he eventually hissed.

"How's that?" I asked, playing dumb.

The Snarl wasn't happy, and he barked into the line this time, his voice lowered another full octave: "I'm askin', are you still there? You can't hear or somethin' all the sudden?"

I grinned at that, delighted that I wasn't on some computer hook-up where the guy could see my face. "Sure," I said. "What time is it, anyway?"

"You got four minutes," The Snarl hissed again. "Don't keep 'em waiting. Do that – keep 'em waiting – you won't like what happens. Like the old guy says in the commercial: I guarantee it."

I mustered up another yawn. "I'll be down when I'm good and ready, if at all. Tell 'em that – whoever 'them' is – and tell your boss the same."

I slammed the speaker down and chuckled, then pulled myself out of bed.

How could I do otherwise? – though it's not every day that you get the chance to mess around with one of AJ Bohn's henchmen.

I forced myself into the broom-closet-sized bathroom, where I studied my face in the mirror and didn't particularly like what I saw staring back through the cracked glass. The euchre tournament had taken its toll, all right. I looked as though I'd been forced to go ten rounds with the reigning middleweight champ, and the bastard had first tied one of my arms around my neck and then strapped it down tight.

"Well, this ought to be a hell of a good time," I muttered. I splashed some water on my face, shuddered a time or two, and did it again. I briefly considered shaving but figured that I didn't have the time. I was willing to let Bohn's minions wait, but I knew that within a minute or so of their arrival, they'd be out of the car and up to the door with knuckles rapping and threats shouted and god only knows what else. I didn't like the thought of my landlady opening her door to that scene. She was upset enough with me anyway, considering my ongoing inability to pay the miniscule rent on time. A scene like that might shove her over the edge and end up forcing me to find a new place to call home, if only temporarily.

Then again, considering what a dump this place is, that might not be such a bad thing, I thought, pulling on the same pair of pants that I'd worn throughout the euchre marathon.

I scrounged in the closet and found a shirt that I'd worn only a few times. I tucked it inside my trousers, looped a belt in place and got it in the right notch, and reached for a sports coat that more or less matched the rest of the ensemble. I thought about adding a tie, decided against it – *It's only AJ Bohn, for god's sake* – then grabbed a Smith & Wesson five-shot revolver from the nightstand and tucked it into the pocket of the sports coat. It's not my favorite carry piece. But it was handy, and I didn't want to dig around in the gun safe at that hour for one of my Walthers.

I started toward the door, realized that I wasn't wearing shoes, and fished around the side of the bed until I located a pair of well-scuffed Oxfords.

Close enough for government work.

In order, I stopped at the dresser to pocket some spare change, the apartment key, and my wallet; fished in the nightstand again for some extra .38 Special cartridges, which

I dropped into my pocket; and scribbled a brief note on the pad of paper that I kept on the stand near the bed:

AJ Bohn's thugs are coming to collect me, 2:15 a.m. Monday

"A little insurance never hurts – just in case," I muttered aloud, admiring my cursive. I examined the note carefully, found it to be a bit cryptic, and added:

Please find me if I don't return soon … MB

"Better," I muttered, though I doubted that it would help much if things turned ugly.

Then I started wondering about my obligations to my real job: college professor.

Let's see, I thought. *The tournament started Friday night and ran through Sunday. It's early Monday now, and I don't have to be back in the classroom until Tuesday morning.*

Thank god for catnaps and the summer schedule.

That's also when my grim sense of humor kicked in:

Of course, if Bohn decides to have me whacked, it won't matter anyway, though someone will have to cover the 11:30 class …

I looked out the window, peering through the musty curtains at the street below.

"Dammit," I mumbled. Bohn's boys – in a big, 4-wheel-drive SUV with windows that were as dark as the hour – already were in front of the decrepit boarding house, and I grunted and considered waiting for them to come up and issue an invitation. I actually liked the idea until I thought about poor Mrs. Broadbridge. I grabbed my fedora (and yeah, I know what you're thinking, but I'm a college professor; it's expected) and walked out the door, pulling it softly shut behind me, then tiptoed down the stairs.

What the hell, I thought. It was close to 2:30 a.m. at this point – *why needlessly wake the innocent, or the oblivious?*

I could already hear Bohn's boys clattering up the porch steps to the front door, and I stuck my hand in my pocket, grabbed the hard rubber grip of the revolver, and gained a small measure of comfort. I took a deep breath, pushed my way through the heavy oak door, and stepped onto the front porch.

Two men the size of refrigerators, heavy with muscle and menace, pulled up short and grinned in unison. They looked as though they'd stepped right out of the woods – no surprise, considering that we live in the heart of timber country in the Pacific Northwest – and I found myself checking their hands for shovels and axes. They wore matching Carhartt work shirts that must have been at least XXXL in size and still didn't fit. Stretching that much cloth across that broad a swath of human form was a foreign concept for anyone other than the maker of circus tents.

"You Blake?"

"You were expecting the King of England?"

"Save it. Let's get going, now – don't want to keep the boss waiting." His delivery was staccato, rapid-fire – like a standup comedian in some dingy after-hours joint.

"What's this about?" I asked as we headed toward the powerful SUV, the two ushers flanking me and guiding me along in a straight line.

"One thing you should know: We don't answer no questions," the same thug said without enthusiasm. "We deliver packages, and yer tonight's package. That's it. Just shut up and get in – best for everybody that way."

"A bit rude, aren't we?" I said as I clambered into the back seat. "I'd think wise guys working for AJ Bohn would brush up on their manners."

"That so?" the driver said as he settled in behind the wheel. "They said you was a college professor and some sort of part-time PI." He glanced at me in the rearview mirror now, holding my gaze. "They told us to play nice. I like to do what I'm told when it comes to Mister Bohn, so you get the benefit of the doubt. Charlie, on the other hand?" He glanced at the second lumberjack. "Charlie don't pay attention to niceties, I guess you'd say. Charlie does what he likes. I'd keep that in mind, I was you. Ain't that right, Charlie?"

The question prompted a single grunt in reply.

"Who's they?" I asked, ignoring the advice.

"What do you mean?" the driver asked.

"You said *they* told you to play nice. Who's they?"

That didn't bring a response, so I tried another strategy to keep the guy talking. "Charlie doesn't say much." No question attached – just a statement.

It had the intended effect.

"Charlie don't need to, though he does other things might surprise you. Then again, maybe not – maybe you wouldn't be surprised, seein' how yer a college professor an' all," the driver said, swiveling his head to face me. "But here's the thing. I got no beef with you, Mister College Professor. And Charlie's got no beef with you, so far's I know. Still an' all, we like a nice quiet ride when we work for Mister Bohn. And we got our orders, which is to deliver you to the estate in good shape. I suggest you shut up and sit back and enjoy the ride. Starting now."

The driver didn't wait for a reply. He put the rig into gear instead and slammed his foot hard on the accelerator. The big engine roared and sprang forward, and the thrust drove me back into the plush seat.

"Charlie and me, we're a good team," the driver sang out, straining to be heard over the engine. "Charlie goes his way an' I go mine, but we usually meet right in the middle – ya know?" He turned the wheel so hard as he added this last part that I had to fumble for the door handle to keep from sliding across the back seat. The tires reluctantly bit into the asphalt with a screeching roar, although the driver hardly seemed to notice. "Right now, Charlie's job is to make sure you stay safe. Mine, too. Buckle up – ya know?"

"I'd stay a whole lot safer if you'd slow down," I muttered. But even if I'd shouted the words, I doubt that either of my hosts would've heard them above the squeal of the tires and the ungodly roar of the SUV's powerful engine.

I could hear, time and again, the blare of a horn and the shriek of car tires as we sailed down the street at an alarming rate of speed. I kept waiting for the SUV to slow down, for the situation to improve, for some semblance of sanity to return to the moment.

And I wondered, not for the first time that night, whether I would've dozed off by now had I just let the damn telephone ring without bothering to pick it up.

"Next time," I muttered, but it already was too late.

TWO

IN BOCCA AL LUPO

MONDAY, 2:32 A.M.

The drive didn't take long, considering the early hour and the break-neck speeds that we traveled through Oregon's capital city, which I call home. Initially I had no idea where we were heading because my escorts decided to sail through myriad residential backstreets and alleyways before finally squealing onto a major north-south thoroughfare that I recognized from the number of well-lit fast-food establishments.

It also helped that it wasn't raining, something it does with mind-numbing consistency in this part of the country.

The driver, mindful of my earlier admonition regarding his social skills, caught my eye in the rearview mirror at one point and called, "You enjoying the ride, gumshoe?"

Gumshoe? I wondered. *Who uses a word like gumshoe?*

I didn't bother to reply – what was the point of engaging in mindless banter and further occupying the driver's attention? – and instead started looking for landmarks to indicate that we were heading to Raptor's Ridge, AJ Bohn's spectacular mansion on the hill.

The fact that we weren't flagged down by a passing patrol car was no great surprise. Bohn's name alone would cause many a cop in many a town in this dim region of the world to look the other way. The fact that he chose to make his home in our modest community of a hundred and twenty-five thousand rain-soaked, cheerless souls was likely reason enough to give him – and his hired help, as was the case here – a free pass whenever one was needed.

Here's what you need to know: AJ Bohn's extensive timber enterprises for decades represented jobs and money and a good livelihood for the residents of our thriving metropolis on the Willamette River. But his name also was associated with some of the seedier elements of modern society, including political graft and corruption on a scale that was said to reach into the governorships of six Western states, as well as the U.S. Senate and, potentially, beyond even that. Still, nothing had ever been proven; no significant corruption charges, in fact, had ever been successfully litigated. Most residents consequently agreed that a little side action from the great man on the hill – whatever it might be; if, in fact, it existed at all – was a small price to pay for the rest of the glutton-filled package that he brought to the city's table. And that much remained true today, even though timber hasn't been king in our state since the early 1980s.

The car sped through the twists and turns of the city's extended commercial area, five miles from the neighborhood I called home, and soon started climbing the southern hills, where everyone with half a brain knew that Bohn maintained his incredible domicile. The place was an enormous mansion, surrounded by perimeter fences and a massive security gate and trained attack dogs and heavily armed bodyguards and god only knew what else, day and night and through all seasons. I was familiar with the place – to a small degree, at least – from research that I'd done during my reporting days, when I'd worked for a handful of daily newspapers in the region. It was, simply put, a fortress, and a spectacular one at that.

I'll confess that I don't do well when riding in the back seat of car – the motion is the same for me as an ocean voyage in a small boat – and at this point in the trip, the speed and twisting and turning wasn't helping the matter any.

"You all right back there?" the driver called at one point, and he was grinning as his eyes met mine in the rearview mirror. "You look green, professor. Me an' Charlie suggest you don't soil the carpet."

I waved away the concern with a sideways flick of my wrist and wondered again why Bohn's henchmen were hustling me out of town. All sorts of crazy notions crossed my mind – including the possibility of a longstanding grudge from something that I might've written at some point during my newspaper career and subsequently forgot.

Then again, maybe the old boy wants to sign up for a journalism class and needs my signature on the add/drop form ...

The entire ordeal made me long for a drink. But I leaned back in the seat instead and counted the turns and twists in the highway, telling myself that every bend in the road the SUV successfully negotiated was one less that I'd have to tolerate before we arrived.

The rig eventually slowed and pulled to a stop. Big iron gates unfolded with a thrum of gears and electrical motors, and we lurched forward and just as quickly braked to another hard stop.

"All right, almost home," the driver said, swiveling his head. "Time to get out and look sharp, gumshoe."

Gumshoe again ...

I slid out of the car, but it was too dark to see much. The early morning air was bracing, and I took a couple of deep breaths, which actually helped to clear my head.

"Up ahead there," he said, pointing with a meaty finger, trying to prod me along.

"I don't need your help. Thanks just the same," I said, pushing in close and looking him square in the eye.

"Just trying to do my part," he said, his eyes never wavering. "I'd never forgive myself if you didn't feel welcome."

"I'll be sure to let the boss know," I said. "Just tell me what this is about."

The second henchman, the one called Charlie, spoke up then, the first time I'd heard him utter anything besides a grunt.

"All this polite talk don't mean much," he said, and I could see his eyes, which were birdlike in the light cast by the SUV's headlights, dart back and forth. "The sooner we dump you off, the sooner we're shut of yer ugly face and on to the next. Skip on up the road an' keep yer mouth shut."

"He speaks at last," I offered.

"Like I told ya, Charlie goes his own way," the driver said. "But I'd suggest you listen up and get a move on. Already said it won't do to keep the boss waitin'."

He urged me forward, using his hand, and fell in step just behind my left arm, shoulder to shoulder with his helper, steering me toward a light that had abruptly snapped on immediately ahead. We hadn't yet made it to the main house; I looked around and guessed that we were at some sort of way station for Bohn's bodyguards as they manned the perimeter gate.

I was greeted with a hostile glare and a nasty gravel-voiced welcome by a tall, slender man who was wearing a gray suit that was two sizes too large and a pork-pie hat that was at least two sizes too small for his head. His right hand was thrust deep into the pocket of his coat, and it didn't take much imagination to know what his trigger finger was wrapped around.

I took a hard, lingering look and quickly determined that his face was as unpleasant as his gravel voice, though neither realization gave me any great satisfaction.

"You're The Snarl, right?" I said. Given the absurdity of it all, I didn't hesitate to crack a little wise, despite the placement of the greeter's hand inside his coat pocket.

"The what?" he asked, his eyes lifting a bit, and I noted again that his voice sounded exactly like the one that had so rudely greeted me on the telephone.

"The guy who called me out on this nightmare, interrupting my beauty sleep," I said. "That's you. The Snarl. But I don't see Bohn anywhere …"

"It's Mister Bohn to you, bozo," he growled, his eyes instantly aflame. "And I ain't never talked to you before – not till now."

He turned to my escorts and said, "You pat him down?" When they glanced at each other, shrugged, and looked as though they'd been sent to the store for a quart of milk but came back empty-handed, he muttered a couple of choice curse-words.

"Do it. Now," he commanded.

Here's something else you should know about me: When it comes to the fight-or-flight-or-freeze response, I always choose fight – regardless of how reckless and foolhardy it might seem or how nervous I might be. This is likely a throwback to my formative years – I'd grown up in a rough neighborhood with a bunch of pushy little thugs-in-waiting – and I'd used the instinct throughout my reporting career and also from time to time in the classroom. Besides, I'd about had it with the hard-sell clown act at Bohn's front gate, and I took it out on the guy who seemed to be in charge.

"Look, buddy, here's the way it plays out," I said, pulling myself up to my full height and squaring my shoulders, brushing off the clumsy pat-down. "Pay attention or take notes 'cause I'm gonna move fast through the list, and I'm not inclined to repeat myself."

I noted the look of annoyance in his eyes – *These guys are used to getting their own way*, I thought – but continued after a quick breath.

"First off, I'm a private detective, not a gumshoe or a bozo, so knock it off; that part's not optional. Second, I don't take orders from you and don't particularly like you, now that I've attached a face to the voice. That could change, but it's not likely. Third, I'm here out of respect for Bohn" – I purposefully avoided the requisite courtesy title, taking another jab – "and sure as hell not to you. Fourth, I don't like being buffaloed by guys who think they're tough" – I jerked my head quickly toward my escorts – "or by circus clowns fingering guns inside their coat pockets. It makes me itchy. You won't like me when I'm itchy – and I'm itchy now. Last, I don't like to be kept waiting, regardless of who's doing it, or why. So scoot off like a good little soldier and tell your boss that *Mister* Blake is here."

I stopped for a second to see if my words were registering appropriately, then leaned in close to the guy's face and added softly: "I'll give him two minutes. Then I'm using that phone over there" – hitching a thumb toward the telephone that sat on a narrow counter inside the guard station, though I never took my eyes off his – "and calling a cab. You get all that, or do I need to talk slower?"

I was surprised when he laughed, breaking the tension.

"You got sand. No brains, but sand – I'll give you that, Blake," he hissed. "But tough talk don't mean squat to me, and it don't get you past first base, which is all this is. Show me some ID – now. You wanna see the boss, show me who you are." He held out his left hand, impatiently waiting for me to magically produce some paper.

"ID?" I asked. "Your thugs just pulled me out of bed and collected me at my apartment. What the hell do you need ID for?"

"Standing orders, pal. You could be anybody and not the punk-assed private dick with a college degree we're all expecting," he said. "In which case, I'd have to send you packing – direct to a shallow grave. So come on – out with it. Make it snappy."

"And if I don't? Your boss won't be happy about my unexpected demise," I said. "Remember: He asked to see me – not the other way around."

"You'd be surprised right about now as to what he might tolerate," he said. "Anyways, keep it up and I'll take my chances. So let's have it. I got better things to do than stand out here in the dark with the likes of you."

It was my turn to laugh, and I did just that, though I didn't want to overplay the hand. I pulled out my PI's license and turned my face in profile so that he could compare the photo with my actual mug.

"Picture don't look much like you," he grumbled.

The euchre tournament strikes again, I thought.

What I said aloud was this: "Yeah, well, so tell me who looks good in a photo ID … besides George Clooney or Halle Berry."

"Knock it off. You got anything else? A driver's license, maybe?" he asked.

"Sure I do," I said. "And I've got my first-grade report card, too, complete with Sister Rita Mae's signature in nice script at the bottom."

"Good. Hand 'em both over," he snapped. "The sooner we get this done, the sooner I can have Francis and Charles here get you up to the house. Frankly, I'm already sick of lookin' at you and sicker yet of hearin' you talk."

I thought that he was joking until he held out his hand. I shook my head in disbelief and produced my wallet again, pulling my driver's license and handing it over.

"And the other you mentioned – the report card thing?" he said.

"Seems I left it behind with my *Flintstones* lunchbox," I offered. "How about my Fraternal Order of Police membership card? I'd give you a logger's union card, but they forced me out for non-payment of dues."

He looked annoyed and snatched the wallet from my hand, then started looking at the various identification cards it contained until he was convinced that I was who I was supposed to be and not some impostor pulling a fast one. He flipped the wallet at me, grudgingly handed over the driver's license and PI card with a grunt, and snapped his fingers at Francis, the SUV driver.

"All right, back in the car – let's go," Francis said. "We still got a quarter-mile to the main house."

"I can hardly wait," I muttered, but I was already being bum-rushed backward and then pushed inside the back seat of the big gas hog.

This only gets curiouser and curiouser, I thought.

Without a better option available, I snapped my fedora in place and sat back to enjoy the rest of the ride – if such a ride can be enjoyed at all.

THREE

A BIT OF A NASTY SURPRISE

MONDAY, 2:57 A.M.

I'd met AJ Bohn once before, albeit briefly.

I'd inadvertently gotten him out of a jackpot a couple of decades earlier when I was still doing investigative reporting for a decent-sized metropolitan daily newspaper, the name of which you might even recognize. He'd only recently moved back to our fair city after a dozen years in Seattle, where he established his reputation as the go-to guy on the West Coast for all things pertaining to timber, lumber, hardwoods, pulpwood, wood byproducts, board feet, enormous government projects involving timber sales and logging rights and slash burns on the hillsides – the works.

He was big then, too, but nowhere near the big shot that he was today.

Today, in fact, by reputation alone, he was the Microsoft and Nike and General Motors Corp. of timber, all rolled into one package – even if logging was an industry in steep decline.

Much like newspapers, I guess.

As I remembered the story, and it's been awhile, he was being jammed up by a couple of high-ranking Seattle city officials who were angry because he was moving his lumber/timber empire to Oregon. The accusations involved state and federal income tax evasion and a number of related charges, extortion among them – all of which turned out to be entirely bogus; the whole setup was a power play by two corrupt upper-level Seattle insiders who were miffed at being eliminated from a potential piece of the AJ Bohn pie, which admittedly was enormous. But the first-day headlines were nothing short of scandalous, if not sensational, and the thing dragged on for weeks and picked up daily momentum as it steamrolled into the nation's newspapers and weekly magazines and the nightly TV news.

I eventually got a tip from a guy who knew a guy – sorry; a good journalist never reveals a source – and was the lone reporter who even looked at the possibility that Bohn actually might be innocent. I eventually uncovered some incontrovertible evidence that I was happy to put into print and, as a byproduct, into the hands of Bohn's defense attorneys as well.

The result was that Bohn went from scoundrel to victim to redemption in the twinkling of a Starbuck eye, and the Seattle twins who'd perpetrated the scam found themselves facing ten-year jail terms before the crisis management types and a multitude of lawyers stepped in and plea deals were arranged.

Bohn shook my hand one day after a federal court appearance, where he testified against the two dirty officials and a couple of their aides and a few lesser luminaries who were in on the scam. He said, as simply as you can deliver the line, that he owed me one. I didn't see it that way, told him so, and didn't think much about it afterward. I hadn't written the story to make his day, after all: I was just a good reporter who played by the rules and let the horseshoes drop where they were pitched. My role in the matter was nothing more than setting the facts straight and telling a decent tale of journalistic non-fiction in the process, something I'd done a thousand times before.

Had Bohn been the bad guy instead of the two city twerps, in fact, I'd have reported that as well and told him as much at the time.

While I'd never heard from him directly after that day, I did learn through my network of professional yappers and go-betweens and sources and informants who drifted in and out of the newsroom, police headquarters, and city hall on a regular basis that he still considered the debt to be unpaid.

I figured now, as I climbed out of the SUV, that maybe he wanted to settle the account for some reason – a better-late-than-not-at-all effort on his part. Then again, he'd sure picked a strange time to say thanks, seeing as how it was as dark as a drain and pushing 3 a.m.

A half-dozen other possible scenarios started running through my head, though none of them seemed to make much sense.

So why would he invite me up for a visit at this time of night, or day, or whatever the hell it is – all these years later? I wondered. And I started kicking that thought around.

It was no secret that I hadn't been in the reporting game for years – not since I'd quit the business in disgust. I was a full-time professor at the local college now, teaching kids how to write and edit and appreciate if not understand the mass media, for at least the duration of a single college term of eleven weeks. And because the job didn't pay much to begin with, and I still had an ex-wife with expensive tastes, and she had on retainer a greedy lawyer representing her interests, I had turned my reporter's investigative skills into a sideline as a private detective of sorts because the money was decent when I could find work.

Maybe he needs a PI, I thought.

I instantly reconsidered. *Nah. That's just stupid. This guy has more money than Phil Knight and Paul Allen and Steven Spielberg and Bill Gates and Oprah Winfrey, put together.*

I looked for Bohn as we drew closer to the mansion's entrance, happy to be out of the SUV. I was trying to appear casual and unflappable, though still wary of the two gorillas who were nipping tightly at my heels, no doubt expecting me to make a break for it. But I didn't see Bohn, and I didn't see anyone else I recognized among the handful of men who were stationed at the front door, apparently awaiting my arrival.

I turned to my escorts and flashed a questioning look, hoping that they could see it in the gloom and would offer some help, though the last thing I wanted was another one-way conversation with Francis, the SUV's surly driver.

When neither reacted, however, I was forced to give it another try.

"What gives here, boys?" I asked. "My time's valuable, and so is my sleep. I've got places to go and things to see and do."

They stopped abruptly, like soldiers marching in formation, and folded their arms across their massive chests at virtually the same instant, their faces turning into impassive masks.

"Thanks. You've been a big help," I said, then faced the entrance again and called out: "Private Blake here, reporting for duty as ordered." I snapped off my best imitation of a military salute and waited.

"Knock it off and step up here," a familiar voice called back, and I started moving ahead again. "And be prepared to stand for another frisk."

I laughed at that, surprised that they'd feel the need to search me again, and even more surprised to find that the man I'd earlier nicknamed The Snarl had somehow arrived at the main house ahead of me.

"How'd you do that?" I asked as I hopped nimbly up the steps, where the light was better because the heavy oak entryway door was wide open.

"Do what?" he asked.

"Get here before me. I left you back at the shack down the …"

"That was my brother," he said.

"Your brother?"

"You don't hear so well?" he said. "That's OK. I got problems of my own."

"So you're the guy who called me on the phone?"

"What of it?"

"I'm just checking to see who the real Snarl is around here," I said.

"The real snarl? What the hell are you talking about?"

"Forget it," I said.

"Whatever – but first, you stand for the frisk …"

"The first one wasn't good enough?"

"Orders," he said. "My orders."

"I'll make it easy for you," I said, marveling at the resemblance between the two siblings, right down to the timbre of their voices. "I've got a revolver in my jacket pocket."

"They let you get this far with that?"

"They were preoccupied."

"Real nice." The Snarl glared at the twin gorillas momentarily but quickly turned his attention back to me. "You should use a holster," he said, stepping forward with an outstretched hand to collect the piece. "You could snag it in the lining and not get it pulled in time."

"I do all right," I said.

"Always a first time. Hand it over now – take it slow. Butt first – no mistakes. Lots of eyes watching."

"Sure," I said and did as I was told. "You want to see my ID again?"

"That's not necessary," The Snarl said, gingerly taking the revolver from my right hand, pointing the barrel into the ground.

"OK, so how about telling me what this is all about?"

"Not me. I'll take you inside and you can talk to McClinton."

"To or with?"

"Now what the hell are you talking about?" The Snarl snapped in that low, growling voice that sounded like deep thunder mixed with road gravel.

"Forget it," I said. I knew McClinton's name, as would most people who paid attention to legal proceedings in the state, and it surprised me, though this seemed to be a day of surprises.

Or is it still night?

"Why the lawyer? I thought I was here to see …"

"Just get your ass inside, for god's sake, Blake. And shut up while you're at it. You'll get answers soon enough," The Snarl growled, waving his hand in the general direction that he wanted me to go. "Head to your right, over there," he added as I moved through the threshold, and I stepped into a mammoth foyer that featured marble floors and rich tapestries and what looked to my untrained eye to be artwork from Old World masters on the walls. I spotted a massive stairway well ahead of me, with doorways and rooms fanning off on either side, but I turned to the right and walked through the enormous French doors and into a sitting room that was larger than my apartment – hell, it was damn near as large as the apartment building. A man was seated on a leather divan, and he stood when he saw me and straightened his suit coat, unconsciously fastening the middle button.

"Mister Blake, my name is Edward McClinton, though most people call me Ned. I am Mister Bohn's personal attorney," he said.

"I know who you are, by reputation anyway," I replied, shaking his proffered hand. "And I hope you don't think I'm rude, Ned, but in case you haven't noticed, it's pushing 3 a.m. and I'm missing my beauty sleep and am wondering exactly …"

"… why you are here," McClinton said smoothly, finishing the sentence. He waved his hand toward a chair that was overstuffed and at least comfortable to look at, if not sit in. "Of course. I understand the inconvenience we've put you through. Please, have a seat, if you would. I'll explain everything."

I plopped down in the chair, setting my fedora on my knee, figuring that I'd give the lawyer a minute or two before making another stink.

He waited until I was comfortable and then sat down again and leaned his body forward in a rigid, earnest fashion. He was a tad short of being called a handsome man, but he was a damn sight easier on the eye than The Snarl, or The Snarl's brother. The lawyer was well groomed and immaculately tailored, as you'd expect of someone in that profession, with a sparse head of hair that had once been blond but was turning both gray and coarse. His eyes were a touch too narrow in his face, although it might have been the wire-rimmed glasses, which gave him a pinched appearance. Then again, I wasn't going to suggest that he change lens-fitters.

"Would you like something to drink?" he asked politely and by rote, with a hint of nerves showing. I found this odd, seeing as how he controlled the setting and was the puppet-master of record – for the moment, at least.

Frankly, I hoped to change that fact.

"Sure, but not as much as some answers," I said.

"I understand. First things first then." He waved his hand, and a butler appeared through the French doors. The man was in late sixties, I guessed, immaculately groomed, with close-cropped hair and a military bearing. He carried a tray with a half-dozen offerings: soda water, a dark red wine in an etched goblet, a tumbler containing what appeared to be either whiskey or bourbon, another that might have held gin or vodka – the guy was an alcoholic's nightmare.

"Whiskey?" I asked, pointing to one of the glasses.

"Indeed, sir. It's the very best Irish I could find at short notice."

"Perfect. Thanks. You read my mind."

I took a sip and was tempted to ask the butler for the brand when McClinton interrupted.

"That will do nicely, Mister Vineyard. Thanks so much." The butler nodded at the lawyer, gave me a stiff bow, and backed away for a few steps before turning smartly about and disappearing through the French doors.

"All right then, let's have it," I said. "You either produce Bohn right now, or I'm heading out with the whiskey. And, just so you know, I intend to collect my revolver along the way."

I started to stand, but the urgency in his voice stopped me cold.

"Please. I'm – I'm, well, I'm afraid that Mister Bohn can't join us this evening," the lawyer sputtered. "You see, he was killed tonight – in this very house. If you like, I can take you to see the body … right now."

I'll admit that this was one hell of a news flash, and I had a hard time maintaining a poker face – something I take pride in, even in the tightest of circumstances.

"Killed?"

"I'm afraid so."

"How?"

"Mister Bohn was shot. Several times, in fact."

A dozen or more questions raced through my mind. But I paused and stared hard at the lawyer for a moment, taking some additional time to process what he'd told me. I chose the obvious question.

"So why call me? Why get me involved? Why not call the cops, just like everybody else does?"

"Well, you see …" McClinton paused here, turning his face to the side as he groped for the right words, and it took him a full minute before he spoke again.

"First off, Mister Bohn is – was – not like everyone else, as you no doubt know, Mister Blake. Secondly, I'm also afraid that involving the cops, as you call them, is out of the question. The cops, you see – the police – killed Mister Bohn. Not more than an hour ago."

Let me tell you, that pulled me up short, and I let my jaw drop for the second time in what amounted to little more than seconds. I gulped the remaining whiskey and looked around for the butler.

Still, I've heard about this sort of thing. My great-great-grandfather was a federal marshal in the old Arizona Territory. He was a man who was known to be quick on the trigger – to shoot first and forget about asking questions later – and some terrific stories had been passed down to me through generations of Blakes. But there's a far cry between a bedtime tale from the Old West and the real deal in the here and now, let me tell you.

The best I could manage?

"That's a bit of a nasty surprise, all right. Maybe you'd better let me see where this happened and tell me everything you know – starting with why you called me."

"I suggest that we get started then," McClinton said, and he stood and headed toward the doors, with me following fast on his heels.

FOUR

ANOTHER DAY IN PARADISE

FIVE YEARS EARLIER

He didn't know where the money would come from. Even at that – even though his life might depend on it – he admitted that he didn't much care. What he knew for certain – all he knew for certain – was that services were rendered, and it was customary that payment was due, in full, at the time of completion.

Hell, that was understood in any town in any state on the map – something else he knew perfectly well.

The police officer leaned in again, jutting his chin within inches of the frightened man who was squirming in an overstuffed chair, and whispered menacingly.

"I'm not screwin' around here. You know that, right?"

He paused, dramatically, flashing his teeth without the slightest hint of a smile, and added, "You do know that?"

The chump in question, a small man wearing a trim, three-piece suit with a fashionable straw cowboy hat clutched in the sweaty palm of his left hand, swallowed loudly. The act made the officer think of scenes that he'd watched in bad, late-night movies on TV when he was a kid.

The little man nodded his head vigorously.

"Sure I am," he gulped, his eyes flaring wide with fright. "You kn-kn-know – you know, sir," he stammered, flustered now and unable to control his otherwise precise speech, "that I'm g-g-good for it. Don't you, Mister Downing?"

Charles V. Downing – Chucky to his friends, though he didn't have many of those, and none whom he could trust near his money, his booze, his cigarettes, his women, or his shakedown schemes – pulled his face back and laughed, mirthlessly and briefly. He allowed his hands to swing freely, away from the arms of the chair that he'd been hovering over, and he turned his broad smile into a menacing leer. His hard, gray-black eyes, like pieces of flinty coal, indicated a coldness that forced the little man to squirm in the chair's stuffing again, wilting under the officer's unrelenting gaze.

Norbert Gallagher, Downing's chump of record, gulped and repeated, for emphasis, "You d-do know that. Right? That I'm g-g-good for it, I m-m-mean."

"You presume too much and hope for too much," Downing snapped. "I'll tell you what I know, and then you'll know it. Got that?"

"Y-y-yes sir."

"All right then, here's what I know. I know you wanted me to perform a service, which I was happy to do. I'm in the service industry. It's why you called me. Right?"

Gallagher again nodded his quick assent. "Y-y-yes sir," he stammered.

"So now it's your turn. Now you need to pay me."

Downing pressed his face in close once more, this time forcing his prey to visibly cringe. "And I want the money now," he said, the venom leaking like thick drool from his lips.

"I … but I … I d-d-don't have it with me," Gallagher stammered, his eyes wide and haunted and flitting wildly about the room.

Downing decided to push in closer. When Gallagher saw the angry, menacing look that swept across the officer's florid face, like an in-rushing tidal flood, he quickly added, "But I c-c-can get it."

"Great," Downing said, stepping quickly away from the chair. He pointed to the cowboy hat that his client clutched in his hand. "Stick that idiotic thing on your head … let's go."

"Well sir, what I m- m- meant to say was that I c- c- can't get it just now. I mean, I can g-g-get it, all right – but I can't get it j-j-just now. I … I'm sure you understand."

Downing scowled and leaned in again so that his nose was little more than an inch from Gallagher's. His fingers flexed in and out, making rock-hard fists each time, and he held them close to his waist, where his Glock 19 semi-automatic handgun was secured in a leather holster that was tightly strapped to his hip.

"Understand? Did I hear that right?" Downing barked. "You really asked me that?"

Gallagher didn't trust his voice; he nodded his head up and down, so quickly that it looked as though he'd acquired a feverish chill and was fighting hard to warm himself.

"I'll tell you what I understand. You owe me money – not much where you come from, maybe, but a hell of a lot to me: twenty-five large."

Downing paused, grinned for an instant, then started again.

"I get it, Gallagher," he said. "Chumps like you light cigars with that kind of money and blow through it in a night of booze and babes. But me? Guys like me work hard for money like that, and that's what I did. I worked hard for it. I keep this town clean of scum, just like the scum I scraped off the bottom of your shoes – scum you'll never have to worry about again. Now it's time to pay."

Gallagher cringed and sunk lower into his chair.

"I want it," Downing continued, "and I want it now – no song and no dance. Know why? 'Cause you can disappear – just like that piece of scum you wanted gone. He disappeared. So can you."

Downing moved his head slightly and pushed his lips next to Gallagher's left ear.

"Just so you know, you're playing a song and dance, and I damn well know it," Downing whispered, his tone conveying pending violence. "I don't like it. I want my money, and I WANT IT NOW."

He shouted the last four words, so loudly that the little man turned his head away and visibly trembled, his face blanching.

"I … I u-u-understand. Really I do. It's j-j-just that I, well sir, I – what I m-m-mean to say is that I …"

Gallagher's voice trailed off, and he threw out his hands in a gesture of defeat and dropped his frantic eyes to the floor, looking thoroughly deflated.

"You telling me the car's empty?" Downing asked. His muscular arms were folded across his broad chest, and he held his chiseled frame tall and erect, accentuating his dominance over the smaller man.

"N-n-no – n-not at all, Officer D-D-Downing," Gallagher said, striving to inject some indignation into his voice but failing miserably as the stammer took hold once more. "If y-y-you are implying that I'm n-not flush – that I'm not a man of m-m-means …"

"Good," Downing snapped, cutting him off. "Here's what we'll do. You pick that phone up and call your bank. Go ahead – pick it up." He flicked his hand toward a cradled telephone, extending his fingers outward. "Come on – right now. Tell 'em you want to get your money. Tell 'em you're on your way over to get it."

Gallagher glanced first at the telephone and then quickly back toward his tormenter, sheer panic sweeping across his face, his eyes again wide with fear and self-loathing, silently pleading for help that he knew would not be forthcoming.

"Do it," Downing snapped.

"I c-c-can't," Gallagher whimpered.

"Why not?"

"My … m-m-my wife f-f-froze my a-a-accounts. It h--happened this morning. She thinks I'm … that I'm ch-ch-cheating on her."

Downing's face turned from vicious hostility to genuine humor in a heartbeat.

"Cheating?" he said, his eyebrows arched in disbelief. "Did I hear that right? You?"

"What m-m-makes you think I'm not m-m-man enough to have an a-a-affair?" Gallagher whimpered. He was too badgered to try for indignation, but his pride wouldn't let the challenge go without some sort of rebuttal.

"You let her do that – push you around like that?" Downing asked.

When Gallagher didn't reply (his eyes were now glued to the carpeted floor), Downing tried again.

"That's it? You got nothing else?"

Gallagher's eyes remained on the floor. Downing pulled the thick fingers of his right hand off his belt buckle and grasped the hard polymer grip of his Glock, pulling it straight out from its holster.

"I guess," he said softly, "we'll have to try something else."

Gallagher didn't react.

"You understand what I'm saying – right?" Downing asked.

Gallagher's eyes were closed now – his head was hanging low, close to his knees – and he started to make a low, eerie keening sound that was more comical than miserable to Downing's ears.

"Keep it up, buddy boy, but you ain't gonna like what comes next," Downing said.

The keening stopped abruptly. "Y-y-you aren't g-g-going to s-s-shoot me? Are you?" Gallagher muttered. "Like you did the, to the …"

"Of course I'm gonna shoot you. What'd ya expect when you don't pay me straight off – I'm gonna head up a parade down Liberty Street? Enlist the mayor, maybe even the governor, to lead a marching band in your honor? That's what you expect?" He laughed, but there was no mirth in the guttural sound that erupted from his throat, and he ended it as abruptly as it began. "But you gotta understand, chump, I ain't gonna shoot you dead. If I shot you dead, how in hell would I get my money?"

Downing's voice rumbled, as though the words were so loathsome to his ears that he could hardly get them out of his mouth.

"Sure, I'm gonna shoot you, but … here, I'll tell you what. Let's just see what I'm gonna do."

He hoisted the Glock close to Gallagher's ear and slowly rubbed the slide against the man's clammy skin.

"You get the idea?" he asked. "First one ear, then the other. Then your nose, maybe. Then your fingers – one at a time. You understand?"

"Y-y-yes sir."

"Good. Make the call – if not to the bank then to your wife. Right now."

"Y-y-yes sir," Gallagher mumbled once more, reaching for the telephone.

Charles V. Downing, police lieutenant and trusted public servant, laughed at the absurdity of this venture. He was swimming in bucketfuls of cash, and god only knew he could use the money. When you have kingly tastes and live on a cop's paltry salary, you needed a hell of a good source of supplemental income.

And he had to admit that this was a hell of a good source.

Loan shark, shakedown artist, bounty hunter, man for hire, jack of all unsavory trades, with no calling card, no confirmed residency, no established place of business or set hours, and no fear whatsoever of retribution – how in hell you could you top it?

It paid the bills, and it paid them in cash, with no questions asked, and it still left a hell of lot of money to stash away.

Now that he was flush again, he laughed aloud and thought about the various ways that he could expand his burgeoning enterprise. He had the mayor in his confidence, thanks to a number of overlooked drunken-driving violations, as well as a friendly district court judge who was overly fond of little boys. He figured that the payouts he made were worth the protection, considering the potential for risks. He also figured that with an expanded empire, he could bring in far more money than he'd ever have to pay out. He knew a few trusted men on the force who would want in on the action – Billy "Buzzsaw" Stone among them – and he had big ideas that would make them all a bundle.

Big ideas meant bigger risks, sure, but it meant bigger profits, too.

The trick is staying a step ahead of the law, he thought. But that, too, made him laugh.

When you are *the law, what the hell difference does it make?*

FIVE

ANOTHER FINE MESS

MONDAY, 3:17 A.M.

The place was a mess; that much was plain enough. In addition to the dead body and the circular pool of blood staining the carpet on either side of AJ Bohn's torso, it was clear that the room had been tossed by someone who was in a hurry.

Maybe it was a lot of someones.

I didn't find that idea to be particularly surprising, given Bohn's reputation; it was just something that I filed away at the time.

Ned McClinton, his lips pursed tight, his face pinched and ashen, stood just inside the doorway once he'd shown me into the room. The lawyer seemed to be greatly troubled by what he saw, though I had a hard time working up much sympathy for him.

When you lie down with dogs, and all that, I figured.

Still, I kept it to myself and started slowly taking in the room, allowing my years as an investigative reporter who'd seen a fair share of crime scenes, and my subsequent life as a halfway decent PI, to take over.

Bohn's body was lying on the floor of his sprawling, palatial bedroom, seven feet from the massive French doors that opened into a wide and spacious hallway, immediately ahead of the staircase.

Looks like he was trying to hightail it out of the room when the shooting started ...

The body was twisted grotesquely, the left arm tucked awkwardly behind the back, as though it had been wrenched, and the right leg was bent at an impossible angle. I got the idea that he'd been kicked savagely, given the position of the limbs and the bruises that were clearly visible on the face and neck.

Just a guess, though – I'll need to hear what the coroner says ...

The beating wasn't the cause of death, however. That much was easy to determine after I walked around the corpse a few times and viewed it from a variety of angles. I counted two bullet holes in the man's back, another in the left shoulder, and at least two more in the right arm. But I would've been forced to move the body to confirm the exact number of holes, and I wasn't anxious to touch it until some sort of official medical examination by trained personnel had been made ...

... by someone more qualified than me ...

Then again, I'm not anxious to touch the damn thing at all ...

The damage to the right arm made me wonder whether Bohn pulled a gun to defend himself – you tend to shoot at the immediate threat, and a gun drawn in self-defense presents a clear threat – and I started looking around for an abandoned firearm. I didn't immediately spot one and glanced at McClinton, who'd turned even pastier in the time that we'd been inside the bedroom.

"Did he own a gun?" I asked.

"Several," McClinton said. His face was turned toward the ceiling, and he maintained his view of the far corner of the room as though some great mystery was about to reveal itself. I glanced up, saw a stylish Cornish arch and elaborate crown molding, and turned my head toward the lawyer again.

"All right, did he have access to them here?"

"To what?"

"To the guns that he owned, counselor. Focus for me, all right?"

"Certainly. He always kept a loaded pistol at his bedside," McClinton said.

"Where, exactly?"

He pointed to a nightstand close to the bed, and I walked briskly over and found nothing on top, then opened the stand's three drawers, one at a time, but failed to turn up any hardware.

"It's not here," I said. "Do you know if he used it to defend himself?"

"I suspect he would have, had he had the time to reach it," McClinton said. "He was proficient in the use of firearms."

"All right, did *you* find any sign of the gun?"

"Me? Personally? No."

"Did *anyone* find any sign of a gun then – or anything else that might be useful in shedding some light on what happened here?"

He remained silent.

I was starting to get annoyed.

"Counselor, did you find any casings?" I asked.

When he still didn't respond, I tried again with this: "The spent brass from a pistol?"

"The room has remained untouched since the departure of the police officers who killed him, so far as I know," he said at last.

"All right, let's try this: Do you know how many cops were up here? That might tell me how many shots were fired."

"I don't know, Mister Blake," he said. "I'm sorry, but I was not in the house at the time."

"Someone must know," I suggested.

"Yes. I'm sure that's true."

All right, so I'll admit it: That last remark got to me, and I moved toward McClinton at a rapid pace. I got close enough to make him uncomfortable, then pushed in closer still, and he eventually stopped staring at the ceiling and looked at me with haunted, red-rimmed eyes.

Bohn's death is taking a toll on the shyster. Interesting. Or is it just an act? I wondered.

But I didn't offer any of that. "Time we played hardball," I said instead, unable to contain my growing frustration. "If you want me in on this – and it's a big *if* right now – I'll need full access to everything you have and everything you know. And thus far, you haven't offered me anything. So talk, dammit, or I walk out and make a phone call. You can try to stop me, but the word is going to get out, one way or another."

McClinton blinked once, then again, and he slowly nodded his head.

"What do you want to know?" he asked.

"Let's start with why I'm here."

"Mister Bohn admired you, Mister Blake – for whatever reason. He'd provided explicit orders, in writing, in his final will and testament, that should anything untoward happen to him, the first call was to go to you."

"Me? Seriously? In his bloody will?"

"Yes. Exactly."

"Well, this can be classified officially as *untoward*, all right," I muttered.

"Yes. It is that."

"I'd actually call it a hell of a mess."

"I would agree, Mister Blake. But to answer your question directly, in accordance with Mister Bohn's wishes, I was to offer you *carte blanche* – anything you want, in whatever form or denomination, legalities aside – to retain your services. I was never told why he wanted you and not someone else, and he once forbade me from even asking, not that I would have; that was simply not my place. But that, and that alone, is the reason why you were called."

He paused before adding: "Do you, Mister Blake?"

"Do I what?"

"Do you know why I was directed to call you?"

I thought about it again, and the only thing that came to mind was the brief encounter that we'd had many years before, in Seattle.

"I've only had a single meeting with AJ Bohn. It was a long time ago and didn't amount to anything," I said after thinking it through again. "Why I'm here is anybody's guess, seeing as how your boss can't shed any light on the subject."

"I see." McClinton hesitated again, as though considering some idle thought, and he added, "Well then, for reasons that neither of us understand, Mister Bohn wanted you and you only, which is the reason why you were called once I saw what happened."

"And the expectation is that I investigate his death?'

"Yes sir."

"And I can name my price?"

"Those were Mister Bohn's specific orders, sir. I have it in writing."

"I'd like to see that."

"Absolutely."

"Fair enough," I said, trying to keep my mind on the specifics of the case rather than the number of zeroes I'd add to the invoice once my services were rendered, and I paused for a few seconds to reorder my thoughts.

"Explain it again: How do you know it was the cops who did this?"

"I received a call from Mister Vineyard that the police entered the house with a search warrant. I directed Mister Vineyard to keep the officers in the foyer until I arrived to examine the warrant. By the time I got here – twenty minutes later, I would estimate conservatively – the damage had been done. Mister Bohn was … well, exactly as you see here, and the police were no longer on the premises."

"And Mister Vineyard is the butler I met earlier?"

"Exactly."

"All right," I said. "So … you don't know that it really was the cops who did this? For all you know, it could've been anybody, dressed as cops and with phony papers and badges."

"No. Mister Vineyard told me that he recognized at least two of the officers from previous visits to the estate."

I'll need to talk to this Vineyard, I thought, and it occurred to me that another two fingers of the Irish whiskey he'd served earlier would make a charming prelude to the conversation.

First things first …

"All right, let's say for a minute that everything you've said is true. Explain to me why the cops would come here in the first place. What was the point of a late-night visit – especially one with a search warrant?"

"I have no idea. Mister Bohn was not in any legal jeopardy. He was not party to any action that would prompt such a visit, so far as I know, and I can think of nothing that has transpired at Raptor's Ridge in recent weeks or months, of a legal nature, that would justify this. Nothing at all."

"And if not of a *legal nature*, as you put it, something else, perhaps?"

He shrugged his shoulders but said nothing.

I thought about that for a moment. "You just told me that Vineyard recognized at least two of the cops from previous visits. Why were the cops here previously?"

"Mister Bohn had business dealings with many people on the police force. I'm sure it was related to that."

"To what?"

"To the business dealings he had with the police."

"Look, Ned, that sounds more than a bit suspicious," I said. "I'm forced to guess that he was involved in something illegal, perhaps?"

I'll admit it: I took a chance with that one, but I wanted to see how he'd react. To his credit, he passed the test.

"I take that as a personal affront, Mister Blake. Mister Bohn was …"

"Call me Max," I interrupted.

"Fine. Mister Bohn was a gentleman and a keen – no, an extraordinary – businessman. He was not a man prone to illegal dealings of any kind, and I am insulted that you would suggest that I would be a party to …"

"Save it, counselor. AJ Bohn was no saint, and we both know it. Nobody who carves out the type of empire he managed, and for as long as he did, ever is. I know what the rumor mill says, and I also know" – though I was bluffing here – "a few choice tidbits that could be sworn to in a court of law. I'll bet you know a whole bunch more, being an insider and all. So forget the innocent act here. It's too little and too late."

"You can think what you want; most people do. But I know better. I know – I knew – Mister Bohn for more than twenty years … knew him well, in fact. I am here to tell you, Mister Blake …"

"It's Max."

"… Max, that I am not privy to anything that would prompt such an attack – and I am privy to much of what transpires at the mansion. Whatever took place here was … off the books, I suspect – both for Mister Bohn, and for the police."

"Off the books?" I said incredulously. "I hope to tell you it was off the books. You don't do something like this" – I jerked my thumb in the direction of the dead body – "by the book."

"I understand. I just don't know how else to describe it," McClinton said.

"You could try cold-blooded murder," I said, but he remained silent, his eyes averted.

I pondered the situation again, then went at the lawyer from another angle.

"If the cops really did this, as you say, why not call in the State Police and have them deal with it? Or, hell, why not call the governor, or even the feds, or both at once, maybe? AJ Bohn was a man of prominence, regardless of how people might feel about him. Such a call wouldn't be considered out of line, given the circumstances."

"Again, Mister Bohn provided specific orders: I was to call and hire you and no one else, and at whatever price."

"You don't exactly hire the State Police or the governor – or the feds," I said.

"Mister Bohn's paperwork was quite explicit on the matter. And did I say that I was to hire you *at any price*?" he added, emphasizing that last three words.

So we're back to that again ...

"Yeah, well, I can't wait to stick you with a whopping bill to cover the inconvenience of this early-morning visit, but I'm still confused – about a lot of things. Hell, I'm not even sure what to do next. What do you propose for the body, for example?"

"I assure you, sir, that I have no idea. Based on my instructions, that's entirely up to you."

"So if I tell you to call the coroner, you'll make the call?"

"I would think, Mister Blake – Max – that a call to the coroner would prompt an immediate call in turn to the local police, certainly to the State Police, and we would be right back where we began this evening."

"True enough," I muttered and looked toward the body again. "But you've presented me with a hell of a fine mess all the same."

"I suspect, sir, that this is just the start of the *fine mess*, as you call it, that I'm presenting you with," McClinton replied, and he almost sounded apologetic. He looked toward the far corner of the room again, sighed deeply, and pulled his eyes off the ceiling and added: "I am almost hesitant to say that I have still another *fine mess* for your consideration."

"There's more? Seriously?"

"Most assuredly, sir."

I laughed. "All right, let's see you top that," I said, pointing toward the dead body.

"Allow me to suggest, Mister Blake – Max – that you check inside the bathroom." He raised a shaky left hand: "It's over there, to your left."

Yeah, I know what you're thinking: I just had to ask …

SIX

DEAD DAMES TELL NO TALES

MONDAY, 3:48 A.M.

By the time I got into the master bathroom, I was damn curious to see what tricks the lawyer had stuffed up his lengthy sleeves – fee or no fee.

And yeah, dollar signs were still running through my head, despite the oddball nature of the situation. But even at that, I wasn't prepared to see Audrey Flowers' corpse in the bathtub, as naked as the day she was born, a single bullet hole through her right temple.

I'll admit here to an inadvertent double-take and a scattering of flippant thoughts at the sight. Chief among them:

Now there's something you don't see every day ...

"What was that, sir?" Ned McClinton asked.

"Nothing," I muttered and began to wonder, as bizarre as things were at the moment, whether I could at that instant distinguish the difference between thinking to myself and speaking aloud. I glanced briefly at McClinton, who'd halted his forward progress at the doorframe and stood with his hands clasped behind his back, frowned, and turned my attention once more to the body in the bathtub.

Like most every red-blooded male on the planet, I've long dreamed of seeing Audrey Flowers in the buff, and not just on the silver screen. But this was an eye-opener that I wished on no one, and it brought to mind that old saw about being careful what you wish for …

… because someone might hear your wish and grant it. And then what?

At least she looked at peace, lying there.

Hell, ignore the hole in her head and she looks as though she's sleeping, I thought.

Audrey Flowers was the biggest genuine movie star our community has ever seen – a true local-gal-makes-good success story of world-class order. She was a true beauty – she'd been a true beauty, at least, before someone dimmed her good looks with a single gunshot – who'd made a half-dozen romantic comedies that did better-than-average box office by Tinsel Town standards and turned her into a nationwide celebrity.

Her salad days were behind her by a few years, and she hadn't been on the big screen in anything recent that I could remember. But it didn't mean that she no longer drew a crowd or turned heads when she stepped foot inside the local Nordstrom's or Saks Fifth Avenue outlets or the extravagant Jackson Jewelers for a little shopping spree, or when she traipsed into the city's better restaurants with a small entourage of hangers-on in tow. No, she was still a radiant star on the streets of the capital city.

I couldn't recall hearing her name associated with AJ Bohn's, however.

"You want to tell me how she got here?" I asked McClinton, who was waiting patiently, his eyes again fixed on the distant ceiling, his face still on the pasty side.

"From what I can observe, she didn't move after she was shot to death in the bathtub," he offered dryly.

"I'm talking about how she got here in the first place, genius. Sorry about bothering you again, Ned, but it's fairly plain that she's not going to tell me anything."

The lawyer cleared his throat and considered his words carefully.

What he gave me was a doozy, by tabloid standards, anyway.

"Miss Flowers and Mister Bohn were seeing one another romantically," he eventually replied in a hushed voice, as though he were providing confidential information that I wouldn't otherwise be privileged to hear unless some profoundly peculiar twist of fate made it possible.

Which, of course, was exactly what'd happened that placed me at the Bohn mansion in the first place.

"Wonderful. Anything else you can tell me off hand, or do I need to see the butler on this one, too?"

McClinton, who was struggling to maintain his composure, steeled himself.

"They were seeing each other for well over a year – perhaps closer to two," he said. "She was here on average twice a week, at least – sometimes more often. They seemed to genuinely enjoy each others' company, despite the difference in age."

"Which was?"

"I don't know – thirty-five years or more, I'd guess. I never asked. It was not my business or my place."

"Did she spend the night?"

"I couldn't say. I never do."

"You never do what?" I asked.

"Spend the night."

"Sure – all right. So let me ask you this: Is anything missing?"

"Missing? In what way?" he asked.

"Missing from the scene."

"I'm not sure that I ..." He paused, seeking an explanation for my question.

I tried again: "Was anything stolen, counselor? If Bohn had a pistol, I didn't find it – not yet, anyway. So where is it? If Miss Flowers had jewelry stashed about, is it still here? That sort of thing – that's what I'm asking. Theft could go to motive."

"I see. I can check, of course."

"Good," I said. "Please do. It could be important"

"All right. Anything else?"

"Can you think of anything that might be even remotely helpful?" I pressed.

"I assure you, sir, that I can offer nothing more than the obvious. Miss Flowers is dead in Mister Bohn's private bath, and Mister Bohn is equally dead in the next room. That she was here at the time this happened is a pity but no great surprise. That she is dead, along with my former employer, is not only a colossal revelation to me, but one that constitutes a sad and untimely demise to a genuinely elegant lady."

"You should write obits for the local newspaper," I said and stared hard at McClinton, although he again refused to meet my gaze. It made me wonder if the lawyer's alibi would hold up to any serious scrutiny – if, in fact, he even had an alibi.

Maybe he loved Audrey, told her the truth, she laughed at him and mentioned it to Bohn, and the lawyer was forced to pop them both once the sparks started flying ...

"Nah, that's nuts," I said aloud, which drew a quizzical wrinkle from McClinton's forehead but still no eye contact. I asked him instead, "What time did you get here?"

"I can't say with exact precision, but I would guess that it was sometime between 1:49 and 1:52 a.m. You could check my exact arrival time in the log books at the guard station, however," McClinton offered. "Why do you ask?

"And the gaggle that's outside – the hired guns? What time did they get here?"

"They are always here. They were here when I arrived."

"They were inside the house when the shooting started?"

"That's highly unlikely," he said. "Only Mister Vineyard was in the mansion, to the best of my knowledge – besides the police officers who are responsible for this ... tragedy."

"Along with Bohn and Audrey," I said. "They were here, too."

"Yes, of course. What I meant was that Mister Vineyard is the only person who was still alive after the gunfire ended and the police left."

Something didn't feel right.

"The bodyguards were where, exactly, while all this" – I waved my arm in a broad sweep toward the bathtub and then back toward the master bedroom – "was going on?"

"At the guard station, I would imagine. That was standard procedure when Miss Flowers was in the residence. They were to remain at the guard station to afford Mister Bohn and Miss Flowers some appropriate privacy."

"The guards didn't see the cops arrive at the house?"

"To gain entrance to the estate, the police had to check in at the guard station. That, too, was standard procedure," McClinton said.

"So why not take down the cops as they're leaving? The boss has just been killed, his girlfriend has just been killed – why would the guards let them waltz through the gates again?"

McClinton said, "I would speculate that the guards had no reason to believe anything was amiss. It was only after I arrived and, despite Mister Vineyard's protests, went upstairs to meet with Mister Bohn to ask about the warrant that I discovered his body – and, of course, Miss Flowers' body moments later."

"So you didn't know that Bohn was dead when you got here?"

"That is correct."

"And so far as you know, this Vineyard fellow didn't hear gunshots while the police were upstairs? Do I have that right?" I asked.

"That is my understanding, Mister Blake – Max."

"Is he deaf?"

"The house is quite large, sir. But you really should speak with him."

"All right, I want to do exactly that – right now. But I also need medical examinations on the bodies – both of them. And because of this crazy set of circumstances, it's safe to say that we can't get that done in the usual way. I'm guessing that Mister Bohn had a personal physician in addition to a personal lawyer?"

"That is correct."

I waited, but McClinton didn't offer a name, forcing me to ask, "Care to share, counselor?"

"His name is Doctor Strand."

"Floyd Strand?"

"Exactly – one and the same."

That's convenient, I thought, though why that notion popped into my head at that moment, I have no way of explaining, even now.

I knew the name via the newspaper's society pages. Strand was, as the local media often reported, a man about town. Among a sweeping variety of other talents, he was a single-digit-handicap golfer who both organized and played in various tournaments for charitable causes at the local country club and throughout the region. He also was a generous donor to any number of do-gooder organizations, a member in good standing – so far as I knew – of the local private university's board of directors, and was something of a ladies' man.

I recalled that he played the piano, although not particularly well.

The fact that I had no knowledge whatsoever about his medical skills told me at least something else about the good doctor – or at least, I thought that it did at the time.

"All right, Ned," I said. "Would you give Doctor Strand a call and ask him to come out to the house? Don't tell him anything. If he insists on a reason for a call at this hour, tell him that Bohn asked for him – leave it at that."

"It won't present a problem, I'm sure. This won't be the first time he's been called to the mansion at odd hours," McClinton said.

"Really? You'll have to tell me more," I prodded.

"I meant nothing by it. Doctor Strand was a confidant of Mister Bohn's, after all, and a frequent guest here."

"Sure. If you say so. Give him a call."

"Of course."

"And McClinton … Ned …"

"Yes?"

"One other thing: Why didn't *you* call me with the news? Why ask The Snarl to make the phone call?"

"The Snarl?"

"Yeah. The Snarl: The guy who called me … he snarls when he talks – whatever his name is …"

"Deeker. His name is Paul Deeker. His brother Tom also works – worked – for Mister Bohn."

"All right, so why ask this Deeker to call me? Why not call me yourself?"

"I was occupied elsewhere, sir."

"Doing what, exactly?"

"Among other things, I was doing my best to exactly recall Mister Bohn's instructions regarding what I was supposed to do should the … ah, should the worst happen."

Well, that makes some sense – on the surface, at least … but it still smells fishy.

"All right. Call Doc Strand. I'm going downstairs to roust the butler."

SEVEN

QUIET NIGHTS AND QUIET STARS

MONDAY, 4:14 A.M.

It didn't take much of a genius – or even a competent detective, which I consider myself to be, incidentally – to figure out that Russell Vineyard didn't pull the trigger on either his boss or his boss' lady friend.

When I found him in his suite, in a far-flung corner of the mansion that is seemingly a city block or more from the main hall, AJ Bohn's butler was listening to Mozart's 40th, the one musicologists call the Great G-minor Symphony.

I was at least impressed with his musical tastes. How can you not like Mozart?

"I was expecting you, sir," he said when I knocked. "Would you like a taste of the Irish you sampled earlier? I expect by now that you could use some."

I'll confess it: He was off my official suspect list with that greeting. But I still had questions to ask, just to get the pieces of the puzzle in the right order in my head. I said yes to the whiskey and asked him to spin his tale of what had taken place that night at Raptor's Ridge.

"When the police arrived, demanding to see Mister Bohn, I asked them to wait in the grand foyer and immediately placed a call to Mister McClinton," he said, speaking calmly while pouring both of us a drink after dialing down Wolfgang Amadeus a notch. "He told me to 'stall them' until he arrived – I believe those were his words – so I informed the officers that they were instructed to wait where they were until Mister McClinton arrived to examine the paperwork."

"You didn't tell Bohn?"

"No sir. He had issued a standing directive that he and Miss Flowers were not to be disturbed under any circumstances – unless he required my services, of course, in which case he would call me directly."

"All right. So you call the lawyer. Then you tell the cops to wait where they are – is that right?"

"Yes."

"So how'd they take the news?"

"Poorly, sir. Lieutenant Downing, who was in charge, told me that he'd be damned if he'd wait around for some 'yahoo lawyer' – those were close to his exact words, sir – and he headed up the stairs despite my protests. Two additional officers followed. Three more waited in the foyer, to ensure, I would guess, that I did not follow the first three up to Mister Bohn's room, which I initially tried to do."

"Downing, huh?" I muttered. I knew of Downing, all right. It's hard to pay attention in town and not know Chuck Downing's name. "You knew him, I take it?" I asked.

"Him?"

"Downing."

"Oh yes – Lieutenant Downing has been to the mansion many times in recent months. It was no surprise to see his face, even at that late hour. I found it strange that I was not notified beforehand that he was coming to Raptor's Ridge; that had always been the case previously. It also was odd that he brought so many other officers with him this time; that, too, was unusual. But yes, it is fair to say that he was a frequent guest of Mister Bohn's."

I made a mental note to ask why Downing was such a frequent guest at Raptor's Ridge, but I wanted to keep the butler focused for now on the events that had taken AJ Bohn's and Audrey Flowers' lives.

"So what happened next?"

"No more than two minutes later, if that, he and the other two officers marched down the stairs again. He said to me, and these are his exact words: 'False alarm. Call the lawyer and tell him never mind.' All of them then marched out the door. I did not see the vehicle they arrived in, but I heard them drive away while I stood at the front door."

I waited for more, but nothing else was forthcoming. Instead, Vineyard neatly sipped the whiskey that he'd poured for himself.

"So that's it?" I finally asked.

"Until Mister McClinton arrived several minutes later, yes. That's it, as you phrase it, sir."

"And you didn't hear anything from upstairs?"

"No – not a thing, sir."

"No gunshots, no bodies falling, no scuffling or fisticuffs – nothing at all?"

"I assure you, sir, that I didn't hear a thing. Had I heard something, I likely would be dead right now as well, and you would have three bodies to deal with instead of two. And had I known that something was amiss upstairs at the time, I most certainly would have called down to the guard station and alerted Mister Deeker and his group to the issue, once Lieutenant Downing and his people left the mansion."

"Did you call McClinton and tell him it was a false alarm, as Downing suggested?"

"Hardly, sir. I knew that Mister McClinton was on his way. I also knew that he would want to check for himself and would not be swayed by a telephone call from me. We are both thorough when it comes to protecting Mister Bohn. I should say *were*, I suppose ..." He let the sentence die off, as though he'd momentarily lost the thought.

"All right, Mister Vineyard, if that's the case, why didn't you go upstairs, once the police left, to see that your boss was all right?"

"I had no reason to believe that something was amiss. I heard nothing, as I have already indicated, to make me suspicious. Besides, I had orders from Mister Bohn that he and Miss Flowers were not to be disturbed. I could not be held responsible for the conduct of the police, but I most certainly would be held responsible for my own conduct, sir."

"Of course." I stopped, thought it over again, and retreated a few yards. "Just so I have this straight, you were waiting the whole time in the foyer with the other three cops while Downing and two more went up the stairs – is that right?"

"Exactly, sir."

I found this odd – despite the fact that I liked the old man – and broke the news to him gently. "I don't get it. Something's not right," I said.

"I understand your skepticism, sir," Vineyard said. "While it may not seem plausible on the face of it, it is exactly what happened, I assure you. I have no reason to lie to you – nothing at all to gain. I liked Mister Bohn a great deal and enjoyed working for him. I also enjoyed Miss Flowers' visits to the mansion. She brought a touch of elegance and class to Raptor's Ridge."

"All right," I said, "but something still doesn't add up. I'd wager that I could hear gunfire from in here, Mister Vineyard. And you were considerably closer to the action – in the foyer, to be exact – when the shots were fired. Right?"

"That is true, sir. But it does not change the fact that I didn't hear anything – nothing out of the ordinary, certainly, but simply … well, simply nothing at all."

Then it hit me: *The cops must have had cans on their pistols … that would explain it.*

Vineyard no doubt noticed the look of understanding that crossed my face. "Do you know why I didn't hear the shooting, Mister Blake?" he asked.

"They were probably using silencers. From where you were, you wouldn't have a heard so much as a spit, which is all that a good silencer will allow."

"I see. Yes, of course – that would make sense, I suppose."

"Tell me about Downing when he came down the stairs again. Did he seem nervous? Did he act funny in any way – as though something went wrong, maybe?"

"Not at all, sir. I would say that he was as calm as could be, given the nature of the circumstances as I understand them now. He said that it was just a false alarm, as he put it – that I should call Mister McClinton and tell him that. And now that I reconsider his words, he even apologized for taking up my time."

"Apologized?"

"Yes."

"All right, that's interesting. And the others who were with him: Did they do anything – act funny in any way, maybe?"

"No one else said a word, sir. I frankly did not pay them any mind. It was clear to them, as well as to me, that Lieutenant Downing was in charge, just as he was each time he visited the estate."

"All right then, Mister Vineyard," I said after another brief pause, "did you recognize any of the other officers who were with Downing?"

"Yes. In addition to Lieutenant Downing, Sergeant Stone was there."

"William Stone? The guy they call the Buzzsaw?"

"Yes. The other four I didn't recognize at all, although one of them was a female officer. But I did know Sergeant Stone and Lieutenant Downing from previous visits."

"I'll be damned," I muttered, trying to wrap my head around the whole thing. "Stone and Downing both, and a woman cop to boot."

"You appear as though you could use a refresher, sir," Vineyard said, and he picked up the whiskey bottle and poured another generous portion, leaving his own glass untouched.

"Thanks," I said and took a sip, allowing the alcohol to linger on my tongue.

"Mister Vineyard," I asked a moment later, "why was Lieutenant Downing such a frequent visitor to the estate?"

"I couldn't say, sir."

"Couldn't or won't?"

"Couldn't, sir. I simply do not know – it's not my place to ask. You would have to ask Mister McClinton."

Pass-the-ball time, I thought. *That's convenient.*

"You have no idea? None whatsoever?"

"None at all, sir."

"How often was he here?"

"At least once a month – sometimes a little more. He would arrive, usually in the evening, meet with Mister Bohn for a few minutes, and leave. I do not believe he ever stayed longer than a few moments at most."

It just doesn't make any sense, I thought. *And somebody around here knows more than he's letting on ...*

I decided to let it go for now and changed direction. "What's next for you?" I asked.

"Next?"

"With Bohn dead, I mean. The estate eventually will be sold, I'd guess. What do you plan to do once that happens?"

"Yes. Of course. Mister Bohn has been generous through the years, I can assure you. I am certain that my needs will be met. Even so, I have invested wisely during my lengthy tenure here. I can sit back and enjoy my golden years. You never know how much time you have left, after all."

Ain't that the truth? I thought, picturing the two corpses.

I needed some fresh air, and I told Vineyard that I was going to go outside and wait for Floyd Strand's arrival.

"Shall I show you the way, sir?" he asked.

"No, enjoy the music. I always do," I suggested, then picked up the glass and left his suite, humming along to the glorious strains of Mozart.

Understand, the place I was moving so casually through was no Gracie Mansion in New York City. It was a far bigger than that, far more impressive, and I poked around as I headed for the foyer, looking into various rooms and wandering along various corridors before returning to the main hallway.

I eventually passed through the grand foyer and stepped out into the bracing air of the early morning. The two Deeker brothers grunted at me suspiciously; the other nearby henchmen were even less enthusiastic.

I nodded at The Snarl. "Did the cops say anything when they left?" I asked.

"Not a word," he hissed. "They didn't even lower the window."

"How about when they came in? What'd they say then?"

He frowned, trying to recall. "Downing was driving," he eventually said. "He lowered the window, stuck out a piece of paper, told me he was expected. 'Nobody said nothing to me,' I told him. 'Why would they?' he says next. So I answer, 'I'm the one lets you in the gate, smart guy' – words to that effect. So he says, 'This piece of paper lets me inside. Call the cops if you like.' Not much to say to that. I'd seen Downing and his boys come out lots of times, after hours like this. So I let him in, though I did call up to the house."

"Did you talk to Bohn?"

"No. To Vineyard – the butler. He was the only one inside besides the boss and the movie star. I told Vineyard I wanted to talk directly to Mister Bohn, but he said the boss couldn't be disturbed 'cause the movie star was there. So I told him

Downing and a car full of cops was on the way up, and he should get ready. Vineyard said he'd handle it and hung up."

"You weren't suspicious?"

"You implying I was in on it, Blake?" he said, and the menace in his voice was as thick as Alaska river ice. " 'Cause I'll settle with ya right now if you are."

"Relax," I said. "I'm just trying to figure out how this could happen, with all the security around the place and nobody hearing, or expecting, or suspecting, a damn thing."

"Like I said, Downing was a regular. Nothing seemed out of place, other than he didn't call ahead. He didn't tip his hand. He was smooth as glass, coming and going. He won't be tomorrow – not once I settle up. But that's the way it was tonight."

Ned McClinton joined us at that moment. He still looked as though he'd lost his best friend, and I was hard-pressed to tell if he was mourning AJ Bohn or Audrey Flowers.

"Doctor Strand is on his way up from the guard station," he said in a terse, off-hand manner. He rocked on his heels for an instant before heading inside again.

Another country heard from, I thought. *What a hell of a night ...*

I looked up past the dark, purple-tinted horizon and enjoyed the riot of stars overhead. The night sky, free from the city's lights, was as beautiful as anything I had ever seen in my life.

EIGHT

WHY LOOK FOR THE LIVING AMONG THE DEAD?

TWO YEARS EARLIER

He was back on the hunt again.

This was better.

Infinitely better.

He moved silently though the room, imagining himself as a slithering snake or a prowling jungle cat, stalking his prey with an omnipotence that rivaled the gods of old, the gods of antiquity.

He could relate to that; he'd always considered himself to be an old soul.

Whether fate or fortune or good planning, or the lunar tides or karma or happenstance or serendipity, brought him to this bedroom now – at this very point in time in the overall ticking of the cosmic clock – didn't matter so much as what he was about to do.

He was struck by the idea that this was superior to anything that he'd tried before ...

... *and there's not much I haven't tried,* he thought.

Killing was as much a part of his being as breathing, or scratching an itch, or tying his shoes before walking down the stairs. It was just ...

... natural, he thought. *It's just the order of things.
My order of things.*

He'd tried it in many forms, many guises, through the years. Ants and crickets and house flies had given way to field mice and rats and squirrels and rabbits, and then cats – many cats – and even dogs and a cow or two. But it hadn't been enough, and he soon tried other game – game that was supposedly far more dangerous, though never at the odds that he played. And when the cops eventually would step in and questions would be raised – tedious questions that he couldn't control; tiresome questions that he couldn't avoid – he would disappear again.

He was good at disappearing.

But he was better at killing.

He'd even gone to war to satisfy his urges. But the Army Rangers and Special Forces and Black Ops missions – all of it was a mistake, interesting though the work was. It taught him many skills, many talents, many proficiencies. Ultimately, however – despite his best efforts and the raw gusto with which he went about his work – it was …

... unsatisfying.

Killing for others, killing on orders, was not in his nature. It was like placing a mountain cat inside a cage and tossing in food from time to time to satisfy the beast's hunger, taking away the thrill of the hunt.

And so he left.

 Disappeared.

Vanished.

It was easy enough. The chaos of the war zone saw to that, and he was good at manipulating others and getting his way. All it took was a body that had been blown into unrecognizable parts, an exchange of dog tags, a helping hand from soldiers who were more mercenary than Army chain of command, a long and uncomfortable ride home inside a casket in the cargo hold of a military transport plane, the proper uniform in place upon his arrival, blending in with the work detail, slipping though the base undetected – all of the skills that he'd learned during his time in Special Ops.

Starting over, with no trace of a previous existence hounding his every move, and no cops left behind to ask monotonous questions, was ultimately brilliant. No one was looking for him, tracking him, attempting to pin down his whereabouts on a given night, or finding it necessary to talk with him, or order him or push him around or yank his chain.

The MPs were good at pushing his buttons, just as the San Diego police had been when they came poking around, asking what he knew about the disappearance of that pretty housewife – shortly before he left the city in the middle of the night and sought refuge in the shelter of the High Desert country in Oregon and then in the Army. How they'd latched onto him was a mystery, even now. But it didn't last; few things ever did. He'd disappeared from San Diego, losing the identity and the menial job and the small, unfurnished bungalow close to the golf course that he'd rented on a month-to-month basis.

He'd learned things in the process.

One thing he learned was to be wary of the cops … *to never trust the cops, to never get close enough for the cops to reach out and latch onto you.* The cops were dangerous. The cops could mean capture and prison – or even the needle.

He'd also learned a far more valuable lesson, one that he'd relied on ever since that first brush with disaster: It was easy to disappear within the system – far easier than he'd imagined. A switch of identities, a change of locations, subtle changes in his features – hair color, adding or subtracting facial hair, eyeglasses, hats, wigs, baggy clothing, lifts in his shoes, a new name with matching documents – and he was on to the next town, the next big score, the next victim.

Always another victim …

From time to time he would return home, probably because he found comfort in the familiar surroundings and a certain swagger, a regaining of his equilibrium, when he temporarily regrouped with his boyhood friends. He'd quickly realized that he knew things they did not, that he could do things they could not or would not do, that he could take chances they would never think of taking, that he could …

… kill and get away with it.
And do it again, and again, and again …

Returning home after the San Diego experience led to his time in the Special Forces, although he was bright enough, manipulative enough, to bring along some company.

The whole thing was brilliant – while it lasted, at least. But the poets were correct: All things must pass; good things come to those who wait; the mulberry leaf becomes a silk gown with time and patience.

He understood patience.

He knew discipline, and attention to detail, and structure and order.

And he was on his own again – just as it should be.

No one looks for the dead. Not the Army; not the San Diego cops, certainly.

Being dead covers a multitude of sins, he thought, and the preposterous nature of the idea almost made him laugh out loud.

And now it was time again.

She looked so peaceful in sleep that it seemed a shame to wake her – especially considering what he was about to do to her.

Patience was one thing. Hunger was quite another. He unsheathed the seven-inch-long stainless steel Cobra tactical knife with a serrated blade and fine bone handle and smiled his very best smile into the face of the unseeing, unknowing darkness.

She couldn't appreciate his smile – not yet. She still had no idea that he was even in the room, nor what was about to happen to her. But that didn't matter in the slightest. He still smiled his finest, most sincere, most convincing smile – the one that said, "I'm truly at your service, ma'am. I'm here to help."

He spotted the gleam of a pendant that was fastened around her neck on a long gold chain and noted how it rose and then slowly fell again on her breast with her steady, rhythmic breathing.

Won't that make a lovely addition to the collection? he thought.

And for the next thirty-six hours, at least, he thought of little else.

NINE

SOME UNDETERMINED
SHOTS IN THE DARK

MONDAY, 4:49 A.M.

The softness of the night was about to lull me to sleep.

All right, so technically it was early morning and approaching daylight; the false dawn already was beginning to filter through the tall Douglas firs and ponderosa pines and sequoias and mammoth oaks that surrounded the estate. I peered into the gloom, dead tired from the euchre marathon, listening for the approaching car bearing the late AJ Bohn's personal physician to Raptor's Ridge, when two rapid-fire gunshots from inside the mansion interrupted the mood.

That will get your heart racing.

Paul Deeker swept past me so quickly that I had a hard time processing what was taking place. I heard him mutter a single violent curse, then a mumbled "Not on my watch," and I turned to follow him inside when, seconds later, another gunshot echoed off the walls. I looked around, trying to determine the source of excitement, and was caught up in the mad dash of a half-dozen of Deeker's henchmen. They shoved me roughly aside as they broke through the entryway, their momentum carrying them past the foyer and into the great room.

Bohn's lawyer appeared at the top of the stairs, grasping his left arm. I could see that his fingers were blood-red, even from where I stood, and it didn't take a doctor or a genius, or even a college professor, to figure out that he'd been in the middle of whatever had taken place.

"He's getting away," Ned McClinton cried, pointing with his good arm toward the east wing of the mansion before clasping it back over his bleeding bicep.

"Who?" Deeker yelled. He'd pulled a no-nonsense SIG Sauer semi-automatic pistol from a waistband holster and had it clasped firmly in his right hand as he ran up the stairs, its barrel tilted toward the ceiling.

"He jumped out the window," McClinton called, and he started down the stairs, appearing as though he were drunk rather than wounded. "He'll get away."

Deeker pivoted deftly on the stairs and pointed to his henchmen. "Quick," he growled. "Find him. Bring him in … alive. I want him alive. Understand?"

He returned his attention to McClinton. "Who was it? Did you get a look at him?"

"I don't know," the lawyer said, his tone shaky, his eyes wide with the fright of his close call. "He was in the bedroom. I surprised him. He was running. I tried to get out of his way. He started shooting, over his shoulder. I tripped, I think, or fell when I got hit. I'm not sure. Then he went through the window. I didn't recognize him."

I was behind Deeker now and poked his arm. "Why don't you go out with your boys – see if you can track him down. I'll help the shyster."

Deeker gave me a hard look, grunted, pursing his lips in distaste, and started down the stairs again, heading toward the front entrance, gaining momentum. He brushed past a dapper-looking man who'd just stepped inside the entryway with an open, quizzical look on his face.

"Sorry, Doc," The Snarl muttered.

"Are you Doctor Strand?" I called.

He nodded.

"I've got a customer for you," I said, pointing toward McClinton. With an honest-to-god physician on board, I could make myself useful again. I hurried down the stairs, following Deeker.

"Hey – who are you? What the hell's going on here?" Strand yelled. But given the circumstances, I was in too much of a hurry to reply.

I raced down the steps and halted abruptly, wondering which direction to take, when a single gunshot barked in the crisp air and, after a brief pause, six rapid replies sang out in turn.

They're going to kill him, I thought, picturing The Snarl's henchmen as I raced toward the action. *Then we'll have nothing ...*

But I was wrong: They didn't get him – at least not yet. Deeker and his boys were milling about as I turned a corner and made my way through a copse of trees. I called out so they wouldn't mistake me for the killer and locked eyes with The Snarl. He was snapping orders as I approached, and he shot me another ugly look.

"Nothing?" I asked.

"Not yet. But we ain't done – he won't get away that easy," he said.

"Will the gunshots attract a crowd?" I asked, thinking about the two dead bodies upstairs and the necessity, at least for the time being, of avoiding police involvement.

"Out here? Not a chance."

I milled around for a few minutes, waiting for more gunfire to erupt or sudden cries of discovery or desperation. But I eventually figured that I was wasting my time and again caught up with Deeker, who continued barking at his crew. "I'm heading in. Maybe I can get something else out of the lawyer," I said. I turned to leave, but he caught my arm and spun me around.

"Blake. What the hell's going on?" he asked. I detected genuine puzzlement in his hoarse voice, if not a trace of panic.

"I was going to ask you the same thing," I said. I took a few steps and then called over my shoulder: "Make sure your boys don't mistake me for the creeper."

By the time I was inside again, Doc Strand had the lawyer in a chair at the foot of the stairway. McClinton's suit coat and necktie were off, and Strand was tending to what looked to be a through-and-through bullet hole in the left bicep, nearer to the shoulder than the elbow.

McClinton didn't like being used for either target practice or medical dummy, and he squirmed in the chair as Strand poked and prodded at the wound. A black leather bag was on the floor beside the physician. While I hadn't noticed, it made perfect sense that Strand must have had it with him when he arrived.

Late-night call and all – why not?

"He fill you in?" I asked Strand as I approached.

"Not yet – haven't asked," he said. "I'll try you instead. How about telling me exactly who you are and what in the name of god almighty is going on here tonight. And, while I'm at it, where in hell is Mister Bohn?"

"Well, that's just the thing, Doc," I said. "Your client's been dead for hours, along with his mistress."

I paused, gauging his reaction. When he stared back, his face a blank slate, I thought, *One cool customer,* and added, "Beyond that, we've got an escalating mystery on our hands. Just a few minutes ago, somebody was rummaging around the crime scene and took a potshot at our lawyer friend."

If Strand was troubled by the news of AJ Bohn's sudden departure from Planet Earth, he showed no outward sign of it. He reached instead into his medical bag, produced a roll of gauze, and started to wrap it, efficiently and professionally, around the lawyer's wound. He sliced the end of the gauze with surgical shears, tied it off, and lowered his face so that he was looking directly at McClinton.

"Ned," he said firmly. "Ned – focus for me. Right here."

"It's just intolerable," McClinton muttered, as though that single word explained everything that had recently happened at Raptor's Ridge.

"Yes. It certainly is," Strand agreed. "Listen to me now. You are going to be fine. Keep the arm elevated for the time being." He raised it to eye level. "Up here. See? I'll take another look in a minute or two – I promise – but you have nothing to worry about. Relax. Take a deep breath or two. All right?"

McClinton mustered a smile. "I guess," he said weakly. "I could use a drink."

"So could I," Strand said. He glanced in my direction again: "Any idea where Mister Vineyard is hiding, or is he dead, too?"

"Last I saw, he was in his room down the hall" – I pointed with a single finger – "enjoying a little night music and a bottle of Irish whiskey."

"We could all use some of the same," Strand said. "Let's escort Ned to Mister Vineyard's suite. Then you can tell me exactly what you know."

"Can't give you much that'll make sense, Doc," I said, "but I'll do my best."

"And I can't ask for more, given the circumstances," Strand said.

We helped McClinton up and steadied him as we walked slowly down the long hallway.

"I'm Max Blake," I said as we started off. It seemed only fair to tell him that much, seeing as how he'd already asked me twice.

"You worked for AJ?"

"Not before this. And, seeing how he's dead, can't say I've ever worked for the man."

Strand smiled. "Well, we all have our moments in the sun – don't you agree?" he said, and it dawned on me that the doctor was all right in the general scheme of things.

TEN

OF CAMERAS AND TAPE RECORDERS

MONDAY, 5:17 A.M.

When you got right down to it, the entire mess at Raptor's Ridge didn't add up. The extra guy in the bedroom wasn't the only reason why the pieces were as jumbled as a well-scrambled jigsaw puzzle – one of the giant ones, the kind that Marion Davies, the silent film star, used to while away the hours up at San Simeon.

Or so the newspapers said, anyway.

It had occurred to me that the more I saw of Raptor's Ridge, the more it reminded me of William Randolph Hearst's mansion in the clouds on the California coast. This place, at least by what I'd seen to date, was every bit its equal in craftsmanship and expensive décor and, yes, even in taste. And I wondered whether AJ Bohn had somehow considered himself to be Hearst and Audrey Flowers to be his own Marion Davies.

The tabloids would have a field day with that ... if only they knew, I thought.

But I didn't want to get stalled on the idea of freelancing a story to the nation's tabloids or *People* magazine, and I put it out of my head.

Anytime I get stuck on a case, I pull out a notebook and pencil and start jotting lists – no doubt a holdover from my reporting days. On one side of the ledger, I list the things that make sense; on the other side, I list the things that don't. Rather than waiting on a report from Paul Deeker regarding his pursuit of the mystery man in the upstairs bedroom, or for Doc Strand to return from the butler's room after tending to the lawyer's wounded arm, I took a seat on the stairs leading up to Bohn's corpse and the body of a woman I'd admired for a long time from afar and started to jot down the facts – or the facts, at least, as I understood them.

But it didn't take long for the ledger sheet to look unbalanced: There were far too many unknowns – far too many items that just didn't make any sense – to offset the ones that did.

I wrote the single word Why? on one side of the ledger and, immediately below it, jotted down, in succession:

Money
Power
Sex
Jealousy
Revenge
Rage
Insanity
That about covers it ...

Beyond that, the involvement of the cops was the next big item that just didn't add up, and I listed it under Things That Don't Add Up in a second column.

Hell, fifty years ago maybe, when corruption was a lot harder to define. But the concept is so damned ... arcane; is it even possible today? I wondered. I jotted it down and kept plugging away, pencil at the ready.

The manner in which Audrey's body was positioned in the bathtub was another item of interest on the *Things That Don't Add Up* side of the ledger.

It's almost as if she were placed in there, and after she was killed.

The lack of immediate security inside the house at the time of the killings became a third item – despite the lawyer's explanation.

I added it, underlined it a couple of times, and made a mental note to follow up with Ned McClinton when he was feeling better. At least I had good reason to hope that he wouldn't take all that long to recover.

The Snarl needs some grilling on this one as well, I thought and placed his name on the list.

But the extra guy in the bedroom was the biggest hole of all, and I added that as well.

It just doesn't make sense. Who is he? How'd he get up there? When did he get up there? What did he see? What does he know?

"And, biggest of all, will I get a chance to find out before Deeker's goons put him down?" I muttered, low and under my breath, still scribbling.

I started adding more items and flipped the page of the notebook for some additional space to write. But I couldn't get the lurker in the bedroom out of my head.

Maybe the cops didn't do the shooting at all, I thought. *Maybe – just maybe – the guy who pulled the trigger was up there all along. Maybe the cops are a ruse, a diversion – a red herring, maybe.*

I headed up the stairs at that point, wondering about the bullet that had passed through McClinton's arm. If I could find the slug, I'd be able to match it against the rounds that took down AJ Bohn and even the one that dispatched Audrey Flowers, sending her off to a final performance that no one but her killer could appreciate.

I heard the sounds of footsteps on the stairs behind me and glanced over my shoulder, expecting The Snarl but spotting Doc Strand.

"How's the lawyer?" I asked.

"As well as can be expected," Strand said, taking the stairs two at a time until he reached the landing. "Looks worse than it is, though he'll be sore as hell and sport a couple of trophy scars to show off at dinner parties … if he's inclined to show off."

"A sawbones with a sense of humor," I said. "I didn't expect that from a man with a low handicap and a medical degree. You surprise me, Doc."

"Unlike competence from a college professor of journalism, of all trades, with a private detective's license. Are you going to surprise me?"

"I might," I replied. "But it's early yet. We'll see."

"You're a man who holds his cards close and his enemies closer, no doubt. So explain the sawbones reference," he said. "You watched *Star Trek* as a kid, maybe?"

I considered telling him about my great-great-grandfather, the federal marshal in the old Arizona Territories, and recalled from family legend that the original Max Blake's best friend was a doctor whom he often called a sawbones. But given the circumstances that we now found ourselves in, I waived off the question and a muttered reference to "Gumshoes, for god's sake" and halted at Bohn's corpse, which hadn't moved since I'd seen it last.

"Allow me to introduce your former client's new look," I said, sweeping my hand in a theatrical gesture toward the sprawled body. " 'Alas, poor Yorick! I knew him well.' "

"Not nearly as well as I knew poor AJ," Strand said, and he stooped low over the body for a cursory examination. "By the way, you botched the quote, professor. Shakespeare actually wrote: 'Alas, poor Yorick! I knew him, Horatio, a fellow of infinite jest, of most excellent fancy.' "

"That's good, Doc. You are a man of many talents, apparently."

"That's what everybody tells me, though nobody's called me a sawbones till now."

He continued studying the corpse, and a minute passed and then another, and I said, "Audrey Flowers is in here," heading into the master bath. Strand popped up from his crouch, ignored a loud pop from his knee, and followed.

"Hmmmm," he muttered, low in his throat, when he saw the body and bent over the tub to look closely at the wound.

I was still troubled at her appearance and said so. "She looks almost … I don't know, at peace," I said.

"She does at that," he offered, though he spoke so quietly that it took a moment for his words to register.

"That bothers me," I said.

Strand turned, a quizzical look on his face. "Why?" he asked.

"Because it tells me this wasn't part of the mess – the activity, for want of a better term – in the other room," I said. "That's out-and-out murder in there. But this? I don't know: It might not be murder at all."

"And you get that from by looking at a dead woman's face? Interesting."

"I'll know more when you give me the bullet that's in her head," I said.

"Give you the bullet? That's not my job – and even if it were, I sure as hell wouldn't give it to you. Last I looked, that's the medical examiner's job – and the city's illustrious police force," he said. He was facing me now, his back turned to the body, the thorough professional once more.

"What did McClinton tell you?" I asked, surprised that he wasn't yet in on the game.

"Aside from your name and occupation and a bit of background, he told me that his arm hurt," he said. "He mentioned it a dozen times, often accompanied by a grunt and the word *'intolerable'* – sometimes all three in unison. Given the circumstances, it's no surprise that's all he said. And, from the looks of things, he's lucky to be talking at all. How about you tell me what the two of you are up to? I can't wait."

All right, so I'll admit it: That last line was delivered with more than a hint of sarcasm. But as I came to know Doc Strand during this sordid affair, I grew to like him and can forgive his early skepticism, when things were still slowly unfolding.

So, where to start? I thought.

"All right, Doc, pay attention 'cause I'll do this quick. We've still got a lot of fish to fry, and mind you, this isn't my tale. It's McClinton's and Vineyard's – at least for now."

I paused, and he folded his arms across his chest, his eyes locked and alert. "Go ahead," he said. "I'll try to keep up."

Sure, he'd just fired yet another zinger – but hey, I get it.

"Before you arrived," I began, "and before the lawyer arrived, and even before I walked in, the city cops came – six in all, with a search warrant. They left The Snarl and his goons at the main gate – though I find that odd – and met the butler, demanding to see Bohn. The butler told them to settle in while he called the lawyer."

I drew a deep breath here and added, "You with me so far?"

"Still here," he said. "Just one question: What, or who, is The Snarl?"

"That's Paul Deeker – one of the bodyguards."

"All right. Proceed."

"Good. So the butler calls McClinton and tells him what's going on with the cops, who are carrying a warrant. McClinton tells him to hold the cops in the foyer until he arrives. The butler is fine with that; Bohn wasn't to be disturbed anyway. But cops are cops, and they aren't buying it. A couple of them say, 'Screw this' – words to that effect, I'd imagine – and head up the stairs. The others wait with the butler. A minute later the cops come down and tell the butler that it's all a big misunderstanding. They head out, offering an apology to Vineyard, who says, mind you, that he hears nothing out of the ordinary while the cops are upstairs – no gun shots, no scuffling, no bodies thumping into tubs or onto the floor. Nothing at all. The lawyer arrives minutes later and finds the bodies when he goes up to ask about the warrant."

I paused here, drawing another deep breath, and added, "The lawyer then calls me."

Strand maintained an empty stare during this recitation of facts and said nothing when I finished. I was tempted to again ask if he'd managed to keep up, but I didn't want to insult the guy. Who knows? I might take a slug in the arm one day and require his expertise.

"So I get here, McClinton gives me the lowdown and tells me I'm the guy Bohn picked to investigate in case something hinkey happened to him, and – just like you – I say, 'It's not my job. Call the cops.' Then he tells me about the cops – that the cops are the ones who've killed Bohn and Audrey, and it's up to me to solve this thing because, as he puts it, you can't call the cops to solve a murder that the cops committed. Which, on the surface, I guess, makes sense."

When I finished, I could almost hear the gears turning inside the doctor's head. He was about the speak at one point, changed his mind, thought of something else and almost spit that out, then abandoned it, all the while rocking back and forth on the toes and heels of what looked to me to be expensive shoes of Italian vintage.

I let him think.

"You didn't need me up here to tell you that AJ and Audrey were dead," he said at last. "You already knew that. So why am I here?"

I grinned then – my best, full-toothed grin … the one that always melts my mother's heart.

"The investigation is off the books – for now, at least – and I need a coroner. You, my friend, are it."

I wish I'd had a camera to capture the look on Strand's face.

It's a good thing that I didn't have a tape recorder running to preserve what he said next, however. My poor mother would've disapproved of both the language and the sentiment.

ELEVEN

A POTENTIAL FLY IN THE OINTMENT

MONDAY, 6:22 A.M.

It dawned on me that Bill Kohlmeyer might be the solution to the entire mess – and to call the situation at Raptor's Ridge something other than a mess would be kidding yourself.

Kohlmeyer is the city's new police chief. He'd been appointed to the job several weeks previously, although he was well-known on the force and throughout the city. He's also a good guy, a man of integrity – a man who doesn't tolerate crime, crap, or corruption, as my flinty grandfather used to say.

With the election of the new mayor months before, sweeping changes were in the air. Kohlmeyer's appointment was the first of many that were announced at City Hall in the aftermath of the vote-counting. He'd been a city cop for thirty years and succeeded at just about every job you can think of during that time, from walking a beat in the early days to motorcycle patrol and then heading up the robbery and homicide divisions, where he was known to dig and scratch and claw for answers like a cat in a litter box. He'd even served as head of the city's SWAT team for a time, and he'd also worked a couple of task force operations with the

State Police force, and with the feds and Homeland Security people as well.

If you needed a door busted open or a full charge into a hornet's nest, Kohlmeyer was the first guy you'd think about to lead the way. You knew that he'd come out smiling – and that your back would be covered.

He'd retired from the force a couple of years earlier but found himself getting restless. The local university hired him to head up campus security as part of its newly upgraded Public Safety operation. Most law enforcement insiders thought of the job as a joke, but Kohlmeyer took it seriously – hell, he took everything seriously – and enacted changes that made the campus a safer place during the day and a thug's nightmare at night.

He'd been on that job for a little more than a year and a half when the new mayor called and offered him a chance to make a real difference. Typically, he charged ahead without concern for the apple carts that he was sure to upend and the chops of the former colleagues that he was certain to bust along the way.

Word on the street was that at least a handful of officers didn't think much of Kohlmeyer's return.

Maybe Downing is one of them ... Downing and Stone both.

I thought of Kohlmeyer now because I'd talked with him any number of times during my reporting days and knew him to be brutally honest – someone who wouldn't excuse the slightest breech of conduct or legal service. I wouldn't call him a close pal, exactly – for all I knew, he still hated my guts because of a serious mistake on a SWAT team encounter that I'd reported for the local newspaper years before. But I knew him well enough to have a healthy respect for the man and his methods.

I hadn't spoken with him in years, though not for lack of trying while I was still writing investigative pieces. But I thought about him now as a possible solution to the problem that was staring me in the face at Raptor's Ridge.

"What's on your mind?" Doc Strand asked as we made the rounds of the master bedroom and the adjoining bath, looking for bullet holes in the walls. "You've been quiet, and I don't like quiet at a time like this."

"You like a man who talks?" I asked.

"I like a man who knows when to talk and has something to say. And I like a man who knows when to keep his mouth shut. With you, I haven't made up my mind – not yet. But right now, I'd rather hear you say something – anything – than to watch you walk around this godforsaken mausoleum saying nothing at all."

I was getting to like this guy.

"All right, I've got one for you: What do you know about Bill Kohlmeyer – the new police chief?" I asked.

"I know him. I didn't just fall off the turnip truck," Strand said. He was looking at the spines of books that were aligned on rows of elaborate shelving that occupied a wall farthest from the bed, searching, at my directive, for a bullet hole.

"Knowing him is one thing," I said. "Knowing something useful about him is something else. Do you know him well enough for that – maybe from his days at the university? You're on the board of trustees over there, I hear."

Strand remained silent for a moment while he considered the question and its deeper implications. I'd noticed that he made a habit of this – of looking at an issue from many sides before forming an opinion or offering a response.

It probably made him a good doctor.

"We don't travel in the same circles," he eventually said. "But I've talked with him at charity events, and at the university when he was still there. I like the guy. I've also heard a fair share of opinion, generally good, from friends."

He was fingering the spine of a title that had caught his eye, but he patted it a couple of times and moved on, using his index finger to slide back and forth, up and down, slowly pacing the length of the extensive built-in bookcase. "What I've heard since the change at City Hall is that some cops are happy he's back, and others would rather be visited by the plague."

"New Testament or Old?" I asked.

"Both," Strand said, "though neither is good for your health."

"Any of those observations come from your late employer?" I asked.

Strand glanced my way momentarily, a cutting look on his face, before moving along the wall of books again.

"Let me give you a heads-up," he said, talking into the titles. "I was AJ's physician. I wasn't his confidant, nor his business partner, nor colleague, nor fellow traveler, nor drinking buddy, nor *bon vivant,* nor man about town, nor Man Friday. I'm not even sure you could call me his friend."

"And you tell me that because …"

"It's plain from your face, your tone, your questions. You think I have information – details, facts and figures, maybe even recordings and videos – about what goes on at Raptor's Ridge. Or, more appropriately, what *went* on here. You think that because AJ had a reputation as a" – he paused momentarily, searching for the right word – "an insider in an insider's world, maybe, that I'm an insider, too, because I worked for him."

"The butler said you were close to the old guy."

"Mister Vineyard, I'm afraid, didn't understand our relationship."

I raised my eyebrows, in a *That's-at-least-what-the-butler-said* manner, but didn't speak.

"Look, Blake," he said. "I don't much care if you judge me, or the choices I make or have made. But I'm not stacked in the middle of this thing, in any sense of the phrase. You can buy that if you want or leave it on the shelf, but there it is."

"All right," I replied, "fair enough. But remember: My initial question was about Kohlmeyer, not about you or your character or whether you were on the inside with Bohn."

"Fine. Based on what I know for fact and not as speculation, I like Kohlmeyer well enough," Strand said after another pause. "The cops who aren't happy to see him running the force are the same cops someone should keep an eye on. And, not to change the subject, but I've got something over here – you might want to take a look."

The doctor was pointing at a hole in the spine of a thick-as-a-board treatise on American hardwoods. The hole looked as though it had been neatly drilled, and I pulled the book off the shelf and opened it. Sure enough, a slug fell out as I flipped the pages.

"Who owns a book about oak trees?" I muttered as I stooped to pick up the spent round.

"Surely you can't be that dense," Strand said. "Aside from being in the timber trade, which explains the book, Mister Bohn had surprising tastes and an interest in a good many topics. Boxing, for instance. He used a phrase that I've since found useful – used it many times myself: 'A man has to be able to punch his weight.' AJ believed that a man who couldn't make a contribution, or couldn't keep up, wasn't a man at all."

"Good for him," I muttered, though I didn't much mean it because my concentration was elsewhere. "And this slug is from a .38, or maybe a 9-mil," I added as I examined the round. I pushed the book back into its spot on the shelf, pulled the pencil from my shirt pocket, and stuck an inch of its sharp end into the hole in the book's spine.

"So the bullet came from that direction," I said, following an imaginary line that stretched away from the pencil's eraser end. "Which means your lawyer pal was somewhere between this point and the shooter when the bullets started flying."

"Or vice-versa," Strand suggested.

"If this round is even from the shooting that involved McClinton."

"Exactly."

"Then again …"

I eyeballed the room, the entrance to the bedroom, the opening to the master bath, and made some quick calculations: The lawyer probably walked into the room and surprised the guy, who turned and fired his weapon twice while heading toward the window.

"Yeah, I get it," I said. "This could be the slug that clipped the shyster, all right, but it also could be from the shots that took out Bohn. Let's keep looking, just in case. No telling what we might turn up."

I pocketed the bullet and drifted across the room again, picking up where I'd left off on the opposite wall.

"Why bring up Kohlmeyer?" Strand asked, his fingers once more running up and down the spines of AJ Bohn's reading material.

"Someone's got to officially investigate. Then again, I'm not sure the cops did the shooting," I said, as much to float a theory as to provide insightful commentary. "Too many holes – too many flies in the ointment."

"So who, if not the cops?" he asked.

"I don't know; wish I did. It would make things a lot easier and a lot quicker. Did Bohn have enemies you know about who would resort to murder?"

"Hundreds, if you believe the rumor mill, though I don't know of any myself," Strand said. "Personally, I liked the guy. He was the real deal – a genuine titan; a captain of industry, as the saying goes – and he was square with me."

"Terrific. We're right back where we started."

"Except for Kohlmeyer," Strand said.

"You're persistent, Doc. I like that about you."

"And you think he can help?"

"More to the point, I don't like the idea of keeping someone at the top of the food chain out of the loop on this crazy case, which is exactly what McClinton's proposing. I can see his point, but I'm not sure I buy it. Not yet, anyway."

"Why not?" Strand asked. "It seems clear, based on what we know so far, that the police were at least a party to the shooting. Put another way, even if the cops didn't pull the trigger, they sure as hell didn't report it when they saw it. That says something."

"True enough," I said. "It's suspicious. But there's still too much we don't know: for example, when Bohn was shot, exactly. Maybe it happened when the cops arrived. Maybe it was earlier. Maybe it was sometime during the day, or even last night. We also don't know when Audrey bought the farm, but it's a decent bet – to me anyway – that she might've been killed first, before Bohn."

I looked at the sawbones again. "You any good at pinpointing time of death?"

There was that pause again. "I'm not a coroner, nor am I a medical examiner," he said eventually. "But I do know my way around a body. The best I can tell you right now is that our victims were struck by gunshots, in the case of Mister Bohn, and a single gunshot, in the case of Miss Flowers. Other factors might be involved – you've noticed the bruising on AJ's neck; someone would have to do a thorough examination. That same someone – a qualified coroner or medical examiner – would have to test for lividity before conclusions can be drawn."

"Lividity?"

"You don't watch *CSI*?"

"Sorry."

"In simple terms, it's the way the blood pools after death."

"All right, Doc. Fair enough. But my point remains. I don't know whether the cops did this. Their conduct's in question, but as to whether one or more of them actually shot Bohn and then shot Audrey, or the other way around? Who can say? Not me. Not yet anyway."

"So that brings me back to the same question: If not the cops, who?"

"Might be the guy who was lurking around up here," I said. "For that matter, it might be the butler" – I ignored Strand's loud scoff – "or even the shyster. And I haven't gotten to any or all of the goons who were on the grounds at the time of the shootings, whenever that was, exactly. All of which takes us back to Bill Kohlmeyer."

"You're wondering whether I think he can be trusted to investigate a mess within his own department?"

"I am."

Strand barked out a brief laugh. "Took you long enough," he said.

"I teach for a living," I said. "Classes last either fifty minutes or an hour and twenty minutes, depending on the day and the number of credit hours. I'm obligated to fill that amount of time for each class I teach, and for each day I teach it. I'm good at stretching out a little to cover a lot – something else I learned in my reporting days."

He served up another brief, humorless laugh.

"But the journey was a good one anyway – don't you think?" I said.

"Not necessarily."

That made me grin, though only momentarily. You didn't need to look far to be reminded that dead bodies still surrounded us.

"As to Kohlmeyer," Strand said, "it's an easy call, based on our current situation and what I know. To my mind, he seems to be, from all accounts, a rock-solid guy. If we are being forced to go into battle, and I think that we are, I'd at least want him on our side."

"You said *we* and *our*."

"I did."

"All right, good. I feel the same about Kohlmeyer," I said. "I sure as hell wouldn't want him on the other side, though calling him in is something of a risk, regardless of which direction I decide to go."

I thought about it a minute longer, then gave it my best *Oh-well, what-the-hell?* look.

"I'll add this," I said. "If I wanted to stick a fly in someone else's ointment, just to gum up the works, Kohlmeyer would be a good choice for the job."

"I never quite understood that metaphor," Strand said, "but I agree."

TWELVE

A FELLOW CONSPIRATOR

MONDAY, 6:39 A.M.

I remained at the late AJ Bohn's magnificent estate for another full hour, running through a checklist of obvious items that needed attention. Sad to say, it was damn pathetic that the job fell to me.

I touched base with Russell Vineyard once more, collecting another set of impressions from him regarding the arrival and departure of the suspect cops. I also figured, after another few minutes of discussion, that if he were lying, he was an absolute master in the art of deception and needed to take his act on the road. I checked him off my list of potential suspects and moved on.

Ned McClinton looked somewhat better than the last time I'd seen him, but only because he'd looked like hell short minutes before. He'd been plied with alcohol to numb the pain in his arm and was tipsy when we talked. But he remained adamant that no one else was to be involved in the investigation, and he asked about the arrangements that I was making to take the bodies for examination.

"Let's leave them here, untouched for now," I told him, purposely vague. "I'm still working out the details."

"I trust you won't take long – for obvious reasons," he said.

"Yeah, I get it. But here's one for you: Do you plan on reporting that hole in your arm to the cops?"

"Absolutely not," he replied, his eyes suddenly focused. "Or at least … not right away."

"You've got some serious counts of failure here, counselor," I said. "A failure to report one or more murders, a failure to report a shooting, conspiracy to hide or dispose of dead bodies, conspiracy to cover up a murder ..." I paused for effect, then added: "So am I missing anything *really* serious?"

He swayed a bit from side to side as he considered a response, then sat down in a heap and said nothing more.

Truth is, he didn't know I was just having fun with him. But any day you can get a lawyer to both sit down and shut up at the same time is something special, a moment to treasure.

The conversation that I needed the most, and the one I was least looking forward to, was with The Snarl. I hadn't heard from Paul Deeker since I'd returned to the mansion while he and his boys were chasing after the mystery man who'd bolted from the master bedroom, winging McClinton as he fled.

I wasn't concerned that Deeker would lie to me, exactly. I was more concerned that he would tell me the brutal truth – that he'd caught The Lurker and was holding the poor sap in some dungeon or cesspool on the estate, torturing him for a confession.

The news I received was equally depressing.

"We didn't find him – at least not yet," Deeker said. "He slipped us."

"Hard to believe," I said, prodding him along.

"Well, believe it," he grumbled, and the look in his eyes was troubling because I couldn't tell whether he was lying to me. "I've got eight men on the estate, including the two who ferried you out here tonight. We know the place inside out. How he got away is beyond me, but he did."

"Maybe he's still on the grounds," I suggested.

"Nope – thought of that. No luck. We had the dogs out and got nothing. Looks like he got over the fence on the east side. The mutts lost his scent near the road. The bastard must've had a driver waiting, or maybe he had a car parked out there. He's in the wind, but I'll get him – you can bet your ass on that. I'll find him, all right."

"And when you do?"

"I'll get some answers, that's what. He'll talk easy, or he'll talk hard, but he's gonna talk to me. That much I promise."

I handed him one of my fancy business cards and told him to give me a call when and if he had something. But I figured that I might as well have run the thing through a shredder: The Snarl wasn't going to play ball with me unless he had no other choice, and we both knew it.

Still, if I was in this thing, and like it or not I was in it – right up to my precious size-fifteen neck – I was going to play it straight, even if the other guys were not.

I finished with Deeker, went back inside, and caught Doc Strand's attention with a discreet wave. He was taking another look at McClinton's arm, talking with the lawyer in hushed tones while he repacked the gauze wrap, and he stepped into the foyer when he finished.

"You done here?" I asked.

"For good, I'd guess, seeing as how my meal ticket has, as the poets say, flatlined after slipping behind death's purple curtain."

The cockeyed euphemism made me laugh.

"You know," I said, "I told McClinton this earlier, but I'll tell you the same thing now: You should write obits for the local paper. It won't pay much, but you have the gift – and you could forget about dealing with gunshot wounds for good."

"Hey, don't write off my medical career so easily," he said. "The lawyer is officially a patient."

"And are *you* going to report the gunshot?"

He gave me that pause again; then he said: "Let's see how it plays out in the next few hours."

"While you're mulling," I said, "how 'bout a lift back to town? I was shanghaied by The Snarl and his goons and don't want to ask them or, worse, hoof it."

"You could call a cab," he suggested with a mischievous grin.

"I could call Santa, too, and hitch a ride on his sleigh. But I figured it was easier to ask you, seeing as how we're out of season."

"Be careful what you wish for …" He let the comment drift off, and I didn't pay any attention anyway, though I recalled the look in his eye more than once later on.

It was fully light as we walked outside – sun and clear blue skies, warming nicely – and I got my first close-up view of the exterior of Raptor's Ridge from inside the perimeter gates. It truly was impressive. It was far more than a house, or even a mansion; calling it an estate didn't do it justice, either. It was built in another time, when craftsmanship and quality and excess stood for something, and it clearly had been immaculately maintained through the decades.

"I can't imagine the kind of money it took to build this place," I said, returning the fedora to my head.

"You probably can't imagine the kind of money it takes to keep it in operation today," Strand replied. "You'd need twenty jobs or more, just to the pay the utilities. Raptor's Ridge has quite a history, you know – long before AJ took over its stewardship." We were walking briskly across the parking lot, ignoring the looks on the grim faces of Deeker's henchmen who were still milling about. "Come on – I'm over here," he said, pointing with his free arm, the fingers of his left hand wrapped around the sturdy leather handles of his medical bag.

I wasn't surprised to see that he was driving a Mercedes with all of the gizmos and gadgets that German engineering provides these days. But I was surprised to learn first-hand that he was a terrible driver, with a heavy foot on both the gas pedal and the brake and a penchant for riding the tail of anyone unfortunate enough to be immediately ahead of him.

"Why don't you push up a little closer and nudge this guy a bit?" I asked at one point as we approached a slow-moving car, though I had the good sense to keep both feet firmly planted deep into the plush carpeting and my right hand clenched on the door's armrest.

"An excellent idea," he said and edged the big rig forward, smiling at the throaty engine's swift roar.

The driver in the forward car must've glanced in the rearview mirror because he jerked his smallish Ford hard to the right, clearing a narrow lane on an already narrow lane, so that we could pass. Strand took advantage of the opening and stomped on the gas again, streaking by in a whoosh, ignoring the blaring horn.

I glanced down and saw that the knuckles on my hand were white.

"You don't perform surgeries the same way you drive, do you?" I asked.

"I don't do much in the way of surgery these days," he said easily. He roared past another sluggish vehicle that was negotiating one of the hairpin turns leading back into town and added, "Might have to take it up again, though. And soon, given the events of last night."

"Something tells me you'll squeak by – if you manage to survive your time behind the wheel," I said, still clutching the armrest.

"I warned you. Don't say I didn't."

"You didn't prepare me for this," I muttered.

"Hey, come on: Don't we want to meet with Kohlmeyer?"

"And you're serious about the *we* part of this equation?"

"Absolutely," he replied. "I'll see this through with you. In for a penny, in for a pound, as they say. I liked AJ, and I'm happy to help. But you're asking me to hang around for some other reason. True, or am I misreading the tea leaves here?"

When I didn't immediately answer, he prodded me: "So are you?"

"Kohlmeyer and I haven't always seen eye to eye," I said. "My thinking is that he might be more inclined to listen to you than he would be to listen to me."

"Any port in a storm then?" Doc said.

"Something like that."

We were nearing the city limits and the traffic was heavier, forcing him to slow down to normal speeds. I won't say that I relaxed, exactly, but I did feel better about the odds of living at least one more day.

"So … what's the plan?" he asked. "Should we go directly to City Hall, or do you have something else in mind?"

"I wouldn't mind tidying up first," I said, having given the question some thought. "But I'd suggest we stay as far away from police headquarters as we can get."

"Why's that?"

"If we sniff around in person, somebody'll spot us – and the wrong kind of somebody. The word's going to get out quick enough. No sense hurrying it along."

"All right, so where to?"

"How about White's?" I suggested. "It's close by. We can get a bite – some tea sounds good about now – and call ahead. I want to talk with Kohlmeyer off the record and well away from his office."

"You think he'll play ball?" Strand asked.

"One way to find out," I replied, though the closer I got to it, the less confident I felt about the entire scenario that I'd been carefully plotting. "The two of us are already conspirators in this mess. Let's see if we can attract a third party."

"Hmmmm – that actually would be six of us in the conspiracy business," Strand said. "Don't forget about Vineyard, McClinton, and Paul Deeker."

That made me laugh. "Toss in Deeker's brother and the rest of his goons and we've really got a mess on our hands," I said. "God help us all."

"All the more reason why we should take it to someone in authority – kick the can up the line," Strand said, gunning the engine to get around a slow-moving pick-up truck before turning sharply once more, leaving another blaring horn in his wake. "Besides, one more person in the know can't hurt at this stage. Hell, it might even help."

But I wondered about the wisdom of that logic as we pulled into the parking lot of White's Diner. I had a queasy feeling in the pit of my stomach about the whole thing.

Then again, maybe it was just the smell of bacon grease as we climbed out of the Mercedes and opened the front door.

THIRTEEN

ANOTHER COUNTRY
HEARD FROM

MONDAY, 8:30 A.M.

In the end, we flipped a coin. Doc Strand paid the bill at White's, which didn't amount to much. I was the lucky guy who drew the short straw and got to call Bill Kohlmeyer to tell him that some members of the department he'd inherited were more than likely corrupt.

The doc ended up with the better deal, even if the bacon was overcooked and the OJ was watery.

As you'd imagine, Kohlmeyer wasn't thrilled to take the call – not after the words we'd exchanged when last we'd talked – and he was even less happy to learn why I was calling now.

But I can appreciate his quandary. It's not exactly the way that anyone would pick to start their day.

I was cryptic enough on the phone. I didn't mention AJ Bohn, Audrey Flowers, Chuck Downing, or "Buzzsaw" Stone by name. I merely indicated that an investment of a few minutes of his time regarding his police force would pay dividends, politically and otherwise, depending on how he wanted to use the information.

"This sounds like a shakedown to me, Blake," he grumbled, and I could picture him behind his desk, his face contorted, his fingers drumming the hardwood, his eyes dark and nasty. "In case you hadn't noticed, I'm not exactly a" – he paused here, weighing his words – "a likely target these days for one of your damn reporting shenanigans."

"It's no shakedown, Bill. No shenanigans are involved," I said. "I haven't worked as a reporter in years. If you don't buy what I have to sell, fine. You can spike my PI's license or have a torrid affair with my ex-wife – good luck with that one – or pin the tail on the donkey for all I care. Just hear me out."

"I might just do all that and avoid you at the same time," he snapped.

"Look, Bill, you may not think so, but I have a lot of respect for you and the police force – despite it all – and I mean that," I offered. "Hear me out on this. That's all I ask."

"And I'll no doubt thank you for it later – right?"

"Doubtful, though you might have to anyway. What I've got is important and worth a few minutes of your day – that much I guarantee. What you do with it, if anything, is your call. But it'll get your attention quick enough – and hold it, too."

He remained silent for a long time – he'd had a way of doing that when he was running the city's homicide division that was maddening, especially to defense lawyers and inquisitive reporters – before he finally relented.

"It's 8:35 now," he said. "Come by at 10 or so. I'll give you three minutes; not a second more."

"No can do, Bill," I replied. "What I have is dynamite. You'll want this off the books and far away from prying eyes around City Hall – at least for now."

"Are you kidding me." He said it as a demand, not a question.

"I wish."

"I'll tell you right now, Blake. You are trying my patience."

"I don't know what else to say, other than this is important. When you hear it, when you hear what I have, you'll understand."

He waited. I did, too. A full minute passed – I know; I counted – as he pondered the dilemma.

"I'm not going to meet at that fleabag office of yours – I flat-out refuse," he said at last. "I don't want to catch something. How about the coffee shop on Liberty Street?"

"Definitely not. It's too public – too many cops use it," I said. "Trust me."

"I did that once. Look what it got me."

"You've done all right. And you're in a position now to do a lot better – for you, for the department, for the city. Who knows? They might pin a medal on you once you've finished up with this."

"So you say."

"So I do. You know Floyd Strand, right?"

"Floyd Strand the doctor?" he asked. "Sure. I know who he is."

"And?"

"And? What the hell does that mean? I'm not part of his country club foursome, if that's what you're asking, but I know who he is. Why?"

"His office is on Mission, a couple of blocks from the hospital. The address is in the book. Meet us there at 10 o'clock."

"Us? As in you and Strand both?"

"That's right.

"Your stable of friends is improving, Blake, if you're doing meet-and-greets with Doctor Strand."

Then that second gear of his kicked in. I'd thought that it might and, in typical Kohlmeyer fashion, he didn't disappoint.

"Hey, hang on just a damn minute," he said, and I could hear the quickening interest in his voice. "I also know for by-god fact that Strand is AJ Bohn's personal physician."

It was my turn to let him dangle on the line, and I did exactly that for a good half-minute. The chief finally broke the silence.

"Does this involve Bohn, or Raptor's Ridge? Tell me right now, Blake, 'cause you don't mess around where Bohn's concerned – not in this town," he said, the words spilling out in rapid succession, like water cascading down a mountain stream.

"I'll tell you everything I know at 10 o'clock, Bill," I said. "See you then."

I didn't want to hear additional threats or badgering or insults, so I hung up the receiver and caught Strand's eye through the glass while I stood at the pay phone, which was mounted on the outside wall near the restaurant's entrance. He'd been exchanging pleasantries with a couple of regulars in one of the booths, and he nodded and pushed through the doorway behind me.

"You need to get a cell phone," Strand said.

"Never heard that before."

"Hey, you never know. So, did he bite?" he asked.

"Yes. That's the good news."

"I'm almost sad to hear it," he said. "What's the bad news?"

"The bad news? We've got to tell him what we know. It's not going to make him happy, or either of us a lifelong friend, you know."

Strand just smiled and pointed toward his car.

"Come on," he said. "I'll give you a lift. You said your place was close by, right?"

"No thanks, Doc. I'll walk."

"You don't like my driving?"

"I wouldn't say that. But I might let it slip, if forced, that a man would have to be a fool, or drunk, or just plain nuts to get into a car with you behind the wheel."

"Hey, you've hurt my feelings," he said. "I'm a sensitive guy."

"You'll get over it. Oh, one other piece of bad news, for those keeping score …"

"What's that?" Strand asked.

"The meeting's at your office – 10 o'clock. I'd suggest you stop for donuts. Cops like donuts."

"Great," he frumped. "Cream-filled or jelly?"

A funny guy, Doc Strand. He was growing on me.

I arrived at his office five minutes early after stopping off at my place for a quick shower and a change of clothing. I also managed a fast check of my answering machine to delete the student queries about missed classes and midterm exams and an even quicker run through the half-dozen student emails that filled my in-box.

Surprisingly, I felt all right, despite the lack of sleep. Adrenaline will do that.

A city-marked car already was in a reserved spot in the lot near Strand's office.

Great, I thought. *No telling what the sawbones has already spilled …*

But Kohlmeyer was out of the car when he saw me and at my side in a few brisk steps.

"This'd better be good," he said.

"Come on, Bill," I said, trying for levity. "No handshake or hug or a slap on the back? Not even a 'Good to see you, Max,' just for old time's sake?"

"Don't press your luck," he said. "You're lucky I don't throw your ass in jail for that stunt you pulled back when – how long ago was it?"

All right, so I detected more hostility than expected … but he was here anyway. It was a start.

I ignored his question. "Well, you look the same anyway," I said as we entered Doc Strand's plush office accommodations. And he did. Kohlmeyer always looked good.

He's about a half-inch under six feet with a build that belongs on a middle linebacker, and there isn't an ounce of fat on him. His face is ruggedly handsome, though his nose is a bit wide from a right cross he caught in a bar riot a decade earlier that involved more than two dozen so-called patrons and an equal number of cops, Kohlmeyer among them.

He's a natty dresser these days. He was sporting a high-quality Seville suit, expensive shoes you can't find at J.C. Penney's or Sears, where I usually do my shopping, and a colorful necktie that managed to match both his sport coat and the shade of his eyes. Rumor had it that his wife, who'd inherited a small fortune when her wealthy parents were killed in an avalanche while on a skiing holiday in France, selected his outfits and dressed him to her own good tastes.

That's likely a good thing. I know for fact that he's color blind and can't match a coat with a tie to save his life. But hell, I'm also told that a rich wife covers a lot of faults.

"You gentlemen are expected," a pretty receptionist said as we entered. The waiting room was empty, and I figured that Doc Strand's easy life was either going to get a great deal easier or a great deal harder, depending on how the conversation went in the next few minutes.

"Right this way, Chief Kohlmeyer, Mister Blake," the receptionist said, and she stood and ushered us into the doctor's private offices.

"This'd better be good," Kohlmeyer grumbled for the second time as we fell in line behind the receptionist.

"Trust me, Bill," I muttered. "You've got to trust me on this."

And all the time I was thinking, *Just don't shoot the messenger ...*

FOURTEEN

ANOTHER RECOUNTING
OF THE TALE

MONDAY, 10:04 A.M.

It would be disingenuous to say that Bill Kohlmeyer was overjoyed to hear the news. But neither did he explode, which I considered to be something of a triumph. In a fight like this, you have to take whatever small victories you can and savor them, knowing that they might not last beyond the next phone call.

In this case, the fact that Kohlmeyer didn't lean over and slug me a few times, propping me up so that he could get some additional licks in before I collapsed, was about as good as it was going to get.

He greeted Floyd Strand amiably enough, shaking hands before sitting down in one of two chairs that were aligned in front of the large cherry-wood desk, behind which the physician sought refuge. Kohlmeyer ignored the proffered donuts – I shrugged off Strand's withering glance – and sat with his feet flat on the floor and his hands folded neatly in his lap. He didn't exactly act like the day's welcomed guest speaker at the Rotary Club, but hell – who could blame him, given the circumstances?

"For the record, I'm here because he's in on this – whatever this is," Kohlmeyer said, waving a hand in Strand's direction. "And I'll say it again, to both of you: This'd better be good." He shot me as convincing an example of *malocchio* as I've ever seen. He even glared briefly at Strand for good measure.

"Look, Bill, I know the last time we …"

"Let him talk," Kohlmeyer snapped, pointing a thick finger at Strand. "I've already heard more than I want out of you – and the clock's running."

I grinned at this turn, though the doc didn't find it amusing. I sat back in my chair, folded my arms across my chest, and waited.

Doc began with this: "I'm hardly the one who should …"

But he hesitated, lost in thought, and Kohlmeyer pounced.

"Just talk," he said. "I'll listen. Then I'll talk. What could be easier?"

Strand, decidedly uncomfortable, glanced imploringly at me, hoping for a rescue line. I felt bad for him – for an instant, anyway – but decided to let it play out. Strand had been tied to AJ Bohn for a lot longer than I'd been on the case – which was what at this point? eight hours? – and he knew the tale as well as I did.

But the poor guy was experiencing stage fright in his first performance at the big opera house, and he would start awkwardly, stutter, stumble for a time, then grasp at another opening, looking perplexed as he considered where it might take him, before he eventually gave up in exasperation.

"There's just too much I don't know," he said – the first coherent consecutive words he'd managed since Kohlmeyer's spotlight hit him dead center.

"For god's sake, just spit it out," Kohlmeyer said, more annoyed than amused. "Pretend you're talking to the medical board instead of the chief of police."

"Bad analogy," Strand muttered, looking desperate.

"Bill," I said, "let me …"

"I want to hear it from him," Kohlmeyer said, pointing at the doctor again. "I want you to shut up."

Strand's eyes were still wide. I figured, *Ah, what the hell; we could be here all day,* and I plunged forward despite the admonition to remain silent.

"Were you followed on the way over here?" I asked, speaking rapidly so that Kohlmeyer couldn't shut me down again.

"I thought I told you to … wait. Followed? I don't know. Followed by who, exactly?"

I didn't bother with a who/whom lecture.

"Good question. Now you shut up. It's my show, and I'll let you know when it's your turn. As you've noted, the clock's running."

Strand slumped back in his chair in relief. He picked up a donut – one of the chocolate-covered selections with custard filling – and nibbled contentedly.

All right, big mouth. Now what? I thought.

Still, where else to start but with the headline in the next day's newspaper – if, in fact, the next day's newspaper would get the story, which was unlikely if we did our jobs correctly.

"AJ Bohn is dead," I said. "So is Audrey Flowers. They're at Raptor's Ridge right now, as stiff as two-by-fours and a little ripe at this point. I counted at least six bullet wounds, likely from two different weapons."

I waited for him to react.

He didn't blink. He didn't even reach for his cell phone, which I'd also anticipated and wasn't quite sure how I'd stop him from making the call to send in the troops.

I took it as a good sign and glanced at Doc Strand.

"You think *rigor* has set in?" I asked, offering up a softball so that he could get his sea legs righted again.

"Absolutely," he replied, relishing the sidekick role. "A careful examination of the bodies will indicate no contradictions to my investigative colleague's initial assessment."

His colleague, I thought. *I like the sound of that.*

"So here's the long and short of it, Bill, and the reason why you were called before anybody else – and I mean anybody – was brought into the picture."

I laid it out for him then, in much the same way that I had for Strand when he'd first come on the scene: the phone call, the early-morning death ride, the lawyer, the butler, The Snarl and his hired goons, the dead bodies, the bullet holes, the late-night cops visit with warrant, Bohn's will and my role in the investigation, The Lurker – the works.

Kohlmeyer is a good listener. He sat still, his hands folded, his focus intense. He was taking mental notes and readying his questions, but he let me talk without interruption.

It's true that his eyes lit up like flares at a traffic accident when I relayed the part about Downing and Stone and the other four cops and their sudden departure from the premises. But he held steady and didn't interrupt the discourse – a real pro, our chief.

I finished the story with the guy who'd been lurking in the bedroom, the gunshot through the lawyer's arm, the goons and the dogs and the futile chase, and the lawyer's entreaty to keep the authorities out of it entirely. Good as all that was, the business with the city cops and their arrival at the mansion was the thing that most commanded his full attention.

I eventually flicked a wrist in the doctor's direction, indicating that it was his turn.

"Mister Bohn and Miss Flowers were the victims of gunshots," Strand said, speaking this time as though he were, in fact, addressing the medical board. "In his case, at least five; in her case, a single shot to the temple, with no exit. I'd guess a .22, judging by the size of the entry wound. AJ's injuries were far more substantive: a 9 millimeter, perhaps a .38 Special, judging by the size of the holes and what I used to see during my ER residency. I can't speculate as to how long they were dead when I arrived, though it was likely hours rather than minutes, given the previously mentioned *rigor.*"

He halted, looked up at the ceiling as though considering the situation again, and added: "I also treated Edward McClinton, Mister Bohn's lawyer, for a bullet wound to the left arm, approximately eight inches above the elbow – a through-and-through."

I picked up the story here. "That one definitely took place after the fact – Bohn and Audrey were already dead. I heard the shots, just before Doc got there. We poked around and dug a slug out of a book in the master bedroom." I extracted the spent bullet and placed it on the desk in front of Kohlmeyer. "Looks like a 9-mil to me, but you're the expert."

"So the guy in the bedroom, the one who shot the lawyer – he wasn't the primary shooter," Kohlmeyer said, a statement more than a question and the first words he'd spoken since I began my discourse.

"Hard to say," I replied. "Maybe he was. Maybe he killed Bohn and Audrey and then shot the lawyer, though at different times, hours apart. Maybe he had more than one gun."

"Unlikely," the chief said.

"Agreed, but at this stage … who can say?"

"And you think Downing and Stone are – what? Responsible?"

"Frankly, I don't know, Bill. I'm not sure. It's the reason I ignored McClinton's counsel, and the old man's will, apparently, and called you. Well, that and the obvious violation of a few dozen laws that I can think of, just off the top of my head."

"That's never stopped you before," he said. But he had a skeptical look frozen on his face, and I took it to mean that he was pondering the involvement of his police officers and not our previous dealings.

Who can blame him?

"No question those two are up to something," I said. "And it's likely no good, whatever it is. But I don't know that they killed Bohn or Audrey. To me, right now, it doesn't add up."

"Tell me why," he said.

Even Doc Strand was leaning forward in his chair.

"For one thing, the butler said he didn't hear a thing when Downing and Stone were upstairs: no gunshots, no bodies falling, no bodies dumped into bathtubs. Nothing. And they weren't up there but a minute, maybe less. I'll grant you, that's plenty of time to kill someone, especially with a couple of shooters involved. But it's still unlikely."

"Thin," he said. "Typical of you, though."

I ignored the jab and continued. "It's what Downing said to the butler when he was leaving. He told Vineyard that he was sorry for taking up his time. Do those sound like the words of a man who'd just executed two people in cold blood?"

"Why not?" Kohlmeyer asked. "Nutty people do nutty things – happens all the time. Someone who's inclined toward murder might do or say damn near anything."

"Yeah, maybe," I said. "But the whole thing still doesn't add up for me. It doesn't make any sense to kill Bohn and Audrey and then walk out the door, leaving the butler alive. He'd be a witness. You wouldn't leave behind a witness – would you?"

Kohlmeyer considered it a moment, then raised the thumbs on his folded hands several times, as though flicking away a meddlesome fly.

"So speculate," he said. "You were up there. You looked around. What do you think happened?"

"If I had to guess, I'd say Downing and Stone were set up – somebody used them to establish a fall-guy. Mind you, I still think they were up to no good. The Snarl said as much when I questioned him."

"The Snarl?"

"Paul Deeker," Strand said. "He's one of Mister Bohn's…"

"I know who he is – and his brother," Kohlmeyer said, pouncing quickly enough that I figured the three of them must've had a run-in somewhere along the line. But I didn't ask, and he didn't give anything up at that point.

Kohlmeyer, in fact, thought about things some more, occasionally shaking his head from side to side, trying to make the pieces fit together, his eyes clouded with what I took for something between seething anger and a decidedly gritty determination.

Or at least that's the way it looked at the time.

"Tell me you haven't had your doubts about Downing and Stone for a long time," I said, speeding him along. "But as murderers?"

He glared at me and turned to our host.

"Can I count on your discretion, Doctor Strand?" he asked.

"Sure," Strand said. "Of course."

Then he turned his muscular frame in my direction again. "All right, much as I hate to say it, I appreciate your dealing me in, Blake," he said grudgingly. "You could've played the cards different. I'm glad you didn't, for both of our sakes."

I decided not to take a bow. "And the next step?"

"I'm not sure, though I want to go up there and look around before deciding anything. And, given the circumstances, we need to keep this quiet for now. You two want to take a ride, seeing as how you already know the lay of the land?"

"I'm in," Doc said, adding quickly. "I'll drive."

"Like hell you will," I said, pulling myself out of the chair and reaching for a donut. "I'd suggest that whatever we do next, we do it discreetly. The eyes are out there – a bunch of them – and they'll be watching."

"You can count on it," Kohlmeyer said, as though he knew more than he'd been letting on. "And maybe even more eyes than we know."

FIFTEEN

A RETURN TO THE SCENE OF THE CRIME

MONDAY, 10:36 A.M.

The drive to Raptor's Ridge was as uneventful as you could hope for, given the unusual circumstances. I was behind the wheel of a Chrysler minivan belonging to Doc Strand's receptionist. Bill Kohlmeyer was in the front passenger seat with an unspoken directive to watch the flow of traffic behind us – a job he took seriously. The doctor, a row back, grumbled the entire time about losing his driving privileges, unamused at this turn of events.

"Trust me, Doc," I said, glancing in the rearview mirror. "I'm doing us all a favor."

"Yeah, well, one man's favor is another man's prison sentence," he grumped.

I had to laugh at that. "Look, Doc," I said, glancing again at the mirror. "We've got the chief of police riding shotgun. If he saw what you did behind the wheel, he'd take your license away for good. Isn't that right, Chief?"

But Kohlmeyer was morose and unresponsive to the casual banter, though his sharp eyes darted back and forth as he watched the flow of cars around us. He was using the vanity mirror attached to the visor, and he'd adjusted the passenger's side mirror for his use as well. If we were being tailed by members of his police force, including those who might resort to murder, he'd spot it.

He wasn't a man taken to brooding, but I could tell that he was clearly troubled by what he'd heard and was no doubt considering various lines of attack to solve the issues that existed within his police force.

"You see that big sedan, right?" I asked him a moment later.

"I see it," he replied gruffly.

But the grey Buick turned onto a side street moments later, well before we started up the southern hills near the edge of town and then began the big ascent to the late AJ Bohn's estate.

"As long as I don't see it again," he muttered.

A minute Strand said, "It might've helped that we took this van instead of my car."

"Or that we left my car in the lot and put the chief's rig in the parking garage," I offered.

"Or that we slipped out the back door," the doc said.

"If we'd been really smart, we would've called separate cabs, or arranged for a helicopter flight, maybe," Kohlmeyer said. "But then, we're not overly bright here, are we?"

"I'd say we're doing all right," I offered.

"Yeah? Consider what you're doing right now, and who you're with, and where you're heading, and why. Then tell me that again," Kohlmeyer said.

"All right, so you got me. But the doc here is pretty smart."

"If he'd been on the ball to begin with, he would've taken on a different client and not associated himself with the city's top ..."

Kohlmeyer's voice trailed off, and he added, "Sorry, Doctor Strand. That was uncalled for, at this stage anyway."

"It's all right," Strand said. "It's nothing I haven't heard before – from a handful of my associates, at least.

But for the record, I never saw anything illegal in the time I was connected to AJ Bohn or Raptor's Ridge. And I never participated in anything that could be considered even remotely questionable, especially as it applies to the application of medicine. You can buy that or not, but it's the truth."

"You aren't in courtroom here, Doc," I said, briefly glancing over my shoulder. "You're among friends, in fact."

"And I'd like to keep it that way," he said. "Then again, I'd like to keep my driver's license, now that you've sabotaged my reputation."

"Penance now, forgiveness and remuneration later," I said.

"Are you really that bad?" Kohlmeyer asked, though he kept his eyes on the traffic flow around us.

"Hell, no," Strand said.

I laughed. "He's worse than you can imagine. Believe it."

The traffic was gone as we neared the final turn up to Raptor's Ridge. I negotiated the winding lane and eventually rolled the van to a gentle stop in front of the big gates, leaning on the horn to annoy The Snarl. Before leaving Strand's office, I'd called ahead on the main line into the mansion, was greeted by Russell Vineyard, and advised him that I was returning with the doctor and another interested party – I left the name blank.

"Let them know at the gate, if you would," I'd added, and he must've done exactly that. The big iron gates swung slowly inward, and three of Deeker's henchmen appeared in the shadows by the guard station, their fingers wrapped around expensive Israeli-made submachine guns.

Kohlmeyer spotted them. "How's that for a warm greeting on a nice, sunny day?" he observed calmly. "What's next? The Confederate flag?"

"I had to stand for a frisk the last time I was here," I said, "but I think they'll skip that portion of the program, now that the boss and his girlfriend are dead and there's no one left to protect."

Kohlmeyer didn't seem to be paying attention anyway.

The Snarl stepped out of the guard's station and motioned for me to roll down the window. He looked inside, scowled when he spotted Kohlmeyer, and glanced at the doctor before returning his eyes to me.

"What's he doing here?"

I couldn't help myself.

"Which one?"

"Kohlmeyer."

"He's here to help," I said.

"His boys is responsible for what's done inside," Deeker grumbled, and he jerked his thumb toward the mansion, the menace in his words unmistakable. "You know it and I know it. Question is, does he know it?"

I knew from my reporting days that Kohlmeyer had a short fuse – it's at least safe to say that he didn't tolerate fools well – and he leaned toward the open window and spoke clearly and crisply: "What you're really asking is whether I'm in on it, right?"

"You got it, pal," Deeker growled.

"I'll say it as a courtesy, just so you know," Kohlmeyer said, his voice neutral. "I'm going to find out who did this, and they won't be happy when I do. I'm looking at everybody: my people, and you and your crew, Deeker. You might not be at the top of my list right now, but you're high up the ladder. Fair warning."

"You don't scare me," The Snarl replied, his demeanor decidedly bellicose.

"That's your mistake," the chief shot back. "You were here last night, on the grounds. It was your job to keep your client safe. You didn't. Who's to say that you, or maybe one of your goons, didn't let somebody slip inside to clip the old man and his houseguest?"

"You listen to me, dammit. I'm not gonna tolerate that from a smart-assed, low-grade, pig-in-a-poke, errand boy who's …"

"Boys – boys!" I said, cutting through the exchange. "First things first." I looked hard at Deeker. "We're heading in."

The Snarl started to protest, but Kohlmeyer said forcefully: "I'm taking a look inside. You want to come along now, fine – be my guest. But you'd best be prepared to answer a whole lot of questions when I'm done. And I'll tell you right now to get a list of names of all your people who were here last night and have it ready for some serious scrutiny before I'm through." He poked me in the arm and added, "Let's go, Blake. Move it."

I gunned the engine; the tires squealed before they bit, and we scooted forward.

"Hey, easy on the rig," the doc called from the back. "I don't pay her all that much as it is."

Kohlmeyer was still steaming. But as he settled himself in the seat again, I thought that I caught the faint trace of a smile lighting up the corners of his mouth.

"Something funny, Chief?" I asked.

"Funny? No. It's just that if it weren't for guys like that, guys like me would be out looking for work."

The butler met us at the door and nodded gravely as we stepped into the foyer. "It's nice to see you again, Doctor Strand … Mister Blake," he replied. "And you must be …"

"He's the chief of police, Mister Vineyard," Strand said.

"Very good, sir," the butler said. "May I get you gentlemen anything before you begin?"

I instantly thought about the Irish whiskey that he'd offered on our first meeting at Raptor's Ridge, hours earlier. But the day was young, and I still hadn't had any sleep. Besides, Kohlmeyer was here now, and I wanted to make a good impression – or at least keep my wits about me while trying to make one – when the chief said, "Scotch on the rocks for me, thanks."

"Make mine a double," Strand said. "The good stuff."

"I'll pass," I said, surprising myself, and then, to Kohlmeyer, "Come on – this way to the scene of the crime. You might want to down the Scotch before you get a look at Audrey, though. It's not pretty."

"Especially when you consider how she looked twenty-four hours previous," Doc added.

"I thought you weren't sure when the murders occurred," Kohlmeyer, ever the detective, said as we started up the grand staircase.

"Give or take," Doc said. "I was speaking metaphorically."

"He does that, Bill – with aplomb. Doc should be writing for the local gazette."

"Better him than you. Besides, if he's capable of writing in complete sentences, he's overqualified," Kohlmeyer said. I wanted to laugh, but we were in the bedroom at this point, staring at AJ Bohn's body.

The passing of a few hours hadn't improved its condition.

Doc frowned, then stood to one side and locked his chin between the thumb and index finger of his right hand, supporting it at the elbow with his left hand.

"Something bothers me about this," he said softly, "but I'm damned if I can put my finger on it."

"Why?" Kohlmeyer asked.

"If I knew, I'd tell you. But something's out of whack here. The same thought struck me earlier, when Blake and I were in here before, but I can't quite get there."

"All right, so what do you suggest?" Kohlmeyer asked.

"Let's bring in Charlie Wilson," Strand said. "He's top-notch, the best in the state at this sort of thing, and he's discreet. I'll make the call if you like. He's an old friend."

"Do it," Kohlmeyer said. "It won't hurt to have the state's medical examiner involved."

The chief looked in my direction next.

"Did you search for casings?" he asked.

"Absolutely," I said. "Nothing turned up."

"So the killer either used a revolver or policed his brass," he said.

"If it was your boys, they didn't have time to pick up after themselves, given the butler's recollection," I said. "You're issuing semi-auto Glocks these days … in .40 caliber, right?"

"And a lot of cops still carry revolvers as back-ups," he said. "But no brass does tell us something."

He walked around the body a couple of times, taking in the scene, getting the picture clear in his head, before he grunted a single time. "Next?"

"This way," I said, indicating with a wave the door to the master bath.

Russell Vineyard was suddenly behind us with a tray balanced in his right hand, and he cleared his throat to get our attention.

"Here you go, gentlemen," he said. "I also took the liberty of bringing you a soda water, Mister Blake. I thought that you might enjoy something, given the circumstances."

"That was thoughtful of you, sir," I said as the others accepted their drinks with mumbled thanks. "I was just wondering, Mister Vineyard, whether you have a camera on the estate?"

"Certainly, sir. It's a digital camera, though I don't know how to use it myself."

"A digital? That's fine. Could I borrow it?"

"Certainly, sir. I'll bring it up right away," he said with a slight bow before wheeling smartly about.

"Might as well get it all while we're here," I said to Strand.

Kohlmeyer, who'd moved into the bathroom in the meantime, called out, "Blake – where's the body?"

"It's in the bathtub," I called and headed in, thinking that he'd somehow missed it.

"Like hell it is – unless there's a second tub I haven't found."

But Kohlmeyer was right. Audrey Flowers' body was gone.

SIXTEEN

AN ALTERNATIVE TO THE FRONT DOOR

MONDAY, 10:59 A.M.

"If this is your idea of a sick joke, dammit, I sure as hell don't find it funny," Bill Kohlmeyer sputtered. "What kind of happy horsecrap are the two of you up to here?"

"The unhappy kind," Doc Strand muttered, and I watched with some interest as he looked uneasily around the master bathroom, doing his best to locate the missing body of AJ Bohn's once-glamorous paramour, just as I had done moments earlier.

"No joke, Bill," I said. "It was here; right there, in fact" – I pointed lamely to the empty bathtub – "before we left this morning."

Kohlmeyer scowled. "And what time was that, exactly?"

"I don't know – 7:30ish, maybe," I said. "We drove back to town, then stopped at White's for a while and kicked around the merits of bringing you in or going it alone. Then I called you at, well, whatever time I called you. What time was that?"

"8:35 a.m. exactly," he said. "I made a note of it."

"Which apparently left enough time for someone to move the body before we got back," I said.

Kohlmeyer didn't like it. I could tell from the scowl on his face and the anger that was flaming, like sparks from a Roman candle, in his eyes.

Strand, god bless him, snorted once or twice before breaking out into a full-forced laugh – one that he quickly tried but failed to get under control.

"What?" Kohlmeyer snapped, shooting a contemptuous glance in the doctor's direction.

"Maybe the butler did it," Doc said, snickering. Neither of us bit, so he added, "Come on – haven't you always wanted to use that line?"

When we still didn't respond, the smile slowly drained off his face. "At least he's a good place to start in figuring out what happened," he said.

"He is at that. I'll go fetch him," I said and started off in search of Russell Vineyard.

I didn't get far. Vineyard was on his way up the staircase, a Nikon camera in hand, as I sidestepped AJ Bohn's corpse and headed out of the bedroom.

"There you are, sir. Very good," he said as he stopped at the top of the staircase, offering the camera.

"Mister Vineyard, could I trouble you for a moment?" I said, using the gentlemanly approach. I waved my hand toward the bedroom and added, "We have a question or two, in here."

"Certainly, sir," he said and trailed behind me. We ignored Bohn's body and moved directly into the bathroom, where Kohlmeyer and Strand were engaged in a muted conversation. They looked up at our approach, and I said, as casually as I could while pointing toward the empty bathtub, "Mister Vineyard. Sir. Could you please tell us what's happened to Miss Flowers?"

He glanced at the empty tub, and a look of genuine surprise creased his face.

"Oh, my," he said, lifting a hand to his right cheek. "Oh, my indeed."

"You've got that right," Kohlmeyer said, and he was far less polite in his delivery than I'd been with the old boy. "Come on, give it up … what do you know?"

"Know, sir? I don't know a thing – certainly not about … that," he said.

"When was the last time you were up here?" Kohlmeyer asked.

"It was just a moment ago, sir. I fixed your drinks and brought them up … just a few minutes earlier, if you'll recall."

"I mean in here."

"Well, it was early this morning, sir … before Mister Blake arrived. I came up to see what had happened after Mister McClinton discovered the, ah … the tragedy. I haven't been back until I brought your drinks, sir."

"Speaking of McClinton, any idea where he's off to?" I asked.

"I can't say with certainty, sir," Vineyard replied. "He left shortly after you and Doctor Strand departed. The pain in his arm was excruciating, apparently, and he wanted to get it properly attended to, sir."

I thought that Strand might take exception, but he didn't react at all.

"So who else has been up here since these two jokers and the lawyer left?" Kohlmeyer asked.

"Why, no one, sir. Not a soul – so far as I know. To gain entrance to the mansion, at least in proper channels, you would come in contact with me, sir. And no one has been up here this morning, or in and out, until the three of you arrived just a short time ago."

"What about The Snarl and his henchmen?" I asked.

"Ah, Mister Deeker. No, he has not been inside the mansion since you and Doctor Strand left, nor have any of his men. I would have known, sir."

This didn't sit well with the chief of police, and you had to be quick to keep up with the exchange that followed.

Kohlmeyer: "They couldn't have slipped past you?"

Vineyard: "I assure you, sir, that it's unlikely."

Kohlmeyer: "So you were standing guard all morning long, monitoring everything that moved in and out of here?"

Vineyard: "Hardly, sir, but still …"

Kohlmeyer: "So it's possible then?"

Vineyard (considering): "If I've learned anything at all during my time on this good earth, sir, it is exactly that: Anything is possible. But in this case, it is highly unlikely, I can assure you."

Kohlmeyer: "I'd say it's damned likely, given what's happened – provided, of course, these two miscreants" – he jerked a thumb in the general direction of the good doctor and me – "weren't handing me a bucket of cow slop in the first place. They weren't doing that – were they? Or you? You aren't in on it with them, are you? Tell me now and I'll let the whole thing slide – a warning ticket."

Vineyard: "Honestly, sir, your tone is highly unnecessary, as are your insinuations. I have nothing to hide, nor can I fathom a reason why these two gentlemen would want to do that. I would say, if you'll allow me, sir, that we all are doing our level best to be as cooperative as we possibly can be. I certainly know that I am."

Kohlmeyer: "And I've got a report on a dead body that's supposed to be right here, and I can't tell what's going on because now there's NO DAMN BODY." He'd raised the pitch of his voice on these last three words, and Vineyard's face cringed.

I grew tired of the back-and-forth. It was like watching a one-sided tennis match. I decided to mount up for a rescue.

"This is getting us nowhere. I can assure you that Audrey was here, Bill – right here, in fact," I said, pointing at the tub again, cutting off Kohlmeyer's next line of attack. "I'd suggest, for starters, that we stop arguing the point and figure out instead who might know something about it. We need to talk with McClinton for sure, and The Snarl – see where that takes us.”

Kohlmeyer pulled his eyes away from the butler for a second. “Agreed,” he said. “But I’m not inclined to let the three of you out of my sight in the meantime … especially you” – and he again glared at Vineyard.

“Hey, hang on a minute,” Strand said. He hadn’t muttered a word since his *The-butler-did-it* line a few minutes earlier, and he apparently wanted to make amends for that ill-timed verbal miscue now. Considering what he offered up next – “Did you tell them about the secret entrances into and out of the mansion, Mister Vineyard?” – I’d say that he redeemed himself quite nicely.

It got my attention, anyway, and it clearly got Kohlmeyer’s as well.

“Secret entrances? What secret entrances?”

Kohlmeyer delivered his reply at the same moment that I spoke the very same words; it struck me as funny somehow, though not nearly as surprising as the revelation itself.

Vineyard’s response was memorable, coming in what you’d have to call classic butler-speak.

“And why would I do that, Doctor Strand?” he asked, his eyes scrunched in disgust. “Secret means exactly that: secret. If we all went around telling the world about the secret passageways that are part of the estate, they would hardly be secret any longer.”

That got a good laugh out of me.

I think that even Kohlmeyer cracked a smile – as much as he ever smiled, anyway, which wasn’t a lot on the best of days, and this was hardly one of those.

Strand just shook his head and gave me one of those *See-what-I’ve-been-dealing-with-all-this-time?* grins that is easier to spot than to describe – though I think you get the idea.

I was still wary of Kohlmeyer’s reaction. This was supposed to be my show, after all, and it hadn’t gone exactly according to the script that I'd sketched out in my head. If you think otherwise, go ahead and lose a movie star's body and see how the world treats you.

Vineyard stood off to one side, unsmiling and unsympathetic, miffed that the secret of the secret entrances had been dumped out of the bag and scattered rather indiscriminately at his feet.

"Is there anything else you require of me, sir?" he asked, looking squarely at Kohlmeyer.

"Three things," the chief said. "No, make it four. One, get the lawyer back up here, pronto. Two, let Deeker know I want to see him before I leave today. Tell him to stick around."

"Very good, sir."

"Next, when you get the lawyer on the line, tell him I want the will. Not a copy, either. Tell him I want to see the original. Maybe we can find a motive."

"Yes. Very good, sir."

Kohlmeyer stopped, adding up the numbers in his head.

"And the fourth thing, sir?" Vineyard asked, nudging him along.

"Stay close," Kohlmeyer replied. "Until we figure this out, I don't want you off the grounds. Got it?"

Vineyard nodded once and turned abruptly, moving at a rapid pace.

"Look, Bill," I said after he was gone. "I may be a lot of things, but crazy isn't one of them. That body was here when the doc and I left the place this morning. If not the lawyer or The Snarl, or both – or maybe even Deeker's henchmen, in concert or one of them acting alone – it was some combination that used the …"

I'd misjudged the police chief, however, because he cut me off at the knees. "Try to keep up, Blake," he said. "I'm sure the body was here when you left. Given the circumstances, there's no way the two of you would make it up. But it's gone now, either out the front door or through one of these so-called secret entrances. I'd suggest we start there, unless you two birds have a better idea."

He waited. When neither of said anything, he added, "Well?"

I wasn't going to bite at that proffered piece of devil's fruit, and neither did Doc.

"All right then," Kohlmeyer said. "How about you show us these secret entrances, Doctor Strand? I'm guessing, along with an entrance, you can use these passageways as an exit, too?"

"You can, indeed – well, so far as I know anyway," Strand said. "What the hell – let's go and find out. Follow me."

We did exactly that.

SEVENTEEN

OF CABBAGES AND KINGS

MONDAY, 11:17 A.M.

You never would have known, and you never would have been able to find them, even if you had known. That was the beauty of the two discreet entrances, in Floyd Strand's parlance, that provided covert access to the estate at Raptor's Ridge.

While it's true that I'm no expert on extraordinary engineering feats, it's not much of a stretch to say that AJ Bohn's secret passageways represented exactly that: genius. They clearly were the creation of a brilliant mind from a bygone era.

The first was in the mansion's lower level. Access was gained through the wine cellar, by adjusting the positions of three bottles of a specific French burgundy that were resting on an otherwise ordinary wine rack. You could hear the inner mechanism of the hidden door lock spin and then click into place, whirring a time or two, and a six-foot section of the wall on the cellar's north side slid inward, exposing a long tunnel.

"The light switch is here, I think," Strand said, moving ahead. "Yup, here it is – got it." The overhead lights popped on nicely. "Been a while since I've been here. It's also quite a hike to get out. Let me show you – you won't believe where it ends up."

The walls and floor were finished with smooth concrete. The ceiling was at least ten feet high and supported well-disguised heating and cooling ducts that provided air circulation, as well as fluorescent lighting placed intermittently along the passageway.

You could call it remarkable, but that would be underselling it.

We walked briskly for five minutes or so. The tunnel took a number of turns and twists, all the while gradually climbing. We eventually reached a set of metal stairs that spiraled upward, with a mechanical trap door at the top. Strand invited us to join him on the ample top step and flicked yet another switch, this one on the upper wall, a few feet below the false ceiling. A motor's hum lifted the trap door, at the same time pushing the final step and the three of us to the top.

"Impressive," Kohlmeyer said.

"Not yet," Strand said. "Wait till you see where we are."

The motor slowed and went silent again. The step stopped precisely even with matching metal decking that formed the floor of a circular room at least ten feet in circumference. The scent of what I thought was pine and tree-bark was striking, and I was about to mention it when Strand found another switch and stood back as a doorway appeared in the wall ahead of us. He walked through to green grass and sunshine, grinned, and waved us through the opening, which was somewhere on the grounds of the estate.

"In case you weren't paying attention in high school, or you aren't otherwise familiar with the genus *sequoia sempervirens*, I give you the species …"

"… a coastal redwood," I finished, though I was as close to being dumfounded as I've ever been – or at least since my ex-wife's sneak-attack divorce smacked me over the head and kicked me a few times for good measure.

"Good god," Kohlmeyer added as he stared upward in disbelief. "It's the whole damn thing – tree and all."

The sequoia towered above us, at least several dozens of feet high, I estimated – a truly incredible creation.

"What's it made of?" I asked.

"For all I know, it's the real thing," Strand said. "The old man showed it to me one day a year ago – I'm not sure whether even he knew how it was built. We were talking about how craftsmanship had become a thing of the past, and he winked in that funny way he had and said something along the lines of, 'Come with me, Doctor Strand. I'll show you some craftsmanship that you won't believe.' He was right. I've seen it, then and now, and still can't believe it's real. But – here it is."

Kohlmeyer quickly returned to business. "Do you know if there's a switch out here – how to activate it so you can get inside the mansion if the door's shut?" he asked.

"No," Strand said. "I don't know that you can. For all I know, it's a one-way ticket, but you'd think that a switch or a button or whatever would be around somewhere."

"Maybe Vineyard will know. Maybe we can get some blueprints. But we'll have to find that out to see if this tree played a role in what happened to Audrey Flowers – whatever that was," Kohlmeyer said after a moment's consideration.

We wandered around the tree for several minutes, looking for switches or triggers that would activate the door, poking in the shrubbery and nearby landscaping, but failed to turn up anything obvious.

"Doc, how about the second passageway?" I eventually asked, still marveling at the sequoia's overall height and the secret that its innards contained.

"Sure," Strand said. "It's impressive enough – you'd love to have one in your house – but I played the trump card first."

"It'll be tough to top this, all right," Kohlmeyer said as we retraced our steps and Strand flicked the various switches to close up behind us. "This thing's every bit as impressive as that Swiss Family Robinson tree you see at Disneyland."

I still couldn't get over the amount of money that must have been involved in not only building but also maintaining a place like Raptor's Ridge. I mentioned as much and whistled as the imaginary numbers rolled through my head. "It's staggering when you think about it," I said.

"Just think what it took to build that tree disguise alone," Strand offered. "I'd be forced to perform a lot of appendectomies, just to cover the bark. But keep in mind that Raptor's Ridge was built with old timber money. It's hard for us to imagine it now, with conservationists and environmentalists and all the rest of the pseudo-intellectuals and phony greeniks and peacenik and whatever they're called who're trying to run the damn planet. But a hundred years ago in these parts? Timber was king, and the man who controlled the empire ran the city, the county, the state, the whole damned region. You know that AJ's great-grandfather built this place, right?"

"I didn't know that," I said. "I thought the original owner was a Carson."

"As in the California Carsons?" Kohlmeyer asked.

"Exactly. It's what botanists call cross-pollination," Strand said. "Men with money often have daughters, and other men who want money propose to those daughters to get a piece of … daddy-in-law's inheritance, if you know what I mean."

We were back in the wine cellar now, and Strand ushered us quickly up the service elevator and out into the expansive kitchen.

"Do you have any idea how large the kitchen areas are in this place?" Strand asked. When we didn't venture a guess, he said: "Almost thirteen-thousand square feet. That's enough room for a dozen good-sized houses. The mansion actually has five separate meal-preparation areas, each one capable of serving up to a hundred guests – 500 people in all.

Ah, to have been a fly on the wall, back in the golden days when presidents and princes and the crowned heads of state were frequent visitors here."

"It's a lot of room to cook a hard-boiled egg, all right," Kohlmeyer, ever the practical cop, said without enthusiasm. "So where's this other passageway?"

"Here," Strand said, "though this pantry – one of five on the property that I know about."

"I thought you said there were two secret passageways. Now you've got five of them?" Kohlmeyer asked.

"I was talking about food pantries," Strand said. "As to the discreet entrances, who knows? I've been coming to Raptor's Ridge for fourteen years, and I don't think I've seen anywhere near all of it. For all I know, another dozen of these things are awaiting discovery."

He opened a door, flicked on a light switch, and an area as large as the wine cellar we'd just visited opened before us. Foodstuffs of all sorts lined the various floor-to-ceiling shelves and refrigeration units, with wide corridors running between them. The area reminded me of walking into a supermarket that was stuffed full for the pending onslaught of Thanksgiving shoppers.

"Impressive, huh?" Strand said casually. "I always got the feeling that AJ was afraid of the Next Great Depression and was preparing for it here – just in case. As they say in the financial reports, gold, silver, and foodstuffs never go out of fashion."

Who reads newspapers any more? I found myself inexplicitly thinking.

But Kohlmeyer had something else in mind. "And I'm guessing he was stocking other goods around the estate?"

"Such as?" Strand asked.

"You tell me, Doctor. You know the place better than I do."

Strand shot a hard look at the chief. "If he used Raptor's Ridge for more than a place to call home," he said, "AJ never told me. And he never showed me anything out of the ordinary – besides the tree entrance, and this." He reached inside a shelf that was stocked with canned goods, fumbled a bit, and finally found the switch he'd been seeking. We could hear a motor thrum to life as a six-foot section of the wall ahead of us moved inward a foot or so, then slid off to the left, exposing a wide corridor.

"That's odd," Strand said. "The lights are already on. You'd think they'd be off."

"Where does this go?" Kohlmeyer asked, moving briskly forward, his hand automatically finding the grip of his holstered Glock.

"Into the garage – the one not connected to the main house," Strand said. "An elevator on that side opens up into a tool storage room – actually, a *big* tool storage room. Well, even that doesn't do it – wait till you see. It must be a thousand square feet."

"The tool closet is a thousand square feet?" I asked.

"At least – maybe bigger," Strand said. "The garage easily accommodates more than thirty good-sized vehicles. Most of Mister Bohn's fleet is stored there, including a few antiques that I'd love to own. He and Jay Leno were friendly – they talked cars a great deal, you know."

Kohlmeyer wasn't thinking about antique automobiles, however.

"Gentlemen," he said, almost casually, moving rapidly ahead once more. "Forget about that crazy sequoia. Thanks to Doc Strand here, I think we've just figured out how the body left the crime scene."

I was tempted to point out that until we had a body and could examine the head wound for stippling and gunshot residue, Audrey Flowers' death might well be a suicide rather than a murder. But I kept it to myself when Strand, tracking at my heels, began to recite a poem that I hadn't heard since my early days in school – a period that stretched back even farther than I cared to admit.

"The time has come," the Walrus said,
"To talk of many things:
Of shoes, and ships, and sealing-wax,
Of cabbages, and kings –
And why the sea is boiling hot,
And whether pigs have wings."

I was tempted to ask what prompted his impromptu performance, but I came to discover during the Raptor's Ridge affair that Doc Strand could surprise you in a variety of ways.

EIGHTEEN

THAT LITTLE VOICE IN YOUR HEAD

MONDAY, 12:47 P.M.

I was back in my office an hour later, pondering the insanity of my life, wondering – not for the first time – what I'd done, exactly, that prompted the otherwise omnipotent gods to look so unfavorably upon my time on the planet. I'd been good to my mother, after all, and I didn't sass the nuns to any great extent during my time in the Catholic schools. Sure, my ex-wife had an apparent beef; I'll admit to that. But who can't say the same about a spouse at some point during any marriage?

I looked at the golf calendar that was hanging on the wall and double-checked the year because I'm not always good at swapping them out when January rolls around. I then began counting off the days before summer classes ended and the start of the fall term began, at which point I'd return to the classroom for good – or at least for another year. We were approaching August, which meant that I had an additional six weeks before my horse-drawn carriage would again turn into a pumpkin and I'd have to trade in my Walther P99 and S&W backup piece for a Sharpie, a laser pen, and stacks of textbooks and course syllabi.

I started thinking about the classes that I'd be teaching in the fall – *Intro to Mass Comm, News Writing, Media Ethics, Editing for Print and Broadcast* – which got me thinking about the numbers of students who were likely enroll in each of course offering. That in turn made me calculate the number of books I'd need to order, and the likely dropout rate after the first two weeks, and the number of emails I'd field in the first forty-eight hours once the term began.

I've got a hell of a lot of work ahead of me, and none of it involves AJ Bohn or Audrey Flowers, I thought.

Juggling my professor's responsibilities with my private detective sideline isn't so bad when I'm teaching by day and finding Mrs. Foster's missing Pomeranian by night.

But when you're in the middle of a murder investigation involving the richest man in the state, and the steady job that pays most of the bills is looming ...

"Ah, to hell with it," I grumbled aloud and lifted my feet onto the edge of the battered desk containing the handful of case files that had occupied my time during the summer – the sum total of almost eight weeks of work as a part-time PI, in fact.

I hate to admit it, but there are times when I detest most all of the work that I do as a private investigator. It's usually dull and often tedious, and the grind – the sheer drudgery of meaningless stakeouts and futile searches for what almost always amounts to mostly nonsense – can wear you down. It's one of the reasons why I haven't been tempted to give up teaching, which has its own set of problems but also offers wonderful rewards.

It's also one of the reasons why I still keep a hand in the writing game, doing occasional travel pieces for slick magazines and Internet sites.

The thing to keep in mind about detective work is that it requires long hours, it's almost always monotonous, and the payoffs aren't much to sing about – if, in fact, a payoff even takes place when the case ends.

I'm also a far cry from being counted among the top-rated private eyes who work for high-priced agencies, the kind of guys who swing a big club and carry a big stick and command a big paycheck. The cases I manage to scrounge up are usually run-of-the-mill affairs that the big firms and the big shots won't touch. Besides the missing cat and/or dog case, a specialty, I get the guy who suspects his wife of cheating on him (it's never the milk man or postal carrier, I can assure you – and yeah, they still have milk delivery where I live), or some daffy dame who's looking for an angle to marry into money (god help them both). I'd had a bit of luck of late doing background checks on potential hires for a couple of the manufacturing plants in town and figured that I might run an advertisement or two in an effort to drum up some additional business along that line – but that was as far as my routine had taken me to date.

One thing was clear: The Bohn/Flowers case was the biggest thing that I'd stumbled into, and it was driving me crazy that I couldn't see past all of the smoke and dust and false trails and the peculiar cast of characters to get a narrow bead on the truth.

I took another look at the calendar and groaned aloud.

Dammit – and I've got another summer class tomorrow

...

It struck me again that in a few short weeks, I'd be back in the classroom for nine solid months, doing my best to teach the basics of gathering and reporting news and the fundamentals of the mass media in the modern age to a bunch of kids. Many of them were fresh out of high school with no good understanding of why they were returning to school and, particularly, why they'd enrolled in my courses.

Other than the obvious: No math ...

The fact that my students enrolled at a community college rather than a big university, a handful of which were within an easy drive, says a bunch about the talent pool, I suppose.

Then again, I'd gotten my start at a community college – they were called junior colleges back then – and I'd done all right.

I was almost looking forward to the change of pace, however, when the phone rang.

Good – they've found Audrey Flowers, I thought as I grabbed the receiver.

"So tell me where you found it," I said as I snapped up the line, expecting to hear Bill Kohlmeyer's voice.

"Where I found it? Found what? Max, are you all right?"

It was Caeli Brown, and I'll confess straight out that it was damn good to hear her voice, even if she couldn't tell me what had happened to my missing movie star. Whenever I need to brighten up a bit, I think of Caeli – and now, here she was, on the phone at the exact moment when I needed a boost.

"Sure, Caeli. I'm fine," I said. "Just a bit worn out is all. It's good to hear you – really good to hear your voice, as a matter of fact."

"I'm glad. I called you this morning – a couple of times," she said. "You didn't pick up."

"And you didn't leave a message."

"I never do. Why don't you get a cell phone and join the rest of the world?"

"Too old and too stubborn, I guess," I said. "All it would do is force me to carry my troubles around in my pocket."

"It could also bring you some help in the middle of the night."

"It would be another bill to pay."

"You could use it to call Triple-A to fix a flat tire."

"It would give my creditors easier access to me. Besides, I know how to fix a flat."

"Ah, but it could save your life in an emergency."

"It would wake me up."

"And it could let me reach you when I needed to."

I paused there; she had me. She always had me. "Well, there is that. I'll give it some thought."

"You're just saying that."

"No, I mean it. Honest I do."

She laughed. "I've heard you say it before, and nothing's ever come of it."

"All right, then I mean it this time. I'll give it some thought. Really."

When she didn't answer immediately, I jumped at the chance to change the subject. "So, what's up, kid? Or did you just call to remind me about my Stone Age tendencies?"

"What's up? Really? OK: You. Me. Lunch? Today? Remember?"

"Oh, right. Sure I do." I didn't, though, god help me.

"Well, it must've slipped your mind. I'm at Jonathon's right now, waiting."

Damn it. Lunch with Caeli. It was back in my head now, despite AJ Bohn's demise.

"And I'm" – I reached across the desk and grabbed my fedora – "on my way. I'll see you in five minutes."

"You mean it? I don't want to sit here alone."

"I can't get there if I stay on the phone," I said, mustering what I hoped would pass for blanket enthusiasm. "I'll see you in five – maybe even less. I'll fly."

So how crazy is this? Less than an hour earlier, I'd been at Raptor's Ridge with the chief of police and the late owner's personal physician, prowling through secret entrances and exits, examining a dead body, wondering what exactly happened to another dead body – the dead body, in fact, of a once-ravishing former movie star who'd been lying naked in a bathtub one minute, a bullet hole in her pretty head, and a short time later ... *vanished.*

And then, out of nowhere, came the less-than-subtle reminder that I was not only late for a lunch date but a damn fool besides.

Crazy stuff, all right.

I'd left Kohlmeyer and Doc Strand at the estate, borrowing the doctor's receptionist's minivan to get back to town so that I'd be able to duck probable tails from Chuck Downing's crooked cops. Kohlmeyer was convinced that Raptor's Ridge was being watched – and who was I to argue? The plan we'd devised was for Kohlmeyer to discreetly call in the state's medical examiner to determine the exact cause of AJ Bohn's permanent departure from Raptor's Ridge – the obvious bullet holes notwithstanding. Strand would assist. And according to the chief of police, at least, I was a third leg in the race.

"What do you want me to do?" I'd asked.

"Stay out of the way," Kohlmeyer replied. "You've done all you can – time for the pros to take over."

"Hey, that's not the way it works," I'd said at the time. "I'm on the case because AJ Bohn wanted me on the case."

"Bohn is dead. I shouldn't have to remind you of that."

"And a contract is a contract, whether he's dead or not. You don't get to push me around, Bill, and you don't get rid of me so easily. I can either work with you, and help, or I can shove around the edges and make a difference that way. Maybe whatever I do will help – maybe it won't. But why take the chance? I'm good at what I do."

"All right, so let's talk about that for a minute," he said. "How's business?"

"How's business? What do you mean?"

"I mean exactly what I asked: How's business?"

"It's fine. Enrollment goes up when the economy tanks. Students take my classes because they want to, not because they have to – unlike the sciences. The dean is happy with the quality of the student newspaper. Ad rates are holding steady ..."

"Save it. I'm not talking college business and what you do there, if anything," he said, cutting me short. "I'm talking about your other life – the one that brought you here. So I'll ask it again: How's business?"

"Business is fine," I persisted.

"Really. Found any missing dogs lately?"

"Sure – funny you should ask. I just closed a case the other day. This woman in the Four Corners district lost her pet schnauzer, and damned if I didn't get the little bugger back inside of forty-eight hours. He was dirty and more than a little hungry, but …"

"Let it go, Blake. You find missing dogs. You snoop around to see who's banging who – or what, for god's sake. If something really big comes along, you do a background check on the guy who ends up being the next comptroller at Nielsen's Tool & Die, or maybe a cost accountant at Norpac Foods. That's what you do. I know. I've asked around. That's as good as it gets."

I cursed once.

"Look, I'm damn good at what I do, Bill. I was always good at what I do – even then, which might be the reason why you're pissed off."

"You haven't seen pissed off, Blake. Not yet."

"And you're being short-sighted and nasty and convenient, none of which are good ideas during a murder investigation. Besides, I could take it to the newspapers," I said.

And there it was, out on the table – the ultimate threat.

"You wouldn't," he said, flaming anger instantly raging in his eyes.

"The paper's not worth a damn any more," I pressed. "But it could blow the lid off this thing in five minutes. All it would take is a single anonymous call. You know it. I know it."

"I could lock you up for interfering with an official police investigation."

"I'd still be entitled to a phone call, and it wouldn't go to my lawyer."

I took a deep breath, gave him my best steely gaze, and continued. "Besides, you wouldn't be here if it wasn't for me. I brought you in, and I could've called anybody … or nobody. I could've called the State Police or the governor or the National Guard, or even the FB-freakin'-I. But I called you instead because I thought you were the right man for the job. So, like it or not, you owe me. Keep it in mind before I do something you'll regret."

He poked a thick finger into my chest, started to say something, gulped it back, opened his mouth to try another line, and then scowled. You don't want to see that look on Kohlmeyer's face, let me tell you – ever. But just as quickly, he retracted his finger, turned his head sideways to fix a crick in his muscled neck, and shrugged.

"All right, dammit. We'll give it a try – see how it goes. The butler says the lawyer's out of pocket, seeing his personal physician. Track him down – see what McClinton can give you on Bohn's will. But when you find him, and when you get the original will, you bring it to me and nobody else. Got it?"

"Sure," I said. "Why would I screw you over?"

OK, so I lobbed up a softball, giving him the chance to swing for the fences. But he didn't – even if I could tell that the thought of it flashed in his mind. Instead, he grinned that little kid grin of his that I'd seen at times during my reporting days – the one that instantly conveyed, *"Don't even think of messing with me, mister."*

What he actually said was far worse: "I know where to find you, Blake. I know what you drive. I know where you work, when you even bother to work, and I know the people you work for. Keep that in mind."

Now, less than an hour later, Kohlmeyer was still on my mind while I was on my way across a few city blocks to see Caeli Brown. She's a dear, long-time pal from my newspaper days who is as good at digging up a story or ferreting out information as anyone I've ever known. We've been friends for a lot of years – more than I'd care to admit. She works some of the PI cases with me, when a female touch is required, and she also fills in for me in a pinch at the college, which provides her with a nice break from the part-time work she handles for a local advertising/PR agency and some media outlets.

I've always thought of her as my Gal Pal.

I've also sometimes thought, during times when I was down or feeling vulnerable, that it was high time to take another step in our relationship – to make her something more than a pal, if possible. I had the feeling that she wanted that as well, although she's too much of a lady to make the suggestion on her own.

Then again, if she were waiting for me to bring it up, she was likely to end up an old maid and unfulfilled ... *or on someone else's arm,* I thought.

Maybe it was everything that I'd seen earlier in the day, but I suddenly found that prospect – that she might end up on someone else's arm – to be highly alarming. And it surprised me that I hadn't given that distressing prospect some serious consideration until that very second.

Maybe it takes a couple of dead bodies to get me thinking straight, I considered as I pulled into the parking lot at Jonathon's Oyster Bar and spotted Caeli's Chevy Malibu a couple of aisles over. I hopped out of the borrowed minivan and stepped jauntily up the stairs, opened with a flourish the big oak door with a brass ship's porthole in its center, and glided inside.

"How many, sir?" a smiling receptionist asked as I entered.

"I'm meeting someone. She's already here," I said, then spotted Caeli in the far corner.

Who knows where this might lead?

She saw me then, waved, and I gave her my best smile as I approached, took the fedora off my head, bent down like the guys in the movies do, and kissed her full on the lips.

To say that she was surprised is an understatement, though I can report without blushing that she returned the kiss with what I judged to be some enthusiasm.

"What brought that on?" she asked a moment later, her face alight with surprise and that rosy glow she gets when she's happy about something.

"My dear," I said, sitting down next to her. I tossed the fedora onto the tabletop and recalled the lines from a favorite old movie, delivering an updated version. "I hope this is a fresh start to a beautiful friendship."

Little did I know, though I had a funny feeling, even then, that I was about to find out.

NINETEEN

'IN THE EVENT THAT SOMETHING UNTOWARD ...'

MONDAY, 2:42 P.M.

I spent more than ninety minutes – ninety minutes I couldn't spare, given what I was working on – with Caeli Brown. I also wished – again, given what I was working on – that I could've spent the entire week with her.

Hell, how about the entire month?

Spending time with Caeli is always easy, regardless of what I'm wrapped up in at any given moment, and it certainly proved to be the best part of my day to that point. Well, that and the idea that I was going to stick AJ Bohn's estate with a whopping bill for services rendered that I hoped would rival the contract offers the New York Yankees, damn them, like to toss out to starting left-handed pitchers.

Even the washed-up closers ...

She instantly wanted to know what had me in such a good mood, and I waited until the main course was served – poached sea bass with steamed veggies and a light tossed salad, dressing on the side, for both of us – before giving her a hint of the truth.

I mention a hint here because I didn't think that I could tell her everything at that point, for any number of good reasons. The most prominent among them, however, was her safety. I had no doubt that I was being watched; it made sense. I also knew that Chuck Downing and "Buzzsaw" Stone were out there somewhere – I'd kept a close watch on traffic as I drove back to town, trying to spot a tail – and I didn't want Caeli to come under their scrutiny because of my own involvement in the goings-on at Raptor's Ridge.

On the other hand, I also knew that shutting her out entirely would be a big mistake. I had too much respect for her opinions, which I often sought, as well as her instincts and her ability to sort through nonsense and arrive at logical conclusions. Besides, I called on her at times to serve as a backup instructor for my classes at the college, and I figured that the case would likely play havoc with my schedule. And so I filled her in on some of the basic facts: AJ Bohn and Audrey Flowers were dead, everything was hush-hush, and I was involved because of a quirky addition that the old man had placed into his will.

I made no mention of The Lurker who'd been hiding in the bedroom, the movie star's missing body, the connection to local police involvement and corruption, the addition of the new chief of police to the investigation, or many – if any – of the gruesome details.

I did tell her that if I played my cards right, the case might pay handsomely.

Some strategic questioning on her part, no doubt fueled by my lack of sleep and a large glass of Oregon-grown pinot noir, also produced minimal details regarding the roles being played by Doc Strand, Ned McClinton, Russell Vineyard, and Paul Deeker. She smelled more to the story, even then, but I made it clear that I was in deep waters and didn't want her to jump in with me.

"What kind of juicy details are you leaving out, Max?" she asked at one point. "You aren't sharing something vital – maybe a lot of somethings."

"I'm telling you what I can. I'll tell you the rest when it's safe, but safety is the only reason I'm not giving you more now."

"Safety? Whose safety, exactly?"

"Let's start with yours and mine, in that order," I said. "You'll have to trust me."

"This isn't the first time I've heard that line from a man," she replied, smiling. "What follows is usually hilarious, though it always ends poorly for someone, and no one is laughing for long."

"I won't lie to you, Caeli," I said. "And I'll let you know more when it's safe. Promise."

"So, trust you. Right?"

"Something like that."

"And it's really the best you can do?"

"At least for now. But I'm dead serious about your safety. I don't want you getting hurt because of something I tell you. I'll give you the details as soon as it's safe."

"All right," she said. "I know you will."

I don't know that it made her day. But her calm acceptance of what she learned – and the measured questions and spot-on observations that she offered with the miniscule facts I'd provided – only further convinced me: Caeli was a treasure that I'd far too long overlooked, if not taken for granted entirely.

I would have to do something about that.

I concluded our lunch with a pact of full disclosure to follow, along with the fresh start that I saw ahead. I also assured her that she was meeting me, the real Max Blake – the new and improved Max Blake – for the first time. I don't know that she bought it all, or believed even half of it. And while much of it took her by surprise, she at least seemed to appreciate the effort.

I gave her an opening, just before we left, to again chide me for not owning a cell phone when I asked to borrow hers so that I could call McClinton. I reached the lawyer on his private number while Caeli freshened up, letting him know that he wouldn't have to make the trip back to Raptor's Ridge so long as I could drop by for a visit. He said I'd find him in his office, gathering the papers for Kohlmeyer.

I kissed Caeli again as I saw her to her Chevy, promised to call her later, and hopped into the van. With a constant eye on the rearview mirror, I quickly drove the twelve blocks to the law offices of McClinton and Clark, which is situated in a new office building off 12th Street, close to the university.

I was anxious to see the paperwork that McClinton was gathering for me as well. *Bohn's directive to hire me – how did he phrase it? – "Should anything untoward happen ..."*

I still didn't like the sound of that, and it got me to thinking:

The only time you'd make an arrangement like that is if you expected trouble – the kind of trouble that could get you killed.

So that must have been it: Bohn knew that he was in over his head, that he'd chomped off more than he could chew, that he wasn't long for this world – pick your cliché.

But it still didn't explain why he'd want me to investigate after the fact. Plenty of good private detectives operated in town, many of whom had far greater experience and credentials. Hell, I was only a part-timer anyway, doing scut work to keep my head above water.

What the hell is this all about, anyway? I wondered, and not for the first time that day.

"Mister McClinton, please," I said when I entered the lawyer's office moments later and was met by a slight, unreceptive receptionist with a thin, cold stare.

"Sorry, but he's unavailable," she replied curtly. "I'll make an appointment if you insist."

"Please let him know that Max Blake is here," I suggested gently. "He's expecting me."

"I see," she said curtly, making it clear that she'd been kept out of the loop. She forcefully punched a button on her desk.

"Somebody named Blake is here," she snapped. "Apparently he's expected." She clicked off the device without waiting for a reply and didn't say another word, tending to the stack of papers on her desk instead, avoiding additional eye contact.

The office door opened seconds later and McClinton greeted me with a wan smile.

"Come in," he said weakly. "I'm just gathering the papers now."

I shrugged off the receptionist's icy glare and entered the lawyer's plush offices. Based on the expensive artwork on the walls, mostly of handsome nautical scenes, I figured that he'd found a good racket. I also figured that with one client, McClinton was in for a rude awakening when he re-entered the real world again.

"Please, have a seat," he said, motioning with his good arm – the one with the bullet hole through it was in a sling – toward the two chairs that faced his chrome-and-glass desk. "It won't take but a second."

"Thanks, counselor," I said and slumped into the plush leather.

"Would you like something?" he asked, mouthing the words absently, as though the question were expected; his attention was attached to a sheaf of papers on his desktop.

"If it means involving the woman at the front desk, no thanks," I said. "She doesn't look pleased."

"That's understandable. She probably blames you for my getting shot." He unconsciously grabbed at the wound with his right hand, wincing as he did. "Besides, I just gave her notice."

"That didn't take long," I said, striving for casual.

"And closing the estate won't take long either, I'm afraid," McClinton said. "The will is air-tight, iron-clad. I know: I'm responsible for almost every word in it. He had no family, no living heirs, no one to contest it, and much of it is going either to charity or to the city."

"By no living heirs, do you mean that Miss Flowers was in the will?"

"Of course; most certainly. As I indicated earlier, they were quite close. With her death, however – well, let's just say that it simplifies things even more, not that there would have been any problems were she still living. It's all rock-solid."

"So you say, counselor. That hasn't always been my experience with matters pertaining to laws and courts, however – especially in this state, and especially in this town."

"Be that as it may …" He let it go, and I didn't want to argue the issue; it was too much like questioning his manhood, apparently.

"How about you, Ned? Are you in the will?"

"To a small degree, yes. Doctor Strand and Mister Vineyard also are represented, and to a lesser degree, so are a handful of the staff who helped keep the estate running smoothly: a cook, three duty maids, three gardeners, an automobile mechanic ..."

"How about The Snarl?"

"Paul Deeker? No, nor is his brother. They were adequately compensated during their brief tenure, I'm delighted to say."

"Delighted because …?"

"Because I won't have to deal with them or their attorneys during probate."

"You didn't like the Deeker boys?"

"I wouldn't put it that way."

"How would you put it?"

"Mister Bohn saw fit to offer them employment a year and a half ago, and they served a useful purpose in his mind, at least. With his death, however, I won't be sorry to see them go."

"You think they'll be angry that they aren't in the will?"

"That's a question you'd have to ask them. I'm not inclined toward speculation."

"All right then," I said after an awkward moment of silence, "three things …"

"Yes," he said, cutting me off. "The first is the will. I have the original here, officially signed and duly notarized."

"Thanks, though I was going to officially ask about your arm. How is it?"

"I'll live, thanks to Doctor Strand."

"I understand that you also saw your own physician this morning."

"Yes, just a short while ago, in fact," he said.

"And is he going to report the gunshot to the authorities?"

"On the advice of his attorney, the answer is officially … not yet. He will make a full disclosure, mind you, but not immediately."

"It only matters to me because of containment, counselor," I said with a thin smile. "But I am curious, seeing as how we all seem to be keeping secrets of one sort of another."

"Yes, well, I trust that your curiosity has been satisfied. As to the third item?"

"Sure," I replied, "and one that is closer to my own heart …"

"Of course … the details of Mister Bohn's specific instructions to retain your services should something untoward happen to him."

"Exactly, and again pretty much word-for-word the way you explained it this morning."

"That's because it reads exactly that way. The wording came directly from Mister Bohn; he insisted on it. I placed it in the will and retained the original memorandum because of its odd phrasings. I wanted to it included in the event that a question would be raised during probate."

He pulled a sealed document from the middle desk drawer and handed it to me. I leaned forward, opened the envelope, and removed a single sheet of white bond paper. There wasn't much to it:

TO: *Edward L. "Ned" McClinton, attorney at law*

FR: *"AJ" Bohn, Raptor's Ridge*

RE: *In the event of my death ...addendum*

Ned:

Please add this to the will, forthwith:

In the event that something untoward should befall me, and in the event that normal channels are deemed unsatisfactory to conduct a proper examination of said untoward events, which could well be the case, I hereby designate that Mr. Maxwell Blake, M.A., former reporter, holder of a state private detective's license, and currently a professor of journalism at the local community college, should be retained to investigate the circumstances surrounding my demise. I further deem that he shall not rest until he and he alone is satisfied with the results and determinations of said investigation.

For that service, Mr. Blake is to be paid and provided whatever amount and/or resources he requests to cover his time and expenses from the settlement of my estate, within reason, as determined by you at the time of the completion of this contract.

Because Mr. Blake is an honest man, perhaps one of only a dozen in the city, I am declining at the time of this writing to set a ceiling on the amount due him at the execution of the will. Further, I am directing you to be creative, if need be, in settling this account. I trust your judgment, just as I trust Mr. Blake's.

Signed,

Da. "AJ" Bohn

And there it was, just as the lawyer described it. I read it again, then a third time, trying to make sense of it all.

"You seem confused," McClinton eventually said.

"As confused, maybe, as you've been, counselor?" I asked.

"When I first saw it, I asked him – only once – if he were absolutely certain that he wanted to keep it intact, in the exact language you see here. He scowled at me. I never asked about it again."

"Well, I don't know a lot about these things, but I'd agree that the wording is … unusual."

"Unusual hardly covers it," McClinton said. "No attorney, or at least no attorney I know, would have written it that way or agreed to allow it to stand in that fashion unless so ordered by the client, which was the case here."

"It's not dated," I said.

"I recorded the date at the time that I took possession of the document. It was Aug. 15, 1993. Does that mean anything to you?"

Sure it did. It was the date that I'd resigned from my last newspaper job. But I didn't let that cat out of the sack in front of the lawyer, and I wasn't sure that it meant anything anyway. Instead, I waved an empty hand – one of those *It-beats-me* motions – and put on a decent poker face.

"He updated it at some point?" I asked.

"Yes, twice more. I have the dates recorded for those as well – in September of 1993 and again only a couple of months ago. On each occasion, I updated the will accordingly."

"Interesting," I said. "Did the wording change greatly?"

"No. In fact, hardly at all. On the first occasion, if I recall correctly, he added that you had subsequently been employed at the college. This last time, in April, he added a clause in the opening sentence."

"And that would be …?"

"*…which could well be the case …*"

"Did you find that odd?"

"Odd in what sense?" McClinton asked.

"Odd in the sense that he's now dead, and this seems to indicate that perhaps he knew it was coming."

McClinton paused and considered the question. His eyes seemed particularly troubled, as though the thought hadn't previously occurred to him. While I'm not an expert at reading faces or accurately and convincingly spotting and then defining human emotions, I still detected a hint of doubt on the lawyer's face. I wondered whether he was thinking that he might've been able to prevent Bohn's death, if only he'd paid closer attention.

"Well," he said after more than a minute of introspection, "if you are able to read that much into six simple words, you are a hell of a lot smarter than I am." He kept his head down as he said this, looking at the carpeted floor in his office, before offering, "Mister Bohn added to and subtracted from his legal documents constantly. I'm not sure what else to tell you."

I considered pressing the point, but what was the use? The old man was dead, it was clear that McClinton didn't kill him, and it was even less likely that the lawyer had somehow arranged for the murder of his boss and lone meal ticket.

Still, it struck me that McClinton would stew about those six simple words for a long time to come.

"All right, thanks for your time, counselor," I said. "I'll take it out to the estate. Kohlmeyer is there, along with the state medical examiner, I'm told, and Doctor Strand. But don't worry; the investigation remains officially off the books … for now, at least."

"Very good. Please ask Chief Kohlmeyer to be careful with that document. If you need anything else, let me know. I'll do what I can. And, of course, when you are ready to settle the invoice for your services, you know where to find me."

"Thanks," I said, and I stood and shook his hand. I actually thought about asking for an advance to cover my pocket expenses but quickly decided against it:

Bad form … and I don't want to look like a piker who's essentially broke.

"Oh, one other thing: What's to become of Raptor's Ridge?"

I already was outside the office door but had stopped to ask the question, just out of curiosity. I'd only seen a narrow slice of the estate that morning, but to say that it was impressive wasn't doing it justice.

Maybe that'll be the bill I stick him with ... the deed to the place.

The answer that I got wasn't so much a surprise as it was a total shock.

"Again, Mister Bohn was quite explicit," McClinton said simply and without apparent emotion, at least none that I could detect. "Raptor's Ridge is to be demolished, with the grounds turned over to the city for the establishment of a park."

That stopped me cold.

"Demolished? As in ... torn down?"

"That is correct," he replied, and a grimace, combined with a trace of defeat, made it clear that the prospect didn't excite him, either. "Every brick, every stone, every timber – everything. Destroyed. You'll find it all there" – he pointed to the paper in my hand – "in the damned will."

TWENTY

A LITTLE FRICTION AMONG FRIENDS

NINE HOURS EARLIER

They met early that morning in a roadhouse in one of the university towns, well south of Raptor's Ridge, far away from the current police activity at the estate.

Paul Deeker ignored the fleet of Hummers and big SUVs that he had access to at the mansion and drove his own beat-up Chevy pickup instead.

He didn't say a word to his brother on the trip down the hill and through the winding back roads that eventually wove their way to the academic town in the heart of the fertile valley, more than twenty miles south of the capital city. Tom Deeker didn't seem to mind. He stared out the window, a half-smile on his face, looking at nothing, concentrating on whatever simple thoughts would pass the time.

"It's over here," Tom said at last, pointing to a shabby, rambling one-story structure that sported *All-You-Can-Eat* and *Beer Here* signs of billboard proportions.

"I know where it is, dammit," Paul snapped. A moment later, after turning into the gravel parking lot, he added, "I hate this stinkin' place. The food is lousy, so is the service, and the swill on tap tastes like panther piss – or, worse, airplane beer."

"Airplane beer? What the hell is airplane beer?" his brother asked.

"You drink one and P38. You ain't never heard that before, huh?"

"Hell, I don't know," Tom said, looking perplexed. "Don't recall it."

"That's funny. I've only been saying it since about 1970," Paul said, the disgust on his face palpable.

"Well, don't matter if we like the place or not. Nick likes it all right," Tom said. "That's all that matters."

"Thought we aren't supposed to call him Nick no more," Paul said. "Or am I wrong about that?"

"Nope – you ain't wrong. Whatever he wants, I guess, and fine by me," Tom replied. "He's the boss."

That got Paul going.

"Look, you simpleton," he said after slamming the truck into park and turning sideways to fix a decidedly unfriendly glare at his brother. "This bastard has us smack in the middle of this, right by the short hairs, and I for one ain't happy about it."

"Come on, Paul," Tom said, his grin widening. "You know he didn't mean nothin' by it. He explained it well enough – said things just got out of hand."

"That's it? 'Things just got out of hand' – are you nuts?"

"Hell no. Look, I ain't happy 'bout it, neither. But what are we supposed to do?" Tom asked. "We gonna cry or pout? Give ourselves up, maybe? How about we turn ourselves over to that bastard Kohlmeyer? What the hell, brother, we didn't do a damn thing."

"We let him in. Hadn't been for us, he never would've had access to the place – you know it and I know it."

"Sure, that's true. But what was we supposed to do? Leave him standing at the door? We owed him that much – after what he done for us back in …"

"That debt was paid a long time ago," Paul snapped. "We don't owe him a damned thing – not ever again. And now he's got us mixed up in murder. Wait. Make that *murders*. Two of 'em, last I checked."

"Like the man says, things just got out of hand."

Tom reached for the handle to the passenger's side door, but Paul smacked his brother's arm with the back of his right hand.

"You still don't get it, do ya, Tommy? Let me spell it out. The old man's dead. The movie star's dead. The meal ticket's gone. *Our* meal ticket." He clapped his hands loudly. "See? Gone. Without the old man, we've got no reason to be at Raptor's Ridge. With him gone, we've got no one to shake down. We're back to Chucky-goddamn-Downing's handouts."

"I don't …"

"Shut up, Tom. I ain't done yet. Just shut up and think. 'Cause the way I see it, without the old man, we've got to move on – and only if we beat a double murder rap."

"Come on, Paul, you know we didn't …"

"Pull your head out and think for a minute, you fool. We're the prime suspects right now. When the dust settles and your buddy is long gone out of town, they'll be lookin' at us … not Downing; he's one of theirs. And Nick's officially dead, so it ain't gonna be him, neither. No sir. Kohlmeyer and his crew are gonna come straight at us. You can bet your ass on it."

"Horseshit," Tom said, though his eyes were a bit wider now, and he seemed less certain of himself. "They can't prove a damn thing. Nick don't exist no more – they can't pin it on a dead man. But that means they can't tie us to him, either, or to the murders. All we gotta do is hunker down and ride things out. Keep our heads down, keep our mouths shut, let 'em spin in circles. Circles is all they got. That's all they're gonna get."

Paul was exasperated – a condition that he often found himself in when dealing with his brother – and he couldn't hide his frustration or his anger, not that he tried.

"I'll say it again, Tommy," he whispered in the low, menacing voice that he used to great effect, this time grabbing his sibling's left arm and squeezing the bicep hard. "The more we let Nick back in our lives again, the worse things'll get. He did it to us back home, and we was lucky to get out with our skin. I'll be damned if I'm gonna let him do it again. You want to follow along like a stupid sheep, go ahead. But not me. I ain't gonna do it."

"All right, all right. Let go, fer gawd's sake," Tom said, tearing at Paul's claw grip. "Ain't no need to get worked up, ya know. What's done is done – time now for us to move on past it."

"Sure – but we gotta move past it now."

"I hear ya."

"Do you?" Paul asked.

"Sure I do, Paulie. We need to cut the cord on Nick again. I get it, all right."

A hard rap on the driver's side window got their attention, and the startled brothers turned and saw Nick Drake grinning back at them. He rolled his right wrist over a few times, and Paul cursed silently and nodded and slowly cranked the window.

"Howdy, boys," Nick said easily. "What's shakin'?"

"Not much," Paul said without enthusiasm.

"Hey, Nick – er, Ax," Tom called across the cab.

"So, are you boys comin' inside or what?" Nick asked. "I'm a sight hungry."

"Sure – you bet," Tom said, his enthusiasm already ratcheting up.

"Good," Nick said. "I got me a hell of a good idea to discuss."

Paul didn't like the sound of that, nor did he like the look in Drake's eyes. He knew from long experience that it always spelled the worst kind of trouble.

"Idea, huh?" he said warily.

"Yup," Nick said, his grin as wide as the All You Can Eat sign across the way. "I'm thinking I'll go back inside that big ol' house on the hill, seeing's how they don't quite know what to make of what happened there last night, and steal me a body – just for the hell of it. What say you to that?"

"Steal a body? Are you completely insane?" Paul nearly shouted.

"Hey, calm down, buddy," Nick said. "Maybe I'll just hide it instead – plenty of places inside. Whatever I do'll turn 'em on their ears. Hell, I'm already laughing about it."

"You're nuts," Paul said evenly. "Completely crazy. Certifiable. I mean it."

"Ah, don't sweat the small stuff all the time, ol' buddy – get over it," Nick said with a grin, although he was seething inside and figured that, somewhere along the line, he and his old boyhood friend would have to come to an understanding about the order of things. But he added now, as though nothing else mattered, "All I wanna do is have me a bit of fun. A man can have a bit of fun – don't you think?"

Afterward, Paul Deeker kicked himself for not putting up a better fight. It hadn't helped that his goofy brother considered the idea to be as good as anything he'd ever heard, slapping his hand on the grungy roadhouse table while Nick Drake outlined the plan.

Only The Snarl seemed to recognize that removing Audrey Flowers' body from its current bathtub resting place would point an even longer finger at those who worked at the estate.

He raised the issue, more than once, and he told Drake – more than once – that he wouldn't cooperate this time out, that he had no intention of going along with the plan, that he wouldn't let his old boyhood friend and Army buddy into or out of the estate again.

"Fine," Nick said, grinning broadly. "Tom'll help out. Won't ya, ol' buddy?"

And at the mere mention of his name, Tom looked just like a lapdog waiting for a juicy bone, shaking his head up and down in joyful agreement.

At that moment, it was readily apparent to Paul that his brother would agree to just about anything Drake asked of him.

Worse, he also knew that he had to once again take care of his brother – *because if things continue the way they're headed now, it'll only get worse.*

"All right, dammit, I'm in," Paul said after more than an hour of arguing and steady drinking, doing his best to put an amenable tone in his voice despite the contempt that he knew he couldn't disguise on his face. "I don't like it, but I'll do it, if only to keep my brother from screwing things up for all of us."

"Hey, Paulie, come on …"

"No – hold on, Tom," Drake said quickly. "Let him finish."

The Snarl didn't need the encouragement.

"Fine. You asked," he replied, staring directly into Drake's dark eyes. "This is a big-time mistake, and it'll come back and bite us all in the ass. I can't say it any plainer. But blood's thicker than water, so I'm in. Hell, what choice do I have?"

"You always got a choice," Nick said through clenched teeth.

But Paul brushed it aside.

"Nope – to hell with it. I said my piece. No need to say more – not now. Later, maybe, but not now. So let's get it done. I don't want to think about it another second."

TWENTY-ONE

SLIPPING DOWN
THE ALLEYWAYS

MONDAY, 3:36 P.M.

I brought it on myself. That much, at least, I'll admit.

When I left Ned McClinton's law offices, I headed straight to Doc Strand's place to drop off the minivan that I'd borrowed a couple of hours earlier while trying and steer clear of the town's crooked cops.

But getting back into my own jalopy was a mistake.

I spotted the tail a minute right away. It was a clumsy effort – *clearly the Amateur Hour,* I thought – no doubt employed by rookies who hadn't been adequately trained. I mean, come on: You don't try to inconspicuously follow someone if you're driving a city-issued, police-marked Crown Vic, for god's sake.

What the hell are these bozos thinking? I wondered.

Unless they don't care that they're seen. Maybe the idea is intimidation?

I didn't like that thought, and I cursed out loud while lumbering down the street in my wheezing, oil-burning, rattling old clunker. I could smell Chuck Downing's hand at work, and I cursed under my breath and did my best to shake the clowns behind me, first by squealing down a narrow, dumpster-lined alley that my compact bucket of Detroit-issued bolts could maneuver through and the big Crown Vic could not. I shot through Third Street, standing on the horn as I blew past a city bus, holding my breath at the same time and ignoring the driver's angry horn blast in reply.

I secretly hoped that I was moving too fast for him to read the license plate and call it in. I also secretly hoped that my clanking car would hold together, if only for a few more miles.

I turned left at the next intersection, powered into another tight alley that ran between the businesses on State and Center streets, then hightailed it into the car wash. I handed the kid a pre-paid plastic sticker and rolled up the window again as he directed me forward.

Once the suds kicked on and I was hidden for the next three minutes inside the soapy bowels of the car wash, I did some serious ass-kicking of my own rear end for walking into both McClinton's place and the doc's office with such a cavalier attitude and precious little thought to maintaining cover.

"Of course they'd be watching both places," I mumbled. "One was Bohn's lawyer and the other was his doctor. What the hell's wrong with me?"

Had it dawned on me then that Downing's contingent might've been watching my place as well, it's doubtful that I would've agreed to meet with Caeli, at least so casually, and I still shake my head at my own careless stupidity in those early hours after the murders.

I knew better. I just didn't think it through well enough at the time.

There's only so far that you can go when you beat yourself up for making a dumb move, however, and I wasn't about to haul out a blackjack and thump myself in the back of the head.

Instead, I hustled out of the car wash and dashed down another alley, maintaining a sharp lookout for the Crown

Vic. I followed the speed limit on Front Street to the next intersection, hung a quick right, and took a quicker left. I ducked into still another alley and eventually wound my way to the back end of Busic Court, where I stashed my freshly scrubbed rig between a painter's van and a familiar old Lincoln that was as big as a boat. Downing's cops would have to be sharp to find me here, though I didn't intend to stay long.

My goal was a breakfast/lunch spot that's run by a buddy of mine, Jim Maddaux, the Lincoln's owner. I pounded on the back door, smiled politely when one of the short-order cooks pushed it open with a wary eye, and was relieved to see that he recognized me and stepped aside to let me in.

I passed some initial pleasantries about his griddle skills with buckwheat pancakes, which made him smile. Celebrity chef Rachael Ray had once featured the place on her TV show, and the pancakes are still a big draw, years later.

"Mad Dog around?" I finally asked.

"Yeah," he said, rolling his head to the left, "in the office. Usual spot, usual tricks, no doubt. Tell him to give me a raise, will ya?"

Even the cook had a sense of humor.

Dog and I have been friends for years. We belong to the same golf club and try to get a couple of rounds in a month – when time allows, anyway. He's a 5-handicap who hits the ball a ton with a homemade swing – one of those guys who never gets enough golf when he's playing well and who becomes even more passionate when he's not.

I'm one of the few guys around who knows how he got the nickname.

"Hey, Max. What's what?" he said, looking up from a massive clutter of receipts and credit card slips and vendor's bills that were spread across his desk like a rancid slather of mayo on moldy rye bread.

Mad Dog is one of those guys you can trust in a tight spot, and I told him exactly that now.

"I'm in a bit of a bind, Dog. I need your office for a minute or two – alone. It's not that I don't trust you, because I don't trust you." It got the laugh I was hoping for, so I gave him the rest of the speech. "It's best if you don't hear the conversation I'm about to have. It might come back to bite you if you know too much, and I don't want that to happen."

He wrinkled his face, like a Chinese shar-pei's, and grinned the same goofy look that you get when he's just dropped a fifty-foot bomb from across the green to take the final skin of the day and soak you for fifty bucks that you don't have in your pocket.

"All right. I can take a hint … go where I'm not wanted," he said.

"It's *when* Dog – *when* you're not wanted."

"Right." He got up from the desk and grinned again. "English professors."

"You mind if I use the phone?" I asked, pointing to his landline.

"Is that going to come back and bite me, too?"

"No," I said. "I'm not calling the group sex hotline. It's a local number."

"Good thing," he said. "I'll be out with the paying customers." He started for the door, then turned and added, "Why don't you get yourself a cell phone, for god's sake?"

Everybody's a critic.

When he was gone, I picked up the telephone and dialed a number from memory.

"Mister Parker's law offices," an efficient female voice answered on the second ring. "May I help you?"

"You bet, darlin'," I said. "Is he in?"

"Hello, Max," Effie Smith said in reply. "Give me just a minute and I'll get him on the line."

I flirt with Effie. She always gets a kick out of it, probably because she's at least thirty years older than I am and enjoys the attention. She must've been a real looker back in the day, and she still looks plenty good even now.

She put me on hold for a moment, and I used the time to carefully consider what I was going to say to Michael J. Parker, Esq., my long-time attorney, friend, and confidant. He's also a hob-nobber in good standing with most of the folks who make the key decisions in our fair state and certainly with all of the folks who make the key decisions in our fair town. So what if he despises golf and those who play it regularly? If you're in a pinch and need a hand, you can't find a better guy … or a better lawyer, for that matter.

Just tell him straight, I wondered, *or sugarcoat it a bit?*

"This can't be good news," Parker's voice boomed as he came on the line. "Though how could I expect anything else? I never hear from you when things are well and all is right with the world."

"Just calling to say hi," I said unconvincingly. "So … how are ya doin', counselor? It's nice to hear your voice."

But folksy wasn't going to work: He's far too shrewd for that. He also can read me like the front cover of a magazine – the kind with the big, bold headlines that you can decipher from the supermarket checkout line that's two aisles over.

"Just tell me you aren't mixed up in whatever's going on up at AJ Bohn's estate," he said, and that caught me by surprise, let me tell you.

"What have you heard?" I asked, and then quickly added, "Better yet, what do you know?"

"Only that some, hmmm, what might well be termed suspicious activity, has been noted around the place in the past twenty-four hours," he said. "Are you in the middle of it?"

"You could say that."

"Terrific. I don't have any details and would love to hear some." He paused here, in the same way that he might in a courtroom, and I found myself anxious to hear what he'd say next. What I got was this: "But you didn't call to trade rumors or satisfy my curiosity. Tell me how I can help, Max."

I stopped there and considered the offer carefully. I knew that we'd be covered by attorney-client privilege, but I also knew that the people who currently were mucking about in AJ Bohn's private affairs – his death as well as his life – didn't give a damn about the legalities and the niceties of things. I genuinely like and respect Michael Parker, and I didn't want to place him in the middle of the same jackpot that I'd found myself in when I first got the call from Raptor's Ridge.

"Come on, Max," he said, prompting me along when the silence dragged on. "It can't be as bad as all that."

"Might be," I replied. "But we don't want to talk about it on the phone. Let's meet for a few minutes, if you have the time."

"I'll make time. Come on over."

"I wouldn't advise that," I said. "I was tailed by the local constabulary after leaving either McClinton's place or Doc Strand's place, not fifteen minutes ago."

"Cops, huh? Interesting, though perhaps understandable, seeing as how we're talking about Bohn's lawyer and personal physician. I'll need to hear more," he muttered at the other end, as though talking to himself. And then, to me again: "It makes sense that if monitoring is in order, for whatever reason, those two would automatically be on someone's radar."

My lawyer is good.

"If I head to your place and they pick me up and tail me, you'll be in it, too," I said. "I don't want to bring trouble to your door."

"I'm a big boy."

"You're also my lawyer, and the cops will know that. They might even have your place staked out as we speak."

"My," he said. "This sounds like real cloak-and-dagger stuff. I haven't been this excited since, well, since the war."

"Which one?" I asked, trying to break the tension.

"I'll ignore that. Where are you now?"

"I'm at Dog's," I said. "Ah, that's Jim Maddaux's place – on Busic Court."

"Yes, the restaurant: good food, large portions, reasonable prices. All right, hold still. I'll be there in ten minutes."

"They might be watching, Michael. They'll tail you."

"I've been around the block a time or two," he said in that reassuring voice of his, the same one he uses when he's convincing a jury that his client was in the Swiss Alps at the same time that the infraction had taken place in, say, Sioux Falls, South Dakota. "Hold tight. Don't move, and don't talk about anything pertaining to AJ Bohn to a single soul, including your friend Mister Maddaux, until I arrive."

"All right."

"Max? One other thing."

"Sure."

"Order me a coffee. Black. And none of that foo-foo crap they're peddling these days."

"Right. I'll have it ready for you."

"Good. See you in a few minutes."

The phone clicked off, and I had to laugh at his demand for a straight cup of coffee.

Good luck in this age of double-shot cappuccinos and triple-shot espressos and lattes up the ying-yang and god only knows what else ...

I stepped outside the office, peeked around the corner so that I'd see into the dining room, eventually caught Mad Dog's attention, and discreetly beckoned him over. He arrived a moment later, his grin still intact, and asked, "Everything all right?"

"Sure, Dog," I said, donning my best poker face. "But I need another favor, buddy."

"If I can, sure."

"Your office for the next thirty minutes or so?"

"We can do that; rent's cheap."

"I'll pay it. I'm working on an expense account," I said. "One other thing."

"Sure."

"Coffee. Black. Five minutes. And none of that foo-foo crap you like to dump in it."

"Coming right up," he said, ignoring the insult to his barista skills.

"You wouldn't have a bottle of something good hanging around somewhere in there?" I asked.

He smiled. "I gave it up years ago. You know that, better than most."

"A man can always ask."

"I'll rustle up a fresh pot of coffee. I'll even bring you a bill."

Michael Parker, good to his word, rolled in eleven minutes later. He's a big man, fit and trim though well into his seventies, with a trademark shock of white hair covering his head and wearing his usual finely tailored Italian suit and lovingly crafted black wing-tips.

It's safe to report that my legal counsel also is something of a character. He'd carried a Mauser Broomhandle pistol in his briefcase when I'd first met him in my reporting days; he told me that it was big and odd-looking and always impressed the hell out of his clients. These days, he doesn't go anywhere without a Walther P5C 9mm handgun that he keeps in his overcoat pocket. Depending on where he's heading and who he's meeting, he also carries a Walther TPH .25 caliber backup pistol in the right-hand pocket of his suit coat – "just in case."

The last time I checked, he'd replaced the Mauser with a Colt M1911A1 .45 caliber semi-automatic pistol that he packs inside an Assault Systems Kevlar briefcase when he's dealing with particularly difficult criminal cases or clients. He also routinely keeps a FN FNP-45 semi-auto pistol in a soft holster in the crack between the center console and passenger's seat of his Chevy pickup truck, out of sight but readily accessible from the driver's seat.

He's nothing if not prepared.

"I can hardly wait," he said without preamble, settling into the chair that I'd vacated as soon as he stepped inside Mad Dog's office. He looked around, picked up the fedora that I'd abandoned when I first arrived, and tossed it aside.

"Are you still wearing this ridiculous thing?" he asked.

"Yet another brutally honest assessment," I said.

"Careful. Honesty coming from a lawyer's mouth could ruin my well-earned reputation. So let's have it, Max: I imagine you have a good story for me." He tasted the coffee, scowled, set it aside, and waited.

"Well, it's a story, all right. Whether it's a good one remains to be seen, though I think that some money's attached."

"That can be both good and bad. But let's begin at the beginning, shall we? We'll see where that takes us."

"Yes, at the beginning."

But I stopped, hesitated, and then brought up a point that had gnawed at me since I'd left McClinton's law office an hour earlier.

"Michael, a question for you first – before I get to the big show."

"You pay me by the hour. Shoot."

"I pay you when I can; you're kind enough to oblige when I can't. And for that, I am forever in your debt."

"Yes you are," he said. "What's the question?"

"What did the AJ stand for? In Bohn's name …"

"You said did. Does that mean what I think it means?"

"It does," I said. "I'll fill you in on the whole deal – and it'll take me a minute or two. This first, though: AJ?"

"Andrew Joseph, I believe," he said, "although his given name was Dashiell – accent on the second syllable."

"Really," I said, a statement instead of a question.

"Indeed," Parker continued. "His mother was a great fan of the mystery writer."

I drew a blank. I do that sometimes.

"Dashiell Hammett, you uncouth boob," he said, prodding me along.

I shook my head. If the name rang any bells in that sliver of time, they weren't tolling for me.

"You aren't familiar with *The Dain Curse* or *Red Harvest*?" he asked.

"I'm coming up empty," I replied. "I do better with the classics and the Romantic poets, and I'm all right with the Irish writers …"

"You're supposed to be a college professor and well-read," he insisted.

"I'm actually a retired investigative reporter-turned-college professor. I know more about datelines and sluglines and the derivation of dash-thirty-dash at the end of a news story than I do about mystery writers."

"Surely you know *The Maltese Falcon*?"

"The movie? The one with Bogart? Sure – I'm good with the movies. I've seen it a dozen times – maybe more. Mary Astor was the dame."

"The term you're looking for is femme fatale, and yes – that was Dashiell Hammett," Parker said. "He also wrote *The Glass Key* and *The Thin Man*. The last was turned into a series of movies with Myrna Loy and William Powell, if memory serves. The initial concept was quite good, though they kept at it too long – typical of Hollywood, where they constantly run a fresh approach into the ground and then keep recycling it."

"And you know all this because …"

"Because I'm not an uncouth boob, nor am I a retired newspaper reporter-turned-college professor," Parker said with a dismissive grunt that might've passed for a laugh had I not known him better. "Besides, I was good friends once upon a time with Mister Dashiell Bohn, commonly called AJ by the rest of the world."

"Huh," I said, at least momentarily appreciative that he'd let the literature lesson go. "Why didn't his friends call him – hell, I don't know – Dash?"

"He hated the name, including any of its shortened variations. He resented it, for some reason – perhaps because of the relationship he had with his mother. It was … complicated, I guess you'd say."

"In what way?"

"It would take too long to explain it, and it doesn't matter anyway. His mother's been gone a long time now and isn't pertinent here. What's important is that AJ was a complex, difficult, usually taxing, often mysterious man. Just when you thought you knew him, the witching hour would strike and he would change into something else entirely, yet another reinvention."

"The rumors are true then?" I asked.

"I wouldn't say that. People like to talk, and Bohn was a guy who was easy to talk about – just because everybody thought they knew something about him. But I don't think that anyone really knew him or understood him – not well, anyway. He wasn't an easy man to get to know, and he was even more difficult to understand."

"You knew him, though, Michael. Right?"

"At one time – a long, long time ago," he said. "We went to school together, which is something you probably don't know. We played on the football team together – quarterback and tight end; use your imagination to figure out who was who. He dated my sister, once upon a time. And if I remember the first car he owned or his favorite recipe, I'll die a happy man. Let's get on with it, damn it, Max. Tell me what happened up at Raptor's Ridge."

I spent the next twenty minutes spinning the tale, making it as fresh as I could, leaving out nothing. He sat still, his face outwardly neutral, asking a question from time to time but essentially letting me spoon out the story in my own good fashion.

Then I told him about the will and the pending destruction of Raptor's Ridge and the odd note to Ned McClinton that had gotten me involved. He asked to see it, smiled broadly when he read it, and handed it back without comment.

When I ended with my call to his office, coming full circle, he leaned forward and rubbed his hands together in earnest.

"All right, two immediate things. First, I want a copy of the will. Let's use your friend's device over there," he said, pointing across the unkempt office space to a compact Xerox machine that was partially hidden amid piles of boxes and assorted clutter. "And second, while you're at it, make me a copy of AJ's note to retain your services."

"Sure," I said, heading to the copy machine. "What are you thinking?"

"I'm thinking, my boy, that we've got some work ahead of us," he said. "And I just might be able to help – far more than you might even imagine."

TWENTY-TWO

ANOTHER ROAD TO WONDERLAND

MONDAY, 3:59 P.M.

Michael Parker often fills your head with ideas and thoughts that, on the face of it, seem as wildly optimistic as anything you can imagine. But in the cold, hard dawn of reality, you come to realize that his advice is so legally sound, well-framed, and well-structured within the law that the dreams filling your head were all of your own doing.

That's a hell of a good trick, and it always struck me that his genius was well served by his profession.

Acting on his astute advice, I snuck across town on foot for a few blocks before taking a cab to one of Todd Wright's used car locations to enact a trade of sorts. Hot Toddy is another golfing buddy, a low-handicapper with a wicked short game and an equally wicked temper. I'd once watched him helicopter a sand wedge such a prodigious distance down the fairway – he resembled an Olympics hammer-thrower at the moment of delivery – that it topped anything he'd managed all day with his driver. My suggestion two holes later for a sure-fire way to increase his length off the tee, using the same technique, was met with stony silence and an ugly glare – at least at the time.

I never get tired of telling the story, however.

"It's just for a couple of days," I told him. "You collect my heap, I use the loaner, everybody's happy. If a little green has to change hands to make it happen, well, I won't kick too much."

"Speaking of your heap, where is it?"

"At Mad Dog's," I said.

"What – it doesn't run?"

"Sure it runs. It runs fine – despite the cough. But I left it at Dog's because I can't be seen driving it right now, and don't ask me to explain. It's a long story that'll only bore you."

"One of those things that only you can come up with, huh?"

"Exactly."

Toddy thought it over.

"What's in it for me?" he asked.

You can't blame the guy, seeing as how I wasn't cutting him in on any of the good stuff that was transpiring at Raptor's Ridge, all of which had prompted the request.

"How about a putting lesson?"

"Like I'd take a lesson from you. Your short game is just like your long game: short."

He smiled.

I did, too.

"Nice," I said. "All right, so how about a sure-fire sale the next time I need a car? I'll buy it from you."

"In a pig's eye," he said. "And the reason you want to do this again?"

"The more I tell you, Toddy, the more likely it is that someone will want to kill you."

"Yeah, right."

"Hey, don't say I didn't warn you."

But Todd is a good guy, and he relented with the proviso that I bring the borrowed heap back to him in good shape and with a full tank of gas.

"You want me to sell your rig if some sap comes along?" he asked. "I can get top dollar."

"Yeah? How much?" I already was thinking about buying a new car with the money I'd get from the estate once the Bohn affair was over, and I wouldn't need two rigs in the big garage that I also was factoring into the deal.

"Let's see – three, at least," he said.

"Three thousand?"

"In your dreams," he laughed. "I was thinking three hundred, but you'd just as likely have to pay me that much to haul it away when the time comes."

I drove out of his lot in a 1985 gray Volvo that stuttered when you applied the gas and had spongy brakes that made me question my decision to see Toddy. But at least the cops weren't looking for it.

Michael Parker also had provided another juicy tidbit – one that would take me on a circuitous back route into Raptor's Ridge, bypassing the main entrance and the front security gate, which by this time would no doubt be well-monitored by Downing's minions.

While my lawyer was busy drafting a contract for the services that I'd render to the Bohn estate – a contract that would sail past the scrutiny of the most rigid probate judge, I had no doubt – I was heading west out of town. Using Parker's detailed directions, I traveled a dozen miles before turning south onto a state highway and followed it for another nine miles before heading east once more on an old logging road that I drove past three times before finally spotting. I crept along, bouncing over terrific ruts and ridges, doing my best to dodge downed tree limbs, looking for a left-hand fork at the 3.7-mile mark. Every now and then along the way, I would catch a glimpse of the twelve-foot-high perimeter fence that guarded Raptor's Ridge.

"There," I muttered when I spotted the fork in the trail, exactly as Parker described it.

Leave it to a lawyer to grease the skids at the front door and slip in through the back.

"I was drinking buddies with the guy long before he became the AJ Bohn most everyone grew to despise," Parker told me before I'd left Mad Dog's. "I've known about this entrance for fifty-plus years, though I haven't used it myself in – well, hell, in almost that long. AJ and I had a falling out, you know. I can't even recall the last time I talked with him – and now, I'll never get another chance."

"Why the break-up?"

"The story is too long and too complicated to go into," he said wearily. "And looking back on it, all these years later, it's of so little consequence that I shudder to even think about it. But the same can be said for much of what happens in our lives."

I'd called ahead before I left, using a borrowed cell phone from one of Hot Toddy's salesmen. When I finally got The Snarl on the line, I asked him to find the rear entrance and wait for my signal.

"I don't work for you, pal. I got better things to do with my time," Paul Deeker grumbled.

"Fine. Send one of your minions," I told him.

"Like hell."

"Look, Deeker, I'm cranky and don't have time for your nonsense. So it's me or it's Kohlmeyer," I said, pulling out what I hoped was a trump card. "Who'd you rather deal with? Pick your poison."

The police chief's name bought me a slight pause. "I don't know where this place is – how am I gonna find it?" he complained.

"Ask Mister Vineyard. I'm told he can tell you exactly where it is – through the woods at the south end of the estate."

"I'm either there or I'm not when you get here," he said, though I figured at this point that it was all bluff and blather with The Snarl.

"I'll find you if you forget," I said, just to let him know that I was paying attention. "I'll bring Kohlmeyer along for good measure."

"You do that. I'd like that a lot," he grumped and snapped off the connection.

Now, fifty minutes later, I parked the Volvo behind a cluster of hardwoods and honked the horn twice in rapid succession before getting out. A vine-covered entry door creaked and then emerged from the perimeter wall. The Snarl was on the other side, grunting as he pushed the well-hidden entrance manually.

"You're a pain in the ass, Blake," he muttered when I walked through. "Come on, dammit, gimme a hand. This stupid thing weighs forty ton if it weighs an ounce."

We pushed the door closed, and he wiped his thick mitts on his pants and started up a trail that led through the woods.

"The estate's a quarter-mile this way," he said. Then he added for good measure, as though he were establishing an alibi: "I had no idea this was here. The place is full of surprises."

I didn't consider his comment at the time, likely because I figured that I wasn't getting paid to exchange banter with The Snarl. He started panting before we crested the first ridge and didn't muster anything more than hard breathing and a grunt by the time I muttered a thanks when we reached the edge of the woods at the southern end of the estate.

"You should get out more – exercise a bit, enjoy nature," I suggested.

He shot a single finger in my direction and headed back toward the front gate, shuffling slowly but resolutely. I laughed and headed up the stairs and into the mansion.

"It's good to see you again, sir," the butler said, greeting me as I entered the foyer. "I'm glad to see you found your way through the back entrance."

"And you, Mister Vineyard," I replied. "Thanks for letting The Snarl know where to collect me."

His eyes clouded over for an instant, but he nodded a simple acknowledgment and said, "Could I pour you a glass of the Irish, sir?"

"Thank you, but I'll pass – it would put me out for good. If you could tell me where Chief Kohlmeyer is hiding, however, I would be most appreciative."

See? I know how to be polite when it's necessary. All those years of teaching college students how to butter up the dean or, better yet, the dean's secretary to get that good scoop has paid off – for me, anyway.

"I believe that he's upstairs with the medical examiner and Doctor Strand," Vineyard said. "Shall I show you the way, sir?"

I declined his offer, started toward the staircase, then turned abruptly and faced the butler once more.

"Do you know Mister Bohn's plans for Raptor's Ridge, now that he's gone?" I asked. I was tempted to say *dead* instead of *gone*, but I'd taken a liking to Russell Vineyard and didn't want to drill him any harder than necessary.

"I'm afraid that I don't, sir," he said. "You would have to ask Mister McClinton about that. I'm sure he would know."

I thanked him again and headed up the towering main staircase, where I found Doc Strand, Kohlmeyer, and Charles Wilson, the state's medical examiner, engaged in an intense discussion in the master bedroom. AJ Bohn's body remained on the floor, but it had been repositioned – no doubt because of the coroner's initial examination.

I nodded at Kohlmeyer and Strand and said hello to Charlie Wilson. I'd talked with him a few times during my reporting days, usually in typically adverse circumstances, and he didn't seem especially pleased to see me now.

"Did you bring the will?" Kohlmeyer asked.

"Yup," I said. "I also picked up a tail on the way out of either McClinton's office or Doc Strand's place – no doubt one of Downing's crowd."

"How do you know?"

"That I picked up a tail, or that it was from Downing's crew?"

"Both."

"Whoever it was drove a Crown Vic belonging to the city, for starters. It said so – right on the side"

Kohlmeyer shook his head in disgust. "I've not only got crooks on my team; I've got crooks who are idiots."

I laughed, but the chief wasn't amused and I let it go. "At least that back way into the place paid off," I said.

"Yeah, that was good," Kohlmeyer said. "Vineyard told us about it. Anything of interest in the will?"

"Lots of good stuff, and that's from just a casual perusal. But try this on for size …"

I paused here for dramatic effect. Even Wilson stopped what he was doing and looked up.

"Raptor's Ridge is to be demolished upon AJ Bohn's death," I said. "Right down to the last brick and board."

"You're kidding," Kohlmeyer said, his mouth hanging slightly agape.

Strand added for good measure: "You have got to be kidding me."

Wilson offered a similar line: "Tell me that you're pulling my leg."

"I only wish," I said. "I damn near fell over when McClinton delivered the news. It's a hell of a shock – then and now."

"I'll be damned," Kohlmeyer said after a moment of silence. "If that doesn't just about beat all."

"I don't know if it does or it doesn't," I said. "But it's something that needs to be looked at – and hard."

TWENTY-THREE

A SHOWING OF HANDS

MONDAY, 5:22 P.M.

"So what are you planning to do about Chuck Downing?"

Bill Kohlmeyer, god bless him, didn't duck the question when I asked it. Nor did he fiddle with his thumbs and move nervously about the room or resort to that most common of evasions and avoid eye contact.

Instead, he stared straight back at me and replied, as calmly as I've ever heard him say anything: "What do you *think* I'm going to do about Downing? I'm going to find the bastard a filthy spot in some filthy prison and let him rot there for a filthy long time."

We were seated in one of the kitchens at Raptor's Ridge. Five of us – Kohlmeyer, Doc Strand, Charlie Wilson, Russell Vineyard, and me – had spent the better part of the past half-hour kicking around the pros and cons, the facts and speculations, of just about everything connected to the case that we could think of.

Among the items on the table:

Who shot the timber baron?

Who shot Audrey Flowers, the one-time Hollywood star and AJ Bohn's mistress?

Who subsequently whisked Audrey's body out of the bathtub without being seen?

How, exactly, was her body removed, apparently under a great many noses?

Who had been lurking in the master bedroom and, when discovered, shot Ned McClinton in the arm before apparently escaping out a window?

How was this same lurker able to flee the grounds, despite a contingent of security guards who were on the premises?

How serious, exactly, was the corruption in the city's police force?

Should the governor or other high-level authorities be notified about the situation?

To many of these questions, particularly the first five, we added still another: *Why?*

Why, exactly, had any of this happened?

Once he'd caught wind of it, Vineyard also was adamant about discussing the provision in Bohn's excruciatingly detailed will, which directed that Raptor's Ridge was to be demolished.

"I don't like the sound of that – not at all," he said. "Surely we can do … something? Anything at all, I would hope? I for one do not want to see Raptor's Ridge destroyed. I can't be alone in expressing that sentiment."

But Kohlmeyer swept the issue quickly off the table. "Important as it might be, and I recognize it's something we'll have to address at some point, it's not the main thing we need to talk about right now," he said. "Not even close."

"Unless we think that it might go to motive," I suggested.

"Doubtful," Kohlmeyer said, though he took some time to consider the idea. "Mister Vineyard," he asked a moment later, "how long has that will been in effect?"

"Years, I believe, sir. Many years, though Mister McClinton would know for sure."

Kohlmeyer waved his left hand dismissively, an indication that we should spend our immediate time, at least, elsewhere.

I had other ideas on the subject – I still thought that the idea of razing Raptor's Ridge might be someone's motive for murder – but I kept them to myself and let the conversation drift back to the main questions.

On the key elements of the crime, at least, all of us could agree.

At one point, we even discussed bringing in the National Guard to take over the city's police force, which was the primary reason why the idea of notifying the governor about the events that had taken place at the estate popped up. Kohlmeyer, as you'd imagine, was dead-set against that suggestion, which came from Charlie Wilson.

The chief's exact words: "That'll happen over my dead body."

I felt obliged to point out the obvious. "If Downing has his way, Bill, that might be exactly the way it'll happen."

And that exchange prompted the next logical question: "So what are you planning to do about Chuck Downing?"

Kohlmeyer was silently seething again, this time at the mere mention of Downing's name. But I thought that he might be holding something back, and I was worried about establishing some lines of trust with the chief and the other members of our little cabal. I also was worn out and fighting sleep, but I did my best to prod him just the same.

"I get that you'll bring him down, Bill," I said. "Everybody in the room agrees. But how, exactly, are you going to do it?"

"Things are already in motion," he said. "Don't ask me to say more because I won't tell you more than what I've already said."

That wasn't good enough for me, however, likely because of my days of dogged determination as an investigative reporter. "I understand that you can't trust your own police force," I tried. "But you can at least trust the people in this room."

"Can I?" he asked.

That response didn't sit well, either. "Is that really what you think – that you can't trust us?" I prodded.

"I've known Charlie here for years," Kohlmeyer said, nodding in the medical examiner's direction. "Him, I trust. As to Vineyard here?" He looked without much enthusiasm in the butler's direction and shrugged his muscular shoulders. "I'm sure he was loyal to Bohn and all, but his sympathies lie there, no doubt, and not with the authorities – especially not with the police. He's of the belief that the police killed his boss, and the available evidence says he should. Hell, I mostly believe it. I don't want to, but what choice do I have?"

Vineyard looked as though he wanted to reply. But Kohlmeyer whisked his hand across the table, as though brushing aside a fly, and moved on.

"And as to Doctor Strand? Well, let's just say that his loyalties also lie in another direction. What's the saying the kids use these days? 'It is what it is' or some such nonsense? I get that."

Strand didn't get it, however.

"I don't know whether to be offended, or whether I should feel complimented and offended at the same time," he replied, clearly puzzled by the chief's words. But Kohlmeyer ignored him and looked at me instead, and I somehow knew what was coming next. He'd been hinting around the edges of it since I'd pulled him in, hours earlier, and he was about to let me know that his memory was as sharp as my keyboard had been in my reporting heyday.

"I already know what you think about me," I said, trying to cut him off before he got wound up.

It didn't do any good. He became a freight train that was greedily burning up the rails.

"I don't think you do," he said. "Not really."

"It was fifteen years ago, Bill."

"It was yesterday to me."

Wilson perked up. "You two have a history? Who knew?"

Strand was still annoyed at Kohlmeyer's earlier dismissive comment, but this exchange had his full attention.

The butler stood and walked to the counter, where he tended to another round of drinks.

"I won't say I'm sorry, if that's what you're looking for, because I'm not," I said. "It was a good story; a fair story. I had solid information. I had a reliable source inside the department. I had two sources inside the mayor's office. I had a source at the county level and another in the prosecutor's office. The story I wrote was factual, and it was balanced. Everybody had their say – or everybody at least had a chance to have their say. And I mean everybody."

"You think it's all so easy, don't you, Blake?" Kohlmeyer said, speaking quickly. "You talk to some people, you make a few phone calls, and then you sit down and scribble in your notebook and hunt and peck at the typewriter. The next thing you know, lives are destroyed, careers are ruined, families are torn apart."

His eyes had taken on a dull glaze, and he recited the words as though he'd memorized them a long time ago and was waiting for a chance to deliver them to the right audience.

Apparently, I was the right audience, and this was the right time.

"Those stories ruined lives – men I cared about," he added.

I wasn't buying it. "The stories didn't do that, Bill," I said. "Mistakes were made, and people on the force tried to cover it up. You know it, and I know it."

"Sure. Easy for you to say. Then again, you didn't have to look Janet Sterling in the eye after her husband put a bullet through his brain – right in her damned living room."

I pushed away from the table and angrily walked over to help Vineyard, though I only succeeded in getting in his way.

The silence in the room lingered for a full minute, then another.

I poured yet another cup of coffee for myself and gulped half of it down while I remained at the counter.

"You know, I read those stories – every one of them," Wilson said at last. "You won't like this, Bill, but it was a good series, and it made a difference. The police department – your department – was changed for the better because of it … accountability became mandatory. That's not an easy thing to do – to effect change for the better from the outside. My advice, for what it's worth, is to let it go. Especially now. We've got new and bigger fish to fry right now."

I looked across the room, and Kohlmeyer's eyes were still narrow, angry slits. But they were no longer aflame with seething fury or lingering contempt. Maybe he'd finally said what he wanted to say for all those years – words that he'd kept pent up for so long that they'd burned a hole into his soul.

I knew a little about that sort of thing; I had pretty much done the same with my ex-wife. It's not always easy to let things go.

"In any event, we've all got a lot of work ahead of us," Wilson continued, as though the matter were settled. "I'm taking the body out of here – through that hole in the wall that Blake so conveniently found. I'd like Doctor Strand to accompany me, if no one has an objection."

"When, exactly, are you leaving?" Kohlmeyer asked.

He may not have been his old self again, but at least he was making a good show of it. When I carried a tumbler of Scotch across the room and set it down in front of him, Kohlmeyer glanced up, grunted, and turned his attention back to the medical examiner.

"Within the half-hour," Wilson replied. "A state ambulance is on the way, with orders for no sirens or bells or whistles. Coming in that back way, it shouldn't raise any interest: Nobody's likely to see it. We'll take the corpse to the lab and make some determinations that might help you figure out what happened here."

"That's good," I said, for lack of anything better to add, and I sat down again, this time with a can of Diet Coke. "How are you getting the body to the gate? It's a long way off through the woods."

"It's under control," Wilson said dismissively, "though Bohn's isn't the only corpse I'm dealing with tonight."

Strand picked up on the comment with a simple, "Oh?"

"The State Police found her three hours ago – a body dump, from the looks of it: white female, late twenties; two GSWs to the head, multiple stab wounds, bruising around the face and neck, ligature marks on the wrists and ankles. Someone wasn't happy."

"Is there a connection to Raptor's Ridge?" Strand asked.

"I don't see how, though you never know until you get them on the table and see what they have to tell you. I'll have to ask politely; sometimes the dead are reluctant to talk – to give up their secrets."

"The priority's here, Charlie," Kohlmeyer said.

The medical examiner looked up, surprised, and I was expecting a retort along the lines of "Don't tell me how to do my job," words to that effect. But instead, he said to Kohlmeyer, "What's next for you, Bill, as you sort through this thing?"

We could tell that the chief struggled with his reply, no doubt still weighing issues of trust with the men in the room. To his credit, he gave us a hint, at least, of what was coming.

"I've made a few calls and discreetly put together a task force of officers I trust," he said. "They were with me when I ran one of the divisions; we've had each others' backs for a lot of years. I've got eyes on Downing and Stone as we speak. We'll bring them down … soon. And you can bet your ass I'll be there when it happens."

The words, the disclosure, surprised me, especially after what he'd said moments earlier.

"Do you know who the other cops are – the ones who were with Downing and Stone?" I asked.

Kohlmeyer's eyes flamed once more. "Every last one. I've got eyes on them as well, and boots on the street. It'll be clean and neat – surgical. I'll get some answers, by god."

"What about you, Blake? What's your next move?" Wilson asked.

I'd thought a great deal about that very question during the past couple of hours of kicking around ideas and theories and admissions of ignorance, and even a brief catnap, as I'd slipped into and out of Raptor's Ridge.

"I want to look at the security force Bohn employed here. When you consider what happened, and what they failed to do, it makes me wonder. So I'll spend my time there, I guess – unless the chief has other ideas."

Kohlmeyer brushed his hand close to the table a couple of times – the fly-removal sweep again. I took it as a sign of agreement.

"Any thoughts about where to start?" Strand asked.

"A few," I said. "A hunch or two, maybe."

"That's not a lot to go on," Kohlmeyer said. "How about I assign one of my guys to work with you? Two heads are better than one. Besides, I still don't like the idea of you doing work that by rights belongs to the department."

I didn't want to argue the point again. But I also didn't want to feel Kohlmeyer's boot in my rear end once he'd brought Downing and Co. into custody and regained control of the police force – and it was clear to me now that he was going to do exactly that.

"Tell you what," I said. "Let me pursue a couple of angles. If they don't pan out, I'll take you up on the offer."

"How much time do you need?"

"End of the day tomorrow, optimistically. A couple of days at most, maybe."

"You keep in touch with me, Blake. I mean it," he said.

"Sure," I said. "Agreed." And I meant it, too – at the time, anyway.

But stuff happens, as my students like to say. Sometimes it's stuff you expect.

Sometimes, though, it just leaps at you from out of the woods.

The stuff that happened next was the result of a phone call.

TWENTY-FOUR

BROTHERLY TIES

TWO HOURS EARLIER

Paul Deeker was in a tight spot and knew it. He already could feel the noose tightening around his neck and, try as he might, he'd yet to figure out a way to break free of the hangman's knot that was strangling the life out of him.

When it was just the lawyer and Vineyard, things were still under control, he thought. *Even when that smart-assed college professor showed up and started poking around ...* and he shook his head again and cursed aloud.

With only those three involved, he'd had no doubt that he could keep up the ruse and break free of the whole mess at Raptor's Ridge.

It was good for the first five hours. Absolutely golden.

But now Bill Kohlmeyer, the city's top cop, was involved, along with the state's medical examiner and the old man's personal physician. And he knew from long, hard experience that Kohlmeyer was a terrier: Once he attached himself to your leg, there was nothing you could do to escape.

Nothing.

Unless you shoot the bastard, he considered. *A terrier takes hold and won't let go, you shoot it ...*

Same with Kohlmeyer. He's the terrier now.

Shooting the police chief was a thought that he didn't take lightly, even as it continued to take root and fester in his brain. It was one thing to expedite a little mayhem for profit. And yeah, he could admit it: The rape-and-robbery scheme that put Nick Drake inside Raptor's Ridge had quickly spiraled out of control.

But that wasn't my fault, dammit. None of it. Drake can't be trusted, and my brother's an idiot. But killing Kohlmeyer?

Well now: That was the heady stuff of real consideration, of maximum commitment, of exhausting all other ideas and possible avenues of escape, of …

… of no turning back.

He knew that if he took the step, any subsequent false move, however slight, would mean far more than a prison sentence. It would mean certain death, either at the hands of the state or of the city's remaining decent cops who eventually would close in on him.

Cops like Kohlmeyer. Smart cops; honest cops. Cops who can put two and two together.

The idea of murder didn't trouble him. He'd killed his share of men who didn't deserve to live, as he thought of it, and he slept just fine at night. But the thought of going after a man of Kohlmeyer's considerable skills was like walking across the hot coals of a raging fire in his bare feet: He knew that it could be done, but he sure as hell didn't want to try it.

He quickly became convinced that an attack on Kohlmeyer would be a suicide mission.

He might not make it out alive. But I know I won't.

And now that it was on the table, he couldn't get the idea of certain death out of his head. Kohlmeyer was too smart, too wary, too quick, too cunning, too good …

… too damn good for me to mess with and live to tell about it.

And if nothing else, I want to get out of this with my hide. I don't want to end up dead, or spending the rest of my days in prison with lunatics.

"Lunatics like Nick Drake," he said aloud.

He cursed again and stomped out of the guard's station near the front gates of Raptor's Ridge.

"I can't kill him without getting whacked," he muttered, and the line became a mantra. He began saying it over and over, repeating it like a prayer, working himself into a trance, a fever, until he was no longer merely muttering the words but shouting them.

"You all right over there, boss?" one of his goons called from the other side of the access road leading into the estate, and the question startled him, snapping him out of the manic litany.

"Yeah," he sputtered, managing a harsh, barkish laugh. "Just thinking about tonight's game is all. Forget it."

That's great, he thought. *He must think I'm nuts.*

But the goon already was gone by the time he looked up again, and Deeker again retreated inside the guard's station. His mind was churning furiously, trying desperately to come up with a solution – any solution – that would get him off the sharp hook that he already could feel, fastened tight to his mouth.

It's gotta be there – somewhere.

The phone rang, and he grabbed it as though he were throttling Kohlmeyer's muscled neck and growled into the line. "What?"

"Mister Deeker? Is that you, sir?"

"Who else would it be?" he snapped.

The line was quiet for a time before Russell Vineyard spoke again. "Mister McClinton just called. He is returning to the estate momentarily and wanted you to know that he'll arrive within twenty minutes, sir."

"Fine."

He slammed the phone down and cursed aloud again.

Just what I need – one more idiot causing trouble.

"That's another bastard I'd like to wring by his scrawny neck and shove off a cliff," he snarled, speaking aloud again, and he looked around quickly when he realized that his words had inadvertently escaped his lips once more.

I'm gonna kill that brother of mine, he thought. *If ever I live so long, he's gonna pay for getting me into this mess.*

The idea of killing his brother, of actually going through with it, unexpectedly struck him as hilarious. He laughed aloud, glanced about, and then figured, *Ah, to hell with it,* and continued laughing until he ran out of breath and tears began to form at the far corners of his eyes.

All I've ever done is take care of Tom. 'Tom gets this and Tom gets that, and Paul, you see to your brother.' Well, I seen to him, all right. And I took care of him all this time. I got him a job. I kept him from doing time. Hell, I even kept the ungrateful bastard alive more times than I can count.

And what kind of thanks do I get?

"What I ought to do is serve him up to the dogs – him and Drake both," he muttered. "That'd fix 'em good. That'd serve 'em both right."

And maybe, just maybe, I'll do exactly that.

I'll just have to do it in a way that Kohlmeyer can't figure out – can't pin it back on me somehow.

"That'll take some thinking. Kohlmeyer's damn clever for a cop. But there might be a way out ..."

Maybe I can set it up so my brother and Drake take the fall ...

Moments later he glanced at the monitors and spotted Ned McClinton's SUV coming up the lane, and he cursed audibly again and activated the beepers that each member of his security force carried, placing everyone on alert.

"I'm runnin' outta time, dammit," he muttered as he eyed the incoming rig. "This'd better end soon 'cause I'm runnin' outta time."

TWENTY-FIVE

A SUDDEN CHANGE ON THE SCORECARD

MONDAY, 6:25 P.M.

"Blake. I want to make a deal."

That was a line I didn't expect and one hell of a nice surprise, considering the source.

The Snarl. I'd recognize that voice anywhere.

I was back in my office, looking over the laundry list of pending issues and questions that I'd compiled earlier, trying to figure out what had happened at Raptor's Ridge. I was fighting sleep while crossing items off my list of possibilities and unanswered questions, at the same time adding new items to consider, when the call came through. There was no beating around the bush or playing cute or asking for a lawyer or clemency or any of the usual nonsense that you'd expect from someone who was in a tight spot and needed a lifeline.

Instead, he added for emphasis:

"Blake, you hear me? I said I want to make a deal, dammit."

Paul Deeker was nobody's stooge or stool pigeon, which made his words doubly surprising – so much so that I had to scrounge around in my head for an appropriate response. I was searching for something clever, something that would put him at ease. But I'd been close to nodding off in the moments leading up to the call, despite the endless cups of coffee and caffeine-laden Cokes that I'd managed to gulp down during the day. Consequently, nothing witty – or even necessarily logical – came to mind.

"I was wondering when I'd hear from you," I eventually said, striving for casual though interested. But I failed in my effort to put The Snarl at ease because I immediately started considered the ramifications of the phone call and what it might do to help break the case wide open, and my pulse quickened sharply.

At least I didn't have to worry about falling asleep at my desk.

I'd talked with him before leaving the estate, a couple of hours earlier, hoping to plant a seed or two, thinking at the time that maybe I'd get him to open up if I pushed. I'd strolled the quarter-mile from the mansion's entrance to the guard's station and found him muttering to himself. He didn't look well – his eyes were dull; his complexion had turned a sickly gray; his hands were nervously fidgeting – and I told him so. He had shrugged it off in that brusque manner of his and grumbled in his menacing whisper, "Who gives a good damn what you think, anyway? Sure as hell not me. What do you want now?"

"I want to know what you know," I'd said.

"You already know what I know," he replied, swatting away my attempt at being both omniscient and convincing with a fixed scowl.

"If I already knew it, I wouldn't be standing here now, having this conversation," I said.

"Last time I checked, a conversation means two people talk, and you ain't gonna get that from me, Blake," he said. "You got no business here – none. Damned sorry I was told to call you when the old man bought it – you of all people. Should have tried another number."

"Cute, but it's not the way it works. Your late boss wanted me here."

"Maybe. Then again …" And there was that look again – the one that spelled anger and furious, barely contained rage and violence and pending mayhem. It's not easy to work all of that emotion into a single glare, but The Snarl somehow managed it with ease.

"It's too late to play coy with me, Deeker," I said. "Why not talk now? Save yourself the grief and aggravation. You know it's coming. Might as well be you talking with me instead of you talking with him." I jerked my thumb back toward the house, where Bill Kohlmeyer was rummaging about, and I could see the hate bubble up to cloud his eyes again.

Mind you, I didn't know any of the history between the Deeker boys and Kohlmeyer at the time; I didn't find out until well after the Bohn case was closed and I did some additional digging – not that any of it matters. All I was doing at the time was running a bluff. I figured that The Snarl knew more than he was letting on, but it was just a hunch – a guess. My logic was simply that a man in Deeker's position wouldn't let the things that had taken place in the past twenty-four hours slip by without knowing at least something about their root cause.

I couldn't say that he was in on it, exactly. But I could guess that he knew more than he'd let on to date, and I was pushing him now to deliver the goods – and to deliver them to me rather than to Kohlmeyer.

All I got was this:

"Screw you, Blake, and the sheep you rode in on. Now get the hell out of here 'fore I do something that'll bring that sorry excuse for a police chief down here with reason."

I tried to tough it out with him.

"Have it your way, pal," I said. "But you'll talk before it's over. You know it and I know it. Might as well be now, when things are fresh in your head. You might even get a sympathetic ear with a decent recommendation …”

“Hey, Blake – go and squat,” he snapped, reaching into the folds of his coat. “Right now – ’fore I make you.”

I put my hands up in classic surrender mode and took a couple of steps back, urging a smile across my face. “Sure,” I said, working hard to appear untroubled by his sudden show of threatened force. “Now’s not the time, apparently. Just let me know when, Deeker. You know where to get me – you’ve got my card.”

I left him then, convinced that I’d witness the Rapture before he’d consider calling me regarding the case.

But a couple of hours later, he surprised me. Damned if he didn’t hear what I’d said to him earlier and make the call.

He didn’t respond immediately when I fed him the line about picking up the phone. So I tried another direction instead, at the same time inserting a damper on the jackrabbit beating of my heart.

“You talk to anyone else?” I asked.

“Hell no. Who would I talk to?”

“No lawyers then?”

“You don’t hear too good, do ya? I said no – pull the wax outta yer ears. All lawyers do is muck up the works. You ought to know that, better’n most.”

“I do know that.”

That’s what I said, at least. What I was thinking was that if he’d talked with a lawyer, it would make it that much harder to get anything out of him now.

“So let’s talk,” I suggested. “But not on the phone.”

“Damn straight not on the phone. And not at that dump you call home, either.”

“My office then?”

“Hell no. Downing’s cops’ll be watching yer every move, fer god’s sake. Wake up. I’m takin’ a hell of chance to even call you. He’s got a long arm, that bastard, and he don’t pay no attention to whether it's legal to run a tap, or much of anything else."

"Let's not jump to conclusions," I said, though I picked up my telephone receiver and turned it upside down, looking for signs of a monitoring device. "Where should we meet?"

"Here, at Raptor's Ridge," he said. "They can't get to me if I don't leave the grounds, ya know."

"Who's they?" I asked. "Who can't get to you?"

But he wasn't biting. "One hour. Same place as before – around the back of the estate. Don't sound the horn. Whistle a birdcall at me. You don't know one, figure it out, or go some place and buy one; they sell 'em at Walmart. I'll open up when I hear it. Then we'll talk."

"All right. Fair enough," I said. "I'll sing like a bird in an hour. I'll see you at 6:25 or so – you good with that?"

"Yeah. I'm good. And Blake," he muttered before I could hang up, "just you. No cops, no lawyers, no courtroom artists, no stenographers, no prom queens in pink dresses, no newspaper reporters or college deans or presidents or the surgeon general with a smoker's warning – just you. Got it?"

That's pretty good stuff, I thought. But I said, "I got it. Just me."

"Good."

The line went dead, my heartbeat started to return to something approaching normal, and I resisted the urge to get up and dance about the room.

I might just crack this thing after all, I thought.

I spent the next few minutes looking for electronic bugs that might've been planted in my office. After the seed that The Snarl planted, I was concerned that unwelcome ears belonging to Downing and his minions might've heard our just-concluded conversation.

I found no trace of a bug, however, uneasily let the idea of covert surveillance pass, and called Caeli Brown instead.

"How'd it go?" she asked when she heard my voice. "I've been thinking about you today – since lunch."

"And you're all I've thought about today – even before lunch," I said.

She laughed – that merry, happy-I'm-here, pretty-as-a-song laugh. But something else I knew about Caeli was that she could spot a line of malarkey as quickly as my mother could. Smart women – the ones in my life, at least – are born with built-in BS detectors, apparently.

"I hope you do better with Kohlmeyer than you manage with me," she said.

"All right, so I was thinking about you off and on from lunch on," I said. "That much, at least, is true."

"I'll accept that. What's up?"

"I was hoping you'd be free for dinner – but before you answer, it might be late. I need to run out to you-know-where again for a bit."

"You know where? Is something happening …"

"No, it's OK," I said, anxious to keep words like Raptor's Ridge and AJ Bohn out of the conversation, just in case. "I'll fill you in later. But this could take a while. I can't give you an exact time."

"It's all right," she said. "Fill me in when you get a chance to call. Oh, wait – you don't have a cell phone."

"Working on it," I said.

"Sure you are." She was still laughing as I hung up the phone.

I slipped out the back door minutes later after changing clothes and tucking my Walther into its carry holster. I wasn't necessarily expecting trouble, but you can't be too careful – not with cops like Downing and Stone running around.

Todd Wright's Volvo was parked three blocks away, in an alley that was used mostly by local residents and meter readers. I hustled down the street, holding instead of wearing my fedora in case some passing patrol car might spot the hat and connect me to it. Not everybody wears a fedora these days, although Caeli says that I look more dashing than professorial in mine, especially when I set it jauntily off to one side and tug the brim low on my forehead.

The Volvo chugged to life after a couple of false starts, and I negotiated the side streets and eventually merged onto the state highway. Before long I was cruising toward the south end of town again, bypassing the normal routes that would take me directly to Raptor's Ridge. I rolled the window down because the air conditioning wasn't working, and the breeze was warm on my arm. I again headed east at the twelve-mile mark, turning onto the old logger's road that Michael Parker alerted me to earlier in the day.

How long ago was it when I met with Michael to talk about this mess? I wondered. *Seems like a lifetime ...*

The Volvo wasn't much to look at or listen to, but it did all right in the ruts and ridges and gulleys and washouts, and I eventually spotted the turnout at the 3.7-mile mark and cruised to a stop, pulling the loaner into the same spot that I'd used earlier. I got out, stretched to get rid of the kinks in my back from the bouncing ride, and put two fingers in my mouth to imitate the sour screech of a barn owl.

Go ahead and say it, but I've got all kinds of talents. Most kids who were in Scouts, even for a short time, still know a bird call or two.

When nothing happened – no creaking gate swinging open, no sound or movement or response of any kind – I risked a normal whistle, the kind that you'd use to get someone's attention from across the street.

Nothing.

I checked my watch, saw that I was on time, and waited, thinking that Deeker might've been delayed. But for the next thirty minutes, at five-minute intervals, I used the barn owl call and heard nothing in reply, least of all the opening of the back gate to Raptor's Ridge.

"The bastard's screwed me over – changed his mind," I muttered. "Dammit."

I thought about how convenient it would be if I could call the house and ask Russell Vineyard to put The Snarl on the line. I thought about calling Caeli to let her know that I'd run into a snag. And I'll admit it: I seriously thought – for the first time in a long time – about breaking down and buying a cell phone.

And if frogs and things had wickets and wings, what a wonderful world this would be...

I let the idea go, climbed reluctantly into the Volvo, and made the slow drive around the estate, knowing that I'd probably pick up a tail when I approached the front gates, which would mean that the Volvo would be of no further use.

Then again, maybe Kohlmeyer has sprung the trap on Downing and Stone by now, and the game's over anyway ...

It took a full twenty-five minutes to loop back around the complex and approach Raptor's Ridge from the front entrance. I rolled the Volvo to a stop, honked the horn, waited, and then leaned on it continuously until I saw someone step out from the guard's station and casually saunter down to the big gate. I climbed out of the car at the same time.

Tom Deeker, The Snarl's brother, stood a few feet from the gate, an AK47 sub-machine gun clutched firmly in his right hand. He had a smirk on his face, and I knew – right then, in that instant – that the order of things had somehow changed inside the compound.

"What the hell do you want?" he called.

"I've got business with your brother," I yelled. "Let me in."

"I got no orders to let anybody in here, you included," he said. "Get lost or I'll sic the hounds after yer sorry ass."

"I need to see your brother," I hollered. "Open the gate."

"Screw you, pal. Get a warrant."

And with that, he spun around and walked casually back toward the guard's station.

Great, I thought. *Now what?*

TWENTY-SIX

THE POT SIMMERS
AT CITY HALL

MONDAY, 8:18 P.M.

With The Snarl missing and his brother leering at me from behind the firmly shuttered gates at Raptor's Ridge, I was momentarily at a loss about what to do next. I sat in the borrowed Volvo for a full minute, staring straight ahead, doing my best to forget the malevolent grin that had graced Tom Deeker's face before he walked away.

I'd like to think that I mumbled something along the lines of, "Well if that don't beat all" – words to that effect. But a few choice epithets were no doubt tossed into the mix.

I was tempted to blow the horn and try again.

Hell, the thought of winding up the Volvo and taking a run at the gate crossed my mind. But I figured that I'd be no further ahead, that I'd have to pay Todd Wright for the damage done to the clunker he'd entrusted to my care, and that I wouldn't make a dent in the heavy iron anyway.

It didn't cross my mind that Deeker and his cronies might actually open fire on me – not until later, anyway, when I already was headed back toward town.

At least I didn't pick up a tail along the way: a positive sign. My guess, and I hoped that it was accurate, was that

Kohlmeyer and his group already had taken Downing, Stone, and their crew into custody. Word would have gotten out, tails would have been pulled or abandoned, and the cops who were on the outside hoping to get back in again – or at least were hoping to stay off the new chief's radar – were more likely to be lying low or writing speeding tickets than they were to be stationed at Raptor's Ridge, looking for me.

Without any more of a plan than an energetic "Ah well, what the hell," I decided to head directly into the mouth of the wolf and steered the Volvo to City Hall, where all city offices, including the police department, are situated in a centralized setting.

I'd always thought, when I was still reporting for the local newspaper, that this was a good arrangement for taxpayers but a decidedly awful one for the people who worked in the building. I'd learned through the years, often first-hand, that most of the employees despised one another, coveted the others' perceived power or title or pay grade or professed relationship with the mayor, and would as soon put a dagger into the next guy's back as they would consider sitting down to lunch with him.

It was getting late, with only an hour of daylight remaining, but I correctly figured that the place would still be buzzing, given all that had happened during the day.

Had I been paying careful attention, I'd have spotted the SWAT officers loyal to Kohlmeyer who were stationed on the building's roof, sub-machine guns in hand. I learned about them later – and a good thing, too. A sight like that might've sent me scurrying back to my pitiful office.

I parked the Volvo in a spot marked for visitors, removed my carry piece and locked it in the glove box, and strolled through the front door. I headed first for the pay phone and called Caeli, just to let her know that something important had come up and that I was heading in to see Kohlmeyer.

"I'd rather be with you, Caeli, but this is vital – something that can't wait," I said.

"It's OK – no problem," she said. "I can't say I'm not disappointed, because I am, but I understand, Max. Where are you calling from?"

Ah, she's springing the Luddite trap on me again.

"The pay phone at City Hall," I admitted.

But she let it go, god bless her – not a single remark about my need for a cell phone. Instead, she said, "Why don't you drop by afterward? I'll make something over here; we won't have to go out."

"That sounds just great; I'd love to. But I might be awhile yet," I said. "This place is buzzing, and it could be some time before I can get in to see the chief."

"No problem; I want to hear all about it anyway. I'll keep something on the back burner until you get here."

I headed next for the information desk – it was surprising to see that it was still staffed at this late hour – and managed a cheery hello.

The sound of my voice at least temporarily pulled the receptionist's eyes away from the funny pages that she was reading in the day's big city metro. I forced a smile and told her that I needed to see the police chief.

"No one sees the chief tonight," she said with a bored huff, glancing up at the clock that was fastened to the far wall. Her eyes returned to the comics, and she dismissively snapped the gum that she was absently chewing.

"I'm sorry," I said, "but *I* get to see the police chief tonight. Please call his office."

What I really wanted to say was this: "I've got a hot date with a special woman I've ignored for too long, and I'm in a hurry here. Snap it up and do your job." But I didn't figure that it would help my case, particularly with this dim bulb.

She again pulled her eyes off the funnies, but her demeanor was even less pleasant than it had been on our first go-round. "Let me make this clear: Not tonight," she snapped. "Come back tomorrow – mayor's orders."

"And I'll ask you again to make the call," I said, more harshly this time. "You don't want to get in over your head here."

"Go away," she said rudely, "or I'll get an officer and have you removed."

Good. Progress at last ...

"Make the call. I'm not going anywhere – not until I see the chief."

"All right – you asked for it." She triple-popped the gum, and the look on her face would've melted varnish off a well-sanded piece of maple.

"Yes. I did ask for it," I replied evenly. "A couple of times, in fact."

She dialed a number using the phone on her desk, working the gum furiously while she waited for an answer, then smiled thinly at me when she spoke into the receiver: "Could you please send an officer up to the front desk? Some guy is here demanding to see the police chief, and he won't leave." She waited until it was her turn again and said, "Yes, I told him that, but …" She glanced down at the funny pages again, her face reddening a bit; then mumbled, "Yes, he's got a funny-looking hat." Another few seconds passed before she said: "All right, wait a second." She looked at me again, her face as dumpish and dour as she could possible muster in a single expression, and said, "Who are you? What's your name?"

"Max Blake," I said.

She repeated it into the receiver, frowned, and hung up the phone without another word. Then she managed a bored look as she returned to the gum-cracking and the comics.

"Down the hall," she said, pointing indifferently, avoiding eye contact. "Second door on the left."

"You'll go far in this job," I said as I started down the corridor. "You might make mayor someday – or state rep, even. Who knows? With an attitude like that, you could become a U.S. senator … or the vice president, maybe. You'd need a shotgun for that, though."

But I already was out of earshot and was talking only for my own amusement anyway. What did I care if City Hall was filled with jaded young *blaguards* who wouldn't know customer service from custard filling?

The new mayor's got more work to do than he might've bargained for with this house-cleaning party, I thought.

Then again, maybe she's the mayor's daughter …

That put a smile back on my face, but it disappeared when I turned the corner into the police division and saw, instead of the normal receptionist, four officers stationed at the door and two more guarding the inner office.

Hardly a normal day at the beach, I thought.

The officers were holding riot guns and wearing body armor; they also had Glock pistols strapped to their legs in tactical holsters.

No one was smiling.

They eyed me warily, weapons ready. I did my best to look as non-threatening as I could, spreading my arms out with my hands open and facing them, as though offering the blessing at church.

"You Blake?" the one nearest the entry door asked.

"That's right."

"Step inside here and show me. Carefully."

"You got it," I said and slowly removed my wallet with my left hand. My eyes remained fastened on the cop, and my right hand was airborne and well away from my body.

"Hand it over – no sudden moves, please," he said when I extracted the wallet from my back pocket, extending an arm. The butt of the riot gun was now balanced on his right hip.

All right, so I was uneasy at this point – I mean, come on; who wouldn't be? – and noted that the cop closest to the inner door had his riot gun trained directly on my chest.

These guys sure as hell aren't kidding around …

I read the name badge on cop No. 1's uniform and addressed him accordingly – an old reporter's trick.

"Officer McDonough," I said, "I've spent much of the day with Chief Kohlmeyer at Raptor's Ridge. He knows me, and I'm sure that if you …"

"All right, Mister Blake," he replied coolly, cutting me off, apparently satisfied that I was who I was supposed to be. "I'll check you for firearms and other contraband now. My partner will have his weapon trained on you at all times, as will the other officers in the corridor, so I'd again advise against sudden movements. Do you understand?"

"Absolutely," I said. "And just so you know, I left my carry piece in the car."

He was good, thoroughly professional, the kind of guy who could get a job with the TSA. I was tempted to tell him that this was the second frisk I'd experienced in the past dozen or so hours but thought better of it, given the mood in the place. The look in Cop No. 2's eyes didn't encourage levity, and I still wasn't yet on McDonough's pool party invitation list.

"All right, sir, have a seat over there" – he pointed toward an empty chair – "and please remain as still as you can manage. It's also best if you don't talk. The chief's been alerted to your presence. He'll see you when he can; that's the best he can do for now."

He pointed to my wallet, which he'd left on the desk, and returned his gaze to the corridor.

I sat where I'd been directed, trying not to make a sound. I glanced across the room to Cop No. 2, smiled, but quickly locked my eyes on the floor when he caught my gaze with a look that somehow matched the one I'd spotted on the face of the surly receptionist at the front desk.

Two hours-plus went by and I was still waiting, without having said a word. I needed to call Caeli and apologize for missing dinner – apologize for not being there for her – and to ask her to cover yet another of my journalism classes. I also needed to use the restroom, and to get up and stretch. But the atmosphere in Kohlmeyer's outer office wasn't conducive to anything but sitting in stony silence … and nodding off from time to time.

God knows I needed the sleep.

Besides stewing about missing Caeli's company, I found myself thinking about Paul Deeker at odd moments, and I decided to find him, and find out what had happened, as soon as time permitted.

TWENTY-SEVEN

A POT OF ALPHABET SOUP

TUESDAY, 1:06 A.M.

Bill Kohlmeyer didn't return to his office until almost three hours had passed. He was accompanied by four well-armed officers, two of whom I recognized from the homicide division. All of them, the chief included, were wearing protective body armor and grim faces.

"Blake," he said when he saw me slumped in the chair that I'd been ordered into by the palace guard. "You're still here."

"I'm not sure I could've left if I'd wanted to," I replied. "Which, by the way, I didn't."

"Nothing better to do, huh? You must lead a dull life."

"More or less," I said, "though the same can't be said for you."

I'd stood when he burst into the room, and I stretched now, stifled a yawn, and followed him now into his inner office, trailing one of the guards who'd kept watch during his absence.

"You can stand down, Patrick," Kohlmeyer said, addressing the guard.

"Right, sir," McDonough said, but he remained on alert near the entrance, his riot gun on his hip, his eyes focused on the door.

"You seem to be in good hands here," I suggested, gesturing in McDonough's direction. "How'd it go?"

"Right to it; no beating around the bush. I like that about you, Blake. OK, so here's tomorrow's headline: Downing and Stone, along with five other former cops, are in the county jail in separate cells," he said, scowling now, his mood as dark as I'd ever seen it. "Two of them were chasing you today in that Crown Vic you spotted. We linked a couple of internal tips and got some names with a bit of arm-twisting, though little else."

"Why county?" I asked. "Why not the city jail?"

"Better there, under the circumstances and knowing who to trust – at least for now," he said, leaning back in his chair and hoisting his feet to the edge of the desk. "I'm working with the sheriff, Bob LeRoy. Don't know if you know him, but he's a solid, no-nonsense guy. We've formed a sort of joint task force, I guess you'd call it. He's been helpful – damn understanding, all things considered. Guess I owe him a favor – maybe two."

"Any admissions from Downing or Stone?" I asked.

"Nothing that matters, and about what you'd expect," he said. "Everybody's innocent, it's all a misunderstanding, whatever we've got is happenstance and hocus-pocus, they must've been framed if this is what we're thinking – the usual line of happy horsepucky."

Now there's a word you don't hear every day, I thought.

"Look, Bill, I don't want to sour your mood …" I left the sentence hanging in the air for a moment, and he jumped in to fill the silence.

"I don't think you can, Blake. I don't think it's possible."

"Let's hope – but let me run something by you first; then you tell me."

"What have you got?"

"It's Paul Deeker," I said. "Before I left Raptor's Ridge this afternoon, just as you were heading out for the raid on Downing, I stopped by the guard's station and ran a bluff on him."

"A bluff on Deeker? What did you have to bluff with?"

"Nothing, but that didn't faze me."

"I suppose not. I've seen you in action."

"Anyway, I told him I knew he was holding something back, everybody knew he was holding something back, and if he didn't tell me about it, he'd damn well have to answer to you for the two murders. I also told him that once you got done with Downing and Stone, your mood would be so nasty that …"

"… I'd take his fingers and toes off, one at a time, to make him talk," Kohlmeyer finished for me. "I get it. What'd he say to that?"

"He told me to stuff my hat in Marine City, Michigan – words to that effect."

"Right – where the sun don't shine, which is about what I'd expect. So what?"

"So he called me two hours later and said he had something. He wouldn't spill it on the phone, whatever it was, nor did I want him to. He suggested that my place might've been bugged by Downing, maybe even by you" – the chief snorted at that – "so we agreed to meet at the estate, using that back entrance again to shake any tails."

I paused here to collect my thoughts, but the chief was growing impatient. It was damn late, and I wasn't the only one who was flat-out beat.

"All right; I'm still here. How'd it go?" he asked.

"That's just it. It didn't. I got there, signaled, waited awhile because I thought something might've come up, and finally drove around to the front gate. This was sometime around 8 o'clock, maybe a little later. I was met by the brother, with no sign of The Snarl at all."

"Tom Deeker was there? But not Paul Deeker?"

"That's right."

"All right. So what'd the brother have to say?"

"He told me to shove it – refused to let me in. He also suggested I'd need a warrant if I saw fit to come back."

"They are nothing if not consistent, those two," Kohlmeyer said.

"I don't like it, Bill. Something's up. I can smell it."

"Why worry about Paul Deeker? He's a big boy."

I sat back in the chair, my thoughts churning. I'd hoped that Kohlmeyer would agree to play cavalry captain and ride to the rescue, taking Raptor's Ridge by storm. On reflection, however, the fact that he wasn't inclined to rush headlong into the teeth of the gale to find my missing snitch wasn't much of a surprise, considering what had just happened inside his police force. But I still had to shift gears to figure out what to do next.

While I stewed, something else occurred to me.

"What about the vultures?" I asked after a minute or so. Kohlmeyer had closed his eyes in the meantime and looked as though he was about to nod off – no question that this had been a long day.

"Yup," he said, maintaining the same pose, his eyes still closed. "They showed up an hour ago. The TV people are all here, filming away in the dark, shooting building lights and windows, I guess. The big paper from up the road had two or three people milling about. No sign of our prosperous little city enterprise, however." He grinned at that.

"They'll probably pick up the wire reports – might wait a week to run it, though," I suggested. He chuckled, enjoying himself, and I asked, "Did you make a statement?"

"Not yet – not sure I will. The mayor is all over it, though. He'll most likely be up all night getting ready. In case you haven't noticed, the mayor likes the spotlight, even when the news is bad."

"Media aside, I'd sure like to know what happened to Paul Deeker," I said. "He knows something, and he wanted to spill it, and now he's … vanished. That doesn't sound good. He could be the key to breaking this thing."

"He can take care of himself – I can tell you that first-hand," Kohlmeyer replied, his feet still propped on his desk, his eyes still shut tight.

"You have a history with that pair. Care to share it? I asked.

"There aren't enough hours in the day – not in this one, anyway," he said. I waited for more, but he folded his hands over his belly and sighed.

I shrugged it off at the time – maybe because I was beyond tired, maybe because the chief's logic was sound, maybe because I didn't care about The Snarl's well-being.

Then again, maybe Paul Deeker found that the heat was too much, and he'd already skedaddled, deciding not to wait around to shoot the breeze with me.

But why call me and say he wanted to talk?

"Look, Blake," Kohlmeyer said, interrupting my somber reverie. He'd lifted his feet off the desk and was showing signs of standing. "It's late. I'm not sure when you slept last, but it's been one hell of a long day. Go home. Get some rest. We'll go back up there in the morning, this time with blueprints for the entire estate. I want to see what old Bohn was up to for all those years. We'll figure out what happened to Deeker, if anything, at the same time. Fair enough?"

"Sure," I said. "Makes sense."

"You start the background checks on the rest of Deeker's crew yet?"

"Haven't had a lot of time, but I've got some feelers out," I said.

"All right," he said. "Keep me posted."

He climbed wearily to his feet, and I took it as my cue to hightail it out of his office.

"Be back here at, say, nine o'clock. That ought to give us all a couple of hours of sleep, at least," he said. "We'll put a squad together. Should be fun."

I knew that Caeli wasn't going to be particularly happy with me when I showed up at her place at this ungodly hour, especially because I'd have to ask her to take over my 11:30 a.m. class.

All thoughts of Raptor's Ridge and the Deeker boys and Bill Kohlmeyer disappeared when she opened the door to her place, however, as did my urge to sleep.

The news vans were still milling about when I got back to City Hall before 9 the next morning. While it's fair to say that I wasn't exactly rested and refreshed after a night with my newfound girlfriend, I can safely report that I was at least invigorated.

I strolled inside, passing the media hounds congregated at the front entrance, and was delighted to see that they were being kept at bay. A couple of TV reporters and one writer from the big city metro recognized me. They all shot me vile looks, typical of the folks who're in the trade these days, and that generated a hearty chuckle.

My spirits, already high, climbed again when I saw that a law enforcement officer in full battle dress had replaced the nasty, gum-chewing receptionist from the previous night. I gave him my name, and he checked my ID, eyed me suspiciously while he looked carefully at the photo on my driver's license and then back at my face again, and finally said that I was expected. He gave me a laminated plastic pass, which I hung around my neck and headed toward Kohlmeyer's lair.

The corridor was lined with city and county officers, all of varying stripes and ranks, and I slowly made my way through them, holding the city-issued ID in my right hand at chin level. But no one paid more than cursory attention once they saw my hall pass, and I took the turn into Kohlmeyer's office, said good morning to Patrick McDonough, who was still on the job, and was shown inside.

Kohlmeyer was behind his desk. He was with the county sheriff, Bob LeRoy, a hard-nosed, no-nonsense, humorless man but a fine, efficient cop. Also present were a high-ranking lieutenant from the State Police, Ken Chichester, who had the reputation of being a department trouble-shooter and problem-solver; a handful of the chief's own men, all of them armed with Mossberg 590 riot shotguns; and Doc Strand, AJ Bohn's personal physician.

That surprised me.

What's the good doctor doing here? I wondered, though I was glad enough to see him and gave him a nod and a quick grin.

The ongoing conversation gave me a better-than-average clue, however, as to why Doc Strand was invited to the party. Clearly unhappy, he was in no mood for amiable pleasantries at my arrival and turned his attention back to the police chief after no more than a cursory glance in my direction.

"Your implication is vague, Chief Kohlmeyer. Why not spell it out for me – in detail?" Strand said, the edge in his voice unmistakable.

The chief was seated at his desk, his hands clasped behind his head, an unpleasant scowl etched across his face, with deep-seated lines running through his forehead.

"Come on, Doctor. It's clear enough to the rest of us," Kohlmeyer said. "It's pretty damn obvious that timber hasn't been king around here since the late seventies or early eighties. As you've already noted, it takes a bunch of money to keep a place like Raptor's Ridge afloat. The speculation is that your former boss was doing more than trading in board feet and government timber contracts."

"Speculation? That's what you want to throw around – speculation? Because I always thought that in this country, at least, you were innocent until proven guilty. Or have I missed something with the change in administration?"

Kohlmeyer shrugged it off. "Let's call it official speculation, if that makes you feel better."

Strand snorted. "It doesn't. That could be you and the mayor. Or worse, it could just be you."

"All right, let's call it agency speculation then," Kohlmeyer said.

"Hogwash," Strand said – or perhaps it was a word that sounded much the same.

"Not so fast," LeRoy chimed in, though he was looking at Kohlmeyer. "What agency are we talking about here?"

"Take your pick," the chief said. "It's all alphabet soup to me."

Strand was sputtering again, the anger in his eyes flashing, his loyalty to the late AJ Bohn showing in both his words and his mannerisms. But the county sheriff was too quick.

"All right, I'll play along," LeRoy said. "Tell me, if you can, Bill, exactly what the 'agency' suspected was really going on up there? You've got my interest."

It was a dandy question, one I would've asked had I been in the room longer, and I liked the way that LeRoy was stressing the word *agency* when he spoke, using the index and middle fingers of both hands to place imaginary quote marks around it.

The implication was clear enough: Prove it.

"Gun-running, among other things," Kohlmeyer said. "As I understand it, we're talking big shipments, too – with fully automatic weapons heading south, to the drug cartels." He turned his body abruptly and started addressing Strand again. "Don't get me wrong: Nobody's accusing you of anything here, doctor. Whatever was going on at Raptor's Ridge was no doubt well above your pay grade – considerable though that probably was."

"It's all bullshit," Strand said angrily. "Nothing but bullshit."

"Look, Doctor Strand, I get it," Kohlmeyer said. "If Bohn's lawyer was here this morning, I'd be taking him along on this little joyride. But he's not, and you know the place as well as anyone – better than most, I'll bet. So here you are instead. Why not relax and enjoy the ride?"

"The same advice you'd give to a rape victim, no doubt," Strand snapped. He then barked out a string of detailed anatomical epithets and waved his hand dismissively. Under normal circumstances, I would've laughed at the sheer absurdity of it all. But these were hardly ordinary circumstances, and nobody was in a laughing mood anyway – least of all Doc Strand.

It also dawned on me that the entire order of things had changed yet again, at least in Kohlmeyer's mind.

"So you think this was a contract killing? A hit, maybe?" I asked from across the room.

"Blake. You're here," the chief said, apparently noticing my presence for the first time. "A contract killing? It's possible – hell, anything's possible. Truth is, I've had an itchy finger to bring in at least one of the agencies, and the bureau, from the minute you called and we confirmed that Bohn was dead. I've been holding back because I don't know yet what to make of the whole thing, especially with Downing and Stone in the mix. Then there's the missing body, which is … just plain weird."

Strand was still angry. "And you don't want to look foolish if this was a simple lover's quarrel gone bad – right?"

"Something like that," Kohlmeyer admitted without apparent discomfort. "But one way or another, I'm going to get a good look around the place today. You know the lay of the land up there as well as anyone, Doctor. I'm hoping you'll share what you know. With you, the butler, and the blueprints, we ought to get to the bottom of … something, at least."

"Or nothing," Strand said.

"Or nothing," Kohlmeyer repeated agreeably. "But that'll tell us something, too. Look, Doctor, all I want to do is get at the truth, which is, I'm sure, exactly what you want. I've got a fistful of rumor and agency conjecture about Raptor's

Ridge that's been kicking around my desk since I took office. I'd like to dismiss what I can and take hold of the things that need to be dealt with, beyond the murders. You want anything less?"

"You'd be better off spending your time looking at the Deeker boys and their crew than spreading lies about AJ Bohn," Strand said. "If there's any gun-running going on at Raptor's Ridge, you can start there – with the Deekers. And you can end there, too."

"I know all about the Deekers," Kohlmeyer said. "And yeah, they're on my radar. Count on it."

When Strand didn't reply, Kohlmeyer stood and started directing traffic.

"We leave in ten minutes," he said crisply. "Ken, make sure the road-blocks are established around the perimeter. And let's be damn sure to keep those idiotic media buzzards out of the mix."

He whispered something to one of his aides that I couldn't hear, then called out loudly, "All right, gentlemen, let's saddle up and ride."

Given the way the session had gone, I wasn't surprised to see Doc Strand head straight out the door, moving brusquely past a half-dozen officers. I remembered reading somewhere that he'd played basketball at Davidson during his college days, and I could sense the same toughness in him now that he must've demonstrated on the court in his hoops heyday.

The chief caught my arm as we waited for the traffic in his office to clear.

"You armed?" he asked.

"It's in the car – didn't think I'd get in here with it this morning," I said.

"Good thinking. Be sure to bring it along. I've got no idea what to expect up there, but I'm going in loaded for bear."

"Makes sense, given Tom Deeker's threat last night."

"Exactly. And listen, Blake – one other thing."

"Sure."

"Keep an eye on Strand, will you? He's mad as hell at me right now. I respect that and, hell, even understand where he's coming from. But he won't be inclined to pay attention to what I say, which is that I don't want either one of you getting close until we know things are clear. If worse comes to worse and all hell breaks loose, I want you to get out of there, or at least to lay low until the smoke clears. And keep Strand with you. All right?"

"Sure. I'm not looking to get my name in the newspapers tomorrow," I said.

"Good. Neither am I. But it might go otherwise."

"So you're officially expecting some action from Tom Deeker today, Bill – or am I misreading the tea leaves?"

His hand instinctively reached for the butt end of the butt-ugly Glock pistol that was strapped to his side.

"We'll see when we get up there, I guess," he said as he headed toward the door. "Not much else we can do but take it a step at a time and try like hell to stay safe."

It was at least a good plan.

TWENTY-EIGHT

A CHANGING OF THE GUARD

TUESDAY, 9:22 A.M.

The first police unit to arrive at Raptor's Ridge, a black SWAT-rigged SUV filled with members of the city's elite force, had just pulled up to the front gate when withering bursts of submachine-gun fire shattered the silence of an otherwise peaceful Willamette Valley morning.

I was in the third car back – with Doc Strand, Bill Kohlmeyer, and Patrick McDonough, who was driving – when the Deekers' glorified goon squad began the assault.

"God in heaven," Kohlmeyer muttered as McDonough hit the brakes and swerved the heavy vehicle off the road, taking us as far out of the direct line of fire as he could manage. Kohlmeyer unlocked his seat belt, yelled at Strand and me to stay put, and bolted out the door.

To hell with that, I thought.

I grabbed the doctor's arm and tugged, and we followed the chief, jumping out the right side of the vehicle, sprawling into a dry drainage ditch. Kohlmeyer was issuing sharp commands, though his voice was nearly drowned out by the staccato bursts of gunfire from the front gate and sporadic return volleys from the officers in the SUVs immediately ahead of us, along with an occasional ear-deafening discharge from McDonough's Mossberg-model riot gun.

The driver of the lead SUV, which was sustaining constant fire, slammed the vehicle into reverse and zigzagged crazily for fifty yards or so back down the road before turning the wheel sharply and cutting the rig sideways into the ditch, almost tipping it in the process. The front tires were destroyed. The windshield was spider-webbed but intact, a testament to shatter-resistant glass and, as I learned later because I bought stock in the outfit, the Pacific Bulletproof Co.

"What the hell's going on?" Strand yelled. His eyes, already wide, registered surprise when he saw that I'd pulled my Walther P99. He added, "Where did you get that? Never mind – where do *I* get one?"

He displayed an excellent beside manner, even in the face of a gunfight.

"Just keep your head down, Doc," I said during a lull in the shooting. I used the moment to grab his collar and pull him as far away from the direct line of fire as I could. We looped around the right side of vehicle – "Dammit, Blake, keep your head down," Kohlmeyer hollered – running fast and staying low, and then sat in a heap, breathing hard, our backs now glued to the rear bumper.

"Stick with me – at least for now," I said.

"I'm damn well not going anywhere," Strand said. He muttered something else, but I couldn't make it out in the din of additional erupting gunfire.

I spotted Bob LeRoy and Ken Chichester behind us. They, too, had abandoned their vehicle and were positioned on its far side, away from the road. Chichester held his department-issued Glock; LeRoy had pulled the riot gun from its stand inside the cruiser and had it leveled in the direction of the main gate.

With his force pinned down but at least momentarily safe, the chief snapped on his combination cell phone/police radio and punched in a coded number. "It's Kohlmeyer," he barked: "10-13. I repeat, 10-13." A pause, then, "We're under attack and taking heavy fire from multiple full-auto weapons." Another pause, then, "10-77 … notify all agencies. Do it now. Kohlmeyer out."

A burst of submachine-gun fire thumped directly into our SUV, and I heard him curse loudly, a sailor's string of choice epithets.

"Blake, Strand – you two all right?" he called out a moment later.

"We're good, Chief," I yelled.

"All right – stay that way."

How can you argue with that?

I could hear him shouting into the cell phone/police radio again, issuing orders to the SWAT officers who were pinned down in various locations along the road. We could hear police sirens wailing in the distance, the pinging of bullets striking metal and iron and asphalt and thwacking into the nearby woods, the crackling of police radios, shouted commands and responses, but mostly the persistent barking of sub-machine guns, riot guns, high-powered rifles, and the occasional handgun.

"What the hell's going on in there?" Strand yelled at one point, talking to no one in particular, least of all me.

Don't ever let anyone tell you that being in the middle of a gunfight isn't loud and dangerous and crazy. I'd seen a great many odd things during my time as a reporter and even as a part-time private detective, including domestic disputes that would sometimes escalate into standoffs with the cops. Hell, I'd even seen a variety of weird events in the classroom: fistfights, heated arguments that included finger-poking and what amounted to fifth-grade taunting, and a few extended crying jags and hissy-fits when final grades were posted. But nothing you've experienced, short of the battlefield, will prepare you for something like this.

Doc poked my arm and said forcefully, "Why don't you fire off a couple of shots?"

"Are you nuts?" I replied, my eyes widening at the thought of sticking my head around the corner of the rig to take aim with the Walther.

"Let me do it then," he said.

"If you want to try something like that, Doc, then *you* must be nuts."

We both laughed grimly at the absolute absurdity of the situation. I poked Strand a moment later when I noticed a sniper team approaching from down the road. The three officers were in all-camo gear with painted faces, carrying their rifles in cases. They stayed low by crab-crawling single-file through the ditch after talking with LeRoy and Chichester.

I waved them in and called out to Kohlmeyer at the same time: "Cavalry's coming in, Chief."

The gunfire was intermittent on both sides now, and every now and then we could hear laughter from behind the big gate. The snipers huddled with Kohlmeyer, pulling out large-scoped rifles and loading them as they discussed strategy.

"Deeker and his boys must think it's some kind of joke in there," I said when I heard more laughter from inside the compound. "They've got to be nuts, too – the lot of them."

"We're all nuts just being here," Doc said.

"You're right. Positively nuts. I'll never complain about summer classes again."

The chief's cell phone/radio rattled, and he was soon involved in a shouted conversation with Russell Vineyard, who was inside the mansion.

"Vineyard, what the hell is going on in there?" the chief hollered as more gunfire sprayed the area. A pause, then, "*Tom* Deeker? Where's his brother?" Another pause, then, "Can you activate the gate from the main house? Say again, please. No? Dammit." He paused again, this time to adjust his thinking. "All right, make sure you keep your head down. I'll get you out when I can. Kohlmeyer out."

He returned to directing-traffic mode, sending the sniper team through the woods west of the gate, ordering a SWAT contingent to the east side, along the 12-foot-high perimeter wall, and then barking into the cell/radio once more: "What about the damn helicopters?"

My face lit up at that, and I poked Strand.

"First the cavalry; now they're sending in the Marines. What's next?"

"The Salvation Army?" he suggested.

It was a good line, all things considered, and I smiled one of those goofy smiles that you give someone when you know they're at the top of their game despite overwhelming odds – like that *Jeopardy* champion, Ken something or other, who won seventy-odd TV sessions in a row before flubbing a question about shipping or … whatever the hell he missed.

It's crazy, the stuff that jumps into your brain when barrages of bullets are flying over your head. It's even crazier to consider how you might react in a similar situation. I've read that some people shut down, others go mad with fear, and some never recover from the trauma. For whatever reason, I chose to think about other things in an effort to disguise the reality of what was actually happening around me.

I recalled a *Golf* magazine issue that was on the medicine cabinet in my bathroom. One of the cover headlines read **Putt Just Like Phil Mickelson**, and I wondered, *Why would I want to putt like that? For starters, the guy's batting from the wrong side of the plate.*

I considered breaking into song at one point and wondered if Strand knew the words to *Summer Wind* – the Sinatra version, not the Lyle Lovett cover.

Yup, crazy stuff, and I was humming *Summer Wind* now and started wondering what might be rumbling through the doctor's head at the same time, which was no doubt even goofier.

Kohlmeyer's voice carried over the incessant gunfire chatter again, and I looked up, expecting National Guard helicopters to swoop in with Robert Duvall playing Wagner on a boom-box. But the sharp crack of the high-powered sniper's rifles, fired in near-unison, was followed by a sudden deathly silence. I glanced for a second at Strand, peeked around the corner of the SUV, and saw Kohlmeyer's grim but determined smile.

The worst of it was over.

The chief's cell/radio crackled to life once more, and we could hear the message from where we were huddled at the back of the SWAT rig: "10-53, Chief. I repeat, 10-53."

"Roger that. Take two teams over the wall now, then advise," Kohlmeyer ordered. His voice, back to a normal pitch now, had remained calm and steady throughout.

A minute ticked slowly by, then another and another. I was eyeing the digital dial on my watch when the steady throp-throp-throp of helicopter blades, cutting the air high overhead, drifted progressively in from the north, and the chief glanced skyward and scowled. He muttered something to McDonough, and his aide grinned, making me wish that we were close enough to hear the exchange.

The all-clear came a moment later, and the big iron gate creaked to life and rolled inward.

"All right, the fun's just getting started," Kohlmeyer said. "Let's saddle up." He waved at LeRoy and Chichester, and the two of them quickly joined the chief and his aide.

Kohlmeyer turned our way next and said, "Blake, I want you two on this side of the gate until I give you the green light. Understand?"

I didn't bother to reply. The chief already was moving up the roadway, asking about casualties and injuries as his men gathered by his side.

Strand poked my arm again and pointed to the Walther, which I continued to hold in a two-fisted grip, the barrel pointed at the ground. "You've got to tell me how to get one of those things," he said. "It's beautiful."

Doc was right about that, too.

TWENTY-NINE

INSIDE PASSAGES
AND DEAD ENDS

TUESDAY, 10:07 A.M.

Kohlmeyer was right: The fun was just beginning.

It just took us a bit longer to get in on the act: forty-five minutes longer in all.

I borrowed Doc Strand's cell phone within minutes of the chief's departure and called Caeli to let her know what had happened and to assure her that I was all right, in the event that she'd hear details of the shootout on the TV news. We talked for fifteen minutes, and I asked her to speak up a couple of times because my ears were still ringing from the previous gunfire.

She expressed concern for my well-being, which was sweet, and told me that she'd cover the 11:30 Intro to Mass Comm class. In the excitement of the shootout, I'd forgotten about the ninety-minute course, and her reminder provided me with an opportunity to talk about something besides gunfire and ricocheting rounds and whether it was Johnny Mercer or Henry Mayer who wrote *Summer Wind*; turns out, it was both.

"Anything in particular I should know about the class today?" she asked.

"My notes are on my desk, but we're covering radio this week," I said. "Work in *War of the Worlds* and Orson Welles, Marconi and Tesla, the Canadian inventor Reginald Fessenden, plus Lee de Forest and Edwin Howard Armstrong, and you'll be golden. Oh, and watch out for Shad Russell and Darren Pike. They're a couple of smart-asses, though both are smart as hell. And if Alisa Halverson and Janel Foster sit within ten yards of one another, you'll surrender control of the class entirely."

She laughed, and I could hear her scribbling notes. Before we signed off, I promised to call when I could and let her know any vital details that we might uncover inside Raptor's Ridge.

Doc and I talked about AJ Bohn's autopsy the previous evening, which Charlie Wilson had conducted at his state-run medical lab downtown, with Strand assisting.

"Nothing but the obvious," he said. "Five gunshots, including a shot directly to the heart. The bullets were 9-millimeter."

"Nothing else of help, then?" I asked. "No extraneous DNA under AJ's fingernails, for example? No …"

"Nothing … as routine as it gets – for a murder, anyway."

We also chatted about handguns for a time – Glocks versus Walthers and SIGs and Walthers versus S&Ws and Rugers – and the state's licensing requirements for obtaining a concealed weapons permit.

He called his receptionist, canceled two afternoon appointments, and asked me for the name of the guy who runs my favorite local gun shop.

We came to the conclusion, somewhere along the way as the minutes dragged on, that the shootout would produce a wave of media coverage that would blow away our veil of secrecy regarding the Bohn/Flowers murders – for better or worse.

"The best-laid plans," Strand said philosophically. "All AJ wanted these past few years was to live out his days in peace and quiet, well out of the public spotlight."

"Then why was he spending his time with a movie star?"

"It's not like she was Angelina Jolie, you know."

"At one time, she *was* Angelina Jolie, or at least her equivalent," I replied.

"I don't know that Audrey was ever an Angelina type – even when she was on the screen a great deal, which hasn't been the case for some time," Strand said. "She was much too wholesome, and too much of a comedienne, to compete with big action stars like Angelina – or, I don't know, Sigourney Weaver, maybe."

"During her *Alien* phase."

"Exactly."

"Yeah, I guess that works. I'm just saying that if AJ wanted to keep a low profile, he might have found a less-conspicuous roommate – one who hasn't been on the cover of *Variety*, or even *TV Guide*."

"I guess," Doc said. "But how do you tell that to a guy who has more money than god and who'd done everything he ever wanted to do for every waking moment of his life?"

"I get it. But the media hounds will swoop in now and stick around – some of them for weeks," I said, talking from long experience. "Book deals will be cut over this."

One of Kohlmeyer's young officers eventually returned to collect us, issuing a terse invitation to the party that already was under way inside the gates.

"Stick close," he said as we entered the grounds. "We're still clearing the site, and the estate is freakin' enormous – never seen anything like it. But the chief thinks it's safe enough for the two of you now."

"Easy for him to say," I muttered, out of earshot of the chief's runner.

"I'm not anxious to head in there if the mansion and grounds aren't secure," Strand said, edging closer to the officer. "The last thing I want to be is a target for the Deekers."

"There's no sign of either of the brothers – not that we've seen so far, anyway … unless they've caught 'em since I've been with you two," the runner indicated.

"I'd feel a lot better if I had a gun," Strand grumbled. He looked at me and added, "If you aren't going to use yours, let me have it."

"Relax, Doc – it's under control," I said, mustering some feigned enthusiasm to make him feel better about things, even if I didn't. I reflexively placed my right hand on the grip of the holstered Walther, just to reassure myself that it was close by.

"I'll relax when I'm back at the country club in a five-dollar Nassau with three chumps," he said, his eyes constantly darting around the landscape. "Frankly, I can hardly wait."

I checked our escort's nametag, then asked, "Officer Fults, how many of Deeker's men are we talking about here – the ones who were manning the gate?"

"Three are down, so far as I know. One's over there" – he pointed east of the gate – "and two more are over there," he said, his hand sweeping across the roadway to a lush landscape of decorative flower beds and rosebushes and young saplings at the edge of the gate and the perimeter wall. "Five men are in custody up at the mansion, last I checked. They ran in that direction when we took down these three, but they gave up quick enough as we moved through. The chief sent for a wagon to transport 'em back to town – ought to be here any time."

"And you're sure the Deekers haven't been rounded up?" I pressed.

"So far as I know," Fults said, walking at a brisk pace. "But the chief'll know for sure – you can ask him. Something might've changed, I guess."

I considered again the conversation that I'd had with Paul Deeker the night before. His absence might mean everything or nothing, but I was surprised – damned surprised, really – that the goons had taken any actions without The Snarl, or his brother, calling the shots.

"What are you thinking about?" Strand asked as we drew within sight of the mansion.

"Paul Deeker," I said. "He was going to meet me yesterday, at that back entrance on the south wall, and he didn't show. He's not here now. I think something's up."

"Yeah," Doc said. "Smart man. He saw this coming and got the hell out while the getting was good. I'd've done the same – same as you, I'll bet."

"So who was giving the orders in here if Deeker's gone, along with his brother?" I asked.

Doc hesitated a moment. "Hell of a good question," he said at last. "I'd suggest that if Kohlmeyer's crew hasn't found them yet, one or the other of the brothers, or both at once, are either still on the grounds somewhere, or they went out through one of the tunnels and are long gone. If they had any sense, they would've bolted when things went south – which for me would've been before the first shots were fired."

"But The Snarl wasn't here yesterday, either," I insisted. "He told me he wanted to spill the beans, but he didn't show. I saw his brother at the gate last night, but no sign of Paul. Best I can figure is he wanted to talk, but somebody kept him from doing it."

"Or he was here and simply changed his mind," Doc said.

"Or somebody changed it for him," I pressed. "I still think something's up."

We were at the front steps now, and Fults waved us forward. "The chief's inside, expecting you," he said. "I'll leave you to it."

Three officers were stationed at the door; two more were inside, riot guns on hips, and I was expecting an order to produce some ID and stand for yet another frisk when Russell Vineyard entered from the side room nearest the foyer and bowed slightly when we saw him.

"Doctor Strand, Mister Blake – so good of you both to drop by again," he said calmly.

I couldn't help but smile at the old guy's aplomb.

"Are you all right?" Doc asked, expressing genuine concern.

"Certainly, sir. Thank you. And how are you faring, sir?"

"We're both fine," Doc said. "Where were you when the shooting started?"

"I'm not certain, exactly, because I'm not exactly certain when it began," he said. "It was only after Chief Kohlmeyer alerted me with his phone call that I learned things were amiss at the estate. That is when I knew to seek shelter."

"You sought shelter?"

"Certainly, sir – in the passageway through the kitchen pantry. I only came out after Chief Kohlmeyer called again, when the excitement ended. I'm happy to report that I missed it."

"I'm glad to see that you're safe, Mister Vineyard," I said. "You have the steadiest hand in the place."

"Why thank you, sir. Would you care for a glass of the Irish now, perhaps?"

"A gracious invitation, but no," I said.

"Very good, sir. Chief Kohlmeyer is in the master bedroom. He asked me to direct you there when you arrived. Shall I lead the way?"

"That's not necessary, Russell," Doc said. "We know where to go."

"If you say so, sir. Can I bring you anything, Doctor? Scotch, perhaps?"

Strand also declined the butler's offer, which strikes me as surprising as I look back on that moment. You'd think that all of the shooting we'd just witnessed, including the moments when our SUV was raked by submachine-gun fire in the initial gunfight, would've prompted a quick reach for the bottle once the air cleared. But I was happy to let it go, for whatever reason, and so was the doctor.

"It'll taste better later on," Strand said by way of apology to the butler as we headed toward the stairs.

"Very good, sir," Vineyard said. "Do let me know if I'm needed." He bowed slightly and disappeared again through the doors of the sitting room.

"That guy's a class act," I said as we headed up the staircase.

"There's more to him than meets the eye," Strand said. "I've gotten to know him a bit in the time I've spent at Raptor's Ridge. He was a war hero: Vietnam, 1968. He won't talk about it, but I did a little research – it's an amazing story. I'd also bet that he could still hold his own in a pinch."

"Good things come in well-disguised packages," I muttered, though I was tempted to turn around and shake Vineyard's hand. But Kohlmeyer already was waiting for us at the top of the stairs, and he looked as if he'd discovered either the Fountain of Youth or the secrets of the universe.

"What took you so long?" he called. "Come on – hurry up while I show you."

He spun about and hustled through the big open doors leading into the master bedroom, and we followed as quickly as we could but didn't see the chief when we stepped inside.

"Where'd he go?" Doc asked, talking to the walls as much as to me.

"Hey, Bill," I called out. "Where'd you go?"

The question went unanswered, and I called out again, but the silence ensued. After exchanging a hand gesture, I headed toward the walk-in closet while Doc went to the master bath, where we'd discovered and then lost again the body of Audrey Flowers a day earlier.

The closet was enormous, constituting an area as large as Mad Dog's entire restaurant. It was filled with section after section of suits, casual wear, various racks of expensive trousers and silk shirts in a variety of colors, sweaters and vests, an entire wall of braces and belts, business-appropriate and colorful after-hours ties and scarves and assorted neckwear, drawer after drawer of socks and underwear, shoes of all styles and designs – but no police chief.

I went back into the bedroom and called out to Strand: "Hey – any sign of him, Doc?"

"He's not in there that I can see," Strand said as he entered the bedroom again. "So … he's not in here either?"

"The wardrobe alone must be worth a million bucks, but there's no sign of Kohlmeyer," I said. "We did see him walk in here, though – right?"

"We did. It must be one of those crazy secret passages again," Doc said.

"I thought you knew where they were," I offered.

"I know about two of them – the ones I showed you. For all I know, there might be a dozen of the damn things spread around the place, large as it is."

Kohlmeyer stepped out of the closet at that point, chuckling.

"So far we've found, thanks to the original plans and some reluctant help from the butler, seven passageways that we didn't know about yesterday," he said. "That includes the one inside this closet. Come on – take a look for yourself."

Kohlmeyer disappeared again, and Strand and I, intrigued, followed.

"You know what this means?" Doc asked, nudging my arm.

"You bet," I said. "It explains the mystery lurker who shot McClinton."

"It gets better," Kohlmeyer said, pointing the way. "There's a set of stairs that head up to an entire astronomical observatory, I guess you'd call it. It's incredible. And there's a second stairway leading down, I don't know, a couple of flights, probably, that takes you into the same tunnel Doctor Strand showed us yesterday – the one that goes to the garage and tool shop."

We entered the narrow staircase as the chief activated a switch that opened up a disguised entryway in a section of the closet that was packed with dress suits.

"This explains how The Lurker got inside, all right," I said as we took a right turn and started up the well-lit stairs. "But why hang around, and why jump out the window instead of sneaking back into the passageway?"

"I've been thinking about that," Kohlmeyer said as he hiked the stairs ahead of us, talking over his shoulder. "He might've wanted something in the room – the spent cartridges, maybe, or maybe a pistol – and was waiting for the right moment. Then he must've gotten spooked by the lawyer and didn't have a chance to get back inside."

"Or he stood on the balcony until McClinton was out of the room, then hightailed it back to the closet again," I suggested, thinking of another possibility. "That would explain why Deeker's boys didn't get him on the grounds."

"One theory is as good as the next, I guess – if you want to swap theories," Doc said. "I'd like to know who told him about these passageways. I've been around Raptor's Ridge for years now, and I didn't know about this. How in god's name did this guy know?"

"Hell of a good question," Kohlmeyer said. "When we find him, we'll get an answer."

We crested the top steps, and Kohlmeyer moved to the side as we took in the room.

The observatory was incredible, even by Raptor's Ridge standards. I counted a dozen high-powered, motor-driven telescopes strategically positioned to provide panoramic views of the night sky through enormous skylights. A writing stand was positioned beside each one, holding leather binders packed with extensive star charts and, as we looked more closely, AJ Bohn's detailed notes and observations from each station. An entire bedroom suite, leather couches and matching leather chairs, and a kitchen area and separate bathroom filled the far end of the room.

"Impressive," Kohlmeyer said. "Who knew?"

"I knew he could talk constellations," Strand said as he headed toward the kitchenette. "I didn't know about this."

"It doesn't help us figure out what happened, though," I said. "And it doesn't explain why Audrey Flowers was in the bathroom one minute and gone the next. Much as I hate to say it, we're wasting our time up here."

"Not true," Strand called from the far end of the room. "Take a look over here."

We headed toward the tidy kitchen, where a refrigerator, microwave oven, four-burner range, double sink, dishwasher, and freezer chest all were neatly situated in rich oak cabinets that stretched around an antique table with eight matching chairs.

Strand had the freezer door open, and Kohlmeyer muttered, "That doesn't bode well," as we approached.

But once we looked inside, it did explain where our missing movie star had gone.

THIRTY

UNSCRAMBLING THE LOCKS

TUESDAY, 11:49 A.M.

"He used to say, 'Think big.' I can still hear him: 'Think big, Doctor Strand, and the rest will take care of itself.' I always wanted to ask, 'The rest of what, exactly, Mister Bohn?' And now I'll never find out – I'll never get the chance to ask him what he was talking about."

We were sitting in the third kitchen at Raptor's Ridge, and Doc Strand was reminiscing about the time that he'd spent in the mansion as the owner's personal physician. Russell Vineyard had joined us, and the three of us were enjoying a glass of the butler's choosing: an exquisite, 140-year-old cognac, Hardy Perfection, which, we'd been told, cost thirteen-thousand dollars for a single bottle.

"It's the oldest unblended cognac in the world," Vineyard said. "Its run was limited to 300 crystal decanters from Daum. To say that it is exceedingly rare is understating the obvious. Mister Bohn bought a half-dozen bottles on a whim."

"It tastes a bit like coffee," I said after a sip, trying my best to look suave in front of what I jokingly thought of as the hired help.

"Yes, with a hint of oak, maybe, and …"

"…chocolate," Vineyard said, finishing Doc Strand's observation, and we raised our glasses in a toast, content for the moment.

The cognac was all right, I suppose, but I wouldn't be ordering any at Windjammer's, my favorite local watering hole, anytime soon – even if it cost thirteen dollars a bottle … and it would have to on my salary.

We'd sought refuge in the kitchen on the advice of Bill Kohlmeyer, who ordered us to stay out of the way of his crack forensics unit but to remain available in case we were needed.

"Get a drink or something while we poke around and make sure everything's secure," he'd suggested. The police chief also issued me a separate command: "Keep your piece handy and your wits about you – just in case."

I found the part about having a drink better advice than his secondary directive, but I still was cautious about what I was trying – and how much I might consume.

For the past two hours, the area's best forensic specialists – gathered from the State Police crime lab, the city's team, and the county's three top experts – were busy sweeping every room, hallway, corridor, passageway, nook, cranny, floor, wall, ceiling, piece of furniture, adornment and knickknack, fixture and feature, item of clothing. An entire team of computer experts arrived and set up shop in the sitting room near the foyer. Literally hundreds of fingerprints were being captured and run through AFIS, the national Automated Fingerprint Identification System. Blood-work and other evidence also was being collected and entered into the computer banks.

The effort was nothing if not efficient.

The paddy wagon had arrived earlier to cart the five surviving goon squad members back to the county jail, with Bob LeRoy, the tirelessly efficient sheriff, overseeing the transfer.

No sign of either Deeker brother had been found.

The media hordes also had surrounded the estate and were being kept at bay for the moment by Ken Chichester's State Police troopers.

Charlie Wilson again returned to Raptor's Ridge, this time to oversee the removal of Audrey Flowers' frozen body from the astronomical observatory, where it had been unceremoniously forced into a freezer chest. The city's ME was on the site as well, dealing with the three dead goons near the front gate.

We could hear Kohlmeyer and his minions from time to time, calling out directives or noting discoveries or asking for certain trained personnel, and the entire process became tiresome after a time. We'd been happy to seek refuge in the kitchen, with nearby access to the cellars and AJ Bohn's extensive stock of intoxicating delicacies.

Once we'd exhausted theories about how and why Audrey Flowers ended up in a food freezer – and no one had a logical thought on the subject – the conversation turned to Bohn. The stories, and the liquor, began to flow.

Strand was more likely to share a remembrance or an amusing anecdote than was Russell Vineyard, who needed to be prompted – sometimes more than once – to register an observation.

"Yes, Mister Bohn was quite an authority on all things pertaining to timber and lumber," Vineyard admitted after some encouragement. "He could talk for hours about the various species of hardwoods on the estate, referring to them always in their Latin names. He would sometimes regale his guests with stories from his youth, when he would climb into the tallest of trees, just to enjoy the view. He told me once that he lashed himself to the top of a Douglas fir during the height of a Pacific storm to imitate the actions of one of his heroes, John Muir, the naturalist. I always found the stories to be fascinating, though I have no idea whatsoever as to their veracity."

Vineyard also referenced Bohn's interest in the stars. "Sometimes he would stay in the observatory for nights on end, taking late meals there, sleeping during the day, all the while issuing strict orders that he was not to be disturbed under any circumstances, no matter how important the business was supposed to be – unless, of course, it was Miss Flowers. He would relent when told that she had arrived unexpectedly on the estate."

He paused wistfully, then added, "Mister Bohn had a child's fascination with the stars, I believe. I can think of no other adequate explanation for it, though I have no idea what prompted his initial interest."

"Maybe he watched Buck Rogers or Captain Video as a kid," I suggested.

"Perhaps," he mused. "Perhaps he did."

I also got the feeling that Vineyard would rather undergo root canal surgery without the appropriate anesthetic than provide details into his late boss's character – and certainly not into his business dealings. Even Doc Strand concentrated on positive points and events that he'd personally witnessed, steering clear of gossip. I came to think of it as happy talk, though I was less certain that the doctor would've been privy to the day-to-day goings-on at Raptor's Ridge, as had Vineyard, and perhaps didn't know any out-of-school tidbits.

In all cases, everything that was said about the dearly departed for the past two-plus hours was highly favorable, and it struck me as odd. Bohn's reputation was hardly that of an angel or a white knight or sainted humanitarian – even if he was a regular contributor to a variety of charities operating locally. I figured that with all the smoke surrounding the man, a fire must be smoldering somewhere at Raptor's Ridge. I soon found myself wishing that Ned McClinton, the attorney, was in the room and, plied with expensive alcohol, would open up about Bohn. I even considered calling him and inviting him out to the estate.

But then I'd have to borrow someone's cell phone ...

The more we talked, and the more we sipped the ridiculously expensive cognac, the more curious I became. I eventually found myself determined to draw something out of either Strand or Vineyard that might prove useful to the case.

"You two never seem to have a bad word to say about your old boss," I said after another sip of the Hardy Perfection. "I can understand why that would be the case with Audrey Flowers, but with AJ? Come on: The rest of the world – or at least the rest of the town – talks about the man as though he ran a dog-fighting ring on the back forty and ate baby kittens for breakfast. Not the two of you, though. How come?"

"You're starting to sound like Kohlmeyer," Strand said sharply. Then, a moment later, he softened his tone: "I've heard all those stories, of course. I never put any stock in them because I never saw that side of AJ – if, in fact, that side ever existed. He was always a total gentleman in my presence, and he always treated me accordingly."

"He was that, sir," Vineyard added. "He was forever a gentleman, right up to the end."

"Well, here's something I'm curious about then: How did AJ Bohn, gentleman that he was, become connected with the Deeker brothers?" I asked.

"Paul and Tom Deeker, and Charles Downing, lived in one of those small towns in the eastern portion of the state – John Day, as I recall. I believe they were close friends," Vineyard said. "Mister Bohn's unfortunate association with Lieutenant Downing brought a great many unsavory characters to Raptor's Ridge, with the Deeker brothers and their so-called bodyguards chief among them."

"So why did Bohn think he needed bodyguards?"

"He didn't," Vineyard said. "That, again, was Lieutenant Downing's plan. You see, Charles Downing was running – in your vernacular now, Mister Blake – a scam on Mister Bohn for the past year and a half. I was a sad witness to the proceedings, but I couldn't for the life of me get the message across to Mister Bohn that he needed to sever the tie completely. It wasn't my place, of course, but I still did my best to convince him of that – as delicately as I could, given my station here. I'm sad to say that he had far more money than sense about some things, at least. This mostly involved matters of the heart – and Lieutenant Downing knew how to activate that weakness in him."

Even Strand was intrigued. "If it all comes down to Downing, how was it that he could exercise such control over AJ?" he asked Vineyard. "Why would AJ play along with a guy who was running a game on him? That doesn't make sense – especially when you consider what a savvy businessman he was."

The butler was uncomfortable with the topic. He squirmed a bit, but he didn't dodge the question.

"Charles Downing, I'm afraid, discovered Miss Flowers in an act of – my, how should I put it? – a bedroom indecency. He threatened to report it to the media, and especially to those dreadful tabloid newspapers. Miss Flowers was already spending considerable time with Mister Bohn by then, although the indelicacy of which I speak did not take place at the estate, nor did it involve Mister Bohn in any way. Most anyone else today would have laughed it off, I suppose: 'What takes place in the bedroom stays in the bedroom,' as the saying goes. But Miss Flowers was a genuine movie star, with a reputation to protect and an image to uphold. She was quite frightened – horribly so, I imagine; perhaps even unreasonably so. She wanted to one day return to her glory days in Hollywood and thought that a scandal like this could ruin her reputation … and her chances of again attaining stardom."

He stopped to sip the cognac, swirling the liquid vigorously about in the delicate crystal, before again picking up the tale.

"I recall full well the day she came to Raptor's Ridge in a state of panic, asking Mister Bohn for his help. And, of course, he obliged. He always obliged her every wish. He was madly in love with her, you see, despite the differences in their ages. I think he would have done anything for her. Providing an unsavory police officer with hush money was nothing to Mister Bohn – spare change was all that it amounted to, really, or at least at first. But once the rat came scurrying in through the front door, he continued to demand a larger piece of the cheese."

"And that rat was Chuck Downing," I said.

"Exactly, sir."

The butler paused, stood for a moment, his eyes distant and fixed on a far corner of the room, and walked slowly to the counter and examined the bottle of cognac.

"Should I pour more of the Hardy, or would you like to try something else?" he asked. "It seems a shame to let all of the stock go … unused and unappreciated."

"You're the master of ceremonies," Strand said. "Lead on, Macduff, and I'll follow you anywhere."

"Agreed," I said. "But please continue your story, Mister Vineyard. I'd like to hear the rest of your thoughts on the relationship between Downing and Bohn."

"Very good, sir," the butler said, speaking softly as he worked the counter. "I believe that Lieutenant Downing began to manufacture evidence. This would have happened at about the six-month mark in his scheme to extort ever-larger sums of money from Mister Bohn and, by default, from Miss Flowers. By this time, finally, Mister Bohn had clearly had enough – he actually told me one day that he should have listened to my counsel in the first place."

"I wish he would've said something to me," Strand said. "But what really amazes me is that he didn't speak to McClinton about the whole thing – unless, of course, he did."

"No. Mister Bohn was tempted to take it to the attorney, and I suspect that once the escalation began, he was about to. But then Lieutenant Downing and his associates cemented the relationship by, I believe, killing the man with whom

Miss Flowers had shared an unsavory bed. I suspect, but have no way of proving, that this man was in on the ruse from the beginning and was hired by Lieutenant Downing – or perhaps it was the other way around – to make some easy money. In either event, I read about the man's death in the newspaper one morning and took the information to Mister Bohn. He was in the observatory – he had spent the night there, as he often did – but he already knew of the man's death and the circumstances surrounding it. When I asked how he knew the details before the media reports, he pointed to a large manila envelope containing the most dreadful photographs and insisted that I look. Lieutenant Downing had somehow made it appear as though Miss Flowers was not only present at the time of the murder, but that she had been the killer as well."

"That would do it," I said.

"Indeed, sir. Miss Flowers' reputation – her legacy, I would venture to say – meant too much to both of them to allow it to be sullied in such a tawdry fashion ..."

"... and Charlie Downing knew that he had a meal ticket for life," Strand said, finishing the thought.

"Exactly, sir."

The room was silent for a moment, broken only by the steady beating of an antique Seth Thomas kitchen clock that was fastened to the wall above the archway leading into the pantry.

"The entire affair said much about Mister Bohn's temperament, and of the unjust accusations that were often made against his character," Vineyard said after a time. "If he were actually the unsavory personality he was so often made out to be, he would have 'taken care of the situation,' as the saying goes, a long time ago, with no one the wiser. But that was not his way. It never was – not in all the time that I worked for him, at least. From what I understand, he put all of that behind him when he left Seattle. In my view, he actually was little more than a simple man with simple needs. He just had amazing amounts of money – and, of course, Raptor's Ridge."

"Mister Vineyard: A question, if I may?" I said a moment later, when the significance of what he'd disclosed became apparent.

"Certainly, sir."

"Why not tell all of this to the police yesterday, immediately after the murder?"

"Because, Mister Blake, you asked me, and the police did not, and I do not make it a habit of providing information unsolicited. No man in my position would dream of it."

I sat dumbfounded, my eyes wide, my mouth at least somewhat agape. Even Doc Strand was amazed.

"It's all a matter of discretion," Vineyard added. "Mister Bohn demanded discretion. It was the primary tenant of our relationship."

"But he's dead."

"To you, perhaps, and to Doctor Strand, and certainly to the police … but he's not dead to me. Mister Bohn lives on through Raptor's Ridge. As long as the estate survives, he remains alive."

I didn't have the heart to bring up the old man's will, which stipulated that Raptor's Ridge was to be razed upon its owner's death. I was afraid of what it might do the butler's ticker and didn't want to take a chance on having him clock out on us – even with a first-rate physician seated in the chair next to me.

I picked up the tulip-shaped crystal and swallowed the remaining cognac. Strand raised his glass, muttered a heartfelt "Bottoms up," and followed suit.

I was about to call for another selection when Kohlmeyer joined us.

"You look like you're having a merry time of it," he said unceremoniously. "But while you've been sitting around, drinking swill and swapping lies, the forensics people found something interesting."

"Pray tell?" I muttered, still thinking about Russell Vineyard's revelations.

But Kohlmeyer brought me around once more.

"After eliminating all staff members and the known and frequent guests – including the three of you – we came up with a set of prints that we can't identify. They match a set taken into evidence at an unsolved murder a few years ago, in San Diego."

"Who was the vic?" I asked.

"A Terri Ann Walker – local housewife," he said, examining a small notebook.

"Any known connection to anyone here?" I asked after a moment's consideration.

"Not so far. But, by god, we're checking on it – you can bet your ass on that."

THIRTY-ONE

AN ACADEMIC INTERLUDE

WEDNESDAY, 9:11 A.M.

I spent part of the following morning at the college, where I had some catching up to do and apologies to make to my dean. He's a decent man with a good heart, and he has three basic rules: 1) He expects faculty members to be on time and in the classroom when we're supposed to be; 2) he expects us to honor our posted office hours; and 3) he's absolutely adamant that students' grades are posted on time.

Do those things, and teach a bit, and you're golden.

Don Brase also fancies himself to be something of an armchair detective. He knows my background as well as anyone on the campus, and he's equally fascinated with my side job: I've often thought that it was the reason why he saw fit to endorse my hiring over a number of candidates with greater academic credentials.

He's forever reading about high-profile criminal cases on the Internet – the ones that the national media report with vigor and blazing detail – and asking me for an opinion about what might've happened and who was likely responsible and what, if anything, will happen next. We've had far-ranging discussions about the O.J. Simpson fiasco and its Las Vegas reprise, the gruesome Addie Hall murder investigation in New Orleans, the sad case of Susan Smith and her two sons, the Martha Moxley murder from 1962, and nut jobs like Dennis Rader, Ted Bundy, David Berkowitz, Karla Homolka, and Diane Downs.

Downs is actually something of a local fixture – a curious oddity, perhaps – and is often in the news in our neck of the woods because of it.

One thing is certain, though: She's a deadly curious oddity.

Downs, who killed one of her own children and tried to murder two others so that she could better attract a man, is an Oregon product, from a small community just outside of Eugene. She was shipped to a prison in California after she successfully escaped for a few days from the Women's Correctional Facility in Oregon's state capital. Parole hearings are now conducted via teleconference, and the college where I work has the necessary equipment to accommodate the legal proceedings. The state's parole board has twice come out to hear her continued pleas of innocence and has twice denied her parole.

The hearings are open to the curious, and any number of students, staff and faculty, and members of the city's more morbid population enjoy attending the well-publicized events.

I doubt whether Brase developed his fascination with high-profile killers because of Downs' nebulous connection to the college, but he does sit front-and-center in the studio classroom down the hall from his office when she shows up on the TV monitor. He also always seems to cut me some slack when it comes to my detective sideline, especially when I take the time to fill him in on the details that you won't read in the morning newspaper or hear on the nightly broadcasts from the four local outlets operating in Portland, forty-five miles to our north.

He was generous again with me on this day.

"So long as you cover your classes," he said when I told him that I couldn't guarantee my presence in the classroom for each of my scheduled course offerings during the remainder of the summer term because of what was happening at Raptor's Ridge. "Caeli Brown is more than capable. We never seem to miss a beat when she fills in – certainly no student complaints are directed my way."

"That's true," I said. "You'll want to hire her if I ever get run over by a truck. Shoot, you might want to hire her anyway, Don. She's far better qualified than most of the candidates you're likely to find, me included."

"You aren't thinking of leaving, are you?" he asked.

The question caught me off guard, and it probably showed on my face. Maybe I was thinking again of the big invoice that I'd submit to the Bohn estate – hard to say. But I covered nicely and said, "I'll let you know when the time comes, and I don't see it coming anytime in the next couple of years or so, at least. I just wanted to put a bug in your ear for Caeli – for when the time does come. She really is an excellent instructor; she knows and understands the media business as well as anyone – certainly as well as I do."

"Agreed, though you know how it is with search committees and college rules and such."

"Sure. Anyway, I appreciate the leeway, Don," I said. "It's just that things are in flux right now with this case, and I'm … well, sort of right in the middle of it, as you know."

"Yes. I've been seeing your name in lights. So what can you tell me that no one else knows?" he asked, rubbing his hands together as we sat at the small table in his office. "I want to hear it all – spare no details, please. You want some coffee?"

"No thanks," I said. "I don't have a lot of time – I'm actually scheduled to meet with the police chief and the State Police boys in awhile. And I'm not sure I can tell you much that you don't already know from reading the papers or watching the TV news."

"Really?" He looked offended.

"If I had something good, I'd share it. But that's just it: We have more questions than answers, and it's driving me nuts. Hell, it's driving everybody nuts."

"At least tell me why you're involved. The newspapers reported that you're 'assisting with the investigation' – I think that's right. But they don't say why, exactly."

I laughed, though briefly. "It's because of my wit and charm," I said. "Well, that and my connection to the college."

"I'd like to think that last part is at least partially true," he said. "But I'll add without fear of contradiction – on my part, anyway – that your name, in association with the college, doesn't do us any harm."

"I'm not sure Berger or Ford would agree," I said, referring to the college's president and executive dean. "The thing of it is, I'm hard-pressed to explain why I'm involved, even now. AJ Bohn specified in his will that I was to be called in to investigate if something happened to him that couldn't be explained as natural causes. The situation at Raptor's Ridge certainly qualifies."

"Huh. So you were up there right away?"

"Right after the bodies were discovered – even before the police were involved."

"I'll bet that didn't go over too well downtown," he said, prompting me for a bit of gossip.

"Well, most of them have gotten used to it – to a degree, anyway."

"Did you actually see the bodies?"

"Up close and personal."

"And …"

"Trust me, Don. These are details you don't want to know. I wish I could get them out of my head – especially after seeing Audrey Flowers. Not a pretty sight, I assure you."

"All right, I'm glad that you brought her up. What's the connection between her and Bohn? The age difference was – what? – thirty years or so?"

"More like thirty-five, I think."

"And?"

We continued the banter for another twenty minutes, and it's safe to say that I kept him interested without giving away anything that would come back to bite me – even though I trusted Don to keep what he heard to himself.

I walked across campus to my office and checked my messages for a few minutes. I even took the time to answer a few, assuring concerned students that the world had not ended because they'd overslept or missed an assignment because of their work schedule (I could relate to that one) or somehow lost their notes from the previous week. Sure, some of it was malarkey, but consider for a moment that the average age of our students is thirty-six. Most of them are hard workers who want to do well, learn a trade or craft or skill, and move on. One of my colleagues in the English Department likes to call the college The First Church of the Second Chance. It's an accurate description of the clientele we serve, and it's one of the reasons why so many people feel good about the place and what it does for the community.

I spent the next hour pulling some lecture materials from previous classes. I laid them out in order on the desk, just in case I wouldn't be able to make a class and Caeli would have to fill in. I marked the lecture notes with some hand-written comments, tucked each one inside a folder, and dated the folders to indicate which class period should be matched to the various sets of materials. I felt better about the situation – for Caeli's sake, certainly. And I also felt a bit better about the circumstances that I was leaving my students in – just in case I was forced to miss more than a few classes consecutively.

I'll also admit that even though I was preparing lectures for future classes, I couldn't keep my mind off the events that had taken place at Raptor's Ridge. I've experienced this sort of thing before. The academic environment can drive you nutty, and not everyone is cut out to enjoy the life, as terrific as it might seem to an outsider.

Consider the fact that I'm not a scholar – far from it. I scraped by in school and was happy to leave the textbooks behind and get a real job, working initially for a tiny weekly newspaper with a subscription base of a few thousand readers. I was there for a year, covering sports and government meetings, before hiring on at a small daily newspaper with a circulation of thirty thousand subscribers. Two years later I found a job with a larger daily that was close enough to drive to without being forced to relocate.

I worked as a reporter for years, gradually climbing the ladder with each successive move, finding jobs at larger operations as my skills increased. But reporting is no job for people who want a life outside the office. The hours are brutal, especially if you do it well: It's not an occupation that can be contained within a forty-hour workweek.

When I saw the writing on the wall in the early 1990s, with computers leading to the Internet, which in turn led to free news and information – and of the crazed reactions to those changes by the inept bozos who were running the nation's newspapers – I decided to get out. I'd written a couple of stories on the local community college, and the president and I were friends because we shared a mutual interest in golf. I confided one day that I was thinking about another line of work, and he told me about a pending opening in the journalism department.

It turned out to be a hell of a deal.

For starters, I was decent at it. My first-hand experience gave me insights that in many cases resonated with students far more than the dry, dusty examples served up in overpriced textbooks. But academic life is far different from the fast-paced ebb and flow of the news business, and it sometimes drives me batty.

That's where the private detective's license comes in: I know how to dig for facts, and it keeps my hand in – even as it helps keep the creditors at bay.

I'm forced to try many approaches to fit in at the college, however. For example, I began wearing the fedora after my second year. Believe it or not, it helps. My colleagues seem to think that if you look like a college professor, you must be a college professor: Mine is not the only fedora in the room at faculty meetings. I sometimes also keep a pipe in the breast pocket of my sports coat and will pull it out at times at department gatherings, where I poke and prod at it a bit with a small jackknife. God forbid that I'd smoke it. Smoking is not allowed anywhere on campus, though I gave it up years ago anyway. But the pipe still provides a certain cachet in an academic setting, silly as that sounds.

The whole thing can make your head spin.

Before I left the college that morning, I went to the library and conducted a search on active West Coast serial killers. I spotted a curious pattern or two, made some notes that would require additional research, and was about to leave when I ran into three of my better students. They'd dropped by to see if I was around, asked politely about whether I'd be teaching the next class, and – just as my dean had done – wanted me to fill them in on what was taking place at Raptor's Ridge.

I was at least happy to see that they were reading newspapers instead of dinking around with cell phone video games or social media deathtraps like Facebook and MySpace.

"Come on, Professor Blake," Cody Mann, an energetic student with a flair for absurdity, pressed as we ambled down the hall. "I get why you'd keep the good stuff from the other media, and especially from the cops. But you can't hold out on us. Your journalism students demand full disclosure."

"Just remember that I have your student ID numbers on file," I said.

"Yeah, but ..."

"And remember that I can go into the system and retroactively change your previous grades at any time. You know that, too – right?"

Mike Nelson, a solid reporter for the school newspaper, groaned.

"Come on, man – that's not fair. You've got to give us something," he said.

"Sometimes the world isn't fair. You ought to know that by now," I said, glancing at my watch and picking up the pace a bit. I'd dawdled at the college too long and didn't want to keep Kohlmeyer waiting.

Caitlyn Lehner, the student newspaper's managing editor, rejected my evasions.

"Professor Blake, here's the thing: You're a key figure in a major investigation," she said. "Your name is in the news and will most likely stay there for a while. That makes you a public figure. Surely you recognize that you have an obligation to talk to us."

"Where does it say that, exactly?"

"There's a sign on the wall in your classroom."

That made me smile.

"All right," I said, drawing to a halt. "Get out your notebooks."

The three of them produced reporter's versions in short order.

"Excellent," I said. "It's great to see that you're prepared."

"Just like you taught us," Mann said.

"OK, so here you go. Pay attention because there'll be a test on this next week."

"Yeah, right," Nelson said.

"Don't say I didn't warn you." I ignored the collective groan and began: "OK, you can start writing now. One, I'm involved in the investigation. Two, we don't know at this point what happened, exactly, or why. Three, some of the best crime-busting minds in the state are involved – draw your own conclusions. Four, it would be premature to provide you with additional information that I may or may not be privy to at this time. But … five, I promise that when this whole thing is over, I'll sit down for an interview with the three of you and give you the entire story, blow by blow, just as it happened. I'll even pose for a picture, and you know how I hate to get my picture taken."

"That's great for later on," Lehner said, still furiously scribbling in her notebook. "But what about right now? What've you got for us right now that no one else knows?"

"Right now? Sorry. All I can offer now, beyond what I just told you, is no comment."

Mann wasn't buying it.

"No comment? We can't let you get away with no comment. You taught us better than that," he said.

"Yes I did, and apparently I taught you well," I said and started walking again. "But it's all I can do for now. We'll sit down when it's over."

"We'll chase you down the hall – out to your car," Nelson said.

"I'd expect no less, but my answer won't change, Mike."

"We'll hold you to it – the interview, I mean," Lehner said. "No, wait: Make that the exclusive interview."

Maybe journalism is in good hands after all, I thought as I headed out to the parking lot and checked my watch again. I'd have to scoot quickly across town to be on time for my meeting with Kohlmeyer, and I didn't want to be late: I had a couple of ideas that he just might want to hear.

Then again, the bastards who run newspapers today refuse to pay anything more than minimum wage for starting reporters and photographers, and worse, they hold their hours to thirty a week. What fool would want to work in an industry like that?

It's little wonder the whole business is dying …

THIRTY-TWO

THE NEED FOR A BREAK

FRIDAY, 2:47 P.M.

The Deeker boys were still missing three days later, which annoyed the chief of police to distraction. Answers in the Bohn/Flowers murder investigation remained hard to come by – despite endless hours of annoying media speculation – and Bill Kohlmeyer figured that the two brothers had some of those answers and, if properly motivated, would spill what they knew.

We just had to find them.

I was troubled by the Deekers' disappearance for several reasons, though primarily because I believed that something had happened to The Snarl. I was convinced that Paul Deeker had been dispatched – a fine word, that; it's one of the great euphemisms – because he knew too much. I just couldn't convince anyone else that I was right, and I'd even thought briefly about leaking the possibility to a longtime newspaper buddy who could take a tidbit like that and generate some extensive mileage. In the end, however, I abandoned the scheme after some careful discussion about its potential consequences with Caeli Brown.

"It's a bad idea all around, Max," she cautioned.

"It might lead to someone finding him – or maybe tell us where he's hiding, if in fact he is hiding."

"It also might get him killed."

"I think he might be dead right now," I countered.

"Then why leak it? It won't bring him back to answer any questions. And if Kohlmeyer knew you leaked the story, especially *that* story, your access to Raptor's Ridge would disappear in a heartbeat."

She was right – she's usually right; she has wonderful instincts – and I let it go. But we still needed answers, and they weren't easy to find.

Charles Downing, the cop who orchestrated the extortion that allowed the Deeker boys access to Raptor's Ridge, was in police custody but wasn't talking. He indicated through his attorney, however, that he would file a multi-million-dollar lawsuit against the police chief and the mayor as individuals, the city as a whole, the city's police department, the county as a whole, the county Sheriff Department and, individually, the sheriff, along with the State Police and its liaison officer, as well as the various television and radio stations that had reported on the events of the past few days and Downing's alleged involvement in them.

For some reason, he didn't threaten to sue the state's leading newspapers, nor did he mention the corporate-owned hometown newspaper. I was told by a longtime source at the big-city metro, forty-five miles up the road, that this oversight greatly annoyed the local publisher and editor. I merely took it as yet another sign that the influence and significance of daily newspapers was over – the kind of anecdotal information I could use in my classes.

I'd spent two-plus hours with Kohlmeyer, detailing Russell Vineyard's accounts of the scheme that Downing had perpetrated on AJ Bohn and Audrey Flowers, piecing in as best I could the puzzle fragments that I'd discovered along the way in my own investigation. I was comfortable in playing this role only after Vineyard determined, despite encouragement to the contrary, that he wouldn't disclose the information personally but had no problem with me explaining what I'd learned from him. I found the inconsistency to be a bit odd, but I respected his butler's logic, if that's what it was, nonetheless.

Doc Strand was in the room with me and helped to fill in the blanks. His memory, as well as his own recollections of some of the events that had taken place at Raptor's Ridge in the past year and a half, were exceedingly helpful.

And while the authorities now had a clearer picture of the events that disrupted the passing scene at the mansion, gaping holes continued to pop up along every conceivable avenue that we pursued.

Downing's people – the cops who were in on his extortion scheme – also had lawyered up, for the most part. One of them, however, a low-ranking beat cop named Ron Clarin, who'd only recently been brought into the scam to provide some muscle, indicated that he could deliver them all if he got a decent plea deal. The district attorney, lower case for a reason, had thus far resisted the offer. This setback was just one more thing that had Kohlmeyer steaming.

"That damned idiot knows nothing about fishing," he said about the DA. "You use a minnow to catch a steelhead, and this Clarin guy is a minnow."

Kohlmeyer, despite his early misgivings, continued to include me in his daily briefings. He'd even told me confidentially at one point that he appreciated my insights. I considered the admission to be a victory, if not a turning point in our professional relationship. He'd also said that I might make a halfway decent detective, in his considered opinion, if only I spent more time watching and listening and less time engaged in speculation.

Of course, he ignored me for the next two days and was cold and distant the following day as well. But I understood the pressures that he was under, and I didn't much care so long as I was still along for the ride – perhaps because so many questions still remained.

Along with everyone else, I wanted to help find the answers, or at least be there when somebody found them.

We still didn't know who shot AJ Bohn, if not Chuck Downing or one of his contingent, nor did we fully understand what Downing was doing at the estate on the night that the bodies were discovered. We did learn that the so-called warrant Downing brought with him that night was a phony. It was discovered, with a variety of other incriminating documents, in a search of his luxurious riverfront apartment after his arrest.

The more that we poked into Downing's affairs, the more apparent it became that his extortion scams had been running for a long time – years, in some cases – and that some of the largest businesses and wealthiest individuals in the city were under the lieutenant's crooked thumb. In time, we figured that a few of them might even come forward.

The deeper that Kohlmeyer probed, the more disgusted he became – and the more he wanted to know.

"I can't imagine why the DA won't cut a deal, if not with Clarin then with … somebody," he'd grumbled that morning. "We need answers to see how deep this thing goes."

If you discount getting direction from beyond the grave, which we did, we knew of only a handful of individuals who, if properly motivated, could help us unlock the puzzle: Downing and Stone, who weren't talking; Clarin, the underling who wanted to talk but most likely couldn't tell us everything, even if the DA did agree to a plea deal; the Deeker boys, both of whom apparently were on the lam; and the mystery man whose fingerprints were found on the freezer in the observatory at Raptor's Ridge and at a previous murder scene in San Diego. We still didn't have a name or a face to attach to the prints, so getting answers there seemed unlikely at best – for the moment, at least.

"We need a break," Kohlmeyer said as we sat in the big City Hall conference room that he'd converted into a command post. Also present were Bob LeRoy, Ken

Chichester, and Patrick McDonough. Notes and photos and official reports and leads and suggestions and timelines were spread about the table or pinned to the wall in varying stages of disarray. We'd been pondering the same material for the better part of the morning, and the chief, fueled by coffee and a handful of donuts and some leftover Chinese take-out, was getting antsy.

"We could use a break, all right," LeRoy muttered as he fingered the frayed edges of the crime scene photographs yet again.

"And soon," Kohlmeyer added. "I'm tired of seeing the same buzzards, morning and night, sticking their microphones in my face, demanding answers, as though the universe depends on what I have to say."

"Or on their interpretations of what you have to say," I added.

"Better you than us, Bill," Chichester said.

"I thought the mayor volunteered to be the primary spokesman," LeRoy said in what might have been construed as a comical jab but, coming from the humorless county sheriff, was delivered with typical deadpan seriousness.

That set Kohlmeyer off again. "Truth is, I'm damn tired of seeing his face around here and would as soon punch him as talk to him right now," he said. "All he wants is answers – just like everybody else. Did I tell you the bozos in the governor's office call twice a day, asking for updates? Twice a day, for god's sake – talk about a pain in the ass. I get calls from state legislators, including the head of the Senate, demanding to be kept informed. You know that living brain donor over in the district that's near the state pen? He called me late last night and said it was my civic responsibility to keep him personally informed so he could keep his constituents personally informed. You believe that?"

"The next time he calls, ask him to spell constituents," I suggested. "If he can do it on the spot, give him what he wants."

The line produced a laugh, but it didn't produce any answers, nor did it make the chief feel any better.

We kicked around ideas and pored over documents for another couple of hours before giving up for the day, and I headed home and called Caeli, making arrangements for dinner and drinks and another round of Twenty Questions. We'd seen each other every day since the murders, discussing the details long into the night; and with each visit, I could sense that our relationship was steadily growing.

I'd learned early on in our friendship that I could bounce ideas off Caeli and would get something of value in return, almost always with far more depth and detail than I'd been able to initially bring to the table. Whenever I was lost, or struggling to keep up, or just trying to make the pieces of the puzzle fit into place, I would turn to her.

In my own mind, at least, I already was giving up my dumpy apartment. I hadn't talked with Michael Parker, my attorney, about the contract for services rendered that he'd drafted for my role in investigating the murders since we'd last spoken at Mad Dog's restaurant. But I figured that I'd gain enough money from the deal to at least make a decent down payment on a flashy engagement ring – once I paid off my various debts and traded in my bucket of bolts for something that was actually drivable.

On this evening, Caeli and I were enjoying dinner and drinks at Bentley's, the town's lone fine dining establishment. We'd found a dark corner where the booths were aligned against the wall and were holding hands when Patrick McDonough surprised me by peering around the aisle way.

His face was somber. I suspected bad news.

"The chief's been looking for you for more than an hour," he said. "He told me to tell you, when I found you, to buy a cell phone."

So much for being all-business, I thought.

Caeli laughed. I merely said, "I trust you didn't interrupt a romantic evening for that."

"We've caught a break, and the chief thought you'd want to know about it from him rather than hearing it on TV tonight," he said.

I was surprised at Kohlmeyer's generosity and said as much.

"Your investigative work was instrumental in making this happen," McDonough said. "We got a call on that tip you gave us – from the sheriff in John Day. Tom Deeker's in custody and is being transported back here right now. The State Police are bringing him in."

"That's welcome news. What about his brother?" I asked. "Any sign of Paul?"

"Not yet," McDonough replied, "but I suspect we'll learn more tomorrow. The chief wants you to be at the county jail at 9 o'clock – if you're interested, of course."

"No classes tomorrow – no problem," I said. "Tell him I'll be there at 8."

And I was, despite Caeli's best efforts to keep me up all night.

Somewhere in the dead of night, I remember lying in bed, thinking about what we knew, and what we could prove, and what still needed to be done to reel in the vicious killer who thus far had managed to so easily stay ahead of us. And Caeli asked, as she often does, "What are you thinking about?"

Good question, I thought ... *especially when I should be thinking about you and only you.*

But I didn't mention that. "I'm thinking about serial killers," I said. "Well, serial killers and William Blake."

She was silent for a moment and then said, "Yes. I understand." And she softly repeated the English poet's lines from memory:

"When the stars threw down their spears,
And water'd heaven with their tears,
Did He smile His work to see?
Did he who made the lamb make thee?"

Caeli got it, all right. It's funny, but Caeli somehow always got it.

I fell into an uneasy sleep after that, dreaming of tigers of a different sort.

THIRTY-THREE

SKILLFUL APPLICATIONS OF DECEIT

SATURDAY: 9:03 A.M.

Tom Deeker was relaxed, even comfortable, in Interview Room No. 1 inside the Marion County jail. He had a cup of hastily brewed coffee in his left hand, compliments of the taxpayers, and he looked remarkably sanguine, as though he were the proverbial feline who'd just swallowed granny's prized caged canary.

He also was aware that he had an audience behind the two-way glass – he'd apparently watched too many crime show reruns on late-night TV – and occasionally mugged for whatever crowd he imagined was there, contorting his face into childish positions and proportions, at one time even pulling his mouth wide with his fingers and sticking out his tongue.

Watching the guy was like monitoring after-class grade-school detentions.

"Can you believe this idiot?" Bill Kohlmeyer said in disgust as Deeker grinned, winked, and raised his eyebrows a half-dozen times in rapid succession. The chief had entered the control room moments earlier and was getting his first glimpse of Deeker's antics.

"He's been going non-stop like this for an hour, Chief," one of Kohlmeyer's aides said. "It reminds me of my kids when they get amped up on too much sugar, and they're 5 and 6 years old."

"Well, he's about to learn that he's not in the first grade anymore," Kohlmeyer said. He glanced at the district attorney, who also was in the control room, and another disgusted look automatically crossed his face.

It's fair to say that the DA, Lawrence Hultz Fuller, is hard to like, regardless of which side of the law you're on. He's a cold, bird-like man with enormous feet and ears and a nose that is long and narrow and hooked at the tip, like the beak of a rooster. The nose is all the more fitting because it matches his unruly reddish-brown hair, which is usually stuck in clumps like thatched straw atop his bullet-shaped head.

Friend and foe alike call him Fuller the Falcon. I always thought that the name was a bad fit, however. Falcons are graceful, handsome birds, and the DA is far from being either graceful or handsome, though he's decidedly bird-like.

My pet name for the guy is Larry the Loon.

"He really hasn't lawyered up?" Kohlmeyer asked. "Seriously?"

"I'd let you know if he had, Bill. I've no reason to hide information like that," Fuller replied, peevish in his answer – and that was something else that described his persona.

"Look, Bill, about the interview," Fuller said. He paused, weighing his words carefully. "I want to make sure we both play this straight – by the book."

"What the hell are you talking about?" Kohlmeyer asked, and his voice was as sharp as a bone knife.

"I don't want anything coming back on us in any way – in a court of law, particularly in an appeal. That's what I'm talking about. I want you to play it straight in there."

"I always play it straight, Larry. Always. You suggesting otherwise?"

"Hey, Bill, I know you do. But I know what's at stake for you and your department, and I'm concerned that, things being what they are, you might feel compelled to …"

Fuller stopped at that point and glanced furtively around. It was clear that he wanted to press the issue, but he didn't want to do it with others in the room.

Kohlmeyer took the initiative instead.

"Forget it. You tend to your tambourine, Larry, and I'll tend to mine. How does that strike you?"

Fuller was straining to get something out. But he hesitated, and then his body relaxed noticeable.

"Maybe we should just count our blessings and get to it," he said.

I heard an aide mutter, "He means we should count our chickens, starting with …" – but I doubted that anyone else caught the line, which was too bad. Kohlmeyer rubbed his hands together a couple of times and headed inside the interview room. Fuller was quickly at his heels, and I couldn't believe my good fortune in having a ringside seat for what might prove to be the heavyweight match of the year.

That was my hope, anyway.

"What was all that about?" I asked after Kohlmeyer and Fuller passed through the side door and into the interview room.

"The Falcon doesn't think cops should lie to a suspect during an interview," the aide said. "That's essentially what he was saying, though I'm sure some politics are at play here, too."

"The Supreme Court ruled a long time ago that lying to suspects is a perfectly legal tactic – a legitimate interrogation tool," I said, puzzled, talking as much to myself as to the aide. "Cops do it all the time. It's how the game is played."

"You know it and I know it and the chief knows it. The DA? I'm not so sure what the DA knows. Hell, nobody's sure about that – him included."

"Pity his poor wife," someone said from the back of the room, and that line produced a couple of snorts.

Fuller went through the usual legal mumbo-jumbo at the start, sonorously droning out the names of those present in the room, the date and time of the interview, and a notification that the proceedings were "obviously being recorded, as you can tell by the microphones that are in front of each one of you" – pointing toward Deeker and Kohlmeyer in turn. He cleared his throat a time or two, glanced at the two-way mirror, and took a moment to straighten his loosely knotted tie, as though preening for both the camera and some added attention, just as Deeker had done.

When Kohlmeyer, who was sitting immediately to the DA's right, gave him a firm nudge, Fuller got to it again. "Yes, all right – let's begin," he said. "The subject of the interview today, one Thomas Snead Deeker of both Raptor's Ridge and the city of John Day, in the eastern portion of the state, has agreed to sit for questions without having a lawyer present. Is that correct, Mister Deeker?"

"You pretty much got 'er nailed there, pal," Deeker replied with a loopy grin.

"I'll take that as a yes – is that correct?" Fuller said.

"You ain't the sharpest knife in the tackle box, are ya?"

Fuller ignored the comment. "I'm going to ask you to sign a legal document indicating that you are waiving the right to counsel." He stared at Deeker, received no reply, and added, "If I may then …" pushing the paper across the table.

"Can't sign without something to write with, genius," Deeker said with a smirk. He looked at the glass and mugged again for those of us who were watching.

Someone in the back of the control room said, "Sure didn't take this guy long to figure Fuller for a fool, did it?" Muffled guffaws followed, but I didn't bother turning to identify the speaker. Eight technicians were packed into the room, and you couldn't find that many people in the entire state who were fans of the district attorney – even if you counted his immediate family.

Fuller frumped audibly before producing a pen from the inside of his jacket. He shot a lingering glare at the two-way glass – *He's like an umpire with rabbit ears*, I thought – before pushing the pen across the table. Deeker picked up the paper, held it close to his face, glanced at the two-way glass again, returned to the document, looked at Kohlmeyer for a time and grinned, looked again to the document, glanced back at Fuller, and finally asked, "So where do I sign?"

"On the line above your name," Fuller said.

"Oh yeah. I see it now." Deeker took the pen, slashed a large X across the paper, and slid it back to the DA, skipping the pen across the table in the process. "We good now?"

Kohlmeyer placed his head in his left hand, rubbing his forehead as though he already were tired of the game. Deeker grinned broadly. "Tough night there, Billy Boy?" he asked.

This might not be much fun after all, I thought, considering for the first time the possibility that Deeker might continue his childish routine for hours.

Fuller cleared his throat again. Kohlmeyer muttered, "Let's get on it with it, Larry," and the microphones nicely amplified his voice in the control room's speakers. I could hear more sniggering behind me.

Fuller: "So I take it that you are acquainted with Chief Kohlmeyer, who is seated next to me … right here? Is that correct, Mister Deeker?"

Deeker: "You mean this guy here?" – he pointed with a bony finger toward the chief.

Fuller: "Yes, that's Chief Kohlmeyer. That is correct."

Deeker: "Ain't that just what I said?"

Fuller: "All right, Mister Deeker." He went at his tie again. "Chief Kohlmeyer would like to ask you a few questions now. Is that all right with you?"

Deeker: "Why not? I got nothin' to hide. I got plenty of time."

Fuller: "Fine; that's good. We appreciate your cooperation, Mister Deeker. All right, Chief Kohlmeyer ..."

Finally ...

Kohlmeyer: "Mister Deeker, where were you exactly when the shootout occurred at Raptor's Ridge on Tuesday of this week, four days ago?"

Deeker: "What shootout?"

Kohlmeyer: "Let's not waste one another's time here. You were seen at the estate before the shooting commenced."

Deeker: "Yeah? By who? That school teacher thinks he's some sort of TV *Magnum PI* or *Five-0* character?"

Kohlmeyer: "Several witnesses place you at the scene immediately before the shootout took place, and at least two more identified you as being on the property once the shooting began. So I'll ask again: Where were you exactly when the shooting commenced?"

Deeker: "Beats me. I been in John Day, ya see, visiting friends. You can ask 'em if you like. I can give you the names and you can look 'em up. I weren't at no shootout. Yer so-called witnesses are liars."

Kohlmeyer: "So you were in John Day at the time of the shootings at Raptor's Ridge that left three associates of yours dead, is that correct?"

Deeker: "Yup." He sat back in his chair, folded his arms across his chest, and grinned.

Kohlmeyer: "And, just so I understand, the people who say they saw you at Raptor's Ridge are mistaken in their belief that you were on the estate during the shootout. Is that correct?"

Deeker: "If by mistaken you mean they're liars, then yeah – you about got it nailed there, pardner. Gotta hand it to you, Chief. Yer a whole bunch swifter'n that one" – pointing at Fuller this time. He grinned again, broadly, clearly pleased with himself.

Kohlmeyer: "Mister Deeker, we have overwhelming evidence that not only places you at Raptor's Ridge at the time of the shooting – reliable eye-witnesses included – but that also places a submachine gun in your hands."

He waited, but Deeker didn't flinch.

Kohlmeyer: "Would you care to revise your story?"

Deeker: "I'd say you got yer facts outta sorts there, Chief. Ain't much surprised at that, though."

Kohlmeyer: "A recently fired Uzi with your fingerprints was found abandoned in the tool shop at the south end of the estate. Ballistics tests indicate this weapon was used to fire at police SWAT vehicles that were on the scene. Would you care to explain that?"

Deeker: "Sure. Easy. Part of my duties around the place was cleanin' the guns and such. That must've been one I cleaned. If it's been fired recently, as you say, then somebody must've used it after I got done cleanin' it. Weren't me that shot it. All I did was clean it."

He paused, grinning.

Deeker: "Anything else?"

Kohlmeyer: "Would you care to explain your relationship with former lieutenant Charles Downing?"

Deeker: "Never heard of him."

Kohlmeyer: "He's from John Day, just like you."

Deeker: "Lots of folks are from John Day – just like me."

Kohlmeyer: "I see. Well, Mister Deeker, he's certainly heard of you."

Deeker: "Lots of folks've heard of me. Hell, you knew me 'fore today. I mean, why wouldn't ya?"

Deeker was playing it cool enough to this point, which was to be expected; this wasn't the first time that he'd gone through this dance with the authorities. But I was hoping Kohlmeyer had discovered something that I hadn't yet heard about, and I drew closer to the glass, waiting for a bombshell.

Kohlmeyer: "So – just so I have this straight – you're saying that you don't know Downing, that you've never heard of Downing before today, that you didn't enter into an extortion scheme with Downing, that you didn't use your relationship with Downing to take advantage of AJ Bohn and Audrey Flowers, and that you didn't conspire with Downing to single-handedly kill Mister Bohn and Miss Flowers – is that correct?"

Deeker: "I'd say that sums it up, all right. Listen, chief, could I get a refill on the coffee – and maybe some donuts? You must have donuts, right? – seein' as how the cops hang out here and all. Maybe you can send one of them little piss-ants behind that mirror yonder" – he flung an arm skyward – "to fetch me something, huh? Come on – chop-chop."

Kohlmeyer: "All in good time, Mister Deeker. But you'll have to play ball first if you want some consideration in return."

Deeker: "So that's what we're doin' here – playing ball? Damn. Why didn't you tell me in the first place? I'd've brought my glove and spikes along. It's been a time, but I could still get some game together."

Kohlmeyer: "All right, Mister Deeker, that's very amusing. But let's try this again: We know from various interviews and first-hand evidence collected at the scene that you personally killed AJ Bohn and Miss Flowers. Would you care to explain why you did that – in cold blood?"

Deeker (his eyes suddenly aflame with anger): "Yer walkin' dangerous ground here, Billy Boy. You'd best be careful yer finger don't poke through the toilet paper – an ugly surprise, that. I didn't kill nobody. What yer sayin' is a damn lie, an' you damn well know it."

Kohlmeyer: "We have evidence to the contrary. Incontrovertible evidence; absolute airtight evidence, according to the district attorney. And we have, as I indicated earlier, testimony from an individual who says you did it."

Deeker: "You ain't got jack, pal. An' in case you don't know jack, which I'm sure's true, I'll put it another way, just so I'm clear: You ain't got squat."

Kohlmeyer: "You forget that we have Downing, and the other former officers who were connected to his extortion ring, in this very jail – right next door, in fact. All of them are talking as we speak. They've been talking for three days straight now. They've had plenty to tell, plenty to say, and it always comes back to you. Not your brother, and not even the rest of the goons you pal around with. Just you."

Deeker (looking troubled now): "Yer telling me ol' Chucky is sticking me with this bill of freight?"

Kohlmeyer: "You really don't think the police would turn on their own, do you? Because if you do, Mister Deeker …"

Kohlmeyer sat back and smiled, without finishing the thought.

It was clear from the look on Deeker's face that the chief didn't have to.

Fuller tried to hide the misgivings that he might have felt at that moment, but he started squirming in the chair and was fighting a losing effort. Fortunately, Deeker and Kohlmeyer were engaged in a grim staring contest, with neither man conceding. To Fuller's credit, he stood abruptly and left the interview room by a side door.

Deeker (giving in at last): "You can tell Chucky for me to stick it. High and hard. Just like the old days. Just like always."

Kohlmeyer: "You can tell him yourself. I'll make the arrangements."

Deeker: "You can stick it, too, Chief. Same way and place."

Kohlmeyer: "Thanks for the consideration. I have one other question for you, Mister Deeker: Where is your brother?"

Deeker: "I want me a lawyer. Now. Interview's over."

Kohlmeyer glared at Deeker for the better part of minute, then stood abruptly and left the interview room through the same door that Fuller used moments earlier.

"Textbook," the chief's aide said. "Way to go, Billy." He poked my arm and asked, "Think that's enough to open up the floodgates?"

"It might be enough to get someone else talking," I said. "It also might be enough for Fuller to agree to a deal with Downing's weak link."

But we both knew that it was hard to say what Fuller might do at any given moment. Sometimes common sense and the DA were mutually exclusive elements that didn't mix in the same salad bowl or solar system.

Still, I had to hand it to Kohlmeyer. He outplayed Tom Deeker and the DA at the same time and in the same room.

Things were looking up.

THIRTY-FOUR

'... AND THEN WE HAD TEA'

SATURDAY, 1:20 P.M.

I finally got in to see Bill Kohlmeyer a little more than three hours after his grilling of Tom Deeker. He was juggling numerous balls, somehow keeping each one in the air through the sheer force of his will – a hell of a testament to his skills.

"Busy, huh?" I asked as I slipped past the cordon of law officers, legal eagles, and his ever-present bodyguards, including Lieutenant Patrick McDonough, who this time greeted me with a crooked half-smile as I entered the chief's reception area.

Progress on a number of fronts, I thought, recalling my first tension-filled encounter with Kohlmeyer's aide earlier in the week.

"You don't know the half of it," the chief replied. "But I wanted to say thanks for the John Day tip. It paid off in nabbing Deeker – looks like we're finally getting somewhere."

I appreciated the compliment, though it had been simple enough: Russell Vineyard told me that the Deeker brothers originally were from John Day, a small town in the eastern part of the state. My reporter's training kicked in, and I called the high school principal to get the skinny on the Deekers.

"Well, thanks. But you did the real work in there," I said, and it felt good to pay the city's top cop a compliment in return.

As things stood at this point, Kohlmeyer continued to be straight with me and, better yet, he continued to honor the odd working pact that we'd agreed to days earlier, when I'd first called him in on the case. With all of the pressure that was bearing down on him – from the mayor, the governor, needy/greedy lawmakers, the media buzzards, even from the straight-arrows in his own department – he easily could've cut me off at any point. He might've even felt justified in doing it, given our history – or at least his selective recollection of that history.

But he hadn't cut me off, and he didn't appear likely to; the man remained good to his word.

"It's just the tip of the iceberg – plenty more where that came from," he said, though I think that he was appreciative of the accolade.

"At least Fuller didn't get in the way," I said, serving up a softball that I hoped he'd swat with gusto. I'd taken my customary seat in front of the chief's desk and settled in, despite the severity of the chair's design.

"He almost couldn't stand it, though I think he might be coming around," Kohlmeyer said. "When he stormed out near the end, just before Deeker lawyered up, I was sure Larry was going to complain to the mayor or file papers to have me removed from the case. Instead, he marched down the hall, made a quick call, and cut a deal with Ron Clarin."

"You're kidding," I said. "I didn't think he'd ever go for that – makes too much sense."

"Well, he's nothing if not political. He heard enough to like Deeker for the whole mess, buying the house of cards I was building. I think he figures that he can make a case against Deeker with some collaboration, and Clarin is his best bet."

"Deeker as a fall guy, huh? Can Fuller make it stick?"

"Beats me, though I doubt whether he cares. All he wants is a decent headline – **Film at 11** – which would take the pressure off him and his office."

"More to the point then, do *you* think Deeker's good for it?" I asked.

"Who knows? I was making it up out of whole cloth in there, but it did strike a nerve with the guy – that and when I asked about his brother. He immediately lawyered up, which sure as hell tells me something."

"Yeah," I said, "I caught that, too. I took it as confirmation that something's happened to The Snarl – something he didn't see coming."

The conversation lagged for a moment before Kohlmeyer picked up the thread.

"At this point we'll just have to see what, if anything, Clarin says, and what it means, if anything. For all I know, instead of implicating Downing or Stone, he'll try to pin it on the Man in the Moon. Richard Nixon. Elvis, maybe."

"Jimmy Hoffa," I added.

"Yup. Him, too." Kohlmeyer chuckled, and he hoisted his feet to a spot at the edge of his desk, pushing his chair back in the process. "We'll find out soon enough, once Clarin's mouthpiece gets here. Then we'll get a crack at him and see what he's got. If we can officially nail the Deekers and tie Downing and Stone to it all, it'll be a hell of a fine day."

"You're not forgetting that extra set of fingerprints, though – right?" I said, mentioning one of the dark clouds still hanging over our heads.

He scowled. "Somebody knows who the guy is," he said. "We'll find him. And once we do, we'll see what he's got to add. He knows something."

"I've been thinking about that," I said. "Answer me this: How difficult is it to go through life without registering a set of fingerprints?"

"Well, damn difficult, I guess," he acknowledged after briefly considering the question.

"You bet. All sorts of occasions present themselves that require fingerprints, starting with your birth. So how is it possible that this guy isn't in any known database?"

"Maybe he's an illegal from south of the border," Kohlmeyer said.

"Or north of the border," I said. "When pressed, Ned McClinton described him as a white guy with a muscular build and a tattoo on his right arm. Does that call anything to mind?"

"Could be three-quarters of the guys in my department. It might be anybody in this town, or anybody in one of your classes, women included. It might be the mayor – he's got a tattoo on his right arm, though I'd call him fat rather than muscular."

"It might be someone who spent time in the Armed Forces," I said, "which is far more likely than the mayor, interesting though that would be. I'm wondering if you can run those prints through the military databases, and especially the Special Forces, black ops folks, Navy Seals or Army Rangers – that sort of thing."

"All right, sure. But why?"

"I've got a hunch," I said.

"A hunch? That's it – a hunch?"

"Don't knock my hunches. My hunches are good," I said.

"All right, but why this particular hunch – why the military or Special Forces?"

"It's the only thing that makes sense," I said. "The Deekers both served, and both of them were in Special Forces."

"I didn't know that."

"I found that out while poking around in John Day," I said. "It's amazing what a few minutes with the retired high school principal will get you."

"That's how you got that stuff?"

I nodded.

"Yeah, pretty good. All right, I'll see to it – right away. I don't know how many hoops we'll have to jump through, but we'll give it a by-god shot."

Progress, I thought again.

... on a number of fronts.

"Here's an idea," I said. "You've got the mayor and the governor and a bunch of state legislators lined up to get their names in the papers and their faces on TV. If you need some political grease to get the fingerprints, start with that crowd – promise a free headline or their names in lights if they help. Both, maybe. They'll jump at the chance. You'd probably have to fight off the offers to step to the front of the line."

"You don't know the half of it," he said, "but it's a good thought." He punched a button on his desk phone, and McDonough knocked once and entered the room seconds later.

"How can I help, Chief?" he said.

Kohlmeyer was scribbling on a piece of paper, and he held up his left hand for a few seconds, index finger extended, while he finished writing, then handed the paper to his aide. "Take that to the DA's office – anybody but Fuller the Falcon – and see if somebody over there can gain us access to these files. It's high priority, Patrick. Have them call me direct if they run into problems."

"Got it, Chief," McDonough said and left as abruptly as he'd arrived.

"That kid's good," Kohlmeyer said once his aide was out the door. "He's got all the tools for the job. I think he'll make a good chief someday. His brother is a cop in one of the Los Angeles suburbs, you know. Another brother is a detective up in Seattle."

That got me to thinking about the Deeker boys again, and what had steered them down the path that eventually led to Raptor's Ridge.

"It's funny how families go," I said after a moment. "You get a set of brothers like the McDonoughs on one hand, and then you get the Deeker boys on the other. How do you explain that – good guys on one side and bad guys on the other? Is it genetics? Family upbringing and values? Environmental factors, maybe? Or peer or social pressures, or maybe something as simple as small-town living?"

"Maybe it's just the luck of the draw," Kohlmeyer said. "Maybe luck doesn't have a damn thing to do with it. Maybe it's just random – like a coin-toss. Who knows?"

"The Deekers might," I said. "Then again, hell, Paul is nowhere to be found, and Tom isn't inclined to say much – about that or anything else."

"Yeah, true enough," Kohlmeyer said, adjusting his frame in the chair. "I'll say one thing about Tom Deeker, though: He may come off like a hayseed, but he's got some smarts inside that head of his. All that shucking and grinning and cornpone horsecrap was just for show. That boy knows the full story. I'm certain of it."

"I sure wish he'd give up his brother's whereabouts," I said. "I've still got a bad feeling that something nasty happened to Paul. He wanted to talk, and now he's out of the picture."

We kicked around a few more random ideas, but I was out of decent suggestions at that point and didn't want to take up any more of the chief's time. I left his office just shy of 4 p.m., using a side door to avoid lingering members of the media horde, and headed back to my place, where I called Caeli and made a dinner date.

But I was thinking again about the McDonoughs and the Deekers and what made the two sets of brothers as different as chalk and cheese as I climbed into my bucket of bolts and chugged away from City Hall.

And the more that I thought about it, the more I was reminded of a fragment from a Dylan Thomas poem that my cousins, Michael and Charles Albus, used to laugh about when they would come in from the big city to visit:

It snowed last year too:

I made a snowman and my brother knocked it down
and I knocked my brother down and then we had tea.

Being brothers, they must have known something that I did not. I found myself wishing that I'd spent more time learning from them – back when we were innocent and our minds, and especially our hearts, were still pure and open.

THIRTY-FIVE

REVISITING THE JERSEY SHORE

MONDAY, 11:22 A.M.

The tale that Ron Clarin decided to spin was either so far off the mark that he was trying to steer the investigation away from the truth, or it was so wild and fantastical that it simply had to be true.

I wasn't sure which possibility was correct, at least not at first blush – and neither was anyone else who initially heard it.

Clarin, Charlie Downing's idea of added muscle for his extortion ring, got a decent deal, all things considered, from the DA's office. All he had to do was agree to talk about his own role, if any, in the Bohn/Flowers murders and to provide a detailed statement about anything else that he might know regarding the crimes that Downing and Co. committed leading up the murders.

For that, in general terms, he was granted full immunity, along with the loss of his badge. He also had to agree to never again apply for a law enforcement position of any type – security guard or rent-a-cop included – in the state. And he had to tell the whole truth and nothing but the truth, get his version of the truth corroborated, and agree to testify at whatever trials resulted.

It made sense that of all the people in Downing's personal crew, Clarin was the lone individual who, initially, at least, wanted to talk. He was the low rooster in the pecking order (he'd been involved with Downing's gang for three days shy of a month), he hadn't been involved in anything particularly onerous – until the Bohn/Flowers murders, at least – and, perhaps best of all, he'd yet to receive a payoff of any kind from Downing.

Or, at least, so he'd told Lawrence Hultz Fuller, the none-too-bright district attorney who had assigned himself to the case.

But Clarin also boasted that he knew things that could, in his own words, "blow the lid off the Downing mob once and for all." And the knowing of things in this case was a currency that was in high demand.

Even Fuller recognized at this stage that placing a microphone and a camera in front of the one-time city beat cop was something that simply had to be done.

What Clarin said in return was fairly amazing, all else being equal.

Much of it was dazzling.

I first read his statement a half-day after its delivery to the DA. I then re-read it, determining that there was too much in it to keep in my head, and eventually got Kohlmeyer to give me a copy.

Striking that bargain was not easy for either one of us, probably because it involved absolute trust on both sides. The agreement I made with Kohlmeyer was that if I ever wrote the book I'd been contemplating since the case first broke, I would have to treat his department fairly: "No hatchet jobs," was the way he put it. He also told me that if I leaked Clarin's statement to the media before a trial took place, he would do damage to my person that no plastic surgeon could make right.

The interesting thing, looking back, was that I fully believed him, especially when he added, "That gal of yours – Caeli? You leak this and I find out and pin it to you? She won't recognize you. Believe it."

I did.

I knew Kohlmeyer well enough to understand that he was good to his word. It's been my intention through this narrative to be equally good to mine.

This is what Ron Clarin had to say, edited here to eliminate the legal niceties and the DA's constant preening:

"IT *was a shakedown racket, straight out of the Roaring Twenties. The Loo* [police slang for lieutenant; he is referring to Downing here], *he liked to think he was Elliot Freakin' Ness. He used to read about the Chicago mobs, used to watch movies and TV shows and such – Netflix, I guess – and figured, 'It worked back then, so why not dust if off and make it work again?' And that's just what he did. It was frickin' brilliant when you think about it. Or not. Depends on your point of view, I guess."*

[Edited segment of two paragraphs, eliminating the DA's posturing]

"So *I got my invite a month before the mess happened up on the hill, at Bohn's place. But I knew what was goin' on up there even before that – about the shakedowns and such. Ya see, one of the guys I know pretty good – have drinks with and such – turns up hinkey after workin' a detail with the Loo, and I press him for the scoop. The day I bring it up, he gets nervous when I go for the jugular regarding Downing, ya know? I'm only guessing anyway, 'cause what the hell did I really know at that point? Nothin'. But I hit the right nerve – plain enough to see. What I don't know is my pal goes back and tells the Loo about my interest, which puts us both in the crosshairs – him and me. Why my guy did it, I don't know. Maybe he thought if he didn't and Downing finds out, it won't end up too good for him, ya know? But too late – he goes ahead and spills the beans. Understand,*

I don't know this at the time – that he's spilled the beans on our little talk. Had I known it then, known he was gonna do that, I'd've damn well kept my freakin' mouth shut and none of this would've happened to the two of us, or at least to me. But I took a chance and pressed 'cause I know him."

[Edited segment as Fuller presses for information regarding Clarin's friend]

"OK, *so before you know it, the Loo comes over and sits me down and says, 'Yer pal tells me you talked about the deals I got going.' This makes me nervous. Downing can hurt me in a lot of ways, including with the brass upstairs. But I try to keep cool. I say, 'Well, yeah, just a bit.' And he says, 'Well, a bit is all it takes, so pay attention and I'll tell you how it shakes out. Yer in on the deal 'cause I say yer in. You do what I say, you keep yer mouth shut, you ask no questions, you get a piece of the pie. You step outta line, you talk to anyone – an' I mean* anyone: *yer mother, yer girlfriend, yer priest or rabbi or minister – they don't find yer body. You get it?' I don't like that, and I tell him, 'Look, why should I jump into something where they don't find my body?' An' he says, 'Tough rocks, kid. You played yer cards, and now yer in fer good or out fer keeps – you choose.' So I say, 'Well, hell, what's in it for me, exactly, if I'm in?' And he says, 'I told you already: a piece of the pie.' So I say, 'Well, I don't know what that means, this piece of the pie you mention. Could be anything – apple or cherry, ya know?' And he says, 'Look, don't crack wise with me. Yer big and ya got muscles and you look like you know yer way around. Be smart; do the right thing. Stick with me, stick close, and you'll get that condo you want at the beach, before the year's out.' And I think, 'How's he know I want a condo at the beach? This guy knows more than he's lettin' on.' So I jump in, if only 'cause I figure it's better 'n gettin' my legs busted, or worse. And hell, gettin' a condo at the beach ain't gonna happen on a beat cop's salary anyway, ya know? I figure, how bad can it be? At least he won't feel the need to whack me. So it's all good.*

But it ain't good. Next thing I know, my pal that's part of Downing's crew gets busted up pretty bad in a 'car accident' and ends up in traction. You can look it up – find LaBuhn's name in the police reports, and in the paper. An' I'm thinkin', 'Aw geez, what'd I get myself into?' I press Biff for info on Downing, he gives me a sniff, and look what happens to him straight off. That ain't no accident – ya know? But even then, it's too late. Biff gets his car rigged 'cause he talked to me, and I know I'm hooked now anyway 'cause there's no frickin' place to go and Downing has this long reach that can take you out with a snap of his fingers."

[Edited segment of seven paragraphs, providing additional details regarding Officer James "Biff" LaBuhn and his so-called accident; the circumstances surrounding the incident were well-covered by various media outlets at the time, although no hint was ever made that the officer's car had been tampered with ahead of the crash]

"*So my first time out on the scam, we go to some shops along State Street. I walk in with the Loo and Stone. They tell me to stand off to one side and look big – their exact words: 'Look big, kid. And don't smile.' So I do that: Stand off to one side and look big and don't smile. The shop owners come out, they see Downing and Buzzsaw – that's Stone – they don't look happy to see those two, and they don't look too happy to see me, either. They talk some. Once or twice I see a finger pointing my way, and I stand there, looking big with no smile – that's it. I don't say nothin', I don't hear nothin' – just look big and don't smile. Then we leave and go to the next place – same thing. This takes a half hour or so – forty minutes maybe. I never see any money change hands, but I get the idea that's what happening. I'm thinkin' to myself again, 'Ron ol' boy, just what did you get yerself into?' Then I think about Biff again, and I really ain't happy about what's going on – ya know? But what can I do? I'm in it now. Big time. So I just keep lookin' big and don't smile and keep my mouth shut.*"

[Edited segment of eight paragraphs, with details regarding the local businesses that Clarin visited with Downing and Stone, the addresses and registered owners, etc.]

"So *I go see Biff in the hospital. He still looks like hell. Two weeks after the 'accident' and he looks like death warmed over, ya know? I say, 'Biff, what the hell did you get me into?' And he gets pissed off at me, see, and tells me it's my fault he's in traction and likely won't never walk right again. I ask him what really happened, and he won't tell me – says I'm nuts to ask, I'm nuts to even visit him, says if I'm smart I'll disappear while I still can so's I don't end up like him. I say, 'Look, Biff, I'm sorry. I didn't know. Tell me what I should do. Tell me how to get out of this frickin' jackpot.' And he says, 'Ain't no way out. You don't mess with these boys. It's dynamite. They got the town locked up. The old mayor? He's in on it. At least one of the guys on the city council? He's in on it, too, and I don't think he's alone. At least one of the district judges, maybe more? He's in on it. Some guy in the governor's office – he's in on it. The guy that heads up the city's building codes and inspection crews? He's in on it, too. The guy from the fire department that investigates arson? He's in on it, along with a couple of his boys.' I say, 'You gotta be kidding me.' I get a funny look in return, like he thinks I'm stupid for not grasping the obvious, maybe. But I can tell he's worried 'cause Downing's network is so big. So I say, 'The city council and the district court and the governor's office and the building inspectors and the fire department – you want me to believe there're all in on it?' And he says, 'Are you really that freakin' dumb? Why do you think the fires that burned out half-a-dozen shops, plus that big furniture store, don't go nowhere 'sides an accident report?' I hear all this and think to myself, 'Well crap, I'm in it now. There really ain't no way out.'*"

[Edited segment of eleven lengthy paragraphs, detailing arson fires dating back three years; these events also received extensive media coverage, although no conspiracy connections were ever made]

"Ok, so I get a call that we're headin' to Raptor's Ridge. It's my first time up there, but I know they've been there a bunch of times 'cause they talk about it some. So on the way up I hear Stone tell the Loo, 'I don't like it, Chuck.' He's whispering, see? – trying to talk low enough so nobody in the rig hears. But I'm sittin' close enough to the front so I can hear what they say. And I'm not stupid. I figure the more I know, the more it might just save my ass. So Stone says, 'Bohn is the goose that lays the golden egg. The rest of the chumps is small potatoes. We ought to just let that end go – sooner or later one of 'em is gonna talk – even if it kills him.' Downing doesn't wanna hear this. 'Shut up and let me do the thinking,' he says. He's mad; I can tell when he gets mad, an' he's mad now. He says, 'It's my racket. I'll do it the way I want.' Stone says, 'Yer climbing in bed with two maniacs. Those friends of yers are hopped up on something. We never should've let them in the place – never should've let 'em get access.' Downing is really steamed now. He says, 'Why do you think we're headin' to Raptor's Ridge now? The Deekers need a lesson. That's why I brought along a warrant. They can't keep us out, even if they try. We go in, we make sure the old man and the movie star is still in our pocket, we clean a little house along the way.' Stone says, 'I still don't like it.' But the Loo just tells him again to shut up. By that time we're up there an' head through the gates. The brothers, Tom and Paul? They're none too happy to see us, 'specially 'cause the Loo brings four extras to act as muscle. Downing an' Stone take somebody else, I think – can't recall fer sure; maybe it's just the two of 'em? – an' head on up the stairs. I wait down below with an old man and two others on the crew. They're up there – I don't know, a minute or less? – an' come wheelin' down and Loo says something stupid and out we go. I don't know what's happened, but we get in the rig an' speed off – back through the gate and back to town,

and we're movin' fast, lemme tell ya. Everybody's sitting in the same spots in the rig, so I'm still close enough to hear. But they don't say nothing the whole drive back. Nothing. It's dead quiet in there — not a word. No police radio, no idle chatter, nothing. I wonder about it, but I'm new to the game, ya know? Then we get back and I hear Stone tell Downing — and I mean, he's whispering this with his back turned to me, but I'm close and I hear it plain enough 'cause he's mad enough to spit nails, and his voice is just hissing like a snake, ya know? He says, 'We been had. Time to cut our losses. You take care of the damn Deekers. I'll take care of the other one.' I can hear Downing get cranked up at this, but they move outta my range and I don't wanna risk gettin' close to hear the rest 'cause I figure I'm already on thin ice, an' one or the other will see me and set me up for some kind of 'accident,' ya know? — just like they did to Biff. But I know something's wrong, and I still ain't seen a dime from 'em, which don't make me happy either. Can't buy no damn condo at the beach when you don't get paid. So when the whole thing heads south, I figure, 'Thank god. This is my way out; just in time.'

"So that's about it, I guess. You got something I can drink around here? A soda pop, maybe?"

THIRTY-SIX

EL GORDO Y LA FLACA

MONDAY, 6:47 P.M.

"It's the damnedest thing I've ever read," I said to Bill Kohlmeyer after going through Ron Clarin's statement. "I mean, it's just crazy enough to be true. Then again …"

"… he's either crazy or he's nuts – or both at the same time, if that's possible," the police chief said, picking up the thought. He was holding the report at arm's length in front of him, and he smacked at it a couple of times with his left hand, punctuating his words. "Or maybe it's a combination of that and something else – I can't tell yet. It sure as hell's got my interest, though."

He tossed the papers on his desk and shook his head back and forth a few times, his face taking on that Don't-screw-with-me look that he gets when he's angry – the one I used to read as meaning take cover when I was still working as a reporter.

I was sitting in the chief's office in the late afternoon, a full week after the Bohn/Flowers murders, chuckling at Kohlmeyer's words. It again struck me how much things had changed during the past seven days. Collaborating with him in this manner a week ago would have been unthinkable.

"I'll tell you something else," Kohlmeyer said. "I'm tightening our hiring practices. How this guy got a job here is beyond me."

"Come on, Bill," I said. "I liked that New Jersey delivery. It even comes across on the transcripts."

"You should hear him live," he said. "He sounds like he was in *The Sopranos*."

"He is from one of the five boroughs, though – right?"

"So is my Aunt Sally, and she doesn't sound like she's in a gangster movie," he said.

I laughed, though briefly. The content of the snitch's statement was dynamite, all right, just as Clarin promised. I figured that heads would roll for much of the next month, around City Hall and beyond, when and if evidence was found to back up the accusations.

I also figured that it would be a good time to be a reporter again, and I thought for a moment – for perhaps the first time since I'd quit the newspaper game years ago – that I missed the hunt for a good story.

All right, so I missed it a bit in that brief instant. I didn't miss the god-awful hours and the horrible pay and the crazy nature of the business, nor did I miss the indifferent audience and the idiotic knuckleheads and vicious, sadistic bastards and megalomaniacs I'd worked for through the years. And I didn't miss it for any longer than a single fleeting second before I again swept all thoughts of reporting and newspapers aside and returned to my conversation with Kohlmeyer.

"When are you going to get a crack at him?" I asked.

"Clarin or the DA?"

Kohlmeyer's disdain for Lawrence Hultz Fuller again made me smile. "Both, I hope, but Clarin first. Seems there's plenty of meat left on that bone – a regular meal."

"Yup. Lots we still don't know, but it's a hell of a good start – even if it all comes down to Clarin's memory of what Downing told him. We've tried Clarin's pal, this LaBuhn character, but he's still laid up and won't say a word or admit to a thing. And I'm frankly having a hard time believing that Downing was able to get that many people in his back pocket. You know Downing a bit – right? How'd he pull that off – if any of it's even true?"

I was impressed that Bill was actually asking for my opinion.

"If Clarin's telling the truth, and that's a large pill to swallow, then money is the most likely angle," I said after some consideration. "People do damned strange things for money."

"True enough. I've watched that crazy TV show where the guy cleans out sewer pipes one week and removes lice from kids' hair the next – one hell of a way to make a buck. Anything's possible, I guess," he said. Then, a moment later, "All right, Blake: What does your gut tell you about Clarin?"

"I can't see why he'd lie; there's no percentage in it," I said. "But Downing might puff himself up in front of Clarin – make the new guy think his empire's bigger than it is. Maybe this was all stuff Downing told all the recruits to … hell, I don't know … impress them, maybe. Clarin included."

Kohlmeyer locked his hands behind his head and swayed back and forth as he thought about it. Then he shook his head slowly from side to side, as though he were riding in a gently rocking train, and said, "The whole thing's crazy: Downing, Stone, shakedowns, high-ranking officials involved in petty corruption – all of it somehow tied up in two murders. It's hard to tell where to even start getting at the truth."

A hundred ideas jumped into my head when I'd first read Clarin's statement. I'd been filtering some of the better ones when I read it a second time, and then a third, before finally convincing Kohlmeyer to give me a copy. An earlier lunch and a long afternoon discussion with Caeli, where we'd talked about Clarin between vigorous bouts of other activities, had solidified my thinking, and I decided to run the best stuff past Kohlmeyer now.

"OK, so try this on," I said. "I don't know if it'll help or not before you actually sit down with Clarin, but …"

"… you've got a hunch?" he said.

"Not so much a hunch as some thoughts on how this might've come about," I said. "Maybe you can use it when you talk with him – if any of it makes sense – to help piece it all together."

"All right," he said. "Let's hear it."

"OK," I said, "the small shops in town didn't matter once Downing got the scam off the ground. According to Clarin's statement, Stone didn't like the shakedowns; he thought it would threaten the overall stability of the scheme – bring down the house of cards."

Kohlmeyer nodded. "But you've got to start somewhere."

"Right. I'm guessing that Downing tried it, to see if it would work, and figured when it did that he was on to something lucrative. Given the nature of the businesses he was picking on – pawnshops and one-horse eateries and small mom and pop operations – he probably threatened the owners with city inspections or trumped-up police reports, or both, if they didn't cooperate. Maybe somebody balked along the way, and he was forced to bring in a real inspector, which is maybe how the players got involved."

Kohlmeyer was pensive. "Considering the people Clarin implicated, that makes sense on the surface," he said. "It also might explain why nobody cried for help. You can't exactly run to the cops if the cops are crooks."

"Nor can you run to City Hall. City Hall authorizes the hiring of cops and other city officials, and Downing apparently made it look as though at least some of the suits were in on it anyway."

"What about the fires?"

"Most were minor – easily contained by the owners."

"And the furniture store?"

"Maybe that was part of the scam; maybe not," I said. "Maybe it was just as reported: an accident. But then Downing used it as another threat – a bigger arrow in his quiver: 'See what happens when you don't play ball?' Figuring that out will take some digging."

The chief circled his hand a couple of times – a keep-it-going motion.

"OK, he puts the fear of god into the bunch he's shaking down, and he puts some people in his back pocket to make the threats real. But he's also got a growing payroll now, full of people he's paying off, and he knows he can't support the enterprise without doing something more – something bigger. He decides to go after big names, big players, to keep his pyramid scheme, for want of a better description, alive. He has his boys on the lookout, either through legitimate means or by planting evidence, and suddenly he's into some pockets that contain real money."

"People like AJ Bohn."

"Exactly. He nails Bohn and Audrey down and hits the big time. And he brings in the Deekers to keep an eye on things."

"All right – hang on a minute." The chief pulled a legal pad out of the middle drawer of his desk and started jotting notes. I figured that he was either making a list of all the well-heeled individuals in town, and there were a few, or that he was making a note to himself to have one of his aides put a big-shots list together.

Maybe he was doing both.

"This makes some sense," he said. "What else have you got?"

"What else?" I repeated. "Geez – that's not half bad for a day's work."

"You'll need acting lessons to pull off the wounded look you're trying for, Blake," he said. "Keep it going."

"Well, the rest is pretty much pure speculation," I said.

Kohlmeyer laughed. "Seems like all of it is."

"Well, sure, but it's speculation based on stuff that Clarin, and Russell Vineyard before him, put into the record.

Downing was looking at ways to get into the pockets of the rich and famous. He starts keeping an eye on Bohn, he discovers that Bohn and Audrey are pals, and he either sets her up or has one of his crew tail her until she makes a mistake, or he forces her to make a mistake – either way works. Given the greed involved, I'm betting that Downing hired somebody to seduce Audrey, and then Downing or Stone kill the guy off – either because he gets greedy or because he threatens to expose the scam; maybe both. But it doesn't matter: Bohn is now on the hook, as is Audrey. The killing frightens them even more – and Charlie and Buzzsaw are in fat city."

I paused here to catch my breath, and Kohlmeyer picked up the speculative tale. "So if it worked with Bohn, he figures it'll work with other fat cats – the rich and famous, as you say."

"Exactly."

I grinned my Cheshire cat grin. The chief grinned back. We were both fairly pleased with ourselves until it dawned on Kohlmeyer that we were missing the crucial link.

"As good as that is, it doesn't explain how Bohn got dead, or how Audrey got dead," he said. "Nor does it explain who made them dead."

"The Lurker is responsible," I said, and it dawned on me for the first time that I was certain of it. "Downing wouldn't have killed Bohn or Flowers. They were big meal tickets. So it had to be The Lurker who killed old AJ."

"And what about our movie star?" he asked. "Do you still think she killed herself, or did this mystery man kill her, too?"

"Beats me," I said. "There was something about the way she looked that first day up there in that bathtub that made me think she might've done it – killed herself – which somehow set everything else in motion. But hell, I don't know. Wish I did. And god knows we might never know."

"You've argued that whole suicide angle before," Kohlmeyer said. "Tell me again why she'd kill herself."

"It's more like a gut feeling that I can't explain," I said. "I can rationalize how it might have happened, though. Maybe she felt responsible – guilty, even – for bringing crooked cops and a shakedown to AJ's front door. Maybe she realized that if she'd just kept her knickers up, Downing never would've had an opening. Or maybe she felt bad about the whole thing and figured that if she were dead, Downing wouldn't be able to maintain leverage."

Kohlmeyer considered that for a time.

"All right, so let's say you're right; let's say she did kill herself," he eventually said. "How does she end up in the bathtub and then show up later in a meat freezer? And, while we're at it, why does Bohn get whacked if Flowers commits suicide – unless you think he killed himself, too?"

"Come on – you're toying with me," I said. "Even I know that Bohn didn't shoot himself five times."

Kohlmeyer chuckled. "We agree on that much. But I still can't figure out what to make of the closet guy. We can tie him to at last one other murder, in California, but what's he doing here, in AJ Bohn's bedroom at Raptor's Ridge?"

He paused briefly again, his thoughtful expression in place. "This whole case is nutty," he said at last. "Why didn't The Lurker kill McClinton on the way out of the estate – why just wing him? Why kill Bohn at all? Or the movie star? And while I think about it, why didn't the businesses in town run to the local newspaper for help? They couldn't go to the cops or City Hall, maybe, but they could sure as hell run to the press. Why didn't they?"

"You're kidding on that last one, right?"

"Yeah – you caught me," Kohlmeyer said, his eyes giving it away. "Twenty years ago that might've worked, but not today. There's no such thing as a local press today – not an effective one anyway. Not here."

"Sad but true," I said.

We both sat quietly for a while. I used the time to think about the days when the local newspaper was a viable resource for citizens and government agencies and entities alike. The arrival of the Internet, which coincided with the disappearance of the daily newspaper's advertising and subscription power base, forever changed of dynamics of the game, however.

I had no idea how Kohlmeyer viewed the passing scene, but I'll confess that it momentarily made me a bit nostalgic.

"If you want facts," I said at last, "we're both out of luck. If you want more speculation, I've got plenty of that."

"Go ahead," he said. "I've got two more minutes."

"I figure that Downing brought in the Deekers because he knows them, and he wants someone on the inside, applying pressure to the scam – keeping the heat on AJ and Audrey. But the Deekers don't like playing second fiddle, and they bring The Lurker in – something they don't tell Downing about. Maybe Downing gets wind of it. Maybe he even tells the Deekers to knock it off – who knows? Then something happens, The Lurker goes nuts, so he kills Bohn …"

"… maybe even kills Audrey," Kohlmeyer adds …

"… all right, yeah, maybe he even kills Audrey, and the Deekers are now stuck holding the bag for both murders. So they alert Downing. They tell him something's up at the mansion and if he's smart, he'll get up there and see it for himself. Maybe they even suggest that things are out of control and he'd better bring reinforcements – even a warrant. Downing acts impulsively; he doesn't know he's being set up."

The chief jumped in again: "So Downing arrives at Raptor's Ridge, finds Bohn and the movie star dead, and realizes he's now in a jackpot he can't wiggle out of without exposing his scam."

"Exactly," I said. "Downing bolts, and as Clarin says, he and Stone argue about taking out the Deekers …"

"… but Ned McClinton calls you in, you call me in, I bring the cavalry in, and things happen too fast for Downing and Stone to get their ducks together."

I smiled again. "Yeah. Something like that. I'm guessing it was a hell of a shock for Downing to run up those stairs and find his meal tickets dead. By rights, he should've killed Vineyard on the spot, just to shut him up."

"But Vineyard already called the lawyer and told him Downing was there, waiting with a warrant," Kohlmeyer said. "That might be why Downing didn't go after Vineyard, or even the Deekers, at that minute. Maybe he was planning another accident for the brothers and the butler down the road – like the one he arranged for Clarin's friend – and figured that he had some time to put it all together."

"Maybe," I said. "It's good speculation, all right, but speculation nonetheless. And it still doesn't get to the issue of who moved Audrey's body, or why."

He hoisted his feet to the edge of his desk once more. "Tell you what: I'm going to run this stuff by LeRoy and Chichester, speculation or not – see what they have to say."

"It would help if we could get Downing to talk, or Stone, or Tom Deeker – or all of them or any one of them to talk," I said.

"You're right. As it stands, it's a house of cards. If we get just one of them to spill what he knows, we'd find out what happened across the board – put a ribbon on the package."

"Find Paul Deeker and get him to talk," I said. "He, at least, wanted to."

"The guy we really need to find, though, is the bozo in the closet."

"Yup. Find him and the answers most likely will come in a flood," I said. "Are your people getting any cooperation from the military on the fingerprint search?"

"Still working on it," Kohlmeyer said. He frowned, deeply, and folded his hands. "Times like these make me wish I was still smoking. And I hated myself when I was smoking. I really did."

THIRTY-SEVEN

A LONG DRIVE FOR
IDLE CHITCHAT

WEDNESDAY, 7:11 A.M.

Someone took a potshot at Bill Kohlmeyer's house a couple of hours after midnight. He'd left the office sometime after 8 p.m., escorted home by two bodyguards, and was in bed by 11:30 after watching the TV news.

The ballistics team later confirmed that the shooter used a .40 S&W-chambered handgun and fired three rounds through his kitchen window, which fronted the street.

The same round is standard issue for city cops.

I heard about the drive-by the following morning. I'll admit that it caught me off guard. I'd actually been thinking that the extra security around his office and at City Hall was unnecessary, seeing as how Downing and his crew had been rounded up and jailed.

But someone apparently hadn't gotten the message.

The shooting made me wonder whether Kohlmeyer had sniffed out all of Downing's rotten cops. It was possible that one or more were hiding in the bushes and decided to have some fun, just to let the chief know that the old order wasn't going down without a fight.

Then again, I considered as I drew a straight razor across my beard, staring into the foggy mirror in my tiny bathroom, it was possible that the shooting had nothing to do with Downing at all. *In the past few days, Kohlmeyer's team had knocked on any number of doors in an effort to learn whom Downing might've been shaking down around town; most of those doors belonged to the locally rich and powerful.*

Maybe someone doesn't like the scrutiny, I thought. Maybe this is someone's idea of telling him to back off.

One thing I dismissed out of hand was a random act of violence. Kohlmeyer's home was not listed in the telephone book, the City Directory, or even on the Internet. You had to know where it was to find it, and even then you'd have had to look hard for it, the way the house was situated well back from the street, guarded by old oaks and tall cedars, an iron security fence, and no visible address.

I called him from my office, left a message, and he called back within the hour, as cool as the supermarket's dairy aisle. I shared my ideas about what I thought might've happened, but he told me that he'd already considered those points and a couple of others besides, including taking a hard look at the previous police chief who was euphemistically retired to make way for Kohlmeyer's arrival. Still, he thanked me for the concern and said the incident only made him more determined, in typical hardball Kohlmeyer fashion.

You don't want to get Bill Kohlmeyer angry at you. It's a bad idea all around.

"Any word on The Lurker?" I asked before hanging up.

"Not yet," he groused. "We're still 'going through channels' with the military boys, apparently – whatever that means."

We kicked around a few thoughts on routing out The Lurker's identify before I told him, almost as an afterthought: "Just to let you know, but I'm driving over to John Day today – leaving in a few minutes, in fact. I'm doing some additional poking around."

"Anything solid, or is this another hunch?" he asked.

"I don't know about solid, but a couple of people agreed to talk. I figure it's better to do it face to face than by phone."

"How long you gone?" he asked.

"I've got a class at the college on Thursday, so I should be back in plenty of time for that. Still, I'll be out of pocket until tomorrow afternoon, anyway."

"Long way to drive for some talk," he said.

"Yeah, but it's better this way," I offered, again justifying the trip in my own head. "The phone's all right if you've got no other options, or if time is essential. It worked well enough when we picked up the tip that led to Deeker's arrest. But you can't tell when someone's lying to you as easily over the phone as you can when you sit down with them and watch how they react and see what they do with their fingers or hands, or with their eyes or mouth."

"Ain't it the truth?" he said. "Can't imagine doing interrogations by telephone. It'd be a disaster." He laughed and added, "All right, be careful. What's it going to take you – five hours? Six? Maybe more if you take that jalopy of yours across the mountains."

"I'm renting a car," I said. "Might as well enjoy the ride and have some fun."

"At least you'll get there. Take one of my business cards along – you've got one, right? Might come in handy – you never know when you need a cop," he said, making me promise to update him on anything useful I might learn while in the small-town home of Chuck Downing and the Deekers.

"And Blake," he added. "Get yourself a cell phone, for god's sake. This isn't 1973."

As it turned out, I wish that I'd listened and had one with me on this venture.

It would have made things a lot simpler.

The state's mountain passes provide a panoramic view of the High Cascades, and I took my time and enjoyed the scenery. The mantle of pristine snow that the mountain peaks acquire in the late fall and winter was long gone by now; the glaciers looked dirty and worn out, like old pairs of sneakers that have seen too many seasons. I'd rented a high-performance Pontiac, a true American muscle car, and stopped twice along the way to enjoy the scenic overlooks. It'd been some time since I'd been up this way – back when I was still reporting – and the memories were good.

West of the mountains, in the foothills and lower elevations, the native hardwoods give way to towering Douglas firs that become stunted and then die out as you climb toward timberline. East of the peaks, the ponderosa and sugar pines take over the landscape, with rich cinnamon bark supporting stately green spires that grow to two-hundred feet or more. John Muir, the Scots naturalist whose conservation stewardship helped save the great forests of the Western states, considered the sugar pine to be the king of the conifers. But I've always believed that you can't equal a grove of ponderosas for pure beauty.

As you approach the Santiam Pass summit, the pines and firs grow shorter, smaller, and then disappear altogether, and juniper spruce dot the landscape. But as I continued east, stopping briefly in the tiny, Western-themed town of Sisters for a bite to eat, even the junipers shrank in stature and prevalence, and the landscape became bleak and strewn with rocky ledges and small canyon rims and buttes.

Still, the High Desert in the central portion of the state has its own stark beauty, and I was able to flex the Pontiac's impressive supercharged muscles on the mostly empty highway and opened the sunroof to feel the warm breeze on what's left of my thinning hair.

I'd like to say that I developed an overall strategy for cracking the case along the way – that had been my intent, at least. But all I could think about was Caeli Brown. I'd asked her if she wanted to come along, but she reluctantly declined because of a firm deadline she was facing at her part-time job. I told her that I understood, and did, and we vowed to take another trip like this one – maybe to the coast; maybe to Seattle or San Francisco – once things settled down.

As I thought it through at the time, gauging my future with Caeli, I recognized that I sure as hell wasn't getting any younger. And I knew all too well that she wasn't going to wait around forever – not for the likes of me.

Maybe I can make something happen when I finish this job and pick up a decent payday, I thought.

But even at that moment, I couldn't get the right words to fall into place in my head as the miles slipped by and I indifferently registered the twists and turns in the highway and the sudden, spectacular mountain views and even the deer carcasses along the sides of the road.

I met Betty Sours three hours later in her tidy home on a dusty, timeworn street near the dreary downtown section of John Day. I'd gotten her name from Lucas McCoy, the retired high school principal who'd talked with me about the Deeker boys via telephone days earlier. She'd agreed to meet with me with only a little coaxing.

"Oh, dear me. I get so little company these days," she said after inviting me into her small but immaculate kitchen. "And it's so very nice of you to drive all this way, just to chat about the old days with a foolish old woman."

"Not at all, Mrs. Sours," I said. "It's my pleasure – a joy to meet you."

"You certainly have nice manners for someone from the other side of the mountains," she said. "So few people do these days, you know – especially the youngsters. They can't read, they can't write except in gibberish, using their la-dee-da computers and even those little hand-held telephones of theirs – silly little things. I hear them driving down the street before I actually see them, you know, with their music blaring unintelligible nonsense, without melody or rhyme, all the while holding those ridiculous gadgets to their ears. I think it's dangerous. I think a law should be passed. You don't use one of those things, do you?"

"No, ma'am, I don't," I said, smiling. But what I thought was, *Uh oh – a wanderer*.

I knew the type well from my reporting days. A wanderer is a person who, during an interview, will start in one spot and end up somewhere else entirely, often in short order. So long as you are patient and have ample time, wanderers can be wonderful people to talk with because they love to talk. You just need to prod them along, keeping them focused on the items you need.

I'd brought with me a sampling of soft drinks, bottled tea, and Starbuck's coffee that I picked up at a local market, along with three different types of store-bought cookies – just to put her at ease. She seemed pleased by the gesture, though she added a few homemade cookies of her own to the tray that she set on her kitchen table.

Hers were the only goodies that were touched as we talked.

"Principal McCoy speaks highly of you, ma'am," I said.

"He should," she replied primly. "I worked at Grant Union High for close to forty years and saw Lucas, and a whole bunch of others, come and go. Some of them wore the name of the Mighty Pacers well. Others did not. Did you know, young man, that Grant Union first started serving students in this town in 1932? Think of all the water that's flowed under the bridge since – the people who've come and gone, families that moved into John Day and then left again, events large and small that took place, presidents who've come and gone … even Democrats. Imagine voting for a Democrat – can you imagine that? What would possess a person to do that? I just can't understand it, and yet … people do. I mean, look what's happened this last time. It's just shocking. I can't find another word for it: shocking."

And so it went for more than an hour of conversation that can best be described as idle chitchat. I would offer a line: "Your cookies are wonderful, Mrs. Sours. They certainly make me ashamed to have brought some in from a grocery store," for example. And she would respond with how the recipe had been handed down to her from her mother's mother's great-aunt and how small markets that were perfectly serviceable had suddenly become supermarkets, "although there's nothing at all super about them," and then she would launch into a discourse about how the departure from a farm-based economy to manufacturing and then to a service industry had essentially ruined the country.

It was an eye-opener.

"Mrs. Sours," I said after sufficient time has passed to make her comfortable. "What can you tell me about the Deeker brothers, Paul and Tom? I understand from Principal McCoy that you knew them well."

"Oh my, yes," she said, "although there are four brothers in all. Paul and Tom, you know about, of course, and, let's see, there's James and David, too. Yes, I think that's right. They lived just down the street from here, though the family is long gone from John Day now, with the parents dead and the brothers scattered to the four winds. I couldn't say where they live now, or if they're all still alive, or what they might do for a living, or where they might work – or even if they work at all. As you know, Mister Blake, many people don't bother with work nowadays and just let the government take care of them, which drains my pipe to no end, I can tell you. Pardon my French."

"Certainly."

"But for those who bother to do the right thing, and by that I mean get a job and pay their taxes and such, a person can make so many choices these days that it's hard to tell what career path is best to take. Why, in my day, a young man could become a rancher, which is a fine and noble profession, or he could clerk in a store and hope one day to buy and operate the business. The timber trade, of course, supported many a young man from these parts, though it's dangerous work, and dirty. Many of the boys from John Day lost a finger or a toe – or far worse – in the logging trade, I assure you. I can also attribute the deaths of more than a few men in this town to work in the forests, directly or indirectly. Then again, some of our boys bypassed all that and sought refuge in the Armed Forces and proudly served their country. Others struck out for the big cities and wanted to find …"

"Ah, Mrs. Sours," I interrupted, offering her one of her own cookies while I broke into her train of thought. "Just a reminder that we were talking about the Deeker boys."

"Oh yes. Of course, dear. You wanted to know about the brothers who lived down the street. They were the nicest children when they were young, even though they didn't receive much parental supervision. Many's the time they came to my house with a bloody nose or a scraped elbow – you know how boys are, I'm sure. I would fix them up and send them on their way, good as new, because god knows their parents weren't equipped for the job, for whatever good reason. The brothers would sometimes skip school, you know, and the truant officer would collect them and drag them back to the house and find that the parents weren't around – both of them worked, which was unusual in those days for both parents to be working and no one left at home to look after the necessary business there. Sometimes it would fall to me to take care of those boys entirely, though others pitched in up and down the street, too, I dare say: I don't mean to take all the credit, you understand. Would you like another cookie, Mister Blake? Can I get you anything at all?"

"No thank you, Mrs. Sours. Thank you," I said.

"All right, well, just ask if you need something, young man – anything at all. So let me see, where was I?"

"You were talking about the Deekers and the people up and down the street who pitched in," I offered.

"Yes, of course I was. So let's see: We've had some real characters in this part of town through the years, let me tell you. Why, Mrs. Simmons, on the other side of the street, used to hang her laundry out her upstairs windows, even in the harshest of winters. It was amazing to see girdles and, well, other unmentionables flapping in the breeze for all the world to see. I think she must have gotten a kick out of it, somehow – leaving her undergarments out there for everyone to stare at all day long. Can you imagine – and with young boys on the block?"

She paused to draw a breath, and I tried to steer her back to the topic.

"The Deekers, Mrs. Sours …"

"Why yes, of course, dear. We were talking about the Deeker brothers – of course we were. As I recall, they played a great deal with the young boy who lived across the street then, two doors down from Mrs. Simmons. His name was Nicholas Drake. Now there was a young man who was the exact opposite of the brothers. The Deekers were amiable lads, you see – for the most part, anyway. I thought that at least two of them actually would've made good teachers – a high compliment from me. But Nicholas Drake was a mean-spirited little brat, even back then – pardon my French. I've always suspected him of killing my dog Checkers. What a great little dog Checkers was – a beagle, you see, and so sweet-tempered. And I'm certain the Drake boy killed Checkers and other neighborhood dogs – cats, too, though I don't like cats nearly as well as dogs, and certainly not poor little Checkers. I'm sure you'd agree."

"Certainly, ma'am," I said. "The Deekers and …"

"Yes, Nicholas Drake. Of course. I thought the Deekers would be a good influence on him, and I'm sure they tried in their own way. But it was the other way around, I'm afraid, for all the good it did my poor Checkers and the other animals nearby. While the Drake boy lived in the neighborhood, you couldn't keep a pet for blocks around. The animals would be here one minute and just … gone the next. Some of the neighbors said it was coyotes, but I never believed that for a second. I knew in my heart it was Nicky Drake. And once he left town – *poof!* Just like that, all of that horrible business with the missing pets and the fires just stopped."

She snapped her fingers for emphasis.

"Fires?"

"Oh dear, but yes. I can't prove it, but many fires were started around the time he lived here: sheds and outbuildings and shunkies in more yards than I can count, a couple of picnic tables in the park one time – that sort of thing. I'm just sure it was him. I can't prove it, of course – but you know how it is when you're sure of something, right? Well, I was always sure Nicky Drake was responsible for most all of our troubles. You could just, well … you could see it in his eyes, if you know what I mean. I say that because, if you've been around the woodshed a time or two, as I have, you can spot things, you know – just by looking into someone's eyes. That's how I know all about those pesky Democrats."

I must have looked skeptical because she quickly added, "It's why I wasn't surprised in the least when all that talk started up about his mother."

"His mother?"

"Oh dear, but yes … his mother. But then, well, let me just say it's a story best told by the authorities and not for the likes of me to share. I certainly wouldn't want Nicky Drake to hear I was saying things out of school about his mother's death, after all. Why, I'm sure I'd end up the same way poor Checkers did – or his mother, for that matter – if he ever found out."

"Are you saying that Nicholas Drake was responsible for his mother's death in some way, Mrs. Sours?" I asked.

"I'm not saying that at all, young man," she replied, quickly and with indignation. "But I would say – suggest, if you like – that you should ask that question of … ah, someone else who might be in a better position to provide the pertinent details. And perhaps that same someone could fill you in on exactly what went on inside that house between mother and son. The whole thing makes me sick, you know

– even now, many years later. But, then again, well … it's not really for me to say."

I waited, but she jutted her chin a bit, and I could see that pursuing the issue was going to take more time that I had.

"So whatever happened to him, Mrs. Sours?" I asked.

"Why, he grew up, and not in a good way. As he got older, he was brought in and talked sternly to, more than once, for any number of offenses the authorities suspected him of, or actually caught him doing. We all talked about it in the neighborhood – the time he broke into the hardware store, for example, or the time he was caught vandalizing City Hall during the Fourth of July celebration – can you imagine that? The nerve of that little … twerp, and pardon my French again. He was hauled in so many times that the chief of police back then, Big Cliff Corn – his son, Little Cliff, is the chief now – gave him a choice: Go off to jail for a long time, with a police record attached to his name, or join the military to acquire some discipline and leave John Day behind for good."

She smiled, drawing a long breath, before starting in again.

"Of course, Big Cliff was a relative of the Drakes, through marriage, as I understand it. But can you imagine? The boy was left to pretty much fend for himself, what with his momma dead, as I've indicated, and his daddy being something of a sot and no help in the matter. Bob Drake, the boy's father, was a low-life drinker and a Democrat for good measure, which is typical, I guess – about what you'd expect from people of that ilk. Anyway, Nicky Drake did about the only smart thing that boy's ever done, so far as I know: He left John Day and joined the service – the Army, I think – and at just about the same time the two Deeker brothers you're so interested in, Paul and Tom, joined up as well. How's that for a coincidence?"

THIRTY-EIGHT

YET ANOTHER FINE MESS

WEDNESDAY, 4:21 P.M.

There was more, of course, although most of Betty Sours' recollections amounted to gossip and conjecture. She speculated, for example, that Nicholas Drake was responsible for the death of an 11-year-old boy who'd died under mysterious circumstances during the time that the Drakes lived in town. The local authorities kept the death hush-hush, she maintained, and it wasn't long afterward that young Nicky Drake was gone from John Day for good.

Circumstantial, perhaps, but it was good stuff nonetheless, and I wanted to stay in touch with her in the event that she thought of anything else that might be useful.

Because I'd purposely left my notebook in the rented Pontiac – the appearance of a pen and paper or a tape recorder will often keep a person from talking – I pulled out the only thing that I had in my pocket to write on and scribbled my name and office telephone number on the back.

"Call me here if you think of anything else of interest about Nick Drake or the Deeker brothers, Mrs. Sours," I said, handing her the business card.

She took it, adjusted her reading glasses, and said, "Oh my. You didn't tell me you were the chief of police back there."

"Oh, I'm not – sorry if you were confused," I said. "That's a friend of mine. My number's on the back – the one I just wrote down. Here" – and I took Bill Kohlmeyer's calling card from her hands and turned it over.

"Oh, there it is. Yes, that fine's then," she said. She walked it over to her telephone, which was fastened to the wall in the kitchen, adding, "I'll keep this right here, in case I think of something else. Did I tell you about the time the power went out in town because of a big windstorm, and the telephones didn't work, either? Looking at the phone made me think of it, you see. This was well before those fancy little things the kids all use now – the ones that aren't connected to wires. My, that was an awful few days. I can't tell you what we had to go through to talk with one another, just to make sure everyone in town was all right ..."

When I finally extricated myself from Mrs. Sours' tales and home, armed with a baggie of her oatmeal raisin cookies for the road, a plan was starting to form in the back of my head. I just needed some confirmation to add a few more pieces to the puzzle. Then I'd call Kohlmeyer with the news. I decided that a trip to City Hall and a thorough search through the John Day property records might pay some dividends.

I also figured that I could locate a telephone there.

I've got just enough time to poke around before they close up shop. And I can still get home in plenty of time for classes tomorrow, and even manage a little time with Caeli, I thought.

I'd no more than stepped out of Mrs. Sours' home on Elm Street when a police car pulled to the curb and the big man behind the wheel, decked out in a uniform of deep blue and gold trim, motioned for me to join him next to his cruiser.

That's odd, I remember thinking once the cruiser rolled to a stop and I saw the officer's beckoning motion. *He surely can't be asking me for directions.*

He motored the window on the passenger's side open, and I ambled over and smiled amiably. I've always found it best to look agreeable when you're in the presence of law officials, regardless of type or stripe or locality.

"Hi," I said. "Can I help you with something, officer?"

"What ya doin' at Mrs. Sours' place?" he asked.

"I was asking her some questions for a project I'm working on and was just leaving."

"A project, huh? Back in the valley, across the mountains, right?"

"Yes, that's true."

I didn't like the way that the conversation began, even at this early stage, and I also didn't like the way the cop looked at me. It raised the hairs on the back of my neck, and I was instantly thankful that Caeli had been unable to make the trip.

"Been hearin' 'bout you," he said. "Don't much like what I hear, neither."

"Oh?" I asked. "How's that?"

"You talked to Luke McCoy the other day – I right about that?"

"Sure did," I said. "Mister McCoy seems to be a fine man, though I've never met him in person."

The officer ignored that. "Luke an' me are members at the Elks Club. He told me 'bout it – said you was fishin' 'round some 'bout the Deeker boys."

"I wouldn't call it fishing, exactly, but I was looking for information about two of the Deeker brothers. That's true. You see, I'm a private investigator in …"

"I know who you are, boy," he said. "I been doin' some fishin' of my own."

He opened the cruiser's door and pulled himself up to his full height, which topped six feet by at least three inches.

He was in his mid- to late-forties, I guessed, solidly built but with a spare tire around the middle. His grey-flecked hair was close-cropped, military-style, and his thumbs were hitched over the middle of his thick belt, which held up an assortment of police necessities, a Glock pistol and two spare but fully loaded magazines included.

"You packin' a gun here-'bouts, Mister Private *Detective?*" he asked, emphasizing the front portion of that last word as though it were something dirty.

"Yes. That's true, Officer …"

I waited for him to supply his name, but he didn't bother. I figured that I'd be able to read his name on the tag pinned to his uniform, and I took a step closer to get a better look.

But he considered the movement to be threatening. He pulled his Glock in a swift motion, aimed it directly at my head, and said – rather calmly, considering the circumstances – "Take another step and you die on the spot. Just you gimme the chance."

I stopped abruptly, reflexively raised my hands high in the air, and no doubt looked both amazed and horrified. I have no way of knowing, of course, but I know how I felt at that moment.

It was not a good feeling.

"I have a permit for the gun," I said. "It's inside my waistband, under my shirt; the permit's in my wallet."

"Take yer gun out with your left hand, real slow and easy-like, then drop it on the ground. You make so much as a twitch or a slip and I kill ya on the spot – understand?"

"Yes. Perfectly," I said. "Have I done something wrong, sir?"

"Plenty," he said as I nervously fished the Walther out of its holster and let it fall into the grass. "I'm gonna snap the cuffs on you now and take you to the jail – 'cross town aways. Then we'll see how much you done that ain't right."

"I don't understand," I said, raising my left hand in the air again. "Am I being charged with something?"

"Let's start with vagrancy," he said with a nasty smirk. "Parading without a permit – didn't like the way you strutted down the sidewalk. By the time we get you cross town, I'll come up with a couple more. All right then – hands behind yer back. You know the drill."

I did, although I'd never previously been on the opposite end of that drill.

He locked me inside a musty cell ten minutes later, shoving me roughly through the opening and slamming the iron doors with a harsh, ringing clang. I caught a glimpse of his name tag then and at least knew who I was dealing with: Little Cliff Corn, the town's police chief, just as described by Mrs. Sours not thirty minutes earlier.

I was still of the belief at this point that the situation could be handled normally. My thinking was that I'd been arrested by a *bona fide* cop, or at least by someone who appeared to be a *bona fide* cop, and that a mistake had been made that could be easily rectified.

It's all a big misunderstanding – nothing more, I thought.

I figured that if I could get my lawyer on the phone, Michael Parker would get me out of the cell within minutes, with all of the bizarre charges that Corn had initially mentioned quickly dismissed. I also could see myself issuing a formal complaint against Corn and the John Day Police Department, and perhaps even the city of John Day itself. But that would come later, once I was out of town and the sorry business at Raptor's Ridge was cleared up.

"I'm entitled to a phone call," I said. "I'd like to make it now, please."

"And I'm entitled to life on Easy Street, but that ain't somehow worked out for me," he said, his malicious, leering grin now spread wide across his face. He needed a shave, and I was close enough to catch a whiff of his breath, which reminded me of fish that had turned bad, mixed with too much whiskey for lunch.

I took a couple of steps away from the bars of the jail cell and said, "I'm not sure what you think I've done, but we can clear up any misunderstandings quickly – if only you'll let me make a phone call."

The grin disappeared instantly. "You keep yer mouth shut, boy," he snapped. "Ain't gonna be no phone calls – not today and not tonight, lestwise. Not 'till I figure out what to do with Big City Snoops that like to worm their way into things ain't none of their concern."

"Look, Officer Corn, I'm entitled to …"

His beefy hands clasped hold of the cell bars, and he rattled the lock back and forth as he shook the heavy iron. "Told you to shut up – ain't gonna say it again. I'm the one gonna do the callin', not you. After that, well, we'll just see after that. But my guess is" – the malevolent grin returned – "things ain't gonna end so good for you. Lots of folks get into accidents on the back roads in these parts. Shame, but that's a fact. You don't strike me as a careful driver, what with that souped-up *ve*-hicle you brought to town."

He turned without another word, moved swiftly down the hall, closed an access door behind him, and left me to figure out what in the hell had just happened.

I called out a few times, demanding a lawyer, demanding to make my allotted phone call, demanding to see a judge or some other higher authority. But Little Cliff gave no indication that he heard me or cared about what I had to say, and I eventually sat down on the concrete floor with my back against the wall farthest from the cell door and cursed silently.

Shakespeare jumped into my head, for some reason.

My kingdom for a cell phone, I thought.

The irony somehow struck me as funny, and I actually laughed out loud, if only for an instant.

But the more that I thought about the situation, the more perplexed I became. My conversation with Lucas McCoy, the retired high school principal, had been nothing but cordial. The man was happy to talk with me, had apparent excellent recall of past events, was willing to share those events in detail, and didn't need coaxing in any way. McCoy actually recommended Mrs. Sours as a potential source for additional details about the Deekers. The idea that he might turn on me and report our conversations to Officer Corn was strange, unless …

… unless he didn't. Unless Corn knows far more than Lucas McCoy, and I abruptly remembered Mrs. Sours' comment that the original Clifford Corn – the former chief of police; the current chief's father, Big Cliff – was related to Nick Drake.

That means Little Cliff also is related to Drake.

"Ah, hell – this whole thing stinks," I said aloud, muttering to myself, again struck by the absurdity of the situation. "I'm sitting in jail, talking to myself, held prisoner by a lunatic who's related to a guy who's probably a serial lunatic. Terrific. Absolutely terrific."

I cursed again, loudly this time, and folded my arms across my chest.

The entire episode reminded me of an old Laurel and Hardy skit that I'd seen on late-night TV years before, but nothing was funny about my current situation. All I could do was remain patient and see what would happen next.

At least I didn't have to wait long.

THIRTY-NINE

A WELCOMING MORNING SUN

WEDNESDAY, 6:22 P.M.

At approximately the same time that I was stuck in a dank jail cell, waiting for Little Cliff Corn to dispatch me to the netherworlds in a staged accident somewhere out in the High Desert, the floodgates to the Raptor's Ridge murder cases were opening at last.

I learned from Bill Kohlmeyer, though I didn't find this out until a full two days later, that The Lurker's fingerprints were matched to a former Special Forces operative who'd been reported KIA – killed in action – during a covert military operation in central Afghanistan.

The operative's name was Nicholas Drake.

He'd lived in John Day, Oregon, as a kid.

Best of all, or at least most telling, he'd been friends with Paul and Tom Deeker and was related through marriage to Little Cliff Corn.

Kohlmeyer was elated at the news, which had trickled in from reluctant military sources inside the Pentagon. But he was troubled at the same time. He had no way of knowing that I was stuck in a John Day jail cell, with its no-account, lone-wolf chief of police growing more menacing, and more intoxicated, by the hour. All he knew for sure was that he had vital news to share, that I hadn't been heard from in more than twelve hours, and that he had no way of reaching me with the news so that I could sniff around its edges while I was in John Day.

Of course, I knew nothing about what was happening on the other side of the mountains at that moment, either, even though Little Cliff – and somehow the moniker was far more fitting than Cliff Jr. or the more colloquial J.R. – was a steady visitor to my cell. On three occasions, he walked clumsily to the cell door and silently stared at me, his eyes hate-filled and glaring, his breath putrid with the reek of cheap whiskey.

An hour after he'd first locked me inside the cell, he returned to report that he'd towed my rental car away from Mrs. Sours' home.

"Gettin' it ready for the big trip – the final one, if you get my meanin'," he said, slurring his words slightly. "Took the cookies, too. Thanks."

"I'm glad – hate to see them go to waste. Who's we?" I asked, for lack of something clever to say. But he left as abruptly as he'd arrived, almost falling down as he whirled swiftly about, and I began to wonder whether this was some form of psychological torment that he'd read about and was trying to use to his advantage.

If that were the case, it wasn't necessary. I could tell that the guy was, in simple layman's terms, as whacky as they grow them in this part of the country. The fact that he was drinking, and hard, didn't help the situation, either, and I wondered again why the law enforcement profession attracted so many quality people on the one hand – people like Kohlmeyer and McDonough, Chichester and LeRoy – and so many paramilitary/Storm Trooper wannabes and nutjobs on the other, a category into which Little Cliff Corn seemed to nicely fit.

He returned to the cell a little after midnight with a tray of food, although it didn't fit the normal jail fare. He dropped the tray on the floor and pushed it with his foot under the cell bars. It contained a plastic cereal bowl and spoon, a single-serving box of Kellogg's Frosted Flakes, and a small container of milk – the kind you'd get in the lunch line in grade school.

"Eat somethin'," he said gruffly. "Don't wanna see ya waste away. I got other plans fer that – other ideas." He delivered the words slowly and carefully.

Maybe he's stopped drinking, I thought. *Then again, maybe he's just drinking himself sober ...*

"I prefer plain Corn Flakes to the frosted variety," I said as I picked up the cereal box. "I'm watching my weight."

"Yup, yer a plenty smart guy, all right," he said, as though I'd invited his opinion. "Then again, how come yer stuck in here, you bein' so smart an' all?"

"I've been meaning to ask you the same thing," I replied while peeling back the cover on the cereal box. But he just waved his hand at me, as though swatting away a fly. Then he turned from the cell and stomped in a clumsy fashion down the corridor once more, his heavy feet clunking loudly on the concrete.

"I'm still waiting to make my phone call," I shouted after him. But he didn't bother to reply or turn around, and the access door slammed loudly again.

Surprisingly, no other police officers made the short trek from the outer offices to the jail.

Maybe he's declared the jail off limits. Or... maybe he's alone, if that's even possible, I thought, unsure of the arrangement the city had with the country sheriff.

The an even worse thought struck me.

Maybe there's no judge, either. Maybe Little Cliff is the whole show – judge and jury.

The prospect was horrifying. And all I could do, as I sat on the floor and ate the cereal and admitted that it tasted remarkably good, though it wouldn't have been my first or even tenth choice for a last meal, was to think about a way to get free of Corn and the town. My mind kept returning to how I could get word to Kohlmeyer about Nick Drake's friendship with the Deekers.

Well, that and to let Caeli know that I'd somehow discovered on the day of AJ Bohn's murder at Raptor's Ridge that I loved her, far more than I might've ever thought possible – far more than anything or anyone else I might ever find in the world.

THURSDAY, EARLY A.M.

I learned later that Betty Sours, god bless her compartmentalized Republican heart, rescued me.

It happened this way:

Little Cliff paraded into the jail at 6 a.m. and banged on the cell with a nightstick, waking me from a fitful catnap. He looked alert, if not exactly chipper, though his breath still reeked of rotgut booze from an extended night of hard drinking.

"All right, bright guy – time to go," he said. "Stand away from the door. Git yer hands up high so I can see 'em."

I took my time crawling from the wretched cot that I'd been dozing in, off and on, throughout the night. I checked my watch, even stretched a time or two, swiveling at the hips as a golfer might do, and eventually reluctantly raised my hands.

"Speed it up in there or I'll fire off a couple of rounds, just to git yer ass movin'," he said. "Sound alone'll make yer head buzz. Hell, might be reason enough to do it anyway." He placed his hand on his holstered Glock and grinned nastily.

"Then again, you ain't gonna be around fer long," he added menacingly.

"There's no need to draw your weapon," I said, trying to sound reasonable. "There's no need for any of this, Chief Corn. You don't have to head in this direction. There are plenty of ways to work things out."

But Little Cliff continued to grin, acting as though he hadn't heard me. He reminded me of the guy who sweeps the floors at a fast-food restaurant and always goes through the same routine, even if there's nothing to sweep and no reason to have a broom in his hand.

"I'm gonna 'cuff yer hands again," he said. "So turn around, hold yer paws behind yer back, and don't stir a muscle. You do that, you so much as twitch, and I whack you upside the head and cart yer ass outside on a dolly. Understand, it don't none matter to me. Coroner won't be able to tell one whack from another, once they pull you from the wreck."

This is not going in the right direction ...

"Listen, Chief Corn, tell me why you're doing this," I said as I turned around to face the wall, joining my hands loosely behind my back. "If you're going to stage an accident, at least tell me why – what you think I know that makes this necessary."

Was I stalling for time at this point, or looking for a way to catch him off guard? It's hard to say, even now. I didn't see the possibility of a rescue being mounted from so far across the mountains, but I also didn't like my odds of getting the jump on the guy – even if he had been drinking. But I was curious, and I figured that if Little Cliff was going to kill me anyway, I might as well know what he knew.

When he didn't reply, I asked it again: "Come on, Little Cliff – what do you think I know? Talk to me."

"Don't call me that. Hate the name – always hated it," he snapped.

"All right, Chief Corn then – explain it to me. Why do you think you have to kill me?"

"You know damn well why," he said as he applied the handcuffs, snapping them tight and pulling them hard again. "A smart guy like you pokes around in business that don't concern him, well, it comes back to bite yer ass, boy. I don't like folks pokin' 'round in stuff that's nobody's business but mine, which is what you been doin' here. You start in on this stuff, it leads down a trail that ain't yer concern. And that's where we are right now. I don't like it none – don't like yer meddlin' – and ain't gonna tolerate it. Not when it puts me an' mine in a bad way."

He was marching me through a narrow corridor that led to the back door while he talked, prodding with his nightstick to hasten me along. We were headed to the parking lot behind police headquarters, where he'd no doubt stashed the Pontiac.

"Worse of all," he continued, "you keep diggin' 'round long enough, you'd find out Nick Drake ain't dead, like they say he is – like he wanted folks to believe. Can't be havin' that. Not for a single damn minute."

It didn't truly register, not until later, but I was still trying to buy some time.

"What did you just say?" I asked.

He pulled me to a halt, jerking hard on the handcuffs at the small of my back, and spun me around.

"Nick was different, even back then. He did things we never did, tried things we'd never try, got away with stuff we'd get caught at. And when he did get caught, well, my daddy always saw to it he come out all right. When it was my turn, and Big Cliff'd catch me at somethin', he'd beat me within an inch of my life. But for some reason, he always let Nick skate. Oh, he'd talk tough enough, but Nick never got the ass-whuppin' the rest of us'd get when Big Cliff caught us at something."

He paused, his eyes momentarily blank, as though he could recall each and every transgression and act of forgiveness and chastisement with certain clarity, one after another. When he eventually returned from wherever he'd gone a moment earlier, his face again took on a hard, malevolent stare.

"Must've been Drake's old lady. She had a way about her, let me tell you: with Nick, with my old man, with a dozen others in town, likely. I don't know that Nick ever got past it – might'a been why he killed her. What do you think? You got an opinion on that, Mister *De*-tective?"

"Nick Drake killed his mother?" I managed after a long pause.

"You surely ain't the brightest bulb on the Christmas tree, are ya?" He spun me around by the shoulders and shoved. "Now open the damn door and say howdy to the morning sun. Gonna be the last time you see it, so enjoy it, best ya can."

I turned to the side and pushed at the security bar with my hip to force the door open, closing my eyes to the sun's harsh glare, which was full in my face.

The next thing I knew, I was knocked hard to one side and was face down on the ground, my head spinning. I found myself spitting dust and dirt because I hadn't been able to use my hands or arms to block the fall, wondering what in the hell had just happened, and why.

I could hear sharply issued commands and grunts and curses and a couple of thwacks and thumps, as though a big fist had been shoved forcefully into a sack of flour, and then someone shouted a single word:

"Secure."

I turned my head to the side, still sputtering, and looked up to see a half-dozen State Police officers surrounding Little Cliff Corn, who was on his knees, his hands cuffed behind his back, his department-issued hat lying in the dust nearby. An ugly red welt already was showing under his left eye, and a reddish knot the size of a walnut was rising on his forehead.

John Day's contrary police chief did not appear to be happy, although he did manage to register a look of stern defiance on his otherwise dour face.

I was helped to my feet at that point, and a State Police officer – youngish, ruggedly handsome in his traditional blue uniform with the snappy Smokey hat perched atop his head – looked me over for a moment.

"Are you Max Blake from the capital city?" he asked.

"Sure am," I said with some enthusiasm, damn surprised at the swiftness of my rescue.

"Excellent. My name's Petrone, with OSP. I bring you compliments from Special Officer Chichester, and from Chief Kohlmeyer. I was instructed to tell you, once we secured the scene and had you in safe hands, that the cavalry's here. I'm guessing that means something to you?"

I didn't bother to reply. I manage a snorted laugh as he unlocked the handcuffs at my back, turned to a nearby officer, and said, "Bag these as evidence." Pointing his index finger in Corn's direction, he added, "And get that piece of garbage out of my sight."

Police radios were crackling, and two squad cars appeared from the far side of the jail building and rolled to a stop, their lights flashing. Corn was hustled inside one of them a moment later, muttering unintelligible phrases punctuated with curse words, and I looked again to Lieutanant Timothy J. Petrone.

"What the hell just happened here?" I asked, taking a moment to wipe the dirt from my hands and then my face. "I'm a bit confused."

"Sure," he replied, mustering a slight smile, as though he'd caught the scent of an inside joke. "Chief Kohlmeyer received a call from a local woman named … hang on, let me find it" – he dug into his pocket and pulled out a notebook, which he opened quickly, scanning the pages – "OK, here it is, a Betty Sours. That's someone you know in John Day, yes?"

I nodded.

"She saw what she described as some funny business taking place between you and Corn outside of her home, after the two of you talked yesterday. Later, when she saw your car being towed, she looked for the calling card you'd given her. It had your name and number written on one side and Chief Kohlmeyer's on the other. She tried you first, apparently, but there was no answer. Then she tried Chief Kohlmeyer and refused to get off the phone until he was found. Once she told him what was going on, he contacted Special Officer Chichester, and we were asked to step in and see that you came to no harm."

"And you just got here? You just now arrived?" I asked, incredulous at the timing.

"Actually, sir, we've had the place surrounded and under observation for some time now – a few hours, at least. I'm still not sure what this is all about, exactly. Our orders were to secure your safe release, take Corn into custody, and arrange for police protection for the town through our department, at least until additional determinations can be made. I'm sorry that it took as long as it did, but we had to proceed with some caution."

"Well, Lieutenant Petrone, you get my vote the next time you run for elected office," I said, still a bit dazed by the whole thing. "I'll tell my friends. All two of them. I promise."

He looked at me strangely – I get that a lot – and then gave me a crisp salute and turned to direct traffic as additional patrol cars rolled into view.

I headed back inside the jail, looking for my Walther, the keys to the rented Pontiac, and a telephone. I needed to get in touch with Kohlmeyer, not only to thank him for sending in the cavalry, as he so eloquently described it, but also to tell him what I'd learned from Betty Sours, and from Little Cliff, about Nick Drake.

It turned out that he knew it anyway, but that didn't make me any less glad to spread the news about Drake's early friendship with the Deeker brothers.

"The pieces," I said after we chatted for a moment once I got him on the line, "are at last starting to fall into place."

"True enough," he replied. "But we've still got as many questions as we do answers."

Typically, Kohlmeyer's assessment was spot-on.

FORTY

A PLACE FOR EVERYTHING

THURSDAY, 2:07 P.M.

I actually thought that Bill Kohlmeyer would be happy to see me when I arrived back in the capital. I'd thought about it off and on during the drive, though I'll confess that everything that had happened in John Day, and at Raptor's Ridge – all of the pieces of the puzzle – ran through my mind again and again.

But first things first: Kohlmeyer had called a meeting of the legal, law enforcement, and civilian brain-trust, as he put it, and I needed to goose the supercharger in the recovered Pontiac to make sure that I arrived on time.

That part, at least, was easy, and I wondered again, as the miles flew by, what GM's so-called top executives were thinking, if anything, when they shut down the company's premiere performance line and decided instead to save the Buick, which I've always thought of as an old man's car.

I also wondered what appropriate gesture I might offer when I saw Kohlmeyer and Ken Chichester, the two men who'd pulled the strings that saved my life. I'd already sent flowers to Betty Sours, whose phone call alerted Kohlmeyer to the danger I was in, and to Caeli Brown, who was filling in for me once again in the classroom. But something told me that the chief and the State Police liaison officer somehow wouldn't appreciate a similar offering.

I thought about a number of options as I entered City Hall, signed in at the reception desk, and was told that I'd better hurry – "conference room, down the hall, second door on the left" – because the meeting already was under way.

Should I slap them a high-five? I wondered, but discarded the idea as being too sports-related.

How about a man-hug? I thought next but quickly nixed that as well: *Nah, too much ... though a handshake is always safe.*

Then again, maybe the fist-bump is the way to go?

Kohlmeyer broke off in mid-sentence and scowled when he saw me, however, erasing all thoughts I'd entertained about a warm and fuzzy greeting.

"Blake," he said gruffly. "Next time I tell you to get a cell phone, dammit, get yourself a damn cell phone."

So what do you say in a situation like that? All I could muster was a weak, "You got it, Chief," as I removed my fedora and smiled half-heartedly in his direction.

"Sit," he said. "We've got a lot of ground to cover."

I took the only remaining chair at the table and glanced around the room. Kohlmeyer had assembled the usual suspects, along with some fresh faces I didn't recognize.

Doc Strand was there, and he gave me a look that was half-grin, half-*What-the-hell-happened-to-you?* Russell Vineyard was next in line, followed by Ned McClinton. Both nodded briefly in my direction. My lawyer, Michael Parker, sat next to McClinton, and he, too, nodded a solemn greeting. On the opposite side of the table were Bob LeRoy, the Marion County sheriff; Chichester; Lawrence Hultz Fuller, the stuffed-short district attorney; two of Fuller's more competent aides; and, in chairs that were lined against the far wall, four people I didn't know and a fifth, a woman, who was connected in some way to the governor. I knew that much because I'd seen her photograph in the newspapers, though I couldn't place her name.

Kohlmeyer was at the head of the big conference table. Standing to his left, a couple of steps behind, was his aide, Patrick McDonough.

This ought to be good, I thought.

Within an hour, Kohlmeyer, Chichester, and LeRoy outlined the essential details of the case as it stood. Among the pertinent facts:

Nicholas Drake was the prime suspect in the murders of AJ Bohn, late of Raptor's Ridge, and his mistress, Audrey Flowers, late of the big screen;

Drake also was the prime suspect in the deaths of more than a dozen women in Washington, Oregon, California, and Arizona in a killing spree that spanned the two years since he'd been reported killed in action while on assignment with Special Forces in Afghanistan;

Drake's current whereabouts was unknown, although it was believed that he'd been using John Day as a base of operations, at least until recently;

The military brass apparently was as interested in Drake as the rest of us, a prospect that didn't particularly excite the chief or the DA;

The Deeker brothers, Paul and Tom, were suspected of allowing Drake to gain access to Raptor's Ridge, although the why of it was a lingering mystery;

Paul Deeker's whereabouts remained undetermined; there was some speculation that he might be traveling with Drake;

A nationwide, all-points bulletin had been issued for Drake and Paul Deeker;

Little Cliff Corn was being held in the Grant County jail in Canyon City, a few miles south of John Day;

Tom Deeker, who was lodged in the Marion County jail, refused to talk or cooperate with his court-appointed attorney, even when notified that his boyhood pal Nick Drake had been identified as a suspect in the Bohn/Flowers murders;

Charles V. Downing and William "Buzzsaw" Stone, the two police officers whose shakedown racket/pyramid scheme had seemingly helped to precipitate the murders at AJ Bohn's estate, also remained in the county jail, as did their minions; all refused to provide additional statements.

Some additional details were added, including a handful of developments that resulted from former officer Ron Clarin's statement against Downing and Stone. All of these points were tied together by detailed notes that Kohlmeyer distributed in a single-sheet handout to help provide some clarity.

Larry Fuller's show, which came next, wasn't nearly as organized or thorough, nor was it as satisfying. Never a man to miss a cliché, he insisted that he'd throw the book at Tom Deeker, Downing and Stone, all of the former officers who were aligned with them, as well as Drake and Paul Deeker – "when they are found, at least, and handed over to me." He also said that he was upgrading the charges against each suspect in the case – "Downing, Stone, the lot of them" – to include accessory to murder in the Bohn/Flowers case. "And I'm still looking to tie Downing and Stone to the murder of Skipper Arnold" – he was the man who'd seduced Audrey Flowers, allowing Downing access to AJ Bohn – "though we'll have our work cut out for us on that one."

If he'd expected applause, which he seemed to when he finished, he was sorely disappointed. He looked around, judging the mostly indifferent faces in turn, before finally shrugging his narrow shoulders and working at the knot in his necktie. He scowled at an aide – I got the feeling that the aide might've assured him that this portion of his speech would be well received – and continued.

"I'll do the same with the rest of that gang. Someone will break, I'm sure of it – someone who can tell us more about the insides of the operation than what former Officer

Clarin could offer," Fuller added triumphantly. "Then we'll bag them all."

He remained adamant that he was in no mood to bargain for lesser sentences with Tom Deeker, Downing, Stone, or with Paul Deeker once he was caught. "And Nick Drake is looking at the death penalty, regardless. He'll get absolutely no consideration from me or my office."

He finished by indicating that he also was inclined to dispatch sheriff's personnel to Grant County to bring Little Cliff Corn into his custody.

The woman representing the governor's office jotted a couple of notes at this last part, turned to the man seated next to her, whispered in his ear, and he got up and left the room quietly. Fuller didn't seem to notice; most everyone else in the room did.

Much as I hated to admit it, I thought that Fuller might've been on the right track regarding Little Cliff Corn, but I doubted that he'd get the chance. Grant County reeked of local politics and small-town propriety and keep-the-hell-out attitudes toward big-city government, state interference, federal intervention – the entire mantra of what's commonly called the right-wing crowd these days.

I figured at the time that Corn would be dealt with locally, if at all, though I also wondered whether the governor might step into the mess because of the potential political fallout.

By the time the meeting fizzled, two hours had passed and the coffee had turned lukewarm and then god-awful. Near the end, Kohlmeyer asked whether I had anything to add. I thought about it, wondering whether I should provide any details from Betty Sours' comments and Little Cliff's intention to arrange my fatal car crash in the vast wasteland outside of town. But there were too many ears in the room I didn't know, and I opted for a shake of the head.

"Not a thing," I said.

"Well, all's well that ends," he said. "It's good to have you back among the living, Blake."

"Thanks to you and Ken here," I said. Nodding in Chichester's direction, I added, "Your man in Grant County, Lieutenant Petrone, is the real deal, Ken. Thanks for sending him to the rescue."

I spent the next ten minutes conversing with Strand and Vineyard while the chief huddled with one of Fuller's aides, along with LeRoy and Chichester.

I shook hands with Chichester as he was leaving, talked briefly with LeRoy, and was surprised to see Michael Parker waiting for me.

"I'm delighted to see you, Michael," I said. "But I've got to ask: What the hell are you doing here?"

"Representing your interests," he said. "Any damn fool can see that. Plus, I charge by the hour and am about to ring up three of them, plus my expenses, which are considerable."

That made me laugh. "Well, I appreciate it, more than you know," I said. "But … well, hell, how did you even find out about the meeting? It's not like the newspaper printed an announcement."

"Kohlmeyer called me yesterday, looking for you," he said. "After he explained that you'd gone missing, I told him I wanted to be kept informed of everything that was happening in the case, at least as it applied to you. When he started to try and wriggle off the hook, I insisted on it."

"Yeah, I can imagine. So what kind of card did you play to get him to agree?" I asked him. "He's not much for lawyers, you know."

"You don't say," Parker replied, chuckling softly. "I told him pretty much what Lyndon Johnson told the *New York Times* when asked why he'd named J. Edgar Hoover the head of the FBI for life rather than firing the no-good bastard, which at that point in his career, Hoover damn well deserved."

"All right, I'll bite: What did he say?"

"LBJ, as the story goes, said, 'It's probably better to have him inside the tent pissing out than outside the tent pissing in.' "

I laughed again. "One thing's for sure: They don't make presidents like that anymore," I said.

"Maybe it's just as well. But Max, LBJ aside, I've got a solution to your contract regarding services rendered to the Bohn estate," he said. "It's one that I think you'll be pleased with. It's also one that the state will be pleased with – in the long run, at least."

"The state?" I asked, surprised. "Why would the state give a damn what I bill Bohn's lawyer, other than as an end-of-the-year tax issue?"

"Come by my office when you find the time," he said, ever the stoic. "Give me two hours of notice once you determine your schedule and I'll get McClinton in the room as well. It'll be good entertainment – worth the price of admission."

"Which will be?"

"Something outrageous, of course."

I was anxious to figure out what he'd cooked up, but Kohlmeyer was at my side at that instant, tugging at my arm.

"You two can chitchat on someone else's dime," he said, talking primarily to Parker. "We've still got some real work to do, and I need a coherent debriefing from this phoneless clown regarding the situation in John Day."

I'll say this about Kohlmeyer: He has a deft way with words, especially when they apply to me.

I told Parker that I'd be in touch, grabbed my fedora, and followed the chief and two of his escorts back to his office.

I'll admit that I didn't mind the time spent with Kohlmeyer that afternoon as I provided chapter and verse and rich detail regarding my conversations with Betty Sours and Little Cliff Corn. But I was far more anxious to see Caeli again.

She and I had some serious catching up to do.

FORTY-ONE

THE UNTIDY HOUSE OF LITTLE CLIFF CORN

FRIDAY, 7:32 A.M.

At this juncture, we were forced both by circumstances and the DA's lack of initiative to either wait for a significant break in the Raptor's Ridge case or push forward on our own.

We elected to force the issue.

Bill Kohlmeyer wanted to kick-start our efforts by heading east to talk with Little Cliff Corn in person. A group of us spent two hours in the chief's office, discussing the situation in detail, and we came to the likely conclusion that Corn knew far more than he'd coughed up to date.

"He at least knows things about Drake that we need to know if we're going to catch this guy," I said as we sat in the chief's office in City Hall, kicking around ideas. Also present were Ken Chichester, Bob LeRoy, and the ever-present Patrick McDonough.

"You were up close and personal with this guy, Blake. Do you think Corn knows where to find him?" Kohlmeyer asked.

"One way to find out, I guess," I said. "Why not get Ken's help again and have the State Police boys on the other side of the mountains grill him?"

But Kohlmeyer jumped in before Chichester could respond.

"To hell with that. Why go half-hog when we can eat the whole damn pig?" he said.

"How's that again?" I asked.

"Come on, Blake, try to keep up. If there's grilling to be done, I'm the one with the knife, not Ken's boys – and no offense meant here, Ken."

"None taken, though my guys are up to the task," Chichester said.

It wasn't that Kohlmeyer didn't trust the interviewing skills of the State Police or Sheriff Department personnel who were on the scene in John Day, exactly. He just trusted his own instincts a hell of a lot more.

To me, his assessment of the situation, and his decision to tackle the problem head-on, was vintage Kohlmeyer: forceful and straight ahead, just as I recalled from my reporting days.

We were in a National Guard helicopter a day later, thanks to an arrangement with Kohlmeyer's new-found friend, the governor, winging our way over the same country that I'd traveled in the Pontiac a couple of days previous. The views were even more impressive from the air, although the steady throbbing of the noisy engine and the thropping of the blades grew quickly tiresome and then become a damned nuisance, despite the muffling provided by the mandatory headphones.

The Three Sisters peaks – North, Middle, and South – were spectacular from the air, even if the mantle of snow that the mountains wear in winter was reduced now to sullied glaciers and crumbling rock. Our pilot provided what he called a cook's tour of the dormant volcanoes and flew in close to the caldera at the top of the South peak. A handful of climbers on the 10,000-foot mountain gave us a hearty wave, and we were soon whisking our way again over the magnificent ponderosa forest and then across the desolate stretch of desert and canyons and the arid, empty countryside that guards the entry to John Day.

The helicopter eventually set down on the Grant County fairgrounds in the heart of town, and we were met by two sheriff's patrol cars and a cruiser from the State Police office. I spotted Lieutenant Petrone at the driver's-side door of the cruiser as we touched down, and he waved as we hopped out, keeping our heads low under the rotating blades. He shook hands with Kohlmeyer, and the two men chatted for a minute. Then he greeted me with a wry smile and said, "You get around for a college professor. You'll have to explain that to me one day."

I would've told him that some of the administrators at my college were less than impressed with my sleuthing efforts and wanted me back in the classroom, considering all the time that I'd missed in the past two weeks. But he apparently wasn't interested in an answer anyway because he motioned us inside his cruiser. We sped toward the south end of town, with Kohlmeyer in the front seat, talking strategy, and me in the back, listening in but essentially twiddling my thumbs.

The two sheriff's patrol cars were in formation behind us.

We made, I suppose, a merry little procession – one that I was happy to be in, considering what had happened to me the last time I was in John Day.

Our destination was the ancestral home of Little Cliff Corn, which he'd inherited when Big Cliff died ten years earlier: a one-story rambler that was as unkempt and bursting at the seams as Little Cliff's midsection. The house was set well back from the road and was fronted by a large hedge that prevented a clear view of the premises from the street. Three outbuildings formed a half-circle in the back.

The place was in need of a paint job and repairs to the porch steps, which provided access to a front door of heavy oak, also in need of a fresh coat of paint. One of the wooden shutters adorning a window facing the street was buckling and about to drop. The eaves drooped in the center and looked ready to fall as well.

The inside was equally disheveled, dirty, cluttered, tousled – definitely the home of a bachelor who'd lost the battle for self-respect, and respectability, a long time ago.

"He could stand a visit from the Merry Maids," Petrone observed, stepping around a stack of boxes and piles of old magazines and other clutter as he entered the living room.

"He could marry a Merry Maid – as if one would have him – for all the good it would do," I said.

"Horsenuts," Kohlmeyer said. "The place is a dump and should be bulldozed, but first things first. If we find any items of interest in here, and I hope we do, we'll have some ammo to use when we talk to the guy."

Two of the deputies and a lab technician from Grant County entered the place with us and were providing Kohlmeyer with details of an earlier cursory search that they'd conducted shortly after Corn's arrest. That effort turned up nothing of interest beyond the clutter. Still, Kohlmeyer was hopeful that something might've been hidden and left behind, and we huddled for a minute while he outlined a plan to pull the house apart if necessary.

"It could be something tiny, or inconspicuous – or something you wouldn't think might be relevant to the case," he said. "So let's take our time and see what we can find. If you spot something that seems odd or that doesn't belong in all this … this filth, sing out. We'll take a look and see if any bells ring. Deal?"

He divided the house and grounds into quadrants, with the lab tech assigned to roam and take photos of any items of interest. We then spanned out and began the search. I drew the kitchen, a hallway, and a mudroom and laundry area with back-door access to the outbuildings.

I started on the outside grounds, looking for signs that something might've been recently buried or disturbed. But I turned up nothing but rusted tools, a decrepit lawnmower, old planters, and stacks of aged cordwood.

Inside again, I found heaps of dirty dishes though few clean saucers and plates, impressive piles of laundry strewn around an ancient stacked washer-dryer combination, cupboards that were essentially empty except for cereal boxes, two cases of Jack Daniels that were stashed in the otherwise empty pantry alongside the refrigerator, some open gin and rum bottles in the cabinets above the cast-iron stove, but little else of interest.

I even emptied the pitifully stark refrigerator of its contents and checked inside the rancid Chinese take-out, the ketchup bottle, and a baking soda box to see if anything had been stashed among the week-old pork fried rice, the Heinz 57, or the Arm & Hammer.

I had nothing, other than a loss of appetite from the ungodly stench of the take-out.

Forty-five minutes into the search, Petrone called out, loudly enough to be heard by all present, "I've got something here. Come take a look." He was inside a closet in a small bedroom, which was stuffed high with boxes and decades of accumulated clutter. He'd opened a trap door that led into the crawlspace beneath the house.

"Looks like it's been dug out under here, most likely by hand," he said as he peered over the edge, lying on his stomach, a large flashlight probing the depths below the floor. "It's almost big enough to stand in. There's a cot down here and a couple of storage trunks, maybe. Looks like cardboard on the floor; hard to tell from here. We'll need to get some additional light before going down if we hope to turn up anything besides the obvious."

He pulled his head up and grinned. "I had to move a couple of boxes and lift a throw rug to find it," he said. "My guess is he was intentionally keeping this covered."

We rigged a bench light from the garage and a couple of table lamps from the living room, each connected to an extension cord and a multiple-plug outlet that I'd spotted during my search of the kitchen, and had the place in decent light minutes later.

Petrone and Kohlmeyer climbed down, flashlights in hand. The chief ordered the rest of us to remain up top while the two of them poked around.

With the deputies hovering over the crawlspace opening, I found a floor register on the opposite side of the room after picking my way through boxes of junk stacked chest high and listened to the muffled sounds from below. I heard Kohlmeyer curse loudly at one point, thought that I heard the word "Rats" but couldn't be sure, and chuckled when I heard a sharp string of curses fired off in rapid succession.

Dank, dark cellars filled with spiders and vermin and god only knows what else didn't excite me much, and I was counting my blessings – simple as they were – when I heard Kohlmeyer call out, "Got you, you bastard."

I had no way of knowing whether he was talking about a rat or something better – or worse – and was tempted to call down and ask. But he was out of the crawlspace a moment later with a cigar box in his hand.

"Found this lodged between the spacers in the floor joists, covered over with a rag," he said. "Take a look inside."

He opened the box, and eighteen pieces of jewelry – rings, bracelets, a necklace, a broach, a set of diamond earrings – glittered in the sunlight that filtered into the room.

"What do you think?" he asked, talking to no one in particular. "Any guesses?"

"Might be his mother's jewelry," one of the deputies suggested. "She's been gone a long time, but he'd have reason to save it."

"Why hide it down there?" Kohlmeyer asked.

"Maybe he didn't trust banks?" the deputy replied. "The guy's not firing on all cylinders, from what I know."

Petrone looked closer at the contents of the box and said, "I doubt that Little Cliff's mother had multiple wedding rings. Off-hand, I'd say they're trophies – souvenirs of some sort."

"That's what I'm thinking, too," Kohlmeyer said. "The bigger question is who the cigar box belongs to …"

"… and who originally owned the jewelry," I said, finishing his thought.

"Exactly," the chief said. "We've got some expensive-looking pieces in this stash, I'd guess – far beyond the means of a simple honest cop."

"And he doesn't strike me as the type to personally wear diamond earrings, either," the second deputy said, chuckling at his own comment.

The lab tech snapped pictures; Kohlmeyer, the deputies, and Petrone all grinned broadly; and I figured that we might be getting somewhere at last as a number of likely scenarios started flashing through my head.

The crackling of the deputies' radios interrupted the momentary reverie, however, and a static-filled voice, weak and unintelligible, called out a couple of times before dying out all together. A deputy whose badge name read Wilcox indicated that he'd field the call in a better location, and he excused himself and stepped outside. Kohlmeyer and Petrone already were back inside the crawlspace, poking around again, when Wilcox returned. He whispered a few words to his partner, looked at me for a second, decided to ignore me, and got down on his knees to yell into the opening.

"Chief Kohlmeyer," he called loudly. "Thought you ought to know: Corn was released from the county jail not more than ten minutes ago."

Another string of curses punctuated the darkness below our feet, and the chief stuck his head out of the opening a moment later.

"What the hell happened?" he asked, his face red with anger and exertion. "Dammit. I thought we had a hold on this guy."

"Local judge sprang him on bail. Not sure who posted it, but Corn's in a Jeep right now with somebody who was waiting for him outside the cell. They're headed northwest, out toward the fossil beds. We've got a patrol car trailing at a discreet distance."

"All right, dammit, let's go get him," Kohlmeyer said, finishing the sentence with a couple of salty verbs.

He ordered the lab tech and the second deputy back to Canyon City with the cigar box, and Kohlmeyer, Petrone, and I piled into the cruiser and took off toward the main road heading west, siren wailing and lights flashing. Deputy Len Wilcox trailed behind in his patrol car.

"What the hell was that judge thinking? Dammit. I want to talk to that bastard," Kohlmeyer snapped.

"The judge or Little Cliff?" I asked from the back seat.

But Kohlmeyer ignored me, which was just as well.

"Let's hope we get to him before he reaches the badlands," Petrone said. "There's places out there that will swallow you whole – forever."

"That's great," I heard the chief mutter as we broke free of the city line and Petrone stomped hard on the cruiser's gas pedal. "Just great."

FORTY-TWO

ROWBOATS ON THE OCEAN

MONDAY, EARLY MORNING
THIRD WEEK

We hunted for three full days without so much as a single sign of Little Cliff Corn, his unknown traveling companion, or the Jeep the two men were in when they left the Grant County jailhouse in Canyon City, a few miles south of John Day, and disappeared into the vast stretch of desert west of town.

The police cruisers and patrol cars were traded in for four-wheel-drive rigs, all-terrain vehicles, and dirt bikes manned mostly by the area's local residents, many of whom happily volunteered to join the manhunt and refused to back off when ordered to stay out of the way. A National Guard helicopter was dispatched from Bend, and two more choppers were flown in from the state capital.

Even the feds were involved. The John Day Fossil Beds National Monument is a part of the U.S. National Park Service, and the higher-ups didn't like the idea of killers, or even potential killers, running loose on their territory – decidedly bad for the tourist trade. It wasn't long before rangers were tearing around the wilderness in their own ATVs, looking for signs of Corn and a man we believed to be his cousin Nick Drake, given the description of the driver who'd collected Little Cliff from the jail.

As the hours dragged on, plenty of false leads and sightings were reported. For each of these, we'd head into the desert with GPS devices flashing digital coordinates, high-powered rifles at the ready, waiting for a sign of the missing Jeep, or a glint of sunlight from a piece of metal – gun barrel or car's fender or hood, or even a reflection off a pair of stylish sunglasses: It made no difference so long as we spotted something.

But the intensive search produced nothing: no sign of the men or their rig – not so much as a single tire track. From the moment the Jeep left the paved road on Friday and swerved onto a whisper of game trail in the vast desert that seemed to stretch out forever, shaking the trailing deputies' patrol car in a plume of dust that rooster-tailed high into the air before evaporating altogether, Corn and Drake ceased to exist as flesh and bone and muscle and sinew and blood.

It was as if the pair vanished from the face of the earth itself. And the quick resolution that I'd hoped for was as ephemeral as Bill Kohlmeyer's good nature and amiable disposition.

It also became clear, as the hours and then the days dragged on, that Little Cliff wasn't one of John Day's more popular citizens.

One of my favorite moments during this part of the hunt took place early on the second day. A local resident – he was in his mid-sixties with a scruffy grayish-white beard, wearing a lumberjack's shirt and denim trousers held up by massive suspenders – strolled by the command post and spoke to Kohlmeyer as casually as if he were asking for the time of day.

"Howdy," he said. "Name's Chancey, Fred Chancey – thought you ought to hear it. This Corn fella yer lookin' fer – Little Cliff? Jest to let you know but he weren't a patch to Big Cliff, the old man. Big Cliff was the real deal. Were he out there now, roamin' with the *cy*-otes an' such, you'd see nary hide nor hair from him again, less'n he wanted ya to. But Little Cliff? Why hell, I don't give him more'n a passin' thought – like cat piss runnin' down a drain. Neither should you, comes to that."

The chief started to ask him a question, but the man turned abruptly and disappeared among the beat-up pickup trucks that were packed into the parking area.

"Colorful" was the only word the chief managed once Fred Chancey disappeared.

We did get a slice of good news after the second day when the lab report came back on the cigar box of women's jewelry that Kohlmeyer found under Little Cliff's house. Five of the pieces were positively identified as belonging to victims of a serial killer who'd savaged the West Coast for the past two years, including San Diego housewife Terri Ann Walker's wedding ring … and a broach that once belonged to Audrey Flowers, late of Raptor's Ridge.

Fingerprints matched to Nick Drake also were lifted from the box and positively identified.

"There's some cause to cheer," I said when we heard the news. "It confirms what we suspected: Drake's our boy – and he's most likely The Lurker."

"Yeah," Kohlmeyer said. "We can prove Drake was here, and recently, and we can tie him to the Raptor's Ridge killings – and to at least four other murders. But we can't do a damn thing until we get him, including prove that he killed Bohn and Flowers. And locating the bastard in this wasteland" – he pointed in the general direction of the fossil beds, which stretched interminably to the north and west, disappearing into the distant horizon – "is pretty much like finding a row boat on the ocean. It's not an easy task now, and it won't get any easier. Fact is, it's damn likely to get a whole lot tougher."

Petrone informed us late on the initial day of the hunt that the judge who'd granted bail was a relative of Corn's, though it was a distant and tenuous link at best. Kohlmeyer confronted the judge by telephone that first night, putting the call on speaker so that we all could hear the conversation. But he got nothing more than a legal brush-off and some huffed-up indignation, and he didn't take well to being told that he was out of both his depth and jurisdiction.

His demeanor at the start of the call could be described as professional, if not overtly courteous. But it quickly moved on to contrary and then disgusted, and Kohlmeyer eventually became livid and went for the jugular.

"Yeah, terrific," he told the judge as the conversation wound down. "You let a certifiable idiot out of jail, and we know for fact that he's traveling with a serial killer and *bona fide* psychopath – both of them apparently related to you. Good luck explaining that in the next election – especially when it gets to the national press."

The tough talk didn't intimidate the judge, at least not outwardly.

"Just what kind of damn fool are you, son? Let me tell you something here that ain't yet obvious to you: We do things different on this side of the mountains, Chief whatever-you-said-yer-name-was," the judge said, stretching his words. "You'd best not call this number again, lest you want to end up on the short side of my gavel, which is something I can accommodate. You hear me all right?"

Kohlmeyer muttered a choice expletive and clicked off his cell phone.

"God in heaven," he snapped. "Killers are running wild around town, the police chief runs the Bates Motel, and the judge belongs in his own jail. What the hell kind of backwater dump is this, anyway? It's like an episode out of … *The Twilight Zone*, for god's sake."

He was right, except that *Twilight Zone* episodes came to an end in thirty minutes, and you could switch channels or turn off the set if you didn't like the story line. At the end of some long days here, we were no closer to finding Little Cliff

Corn and his running mate, the serial killer Nick Drake, than we'd been when we started.

An additional search of Corn's house turned up more fingerprints belonging to Drake, but we already knew that the former Army Ranger was there recently because of the broach that had until days earlier belonged to Audrey Flowers. Kohlmeyer was quick to stomp about, cursing his bad luck, cursing the offending local judge, cursing the fates and the gods and the climate of the High Desert.

In the end, he asked the governor to send in a National Guard unit to storm the entire expanse of the fossil beds, and someone somewhere must've entertained the thought, if only briefly. But when the feds decided that it was a bad idea all around, Kohlmeyer and I got on one of the helicopters and returned to the state capital instead.

The best part of that deal? I spent a full day and two full nights with Caeli once the chopper deposited me back on solid ground. Someone had to repay her for the work that she was putting in at the college, and I'm delighted to say that the job fell fully to me.

Once we took a few minutes to discuss what had taken place in the fossil beds and the investigation's overall lack of progress in locating Corn and Drake, which occupied the first five minutes of our reunion, I gave no additional thought whatsoever to the case.

None.

Then, two days after we'd left John Day, Kohlmeyer called to say that he'd received a report from the State Police in Grant County regarding a possible Jeep sighting in the desert. That got my attention. I raced to City Hall (we had no time to head for Grant County), and the chief and I monitored the police radios for more than an hour until word came through that the sighting was a false alarm: wrong vehicle, wrong color, wrong registration … just some local guy and his girl joy-riding out in the desert.

We cursed our luck, and we both expressed a desire, as the action was taking place in the badlands, to be out there – on the hunt, closing in.

But we weren't, and wishes don't mean much in broad daylight. The simple truth was that our presence there wouldn't have mattered greatly. We both put it out of mind and waited confidently for the next telephone call to come rolling in.

While it wasn't long in coming, it wasn't the one that we'd hoped for, either, although it did add another piece to the puzzle.

State Police detectives, working with the medical examiner's office, determined that the body of a white female homicide victim that had been dumped on the outskirts of the state capital two weeks earlier was a Gladys Richter, age twenty-seven, of Eureka, California. She'd been a waitress/hostess in a restaurant north of the coastal community and had been reported missing six weeks previous.

She was last seen, according to two eyewitnesses, in the company of a white male in his mid-thirties who exactly matched the description of Nicholas Drake.

FORTY-THREE

GLADYS AND AXTON

THREE WEEKS EARLIER

"Look, Gladys, it's no good pretending," he said.

Axton Hoyt, AKA Nicholas Drake, smiled grimly, though his eyes had a haunted look about them. He glanced down at his shoes momentarily, as if he could discern the depths of the cosmos and the full meaning and mystery of worldly existence in the high sheen of the patent leather that was nattily wrapped around his feet.

He eventually pulled his gaze from the floor and stared at her again, and his eyes turned instantly cold and hard. A shiver ran down the back of her spine, and she flinched inwardly. This was the same look she'd seen on that first night, when he picked her up at the bar – before she could politely decline his invitation to have a drink because something about him, far beyond his charm, gave her the creeps.

It was a look that she hoped to never see again.

"Give it up, Gladys," he snapped, his teeth bared and gleaming in the harsh glare of the overhead light. "We can do this any way you like – easy or hard – but you know in the end I'm going to get what I need. I always do."

He paused, squinting, and then rolled his head slightly to one side.

"I'm sure that's true," she said softly, and she worked hard to force a smile.

"You know it's true," he said. He pressed his face inches from hers and added with nasty relish, "Am I right?"

Her eyes were wide with fear now, though she prayed silently that she could at least hide the genuine loathing she felt for him at this moment, as well as the disappointment in herself for not being stronger.

"Sure, Ax," she said after a slight hesitation, attempting to work some conviction into her voice. "I'm with you, all right." She forced a weak smile, but it died beyond the light in her eyes and quickly receded into a caricature of forlorn concern for her own well-being.

He abruptly pulled his body away from hers and grinned that lean, rakish, wolfish leer of his and licked his lips in anticipation, like a beast closing in for the kill.

"Good, Gladys. That's good – very good. Might be some hope for you after all."

When she looked into his eyes this time, they seemed distant and indifferent again, and she drew courage for an instant and chanced trying to talk some reason with him.

"Ax, don't you think if something goes wrong, the cops will – well, you know ..."

"I don't think about the cops at all," he said harshly, pulling himself back from the mental distance that he'd achieved a moment earlier. "Neither should you."

"I know that, Ax. It's just that, well ..."

"Funny thing about the cops," he said, interrupting her as though he hadn't realized that she'd started to speak again. "Just when you think you can ignore them, they reach out and beat your head with a shovel. Just for fun."

He continued to drone on about the cops, but she tuned it out. She'd seen him like this before. He would go on autopilot, talking as if by rote, spewing out the words as though he'd memorized them in some distant past, his eyes again fixed on some faraway place that only he knew existed.

"Don't matter if they're city cops or state cops or federal cops," he said. "Army cops, too. I got no faith in cops – learned that a long time ago. Don't even matter if you know the cops."

He looked up and focused once more, as if he were waking from a bad dream, and he smiled tightly, his eyes ablaze with hate.

"I mean it. Ya know?"

"Sure I do, honey – of course I do. And you're right – like always," she said, though her eyes were flecked with fright and, try as she might, she failed to exude comfort or empathy or any emotion other than raw fear as she softly spoke the words.

It won't be long now, she thought. *He's gonna blow a gasket again, and then god help me ... and everyone else.*

But she remained silent now and at last managed a smile.
It calmed him.

"Here's what happens next," he said. "We get there, my guy opens the door, and in I go – just like that." He snapped his fingers for emphasis.

"That's good, honey," she said.

"You bet. Nothing to worry about – no guards, no alarms, no cops," he said, the wolfish grin in place. "I walk in and no one's the wiser."

He paused, a look of triumph on his face, and started pacing the room again.

"The dame is always dripping with furs and diamonds and expensive stuff. I take the gems ... whatever I want. Even have some fun with her if there's time. Then I slip out again – piece of cake."

She hated this about him – just hated it. He could take the most dangerous, self-destructive, complicated plan and turn it into ... nothing, as though a smile and a single snap of his fingers and a guy on the inside – if there even *was* a guy on the inside – would make it happen.

But she also was smart enough to know that questioning him, or pressing a point, was something that wasn't done. Not at this stage, anyway.

Not if I want to live ...

"That sounds good. Really nice," Gladys said.

"Nice?" he said, wheeling about. "That's all you got to say? It sounds nice?"

"That sounds great, baby. Just great."

He grinned.

"That's my girl," he said. "You stick with me. Good things'll happen. You just wait."

But he already knew that bringing her this far was a mistake, one he'd rectify quickly.

Axton Hoyt – AKA Drake Nichols and a half-dozen other aliases – had no intention of keeping Gladys Richter around …

… not when he was about to pull off the biggest score of his life.

Why he'd let her hang around for this long was a mystery to him, and it had only been a few short days or weeks – hell, he couldn't even remember – since he'd picked her up in a seedy bar down by the wharf north of Eureka. Sure, he enjoyed stringing her along. And sure, he liked what she offered at night. And yeah, when he thought about it for any length of time, he'd admit that Gladys did look something like *she* had looked, a long time ago.

But he knew how it would end – the same way that it always ended.

He just wasn't sure of when, exactly, though her time on the planet was rapidly drawing to a close.

Maybe tonight, he thought. *Maybe I'll put us both out of our misery tonight. Then I can get serious about the job on the hill.*

The thought of the big score at Raptor's Ridge made him smile for the first time that day.

FORTY-FOUR

FROM NOTHING TO A PHONE CALL

TUESDAY, 8:16 P.M.
FOURTH WEEK

I figured that it was over.

A group of us even gathered a few days after our return from John Day and ran through a half-dozen scenarios on what might've taken place in the fossil beds and the dust and sand of the high desert that had swallowed Nicholas Drake, the serial killer, and his cousin Little Cliff Corn, the former John Day police chief, kidnapper, and village idiot.

Restaurateur Jim Maddaux was our host, opening his establishment after-hours to serve up scrumptious platefuls of *hors d'oeuvres* and a half-dozen varieties of Oregon wine.

Doc Strand was there, as were Ned McClinton, Russell Vineyard, and Charlie Wilson.

Bill Kohlmeyer dropped by, though he made it clear that he wasn't particularly happy about it when he said, "I'm only here because of Mad Dog's food, not because I want to hear any more crackpot theories about this damn case." He was accompanied by his bodyguard, Lieutenant Patrick McDonough, who approached even this event as though he were expecting trouble.

Bob LeRoy and Ken Chichester also dropped by for an hour or so.

Todd Wright was invited as a thank-you for supplying me with a set of wheels to duck the bad guys, just before Chuck Downing and Co. were hauled in, but he sent along his regrets.

Michael Parker was traveling on business in Greece, but he sent a text message from his cell phone to McClinton, who forwarded it along to the group: "Please advise MisterVineyard: It's good to know the butler didn't do it."

A lawyer with a sense of humor? It was almost too much to ask.

He followed that message with another, directed at me: "Ned: Please tell MB to see us soon re. his bill for services to Bohn's estate." I'd spent so much time with Caeli Brown, and with catching up on my teaching duties at the college during the past few days, that I'd put business concerns on the back shelf. But I thanked McClinton for the reminder and promised to get with him and Parker as soon as my lawyer returned from his overseas trip.

Caeli, tired of hearing well-placed but single-source theories from afar and willing to offer a few ideas of her own, accompanied me to the gathering. I don't know that I've ever felt more at home or more alive than I did with her beside me that night.

We all had a hell of a good time – perhaps because Larry Fuller, the DA, wasn't invited to the shindig. We snacked, we sipped and tippled, we swapped anecdotes and insider tips and a handful of tall tales, and we came to this inescapable conclusion: It was highly unlikely that we'd ever see Nick Drake or Little Cliff Corn again.

"We might find Corn's body one day. I don't think we'll ever see him walking upright," Kohlmeyer offered before he slipped away. "He's not too bright. He'd be a burden for an Army Ranger in many respects – including an extended flight. There's just no reason for Drake to keep him around – he doesn't bring enough to the table."

"But they're related," Wilson said. "He might keep him around for no other reason than that. Blood is thicker than brains sometimes."

Caeli then theorized that Little Cliff might be as likely to kill Drake as having it happen the other way around.

"Corn would know in a hurry that he's expendable," she said. "And while he's none too bright, he'd understand self-preservation and self-protection. Besides, he carries a gun for a living. He must know how to use it."

"I saw Little Cliff up close and personal – a hell of a lot closer than I'd like," I said. "He's mean, he drinks to excess, he has serious anger issues. He'd kill Drake if he had to. Maybe that whole business with Drake's mother and Little Cliff's father would be enough …"

I let the ugly thought linger.

Doc Strand joined in.

"Lost here is the fact that we just don't know enough about Drake and what drives him – what makes him tick," he said. "It makes speculating fun, in a general sense. But it's still pointless. I'd feel better if we knew more."

"We know that he killed his mother," I said. "If we're looking for an analysis of some sort, we can start there."

"We only know that's what Corn told you," Kohlmeyer said. "We don't know it for sure, though – not yet."

McClinton, who'd been mostly silent for much of the night, spoke up. "Based on what we do know about Corn, at least, I wouldn't want to be locked in a room with him – nor would I bet against him."

"I *was* in a room with him, and I agree," I said.

The room was quiet for a moment, and I could picture Little Cliff looking at me through the cell bars while I was locked in his jail, his eyes as hate-filled as any I've ever seen.

LeRoy broke the silence. "His mother aside, Drake has killed a number of women we know about and who knows how many others we don't know about," he said. "We can't say the same thing about Corn – or can we?"

"Only that he's capable," Kohlmeyer replied.

Russell Vineyard joined in for the first time that night. "They must make quite a pair, don't you think – Drake and Corn, I mean? I must say that I find them to be strange bedfellows, indeed."

Caeli frowned at the observation. "Did you have to use 'bedfellows' in the same sentence with those two, Mister Vineyard? The thought gives me the creeps," she said.

"Surely you speak for all of us on that count, my dear," he replied quickly.

That gave us a good laugh, and we passed the evening in similar fashion, with ideas floated and theories discounted or acknowledged and suggestions of all sorts and varieties extended. We weren't overly serious or melodramatic, either.

Isn't that the way it's supposed to be when friends get together?

The gathering broke up sometime after midnight, with LeRoy, Chichester, Kohlmeyer, and McDonough already gone and Vineyard doing his best to disguise a series of long yawns. The case wasn't solved, nor was the world saved, but we'd bonded again over a shared experience and felt, at that moment, at least, that we were part of something important – if only temporarily, if only from a distance – recognizing that the status quo might be as good as we were ever going to get.

Then I got an unexpected phone call six days later that again turned things upside down.

MONDAY, 9:57 A.M.
FIFTH WEEK

"Would have called you sooner, but it ain't much in my nature," the cowboy voice, gruff and gravely, said without introduction. "Got to thinkin' you'd want to know this, though – that's why I'm callin' up now."

I had no idea who was on the other end of the line and didn't quite know what to make of his unusual approach to starting a conversation. I decided to play along, however – just in case a useful tidbit was lurking.

"Your sound familiar," I said, "but I can't place the voice. Sorry."

"No reason you should – ain't no need to apologize. Name's Chancey; Fred Chancey. Spoke to yer chief of *po*-lice when you was over to John Day some weeks back. Just fer a minute, it was, when everybody else on the reservation was out huntin' Little Cliff in the fossil beds."

"Sure," I said, though I still wasn't totally dialed in.

"Nothin' wrong with sayin' you don't have a clue as to who I am or what I want – or why I'm callin' you and not the *po*-lice chief," he said.

"Fair enough," I answered with a quick laugh. "So who are you, exactly, and why are you calling me and not Bill Kohlmeyer?"

"Ain't in my nature to talk to the *po*-lice," he said. "We fend for ourselves on this side pretty much and leave the law to fend for those it looks after, mostly. But you boys need some help on this one. That's why I'm callin' – to offer some. I'm in a place to do that."

"Wait," I said. The light bulb in my head switched on, and I could see Fred Chancey in my mind, as surely as I could see the telephone receiver in my hand. "I've got it now. You're the fellow who stopped by during the search to tell us Little Cliff wasn't a patch to his old man."

"Yup, that's me. And he ain't. I had a load of respect for his daddy, once upon a time, though lord knows Big Cliff had his faults. But I ain't never much cared for the boy. He's mean, he's mostly a drunk, and he let that job go to his head – something Big Cliff never did, and never would've abided in his boy. The old man must be spinnin' round-about in his grave to see what's become of that kid of his."

He paused, and I could picture Chancey, sitting in some desolate cabin, spitting out the words, driven to talk by an internal force that I couldn't yet spot.

"Can't call him a kid no more," he added a moment later, "but he's a bastard if ever there was one."

"Big Cliff must've been a good man if that's why you're calling now," I said, prodding him to talk.

"Ah, hell, it ain't even that so much," Chancey said, growling as much as speaking the words. "I don't like the idea of Little Cliff showin' up here some night, scarin' the god's holy hell outta folks and doin' god only knows what to who, or why. He's capable of a lot of mischief, that one – always has been – and it's high time somebody stopped it."

"It's not that we haven't been trying," I said. "We just don't know where to find him."

"I know that, dammit, which is too damn bad," Chancey said, the frustration in his voice spilling over with every word he spoke. "So it falls to me to set you boys straight, seeing's how nobody else stepped up and ain't likely to at this late date. That's what really burns me. Understand, I ain't the lone keeper of this stuff. Never have been."

He paused, and I waited. He eventually said, "You with me? You still there?"

"Sure," I said.

"But what? You ain't gonna ask it? "Ask it? Ask what?"

I'll admit it: I was slow at grasping the obvious here. Then it hit me, and I said, "Wait. You know where we can find Little Cliff?"

"That's why I'm on the phone, son," Chancey sputtered. "Don't know for sure he's there or not, mind ya, but I'm gonna tell ya where to look. Rest is up to you."

"How would you know this?" I asked.

" 'Cause I knew Big Cliff pretty well. You got to understand that, back when the territory was first stretchin' out some, it weren't nothin' but cattle and gold country. No one out here gave a hoot in hell 'bout dried-out bones and such – all that fossil beds nonsense with the feds in charge came about after the big gold rush. The old boys pulled millions in gold out of that countryside, and lots of folks still look for the Lost Blue Bucket Mine – a famous tale that some don't think is a tale a'tall. You ought poke around some there – might be of interest. Ya with me so far?"

"Sure"

"Good. High time. Anyways, Big Cliff got hisself a mine he worked fer a lot of years. When he went to pushin' daisies, the lot of it fell to Little Cliff. I expect, if he ain't in Los Angeles, maybe, or in Mexico in some tequila palace with some dainty little Chiquita darlin' – which is where *I'd* be, I tell ya – he's holed up in that cabin of Big Cliff's, out in the middle of nowhere near the fossil beds, layin' low and maybe even workin' the mine."

"Gold country?" I said incredulously after he'd finished and I had time to absorb his words. "Really?"

He chuckled. "You ain't from around these parts, are ya, son?"

I asked many more questions and took some notes, thanked Fred Chancey more than once, and jumped on the Internet to spend several maddening minutes in a maze of assorted state and federal government maps. I also took the time to research the heady story of the Lost Blue Bucket Mine that he'd referenced. Then I dialed Bill Kohlmeyer, waited impatiently for a full seventeen minutes before he finally barked his name into the phone, and tried not to overplay the hand.

"I might have something, Bill," I said when he answered.

"Something's better than what we've had to date," he replied.

"You remember that old guy back at the fossil beds who stopped by to tell us that Little Cliff wasn't a patch to his old man?"

"Yeah. Maybe," Kohlmeyer said, though he didn't sound as though he recalled the conversation any more than I had initially.

"You called him colorful," I added, trying to jog his memory.

"Yeah – I remember now. Don't recall his name, though. What about him?"

"Fred Chancey. His name's Fred Chancey."

"All right, so it's Fred Chancey. What about him?"

"He just called with a tip on where we might find Little Cliff," I said. "Seems that Chancey's been waiting for someone from John Day to fill us in, and nobody has. So he felt obligated, for whatever reason, to step up and let us know about a cabin and a nearby gold mine that Little Cliff's old man had, west of the John Day River and Cathedral Rock."

"Did you say *gold*?"

"I did."

"And this cabin and mine are common knowledge in John Day?" Kohlmeyer asked.

"Apparently. It's hard to say without talking with everyone in town, but Chancey seemed to think so."

"I'll be damned. So where is this place, exactly?"

"It's on Johnny Creek, above the Blue Basin area of the monument, off Highway 19. It'll likely be hard to get at, from what I can see on the map. There aren't any marked roads, so it's ATV or four-wheel-drive rigs only. Either that or we hike. My guess is we'll need to get with the park rangers and make a determination as to what we're dealing with out there."

"This is park land then?"

"No, it's outside the park. But I'm willing to bet that the rangers know the territory better than anyone."

"Yeah, makes sense." He was silent for a moment before adding, "I'll be damned. All this time, and he's close to home, maybe, and gold might be involved, which is maybe what's keeping him close, and nobody offered up a thing."

"Not until now," I said. "Chancey didn't seem particularly happy to deliver the news, either. He called it his duty, seeing as how no one else stepped up. Plus, he thinks there's a chance that Little Cliff might prowl the town again, and it bothers him. Chancey thinks Corn's dangerous."

"He got that much right. Still, we don't know he's there – at this gold mine."

"True. But it's better than what we had before, which was nothing."

The line was quiet for a moment, and I could picture Kohlmeyer on the other end, plotting strategies and potential lines of attack.

"All right, let me make some calls," he eventually said. "Guess I'd better start with the park superintendent."

"What about your new best buddy, the governor?" I asked. "Think he'd authorize another National Guard training exercise if you asked him nicely?"

"Doubt it – doubt I'll even ask," Kohlmeyer said. "I got a look the other day at the price tag attached to our last little helicopter junket. You just can't make this stuff up, Blake. He didn't think taxpayers would be amused, which is why he showed it to me. After looking at the tab, I'd agree."

"Well, whatever you decide, I want to be there."

"Sure," he said. "It's your tip. Besides, if this doesn't pan out – if it goes south – and we ring the cash register up for nothing, I'll have you to blame. I'd much rather have the governor chewing on your ass than mine."

He laughed as he hung up the phone, though I'm not sure why. I didn't see any humor in the remark.

FORTY-FIVE

VISIONS OF DANCING
GOLD NUGGETS

TUESDAY, 7:22 A.M.
FIFTH WEEK

It took Bill Kohlmeyer the better part of a day to plan an assault on Little Cliff Corn's cabin near the John Day fossil beds.

It wasn't an easy task. Kohlmeyer, sensing jurisdictional squabbles and the long reach of the federal government, went directly to the governor to head off potential conflicts before they could develop. That brought another set of variables – politics – into the picture.

But Kohlmeyer believed that the tradeoff was necessary, if only to keep the feds at bay until we could get in and out – ideally with Little Cliff and his cousin, the serial killer Nick Drake, in custody.

If, in fact, Drake was still in the area, or even in the country.

"I almost called the superintendent of the National Monument to give him a heads-up," Kohlmeyer told me that first night, after the plan finally came together. "But I knew he'd kick it up the line, and somebody else would kick it even further up the food chain, and before long word would get out. Then the damn politicians and agency heads would line up to get in on the act, especially if they could get their pictures taken. Next thing you'd know, the media buzzards would swarm in and the damn thing would circle around and bite me square in the ass. Meantime, Little Cliff would get wind of the whole shebang and disappear into the sagebrush again. No thanks."

Instead, he called on the governor, and the two of them agreed on the formation of a small task force that would locate Corn's cabin and gold mine, determine whether the ousted head of the John Day police force was on the premises, and take him into custody in whatever manner was judged to be most feasible. The governor would notify the feds and the various state and local politicians, and then only after the fact.

" 'If this Drake character is still hanging around, then so much the better,' " Kohlmeyer quoted the governor as advising him during their forty-minute meeting. " 'But do your best to avoid a shootout, and don't tromp all over the federal lands out there. Those boys are sensitive, and it's bad enough we're sending you in there without the feds' help or advice. They won't like it, but I don't really care at this point – I'm plenty man enough to take the heat.' "

According to Kohlmeyer, the conversation made him laugh on two counts.

"First off, he's more politician than problem-solver, though I'll admit that he did us a good turn on this one by agreeing to keep the feds out – at least until we figure out what's going on," he'd told me. "And second, the whole time we talked, I got the feeling he was worried about turning us all loose on some sort of Wild West re-enactment. He must think that all we dream about is getting into a shootout with some half-cocked wiseacre out in the pucker-brush. We both know you get your fill of that the first time the bullets start flying over your head."

"The shootout with the Deeker gang didn't help the cause," I said.

"That crossed my mind. But I still get the feeling that if we bag Drake, the governor would find us straight away and stand next to the carcass, holding a rifle with a big-assed grin on his face, smiling for the cameras. He's not against publicity if it'll get him a few votes."

The so-called task force, from our side of the mountains, consisted of Kohlmeyer, Patrick McDonough, Ken Chichester, and me. We were scheduled to connect with Timothy J. Petrone, who headed the State Police post in Grant County, once we reached the Sheep Rock Unit of the John Day Fossil Beds National Monument, forty miles west of Cliff Corn's home town. Petrone also would bring in a local guide who knew the area.

I met Kohlmeyer, Chichester, and McDonough early in the morning at City Hall. We armed ourselves with topographical survey maps, a camera with a long-range lens, three pairs of high-powered binoculars, two sniper's rifles and plenty of ammo, a duffle bag full of what I like to call SWAT toys, a satellite phone, two grocery bags of assorted protein bars and trail mix packages that the chief was partial to, and two cases of bottled water. We loaded up one of the city's SWAT rigs, an armor-equipped black SUV, and headed east on Highway 22, with McDonough driving and Kohlmeyer riding shotgun.

The lone news van that had been lingering around City Hall tried to follow as we started our long drive, but it was pulled over by a city patrol car within five blocks after a quick call from Kohlmeyer. In the old days, I would've considered that to be dirty pool; it didn't qualify as such now.

I stretched out in the back seat, ignored the mundane chitchat, and woke up ninety minutes later when we picked up Highway 20 at the Santiam junction, high in the Cascades. Black Butte, a perfectly shaped cinder cone volcano, soon loomed in the distance. I remembered climbing its well-established trail to the summit one sunny summer morning during my reporting days for a story about antiquated methods of fire prevention. Two months later, a volunteer in the tower lookout station atop the butte spotted a lightning-sparked fire that eventually spread to many thousands of acres and burned until the winter snows finally extinguished its last gasps, long months later. But the spotter's quick action no doubt saved Black Butte Ranch, a resort for the wealthy at the base of the volcano, preserving hundreds of million-dollar homes and who knows how many lives?

You could still see the fire's remnants as we headed across the mountain pass and entered the ponderosa forest and the Metolius River Basin.

I used to think that owning a place at Black Butte Ranch would be the mark of a successful man – something to strive for. After that fire, however, I decided that a place at the ocean would make more sense. What could possibly go wrong there, outside of tsunamis and landslides and the fact that everything made of metal eventually rusts because of the salt water?

We stopped briefly in the hamlet of Sisters and again in Prineville, in each case picking up fresh coffee refills while leaving the remnants of the last cups behind. We'd been on the road for a little more than three hours at this point. Kohlmeyer got behind the wheel, McDonough moved into the shotgun position, and Chichester called ahead to let Petrone know that we were still a couple of hours out. I was content to nap again when Kohlmeyer sang out.

"Hey, Blake, tell us something about the gold discoveries around John Day," he said. "It'll help pass the time."

I considered the question before I answered. "I'm no authority, though I did some reading after my talk with Fred Chancey," I called back, loudly enough to be heard over the whine of the SUV's big tires.

"So what'd you learn?"

"Grant County was a mining hotbed in its early days," I said. "You either raised cattle or searched for gold, and a lot of folks came and went, doing both. John Day and Canyon City were big mining towns in the early days. But the best story of the bunch is the Blue Bucket Mine. And it wasn't really a mine at all – not in the classic sense, anyway."

McDonough scoffed. "So what was the Blue Bucket Mine, if not a mine?" he asked.

I leaned back in the plush seat and pulled what I could recall of the story out of my head as we sailed past Prineville Reservoir and headed into another ponderosa forest as the road climbed steadily, twisting and turning, pointing east.

"It started with 400 or so pioneers from Iowa who were traveling the Oregon Trail sometime in the 1840s. They picked up the Malheur River by Vale as they entered Oregon, then left the river and continued on past Castle Rock. That put them in the vicinity of Willow Creek and Crane Creek. As the story goes, or at least as I remember it, some of their oxen strayed from camp, three men from the party went to find them, and they eventually returned with fifteen to twenty chunks of colored rock that they initially thought was copper. They were asked by the folks back at camp how much of this copper material was in the stream, and they said there was plenty enough to fill up any number of the wooden blue buckets the pioneers carried on the wagons to haul water."

"So that's where the name comes from?" McDonough asked.

"So far as I know."

"All right – so then what happened?" Kohlmeyer asked.

"They didn't give much thought to the copper rocks at the time and continued on," I said, "eventually settling in a variety of spots throughout the Willamette Valley. But a few years later, during the height of the California Gold Rush, a woman from the wagon train named Fisher remembered what they'd found near the headwaters of Willow Creek. She'd apparently been given one of these lumps of so-called copper, which of course turned out to be gold – or so they say. Some of her relatives went back through the years, trying to find the spot. And more than 170 years later, the area has been scoured by all manner of prospectors and geologists and ranchers and god only knows who else, all of them trying to locate the original source."

I stopped, with visions of gold nuggets dancing in my head. Kohlmeyer urged me forward with a simple word.

"And?"

"Plenty enough gold has been found throughout the area," I said. "Estimates are that more than twenty-six million dollars worth was found in Canyon Creek alone during the gold rush of 1862 in the John Day and Canyon City area. But nobody, or at least so far as anyone knows, has ever found the Blue Bucket Mine again."

We sat quietly for a few moments, with only the hum of the rig's big engine and the song of the tires turning on asphalt breaking the silence.

"Sounds like a campfire story to me," Chichester said at last. "A good one, but a campfire tale nonetheless."

"Big Cliff thought it was real enough," I said. "According to Chancey, Big Cliff spent the last thirty years of his life, off and on, looking for that mine, or something like it. That's the reason he built his cabin out in the middle of nowhere and staked a claim. With any luck, we'll find Little Cliff with a shovel or a pick-ax in his hand instead of a Glock."

"And if we don't find him, maybe we'll have some real luck and find this lost Blue Bucket Mine instead," Chichester said with a dry chuckle. "That'd make the trip worthwhile."

"I'd bet the governor would confiscate every bucket we found, seeing as how we're all public employees on the taxpayer payroll," Kohlmeyer added.

"Speak for yourself," I said.

"Maybe we'll get really lucky and find both Little Cliff and the gold," Kohlmeyer said. "But I'd rather have Little Cliff in hand at the end of the day, given a choice."

"Not me," I replied. "Much as I'd like to get my hands on Corn, preferably around his fat neck, I'd trade him for a blue bucket of gold any day."

"You just say that because the alimony check is due," Kohlmeyer shot back, and I caught him grinning as he glanced my way in the rearview mirror.

"Nice detective work," I muttered.

The conversation did get me thinking about Caeli Brown, however. And that in turn got me thinking about my pending invoice to the AJ Bohn estate. I made a mental note to call my attorney once we returned to civilization from desolate gold country, pretty though it was as the miles sailed by like passing clouds on the hot desert winds.

TUESDAY, 2:38 P.M.
FIFTH WEEK

We met Petrone outside the parking lot of the Fossil Beds' Sheep Rock Unit. He was driving his own car, a relatively new red Ford Mustang, and he waved as we pulled alongside.

McDonough ran the window down after a brief conference with Kohlmeyer. "Might as well grab your gear and climb aboard," McDonough said to Petrone. "No sense taking two cars in – not unless you see an advantage."

"No, that makes sense, so long as you've got room for two," Petrone said, and he stepped nimbly out of the Mustang and headed around to the back of our rig.

Monte Simmons, a John Day native, climbed out of the Mustang's passenger's seat and stretched his lanky frame before he ambled over. He was a big man, topping six feet and 250 pounds, and he moved slowly and deliberately, reminding me a brown bear standing on its hind legs. He had a hard, rugged face, a scraggly beard that was in need of a decent trim, and black-framed glasses that were perched low on his nose, making me wonder whether he was near- or far-sighted.

Maybe both ...

Once introductions were made, we loaded up and headed north on Highway 19. Petrone and Simmons occupied the middle seat; Chichester folded his gangly frame and joined me in the back.

"We appreciate your assistance," Kohlmeyer said, his eyes finding Simmons' face in the rearview mirror. "I'm not sure we could locate Corn without help."

"I ain't sure we'll find him yet," Simmons said. "Lots of territory out there to cover" – he gestured with a big hand in a broad sweep toward the desert to the east – "and no tellin' whether anyone's home when we come a'callin'."

"You know where the cabin is, though – right?" Chichester asked.

"Sure," Simmons said easily. "Been some time since I seen it last, but I can find it all right."

"I'm curious, Mister Simmons, if you don't mind my asking: What prompted you to offer your services to us now?" Kohlmeyer asked.

"Heard tell there's a big *re*-ward," he said, adding a sharp accent to the first syllable; a sweeping grin spread across his face as he turned toward Petrone and then swiveled his massive head around so that Chichester and I could enjoy the joke.

"I'm not sure where you heard that, exactly," Chichester said, and it was apparent that he either wasn't amused by Simmons' attempt at humor or didn't realize that the big man was joshing the car's occupants. "The state is paying you for your time, of course, but there's no ..."

"You mean there ain't no *re*-ward?" Simmons said.

"I'm afraid not – you've been misinformed," Chichester said with a bit more force.

"In that case, best turn this here rig straight around and take me right on back home again," Simmons said, his grin broadening even more. "I ain't one to work for the *po*-lice without first gettin' some up-front money." He turned in Chichester's direction again and added, "You did bring the up-front money – am I right? 'Cause I ain't steppin' foot outside this *ve*-hicle if you didn't – and I sure as hell ain't gonna do nothin' without no *re*-ward money to claim."

Chichester was still considering how to answer when Petrone stepped up to rescue him.

"I think Mister Simmons is pulling our leg, Ken," he said.

"Oh." Chichester considered his colleague's comment, and I imagined that he was running the entire conversation through his mind again, just to see where he'd gotten off track. He shook his head slowly from side to side a couple of times, as though he were puzzled by this unexpected turn, and then sat quietly for a time, his hands folded in front of him, his face empty.

"So, Mister Simmons, why help us now?" Kohlmeyer asked again. "Why not make the offer when we were out here days ago?"

"Don't know I got an answer you'll want to hear," Simmons said. "Truth of it is, I don't much care what Little Cliff did or didn't do, and I don't like to stick my nose in other folks' business without good cause. I'd be just as happy to let all this go and you boys work it out on yer own, but Fred asked me to see you through it. Fred's my uncle on my mother's side, ya see. Only reason I'm here is 'cause he asked. Well, that and what I know 'bout the country we're headin' into, which is pretty much everything. I suspect ol' Fred would've taken you in – say ten, fifteen years ago. But he's gettin' on some, so he wanted me to do it. And what he asks me to do these days, I pretty much do. Got a high amount of respect for my uncle. He's good people."

"It's appreciated," Kohlmeyer said.

"I hope you boys brought yer boots along," Simmons said after another mile passed.

"Got 'em on now," Kohlmeyer said.

Simmons leaned over the seat and peered down at Kohlmeyer's feet. "You got on some hikin' boots, near as I can tell. And so do you," he said, talking this time to McDonough as he pointed toward the SUV's floorboards.

"That's right," Kohlmeyer said.

"Best to wear cowboy boots, is all," Simmons observed as he sat back in the seat again.

"Cowboy boots? The damn things pinch my feet. I don't want to hike to this cabin wearing cowboy boots," McDonough said.

"Hike? Who said anything 'bout a hike?" Simmons asked, and he started flashing his grin around once more. "It'd be a helluva long hike in and back again to Big Cliff's cabin, I can tell ya, boots or no boots. I got horses waitin' for us at Cathedral Rock. Hope you boys can ride – makes it a bunch simpler if I don't have to give lessons to greenhorns and lead the parade, too."

"Aw, hell," I muttered. "I hate horses. Horses and boots both."

I don't know if Simmons heard me, but he seemed to be wonderfully amused.

FORTY-SIX

BACK IN THE SADDLE AGAIN

TUESDAY, 3:12 P.M.
FIFTH WEEK

The ride was worse than I imagined.

Far worse.

I may live in the American West and the heart of cowboy country, and my great-great-grandfather may have been a famous federal marshal in the old Arizona Territory – famous enough to have books written about his life and escapades – but I sure as hell wasn't excited about climbing on a horse. I also was damn sure, especially after an hour in the saddle, that once this business was done for good, I wouldn't climb on another one anytime soon.

Monte Simmons was good to his word: When we arrived at the Cathedral Rock parking area, he introduced us to Jim Reeves, a local wrangler who'd trucked in a saddle horse for each of us, plus a packhorse to carry our supplies.

Reeves, a tall, angular man in his mid-fifties who looked as though he'd stepped directly out of a John Wayne movie set, was accommodating as he helped us adjust the saddles and stirrup lengths. He also had a few words of advice, which he offered in a friendly, good-natured manner.

"If you know your way 'round horses, have a good time," he said. "If you aren't used to horses, well, all I can tell ya is to have as good a time as you can manage. Just consider that the horse is a hell of lot smarter than you are." He chuckled and tossed a length of coiled rope inside the extended horse trailer that he'd brought along to transport the animals.

"That's all you got – really?" I asked while sitting atop a handsome buckskin gelding, seventeen hands high. Given his color, the horse was appropriately named Buck. "You've got no other advice besides 'Have a good time, pardner' – nothing else? Because that's not offering much, Ann Landers."

Reeves flashed me a twenty-megawatt smile.

"Hey now – you got the best horse of the lot," he drawled. "He's used to riders who don't know one end from the other, which more or less fits in your case."

"I'm not arguing that," I said, leaning over to pat the horse's massive head a few times. "I'd just feel better if he came with bucket seats and a brake pedal."

The big wrangler laughed easily.

"Relax," he said, "and let the horse do the work – he's good at it. You don't need to spur him or steer him or prod or poke him, and you sure as hell don't need to pet him like a damn dog. That horse knows what he's doing, even if you don't."

"It's true enough that I don't," I said. "I just wish you hadn't told the horse."

"Trust me – he knows. He knows." Reeves chuckled again, then closed and locked the loading gate on the horse trailer.

Simmons, our wilderness guide, eased his horse across the lot and engaged in a brief discussion with Reeves. I caught Kohlmeyer's eye and noted that he was as comfortable in the saddle as he was in his department-issued SUV, despite the body armor that he'd insisted we all wear.

It also was quickly apparent that he recognized my discomfort.

"You're among friends, Blake," he called, but I could sense laughter in his voice.

"Hope I can say the same when I climb down from this beast," I muttered.

"All right," Simmons called out after concluding his business and shaking hands with Reeves. "Time to head out and have some fun. You boys might even catch a bad guy or two if we're lucky."

"Is that what they call this? Having fun?" I grumbled. But the creaking of the saddles and the clatter of horses' hooves in the dirt covered my complaint, which was just as well. No one likes listening to a whiner.

We passed the first hour in relative silence. Simmons and Petrone were at the front of the line, followed in succession by Kohlmeyer and McDonough. I was next, with Chichester, another experienced rider, bringing up the rear of the procession and handling the reins on the trailing packhorse.

Kohlmeyer and McDonough carried the sniper's rifles, which were strapped to the saddles. We all had backpacks and carried an assortment of water bottles and packages of trail mix and nutrition bars that Chichester produced from a large grocery bag before we left. The packhorse carried the gear that was either too heavy or too bulky to easily store on our person: a couple of folding spades, the three sets of binoculars, the satellite phone, a sack of the SWAT toys that Kohlmeyer brought along, and saddlebags filled with god only knew what that Simmons and Reeves oversaw.

We made, I thought, an odd if efficient group, and it dawned on me that a hundred years ago, we would've called ourselves a posse.

Despite his enormous size, my horse had an easy gait and amiable disposition. Still, the insides of my legs burned after no more than fifteen minutes of riding, and my rear end felt battered and beaten in no time. I waited impatiently for

Simmons to halt the procession and give us a stretch break, but he didn't seem to notice my discomfort – and no one else seemed to be greatly bothered.

I began to hum to keep my mind off the pain and numbness and muscle ache and general torture that was consuming me with each stride the horse took. But given the nature of the hunt, my mental versions of Paul Simon's soothing, artful tunes soon gave way to the Sons of the Pioneers, and before I knew it I was singing aloud:

See them tumbling down,
Pledging their love to the ground;
Lonely but free I'll be found –
Drifting along with the tumbling tumbleweeds.

I thought that the impromptu concert was hilarious, even though I don't sing particularly well. But Kohlmeyer turned halfway around in the saddle and made a quick slashing gesture across his throat with his free hand.

"For gawd's sake, Blake," he rumbled. "Why not start up a brass band to let 'em know we're coming?"

"Still got a ways to go there, Chief," Simmons offered. "No harm done – not yet anyways."

We were moving slowly through hot, dusty country that can be described as both bleak and spectacular in the same breath. Red-, white-, and gold-streaked hills, dotted with stunted juniper and sage, surrounded us, with bracken and bramble and thistle fastened to the grim, dusty hardpan that crumbled under the horses' terrific weight.

I was soon tired of eating dust and sore enough that I wasn't sure I could stand again, and I pointed toward a cluster of scraggly junipers that were struggling for purchase along the edge of the creek and called out, "I'll stop singing if we take a break."

Kohlmeyer called ahead to Simmons, saying something that I couldn't hear, and our tracker turned his horse off the wispy game trail he was following and headed toward the stream. He pulled up a moment later and turned his horse to watch us move in, smiling as he surveyed his band of travelers, turning the world into two camps: cowboys, and everyone else.

I fell into the Everyone Else Department, as did McDonough. He was able to disguise his pain better than I was, however, and I almost dropped to my knees when I finally swung my aching frame off Buck and stumbled before catching my balance.

I could hear Simmons sniggering, but I was too beat-up and bone-weary to care.

"How much longer?" I asked.

"Depends on how fast we go," he said, grinning.

"All right, at our current pace, how much longer?" I pressed.

"Another hour at least, and maybe thirty or forty minutes beyond that," he said. "Though I'd think we'd want to walk in the last mile or so – quarter up the horses first. That'll get us close in without bein' heard, most likely. Plus, I don't want the animals to get caught in no gunfight. That'd run up the tab somethin' fierce for you fellas, and my friend Jimmy would be none too happy if he was to lose a horse in this rumpus. If we do that – walk our way in – it'll take a bit more time."

"Makes sense," Kohlmeyer said as he climbed off his mount and swiveled his torso a few times, loosening his back muscles. "How much cover can we expect?"

"It's barren country, much like what you see here," Simmons replied, sweeping his arm toward the nothingness beyond. "Again, been a time since I come this way and longer still since I been to Big Cliff's cabin. Doubtful they'd expect company, though – 'specially this time of day. But don't expect much cover or help, 'ceptin' maybe surprise and the creek bed."

"Yeah – afraid of that," Kohlmeyer muttered, and he huddled with Chichester, Petrone, and McDonough for a time while I headed toward some junipers, my feet leaden and barely responding, anxious to saddle up behind a tree and get rid of the last of the Prineville coffee.

"Hey – best watch fer snakes over toward the water there, buckaroo," Simmons yelled. "Rattlers like it where's it's nice 'n cool, ya know."

I understood well enough that the ornery bastard was enjoying himself at my expense, but I kept a watchful eye regardless. Moments later I hobbled back to my horse. The old boy was content to stand easy and wait for me to remount, but Simmons had other ideas first.

"Best let the horses drink some 'fore we move on," he said. "Just go easy when you take 'em across to the edge, what with the snakes and all lined up along the bank like cowgirls at a hoedown. And fer god's sake, don't let 'em go on slurpin' too long – makes 'em sick. Then we can head on out."

We didn't see any snakes, but I noticed that even Kohlmeyer kept a wary eye on the creek bank as he let his roan drink from the lazy-flowing water.

Simmons looked at his watch a few minutes later, glanced momentarily at the position of the sun, and turned toward Kohlmeyer.

"The cabin sits at the edge of the creek, fifty yards or so up from a good-size bank, as I recall," he said. "The mine runs into a ledge that fronts the creek for a few hundred yards – right smack into the hillside. Place'd be better for some rich city artist to paint than a miner to dig, you ask me, but Big Cliff called it home for a long time and thought it had what he liked to call promise. That always made me laugh. But hell, you can't stop a man from dreamin' big dreams when gold's involved, I guess."

He pulled a packet of chewing tobacco from his back pocket, pinched out a chunk with his thumb and index finger, and tucked it inside his cheek. "If you want cover," he added after settling the plug of tobacco in place, "we might think 'bout timin' our arrival on toward dusk, though we'll pull in so's you can get the lay of the land first."

I jumped in ahead of Kohlmeyer. "If we wait that long and can't tell whether anyone's home, we spend the night in the desert with snakes and lizards," I said. "I don't like the thought of that – not that you asked my opinion."

"We'll know right off if nobody's home," Chichester said. "We play our cards right and catch 'em straight off, we'll spend the night inside with Corn and Drake hogtied and gagged. Then we bring 'em both back at first light."

"And we've got the satellite phone," Kohlmeyer said. "It's not like we're cut off from civilization."

"It's not exactly the lap of luxury, though," I grumbled.

"For god's sake, Blake, take it easy," Kohlmeyer said.

"Hey," I said, "my idea of roughing it is staying at a Holiday Inn without a swimming pool."

That got Simmons chuckling again, and he mounted his big thoroughbred and headed east once more, picking up the trail we'd been following since leaving Cathedral Rock.

"Hey, Blake," he called over his shoulder a minute later. "Know any other cowboy songs?"

"Sure," I yelled back, making myself heard over the rustling of the horses' plodding movements and the creaking saddle leather. "Why? You want to hear one?"

"Hell no." I could hear him laughing again, and he added a few seconds later, "Not in this lifetime."

I ignored the insult and thought instead about Caeli. I began to picture the two of us, driving through the mountain pass in a sleek, high-powered red convertible. The wind was blowing through her long, dark hair, and her eyes flashed with delight as the miles ticked by. The scent of the trees – big pines and firs, towering overhead – lingered in my mind, as did the numerous times that she would turn and smile at me, reaching out her hand to hold mine. I was soon lost in the reverie and ignored the torture of the trail and the horse's bouncing if steady gait and the dust that found its way into my mouth and eyes.

Should've brought a kerchief and covered my face like some Old West outlaw, I thought.

Almost ninety minutes had passed when Buck slowed to a halt, and I opened my eyes again. Simmons and Kohlmeyer were climbing down from their mounts.

Thank god, I thought before forcing my aching leg over the saddle horn and sliding to solid ground once more. I stumbled over to the spot where Kohlmeyer, McDonough, and Chichester were conferring with Simmons.

"It's another half-mile or more up the line," Simmons said, waving in the general direction that he expected us to cover on foot. "We can tie the horses here, head in, see what's what."

"Will the horses be all right?" McDonough asked. "Hate to have them run off with us out here on foot."

"No reason they'd be otherwise, lest somebody comes in to cause some mischief or rout 'em away," Simmons said. "You can leave somebody behind, I suppose, though I don't much see the sense of it. But whatever trips yer trigger works fer me."

Kohlmeyer turned my way with a question in his eye.

"Not me," I said. "I want to see what's up ahead. Besides – you heard the man. What can go wrong?"

Simmons found that humorous and started chuckling again.

"Ya know, I'm right glad yer along on this venture," he said. "Funny guy, all right. A downright funny fella."

I considered a sharp retort, but Kohlmeyer, ignoring the tracker's observations, beat me to it.

"Yeah, he's hilarious. All right, here it is," he said. "We get our gear and head out, single-file. Simmons and I will lead. Ken, you and Lieutenant Petrone bring up the rear. Blake, stick close to Patrick. Remember to stay low and keep quiet 'til we get a look at what's ahead."

I instinctively reached for the butt end of the Walther that was tucked nicely into a black leather holster and, comforted as I was when I found it, used the same hand to check for the twin sixteen-round spare magazines that I carried at the four o'clock position on my belt. I'd packed two additional magazines and two full boxes of 9mm jacketed hollow-point ammo and an additional two boxes of full-metal-jacket rounds into my rucksack, but I found myself wishing that I, too, had brought along a sniper's rifle.

Despite the heat and the discomfort that it caused while I was on the horse, I also was glad at this stage to be wearing the Kevlar vest that Kohlmeyer insisted on for the participants of his hunting party.

We started out moments later, and I was surprised that my heart already was hammering loudly.

Won't be long now, I thought. *One way or another ...*

FORTY-SEVEN

AND THEN THERE WAS ONE

TUESDAY, 8:45 P.M.
FIFTH WEEK

We could see the cabin in the distance. A thin wisp of smoke trailed from a cockeyed chimney made of stacked coffee cans that were somehow secured with chicken wire and weathered duct tape.

"Somebody's home," I muttered. "Or somebody's at least close by."

"Exactly," Bill Kohlmeyer said softly. "And that's exactly what bothers me – not knowing where that somebody is."

We'd snuck up on Little Cliff Corn's cabin in the wilderness east of the John Day Fossil Beds a few minutes earlier and were waiting for twilight to settle in before getting a closer look at the place. Despite steady, attentive surveillance with the three pairs of binoculars we'd brought along, we glimpsed no movement, other than the smoke from a wood fire that we could smell from the catbird seat where we'd positioned ourselves: fifty feet or so up a rocky embankment that overlooked Johnny Creek and the surrounding countryside.

Monte Simmons, our guide through the scenic desolation to this remote way station, estimated that we were fourteen miles east of Highway 19 as the crow flies.

Given the bleakness of the terrain, it might as well have been a thousand miles.

We soon spotted the tail end of a single all-terrain vehicle that was parked on the far side of the cabin, east of where we were positioned. We saw no sign of the Jeep that Little Cliff and the man we thought to be Nick Drake had used to disappear into the desert after the judge in Canyon City foolishly granted bail to the former head of the John Day police force.

The ATV led us to believe that only Little Cliff would be found on this trip.

Or maybe he's dead and Drake is inside the cabin ...

"Might be in the mine – whoever it is," I said, nudging Kohlmeyer's arm as he scanned the area through the high-powered binoculars that he'd carried to the site.

"And he might be on the moon for all we know," he replied, though he swung the binoculars toward the mine's opening, 200 yards northeast of the cabin. "No sounds, though – nothing to indicate anyone's working inside. Then again, it's late. Maybe he's in there and not working."

I could tell even without binoculars that the mine was a ramshackle affair, judging by the mishmash of support beams that framed the entrance on the southern face of the embankment. I shuddered at the thought of working inside it – even if the payout might be a gold bonanza.

"The some tells us somebody's nearby, either in the mine or the cabin, or he's not here at all and somebody else is," I said. "Let's have a look at the place. Why wait?"

" 'Cause you are like to get your ass shot off, for one thing," Kohlmeyer said.

"No windows on this side, though," I countered. "If you're inside, how would you see anyone coming down the hill if there's nothing to look through but walls?"

Kohlmeyer scanned the cabin again, taking his time. I got the feeling that he was checking every foot of the hard-scrabble exterior wall that faced us – a patchwork of plywood and particle board and scraps of hammered tin that'd been molded to fit on the corners – looking for an opening through which an occupant could watch the outside world.

"Sun's dropping fast along that ridgeline," he said after a minute passed, and he waved his free hand back toward the west. "It'll be dark soon enough. Let's hold on – wait a bit. Then we can have a look."

Petrone, who'd commandeered one of the sets of binoculars, pulled the lenses from his eyes and glanced first at Kohlmeyer and then at me. "The dark'll play into his hands more than it will ours," he said. "He knows his way around that layout – cabin and mine both. We don't. That'll give him an advantage when the time comes – if he's in there."

The logic was sound, and Kohlmeyer gave it some consideration. It was one of the things that I'd come to admire about him since the Bohn/Flowers murders placed us in the same orbit: Unlike a lot of high-powered individuals who work their way into decision-making positions, Kohlmeyer doesn't believe that he's always right, nor does he always insist on the last word.

He'd never make it as a newspaper publisher.

"What do you suggest?" he eventually said.

"Only that some careful reconnaissance wouldn't hurt," Petrone said. "I'm willing to have a look around – unless you'd rather have someone else do it."

Kohlmeyer nudged Chichester. "Any thoughts on this, Ken?" he asked.

Chichester gave the question a moment's consideration. "We might be wasting time that could be put to better use," he said. "But I'm not crazy about placing somebody in harm's way to save a little daylight."

"Nor am I, though he makes a good point," Kohlmeyer said. "Still, if anyone's going down there, it's me. It's our case; our lead, thanks to Blake here; our murders to solve, too. But it's my responsibility."

"Not a chance," McDonough said quickly. "With all due respect, Chief, you're too valuable to run down there by yourself. I'll go. It's my job."

"No, Patrick," Kohlmeyer said. "I'll go – the rest of you stay put and keep a sharp eye."

"Forget it, Bill. I'll go down," I said. "It was my lead that got us here and my job to follow it up."

I didn't wait for a reply. I scrambled up and, reaching for my holstered P99, started down the hill.

McDonough grabbed my shoulder and spun me around before I'd made it beyond a few steps. "No you don't, Blake," he said. "Nice try, but you're staying put."

I didn't have the chance to argue. He brushed past me and sidestepped his way down the hillside, moving cautiously in an effort to avoid kicking up dust or having loose rocks and gravel clatter on the slope in front of him.

I'd just made it back to the top of the ridgeline when the first of a half-dozen rapid-fire gunshots shattered the silence. Kohlmeyer grabbed my belt with one hand and tugged me hard to the ground, cursing loudly as he dropped the binoculars and reached for his sniper's rifle.

McDonough, the apparent target of the gunfire, seemed to be unhurt by the initial rounds and was now scrambling a rapid zigzag course directly toward the cabin instead of away from it, as I would have thought, moving quickly but still maintaining his balance. I initially thought that he was crazy, and I could hear Kohlmeyer muttering, "Get out of there, Patrick – get the hell out of there," until it dawned on both of us that no other cover was available.

McDonough reached the cabin's northwest corner and slid safely to the ground, pressing against the building's foundation. Temporarily safe, he pulled his back against the wall and gave us a thumbs-up, indicating that he was all right, before returning both hands to his Glock.

"One gun only," Chichester said in a voice that was little more than a whisper.

Petrone, who was positioned immediately to Kohlmeyer's right, said, "Sounds like a rifle – a brush popper of some sort."

"Hunting rifle, I'd say," Kohlmeyer said. "Maybe a thirty-thirty or a three-oh-eight," he added a moment later, and I was struck again by the calm professionalism of the officers.

"I don't understand how he saw us," I offered. "No windows."

"Must be a spotter's hole we can't see," Kohlmeyer said. "Anyone catch a barrel poking out the wall?"

We all shook our heads, but there didn't appear to be another logical explanation for the sudden gunfire.

Simmons, who was twenty yards behind us, well away from the rim, kept his head low and remained flat on the ground.

"Hey – you all right down there?" Kohlmeyer called, swiveling his head around.

"Yeah. I'm OK," Simmons called back before adding, "considering the lunacy of this whole damn adventure." He spit, dribbling tobacco juice down his chin.

"Got that right. Stay put till I tell you otherwise," Kohlmeyer said.

He looked down the hill toward McDonough, cupped his hand to the side of his mouth, and yelled loudly: "Cliff Corn. This is the police. We have you surrounded. Come out with your hands high in the air. Do it now."

The call was met with silence, and Kohlmeyer waited for another few seconds before repeating the identical phrase, adding the same emphasis to each word.

Nothing.

He swiveled sideways again and nudged Petrone. "What do you think?"

"We need to get your guy out of there in one piece. How 'bout we flank the cabin?"

"Good – clear enough he doesn't want to play ball," Kohlmeyer said before glancing at Chichester. "Ken?" he asked in shorthand.

"Flanking makes sense. How about I head south fifty yards and scramble down toward the creek? Then I'll come in from that direction."

"I'll do the same from this side," Petrone said, "and swing in from the back, the north – unless you've got another suggestion."

"No, that's good," Kohlmeyer said. "I'll follow the ridgeline another hundred yards beyond and take the far side, to the east. That gives us eyes on three sides – and Ken can cover the door."

"What do you want me to do?" I asked.

"Nothing. Stay here; stay out of it – out of the way," Kohlmeyer said.

"Come on, Bill. I didn't come all this way to hide. I can help," I said, angry that I was again engaged in this conversation.

"You can help by staying clear of fire, Blake – and keeping Simmons company."

Before I could argue, Chichester said, "What do you want to do for a signal, Bill? Maybe Blake can help with that."

Kohlmeyer briefly gave it some thought. "All right, tell you what. Blake, you'll be able to see all of us from this position once we get in place," he said. "Wait 'til we're set and each one of us gives you the hi-sign when we're ready – a wave of the arm. Then pump some rounds in the side of the wall down there. Don't rush – just steady fire. You can do that, right?"

"Standard bolt action. Piece of cake," I said.

"Good. And Blake – make sure you shoot that damn thing well away from Patrick. You hit him, god forbid, you answer to me. Got it?"

"Sure, Bill. No problem."

"Good. That'll make whoever's in the cabin keep his head down, and it'll give us time to get down the hill and storm the place. That sound all right to everyone?"

Petrone muttered a muted reply and handed over the sniper's rifle before pulling out his Glock. Chichester already had drawn his pistol and reflexively checked the magazine.

Kohlmeyer glanced briefly at both men, nodded his head almost imperceptibly, and gently whispered, "Be sure to let Blake know when you're set. He sets the tone – got it?" Getting no argument, he added, "All right then, let's be careful. We head out and get this done."

A minute or so later, I could hear Simmons stirring below me. "Hey, Blake," he called.

"Yeah?"

"Be sure you don't point that thing down here."

That struck me as funny, despite the seriousness of the situation, and I chuckled but didn't reply, instead watching Kohlmeyer and Petrone on my left and Chichester on my right as they worked their way into position just below the exposed edge of the ridgeline. I spotted two adolescent eagles in the distance, circling a red-tinged butte, effortlessly riding the air currents, and I began to consider how far we'd come from AJ Bohn's Raptor's Ridge. It dawned on me that the dead timber baron's estate was a place that was as imaginary as any that you were likely to find in a fairy tale – a place that wasn't real.

But this is real enough, I thought, keeping watch as the eagles climbed lazily toward the heavens. *This place – all of the dust and dirt and grit and sand, and those two raptors off in the distance – that's as real as it gets.*

McDonough, who hadn't moved from his position at the cabin's foundation, spread his arms outward, imitating a parson's oratory, asking what was going on. I pointed off toward the south, where Chichester had gone, and then to the northeast, toward Petrone's and Kohlmeyer's path, hoping to convey that a rescue was under way. I wasn't sure whether he understood my efforts at long-distance sign language, especially in the vanishing twilight, but he sent me a thumbs-up sign and clasped his Glock, pointing the barrel skyward, his head swiveling from side to side as he continually assessed the situation.

Chichester arrived first and waved that he was ready. Petrone, positioned directly behind the cabin, signaled next. Kohlmeyer had more ground to cover, and it was another three minutes before I caught sight of his arm, flashing up and down. It would be fully dark in another ten minutes or so, and I figured that now was as good a time as any. I took aim at the center of the cabin's west-facing wall, drew a deep breath, and slowly squeezed the trigger.

The rifle bucked hard into my shoulder, and I cycled the bolt, forcing another round into place, and moved the target line five feet down and to the south – away from McDonough's position. I fired again, caught sight of the three officers moving crisply down the hill, and fired off three more rounds, each time moving the target line downward and to the right as Kohlmeyer, Petrone, and Chichester all found precious shelter along the cabin's foundation.

Now what? I wondered.

"Cliff Corn. Come out of there with your hands high in the air," Kohlmeyer called, his voice carrying in the cool desert air.

"Like hell I will," a voice called from inside the cabin, and I recognized it instantly as Corn's. "Who's out there? What the hell d'ya want? Get off my land."

"State Police," Petrone hollered. "You're surrounded. Come out with your hands up."

"Ain't gonna do it. Come and get me, you filthy bastards," Corn replied. His message was punctuated by two rounds of what sounded like handgun fire, originating from somewhere inside the cabin.

I remember thinking at the time that it was odd – that he'd been firing a high-powered hunting rifle moments earlier and now had switched to a handgun, but I dismissed it as the events quickly unfolded.

"Hold your fire," Kohlmeyer shouted to his men. He waited for a moment and called out again, clearly enunciating each word precisely, as though he were the master at a spelling bee for grade-schoolers: "Corn – only one way this ends well. Come out now and no one gets hurt."

"Piss off," Little Cliff yelled. "I ain't turnin' myself in – not to the likes of you. And I don't care who you are."

I waited for more gunfire, but it didn't come.

"Hey, Little Cliff." The voice made me jump. Simmons had joined me on the ridgeline, and he cupped his hands around his mouth and called out, loudly again, "Monte Simmons here."

That was met with more dead silence until, a moment later, Little Cliff called back: "Simmons? What the hell d'ya want?"

"To save your worthless hide, you prick. Give it up," Simmons called. "These boys is serious – yer surrounded. No chance you get away from this. Ain't no way out save through that front door. Take it 'fore yer full of holes."

Nothing.

"Come on out – then we all go home," Simmons called once more, his thick hands still cupped at the sides of his mouth.

"Did you bring these bastards here, damn yer filthy hide?" Corn shouted after another suspenseful minute passed.

"Sure did," Simmons called. "Happy to. Question is, you wanna live or not?"

"Hell, I ain't sure yet," Corn shouted, and that made Simmons snort and poke me hard in the arm, as though we both were listening to a joke that no one else either heard or understood.

"Well, you do whatever you think best, Cliffy – just like always," Simmons hollered after he composed himself. "Ain't nothing to me one way or t'other."

He was laughing again, and he looked at me with a widespread, lopsided grin, dribbling tobacco juice from the left side of his mouth. "That silly bastard's like to end up gettin' hisself kilt," he said, speaking casually, as though we were conversing in a restaurant or after Sunday church. "Stupid as he is, he likely warrants a good killin' about now. Some folks just don't deserve savin' – despite my best efforts."

He must've found that last line funny because he started chuckling again.

I didn't bother to respond; the situation was so surreal that I was hard-pressed to think of an adequate reply.

It was mostly dark now, but I caught a glimpse of Petrone gesturing toward Chichester and McDonough, and I figured that he'd picked up a signal from Kohlmeyer at the opposite corner of the cabin, out of my range of sight.

"Last chance, Corn," Kohlmeyer shouted, his voice calm and steady. "Give it up and you live to fight another day."

The chief's words were greeted by a lingering silence, and Simmons poked me again. "Why not touch off another round into that side wall – give him somethin' else to think about?" he said.

It wasn't a bad idea, but Little Cliff jumped in first. "All right, dammit. I'm comin' out," he hollered.

"Hands high then; no funny business," Kohlmeyer yelled. "We see a gun, you're dead before you hit the ground."

"I hear ya," Corn called.

He emerged from the cabin a moment later. Petrone and Chichester, who were closest to the entrance, converged on him simultaneously, kicking his feet out from under him and cuffing him once he was flopping on the ground.

"Secure," Petrone called seconds later. Kohlmeyer and McDonough, who'd circled the cabin, emerged from the shadows on the far side, their pistols covering Corn's prone body. I could hear the four of them conferring briefly, though I couldn't tell what was being said.

That's when the high-pitched whine of a hunting rifle cracked the still air again, and Ken Chichester was driven off his feet and landed hard on his back in the dirt. He remained perfectly still as Kohlmeyer, Petrone, and McDonough scrambled for cover once again.

"What the hell?" Simmons mumbled as he slithered rapidly below the ridgeline, abandoning his position next to me.

"We lost track of Drake," I muttered, talking as much to myself as I was to Simmons. "Bad mistake."

FORTY-EIGHT

THE START OF A NOT-SO-FINAL STAND

TUESDAY, 10:09 P.M
FIFTH WEEK.

Ken Chichester hadn't moved since a single shot from what sounded like a high-powered rifle sent him thudding to the ground moments earlier.

I already knew. I was keeping a silent vigil on his prone form from on top of the ridgeline overlooking Little Cliff Corn's desert cabin and mining operation, holding out hope that I didn't believe in.

"Come on, Ken," I muttered, more than once. "Get up and get out of there."

But the State Police liaison officer hadn't moved since he'd been struck down while placing handcuffs on the one-time John Day police chief – or at least he hadn't moved so far as I could tell. The sun had long since set; the only light available was the expanse of stars overhead and a three-quarters moon that bathed everything in faint glow and dim shadow. Even at that, I could see Chichester's dark form on the ground, unmoving.

Everything else was just a guess.

The shooter remained inside the cabin – or at least I figured that he was still inside. Bill Kohlmeyer and his aide, Patrick McDonough, both scattered when the shooting began, dragging the shackled Corn with them. I'd also lost track of Timothy Petrone and had no idea where he was at the moment, though I figured that he'd be somewhere close by, vigilantly watching for movement inside the cabin that most likely shielded Nick Drake.

We could now add sniper to Drake's resume, tucking it into place beside serial killer and psychopath and lunatic and cold-hearted bastard.

I scanned the area surrounding the cabin, peering around the sights of the sniper's rifle, looking for any movement that might indicate what had happened to the good guys. But I saw nothing of interest, even as my eyes continued to adjust to the darkness, and glanced again at the spot where Chichester had fallen. I was hoping for some signs of life – hoping that he might've somehow been merely stunned by the gunshot and had crawled to safety since I'd last looked.

That's when Kohlmeyer again took charge.

"Nick Drake," he called forcefully, his words ringing in the still night air. "Come out of the cabin with your hands high in the air. Do it now."

The deep, commanding voice abruptly pulled my eyes off Chichester's prone form.

An eerie silence followed.

Monte Simmons, who was several yards below me on the ridgeline, began to crab-crawl back to the top. I heard the crunch of the gravel against his forearms and thighs and the scrape of leather biting into the hardpan from his cowboy boots. He grunted as he reached my side and, keeping his head purposely low, poked hard at my arm.

"Touch off a couple rounds into that wall, Blake," he whispered, gesturing with his hand. "Give that boy somethin' to think about. Might even hit him and end this."

"It's a bad idea," I muttered.

"Sounds damn good to me."

"First off, I don't know where our guys are. Second, the bastard in that cabin doesn't know where we are right now, but he will if I start shooting."

Simmons grunted his disapproval. "If that's Drake down there, like we both think, he ain't worth the effort to save," he said. "And he ain't gonna see us up here and him inside that cabin."

"He saw McDonough well enough," I said, still whispering. "Must be holes cut into the walls."

Simmons pondered that. "The chances of him lookin' out one of them holes at the same time you fire a round is damn unlikely," he said. "Shoot the bastard. He deserves it."

"I might hit our guys," I said.

"Hit that wall and you won't be nowheres near 'em. Look, you don't wanna do it, give me the damn rifle. I can hit what I aim at; won't have to worry 'bout shootin' one of yers."

The back-and-forth was interrupted by Kohlmeyer's booming voice.

"Nick Drake. We know you're in there. We know all about you and what you've done. Give yourself up. You're surrounded. There's no way out of this but through the front door."

An unfathomable silence ensued, and I actually began to consider Simmons' suggestion to accent Kohlmeyer's words with some firepower. But Drake – if the shooter inside was, in fact, the serial killer – finally took the bait that Kohlmeyer was dangling.

"You don't know nothin'," he called. "Clear on out 'fore I kill every last one of you. That includes you, Simmons." He paused a moment and yelled out again: "I know yer there, Monte. I know you brung that rabble here. I'll save you 'til last – ain't nothin' to me."

I sensed the sudden intake of breath from Simmons when he heard his name, and his body stiffened when the threat of death was called out. But he didn't respond; he remained stationary on the ridgeline, his eyes just above the rim, staring down into the semi-darkness below.

"What's your history with Drake?" I whispered, but Simmons ignored me. I was about to prompt him again when Kohlmeyer's voice boomed from his hiding place.

"Give it up, Drake," he called. "Walk out now with your hands high. That's the only way you'll see tomorrow."

The call went unanswered, and the seconds turned to minutes and then dragged on as the night grew ever blacker. It was fully dark now, and I was convinced that Drake could simply walk out the cabin door and disappear.

Then again, he could just as easily walk out the cabin door and slit a few throats before he disappeared into the night.

The thought was not reassuring. I pulled my Walther and placed it on the ground near my right hand, just in case the fight came to close quarters and I wouldn't be able to swivel the sniper's rifle fast enough to make it useful.

"Blake," Simmons whispered. "No more screwin' around. Pump a couple rounds in that wall. We gotta stir up some action – make something happen 'fore he gets a leg up again."

"Forget it," I said, surprised at how easily my words carried, and lowered my voice another notch. "Kohlmeyer can do that from wherever he is if he wants. Besides, they might be sneaking up right now, ready to storm the place. I'm not going to chance hitting our crew."

"Well, somebody's gotta do somethin', dammit. Otherwise, that sumbitch is gonna lick on outta here and never be seen again – and that's if we're lucky," Simmons said, his voice a thready whisper now. "If we ain't lucky, he'll kill us on the way by." He paused a moment and added, "All this'll be for nothin'. Can't let that happen."

"How do you know Drake?" I asked him again.

"Long story," he muttered.

"So talk – make it quick," I said.

"Short version is everybody in John Day's related in one way or t'other," he said. "You ain't gotta go far to find the hint of a neighbor in every woodpile in town."

"You're related to Drake?" I persisted.

"More or less."

"That means, by extension, you're related to Corn. Right?"

"Yeah. I guess you could say that."

"I'm not saying it. You are. How close are you?"

"Not all that," he replied. "No need to make a big deal 'bout it. Not one of 'em means much to me – 'specially Drake. He was a bad seed growin' up – everybody knew it, then as now. Trouble was, nobody did nothin' 'bout it. He might'a been stopped back then, ya know – when he was in his teens and the killin' of cats and dogs and strangers was all that kept 'im busy. I guess Big Cliff's to blame, though he tried to save 'im. Then, when the Army got 'im, well, all bets was off. They took a bad seed and made it worse. Can't say I'm surprised how he turned out. Not sure how it could be worse."

"You said strangers. Mrs. Sours mentioned an 11-year-old boy – and dogs and cats. But she never said anything about strangers."

"Likely she never knew. I did, though. So did Big Cliff – Little Cliff, too, more'n likely. An' I'm guessin' ya already know he kilt his own mother."

I was formulating a dozen more questions when the clabber of skidding rock from below drew my attention.

"Blake? You still up there?"

The voice, theatrically whispered but easily carrying to where I was positioned, belonged to Petrone. Judging from the sound, he was immediately below us but well down the ridgeline.

"Yeah," I whispered back. "What's up?"

"We're going in exactly five minutes from now. Set your watch. When you hear the shooting, aim for the middle of the cabin wall and fire 'til you hear otherwise. Got it?"

"Yeah," I whispered. "Got it. How's Ken? Did the vest save him?"

"He didn't make it. Mark your time now – be ready."

The rocks clattered again, and Petrone was gone.

I checked the time on my digital watch, pushing a button to activate the light inside so that I could read the numbers. I tried not to think about Ken Chichester, who was lying dead on the hardpan below us. But Petrone's simple words – *"He didn't make it"* – kept replaying in my head, like an old record that was stuck on the same line of a sad song.

I occupied my time in other ways while waiting for the gunfire to start. A few whispered commands to Simmons produced a rucksack from a stash of equipment down the hill, and I fumbled inside until I located a box of 7.62x51mm ammunition for the FN SPR sniper's rifle. I methodically loaded the rounds and began counting off the time in my head.

Simmons was on my right flank again. I could hear his steady breathing and sensed that he was excited about the prospect of pending violence. I wondered again about his connections to Drake and Corn and what it must feel like to have a serial killer climbing about the limbs of the family tree. But my mind kept repeating the same phrase, again and again – despite my best efforts to put it out of my head:

He didn't make it.

He didn't make it.

He didn't make it.

It was damn depressing. I'd liked Chichester. He was a good guy who cared about the law and the State Police force and the people he worked with and the citizens he served, and I wondered whether he had a family and, if so, who was going to tell them about his death. And I considered how impersonal it all sounded in the cold, dark night of the empty desert. Then another phrase popped into my head, and I mentally repeated it, again and again:

I'm sorry for your loss, ma'am.

I'm sorry for your loss.

I'm sorry for your loss.

I was startled by sudden bursts of gunfire erupting from below – flashes of flame from the barrels of the rapidly firing Glocks – and the booming, echoing sounds that rolled up the walls of the ridge. I aimed at the dark outline of the cabin's west wall and squeezed the trigger, then repeated the action twice more. All the while, the volley of gunfire from below bellowed off the sides of the ridge that framed the cabin and rumbled and cascaded across the darkness.

And then it was over, and Kohlmeyer call out.

"Hold your fire – hold your fire."

Kohlmeyer and Petrone had positioned themselves on either side of the cabin's entrance and kicked the door in while firing dozens of bullets into Corn's rustic slice of heaven, using the thirty-plus-round high-capacity magazines. McDonough was stationed behind them, close to where Chichester's body was unceremoniously lying dead in the dirt, guarding Little Corn while hoping to catch a glimpse of Drake through the open cabin door.

I was waiting for some good news: a call of "Got him" or "Subject's down" or something along that line – the kind of line you'd expect from well-trained officers working in dangerous circumstances.

But instead of a call-out from the cops, Little Cliff started laughing loudly in a strange, high-pitched cackle that made the hairs on my arms and neck stand up.

"Ain't gonna find him inside," he sang out before breaking into another round of eerie, shrieking laughter. "Ain't gonna find him a'tall, lest he wants ya to."

"Dammit," Kohlmeyer called out seconds later. "He's gone – he's not inside."

"Ah, hell," Simmons, who was at my side, muttered. "That surely ain't good, neither."

He slid down the bank behind me at that point. I figured that he was looking for a place to hide and considered, for a fleeting instant, joining him as Corn's laughter reverberated off the cabin walls and the ridgeline and the sparse vegetation of the cold, heartless, black desert that surrounded us all.

FORTY-NINE

A SHOT IN THE DARK

TUESDAY, 11:02 P.M.
FIFTH WEEK

We gathered warily outside moments later, after Bill Kohlmeyer discovered a disguised trap door in the cabin floor that opened to a roughhewn tunnel. Clumsily hacked out of the hardscrabble and supported by scrap plywood and timbers, it dropped four feet into the earth and ran at a forty-five-degree angle back toward the embankment behind us.

Nick Drake was nowhere to be found, and Little Cliff Corn couldn't stop cackling in that same, high-pitched laugh that'd made the hairs on my arm and the back of my neck stand straight up moments earlier.

It seemed odd for our posse to gather without Ken Chichester looming quietly in the background, taking in the various points of view, speaking only when he could add something meaningful.

"Where's Simmons?" Kohlmeyer asked after taking stock of the situation.

"He lit out when he heard Drake wasn't dead," I said, sweeping my hand toward the west to indicate the general direction where he'd fled. "That's as good as I can tell you."

Corn laugh uproariously at that simple declaration, and Petrone jerked hard on the plastic handcuffs that secured Little Cliff's wrists, forcing him to momentarily whelp instead of cackle.

"Knock it off," Petrone hissed in Corn's ear. "I won't tell you again."

Corn grunted once but remained silent.

Kohlmeyer turned his attention to me. "Simmons say where he was going?" he asked, clearly annoyed, though I couldn't tell whether he was angry with Simmons for disappearing or with me for allowing him to vanish.

Maybe he's pissed at both of us, I thought, and the image of Chichester's dead body, lying prone in the dirt, again ran through my head.

"I don't know, Bill," I said. "Maybe he went to get the horses; maybe he skedaddled. He didn't say anything. He was there one minute and then gone. But he said something interesting: He's related to Drake and our crazy friend Little Cliff here."

"That right?" Kohlmeyer asked, his eyes flicking toward Corn. "You and Simmons related?"

"You bet," Corn said, the smile on his face widening. His eyes were wet and shiny from his ongoing laughing jag, and he turned his head far to the right and down to his shoulder, wiping the moisture on his cheek by using the collar of his dirty flannel shirt. He tugged hard at the cuffs again and added, "Everybody in John Day's related in one way or t'other. High time you figured it out – might save you askin' so many dumb questions."

I could sense the wheels turning in Kohlmeyer's head again – likely in the same direction that my own gears were grinding away. We now not only had to be concerned about Drake's whereabouts, but we also couldn't be sure of Simmons' loyalties. It was plausible, in fact, that we now had two enemies hovering in the darkness. And despite my best efforts at instant recollection, I couldn't recall whether Simmons was carrying a firearm.

If he's like everyone else over here, he's probably got at least one pistol tucked away, along with a hunting knife.

Not good, I thought.

I shifted the sniper's rifle from one hand to the other, suddenly aware of its heft.

"Where's the tunnel lead?" Kohlmeyer eventually asked, directing the question to Corn.

"Climb down inside, see for yerself," Corn said.

He started cackling again. Petrone yanked hard on the 'cuffs, which brought the laughter to a quick halt.

"Talk now or later – makes no difference," Petrone said. "One thing's damn sure: You'll talk, and plenty, before we see daylight again."

Petrone's anger was palpable, and I figured that he, too, was thinking about Chichester's death, blaming it as much on Corn as he did on Drake.

"Corn. Where's that tunnel lead?" Kohlmeyer said.

Petrone again yanked on Little Cliff's handcuffs, and the big man grunted audibly and hissed, "A place you bastards won't find him. Not unless you can see in the dark."

"Gotta be the mine," I said. "Where else would it go?"

Corn scowled and inadvertently glanced to the right, where the mine entrance was situated, fifty or so yards away.

"Good place to start," Kohlmeyer said.

"We'll have to wait for daylight," Petrone said. "Can't see much otherwise."

"Wait that long and he'll be gone," Kohlmeyer replied.

"Maybe this'll help," McDonough said, stepping from the cabin with two miner's lanterns in hand.

"What about this fool?" Petrone asked, tugging at Corn's cuffs again. "We can't drag him into that mine."

"Let's hogtie him and leave him in the cabin," McDonough suggested. "Plenty enough rope. We can strap him to a chair – even anchor him to a wall."

"Good," Kohlmeyer said. "Get to it, Patrick. And hand me one of those lanterns."

McDonough offered up a lantern, and he and Petrone tugged Little Cliff none-too-gently up the two crude steps that led inside while I stepped in line behind Kohlmeyer's brisk march toward the mine's entrance, rounding the right side of the cabin.

The sudden crack of a rifle rang out in the same instant that a high-velocity round whistled into the cabin's frame, splintering the wood a couple of inches above the chief's head. He promptly dropped to the ground and scrambled around the cabin's south-facing wall, cursing under his breath as he found cover beside me.

"You all right?" he whispered.

"Yeah. You?" I replied.

"Near as I can tell. God a'mighty."

Petrone joined us near our hiding spot, a few feet from the cabin door. Kohlmeyer was staring at the building's mottled corner.

"That come from the mine?" Petrone asked softly.

"Most likely – didn't see the muzzle flash, though," I said. "Anybody hit inside?"

"Everybody's good – even Corn," Petrone said. Then, to Kohlmeyer, "What do you think, Chief?"

"No good," Kohlmeyer said. "The light's no good. He can sneak out any time and attack, or run – or both. With the training he's had, Army Rangers …"

His voice trailed off, but it was clear that we all were concerned about the prospect of a former Special Forces operative running amok in the darkness.

"Let's pin him down before he can act," Petrone said. "I'll take the far end of the west corner – plenty of cover, and it offers a good look at the entrance."

"Sure – that's good," Kohlmeyer said.

McDonough was out of the cabin again, and Kohlmeyer directed him with a couple of hand motions to stay close. Then he turned his attention to me.

"All right, Blake. Head down to the creek bank and use it for cover to move east, upstream." He pointed with his right hand as he spoke. "Find yourself a spot twenty or thirty yards away where you'll have some cover but can get a good look at the mine. Train that rifle on the entrance. Whistle up a signal once you get into place. Got that?"

"No problem," I said.

"Good. The object is to get inside and hunt the bastard down, or smoke him out somehow – put an end to this thing. But we've got to keep him inside to make it happen, and we need to buy time. We'll take up positions on either side of that entrance and play it by ear from there. You good?"

I nodded, and he said, "All right, let's go. Just be sure to wait for my signal."

"What's it going to be?" Petrone asked.

"You'll know it all right," he said. "Keep your heads down in the meantime – all of you."

I didn't wait for further elaboration and headed down to the creek bank, running hard and staying low, keeping the cabin between my rapidly retreating frame and the mine's entrance. The light, while scant, provided a good view of the bank, and I slipped over the rim and dropped five feet or so to a rocky shelf that lined the edge of the creek bed. I kept my head below the rim of the bank and walked upstream, staying dry for the most part, ignoring the times when I had to wade through the inches-high, gently lapping water.

I counted off the distance in my head and halted when I figured that I'd traveled thirty yards, then started looking for a spot to climb out. I found it a moment later: a depression in the earth where erosion at a gentle rounding of the stream had washed the land into a downward slope. It was filled with hefty rocks and gravel pushed up during times of high water, and it provided me with decent access out of the creek bed.

I dropped to my belly and edged forward, staying low, raising my eyes just above the bank, and eventually spotted the mine's entrance in the distance, a bit to my left now and no more than eighty yards away. The light was lousy, but I could see well enough to find what I was looking for. I set the rifle down momentarily and hefted the largest rock I could manage with two hands, maneuvering it up to the rim and placing it firmly on the edge. I grabbed the rifle again, settled in so that the barrel was just to the right of the rock, which I used for cover, and took aim at the mine's entrance.

Not bad, I thought. *Not perfect by any stretch, but not half bad.*

I considered using my barn owl screech as a signal, but it required a lot of breath and two fingers, so I settled on a simple bobwhite imitation instead. It wouldn't fool Nick Drake, but it would let Kohlmeyer know that I'd reached my destination and was ready for whatever might come next.

It didn't take long to find out: A hail of gunfire from the east and west sides of the cabin barked out in the night, with tiny tongues of flame leaping from the edges of the walls where Kohlmeyer, Petrone, and McDonough were positioned. I fired a round into the mouth of the mine, racked the bolt, fired a second shot and then a third, and slammed another cartridge into the chamber but waited this time. Sparks were flying off the rocks inside the mineshaft as the pistol bullets ricocheted and whined and rattled around the interior walls.

The gunfire died off almost as quickly as it began, and I figured that the three cops would reposition themselves and snap additional high-capacity magazines into their firearms. I was intently watching the mine's entrance, waiting for signs of life or return fire, thinking that finding Drake anywhere near the mine's mouth was an unlikely bet at best.

That's when I spotted what I thought was a shadow edging out of the west corner of the shaft, as unsubstantial as a whisper of wind in a leafless tree.

I inhaled, aimed the rifle barrel at the point where I thought the shadow might logically move to, and pulled the trigger. The rifle's harsh crack boomed loudly, which in turn sparked another vigorous round of gunfire from the three Glocks. I could tell from both sound and flame that two of the shooters were in new positions on either side of the mine's entrance; a third had taken cover behind a gnarled juniper trunk a few yards away from the cabin's northeast corner.

I chambered another round, watching intently. But the gunfire eventually died away, and we held our ground as the time slowly passed: a minute turning into another, five minutes turning into ten and then ten more. I kept waiting for Kohlmeyer to begin a new round of gunfire, or to signal some other strategy, but the night had turned deathly silent, both inside and outside of Little Cliff's mine.

I reloaded the rifle with spare cartridges from my pocket. An hour passed, and I considered heading down to the streambed and making my way back to the cabin. I held firm instead. When I counted another hour's slow passing, I rested the rifle against a rock and pulled my holstered Walther. I quietly slipped down the embankment and stretched for a moment before crawling back into position, waiting.

And waiting.

And waiting.

By the time the false dawn started to appear on the fringes of the hills to the east, I was sore and hungry and decidedly thirsty and absolutely dead tired. It wasn't long before I started thinking about a hot shower and a soft bed and Caeli Brown's gentle company.

A stone, tossed from the streambed west of me, skipped off the gravel near my face, interrupting my reverie. Kohlmeyer was waving at me from a few yards away. "Thank god," I muttered and slid down the embankment, joining him after slinging the rifle and again pulling the Walther.

"Any sign of Drake?" I whispered as I drew within earshot.

"No – nothing. He must've slipped away in the dark."

"Thought I saw someone trying to slither out of the mine when that second round of shooting started up – drew a decent bead on it. That wasn't him?"

"If it was, you missed – so far as I know, anyway. We all did. No sign of Simmons, either," Kohlmeyer said. "Seems he's disappeared, too."

Monte Simmons was a concern, all right – *maybe the bastard teamed up with his cousin and took the horses,* I thought – but we both understood that Drake was the real threat.

"You think Drake's gone?" I asked, gripping the P99 tightly, suddenly more aware of my surroundings and the vulnerability of our position to attack from above, or even from the bank on the opposite side of the creek.

"That's just it," Kohlmeyer said, pointing to a spot where we could climb out of the streambed. "I'm not sure of anything. And I don't like that feeling – not a bit."

FIFTY

INTO THE VIPER'S
PIT ... AND OUT

WEDNESDAY, 6:37 A.M.
FIFTH WEEK

Timothy Petrone stepped confidently into Little Cliff's high desert cabin and motioned to Bill Kohlmeyer.

"Just made contact on the sat phone," he said. "They're flying in two National Guard helicopters from Bend/Redmond, with some extra personnel – should be here in an hour."

"Good," Kohlmeyer said. He was busy surveying the walls of Little Cliff's ramshackle shack in the scrubland, looking for the spy holes that allowed the cabin's occupants to spot approaching trouble.

"Corn causing any more grief?" he asked a moment later.

Little Cliff remained trussed, gagged, and tied to the trunk of a juniper tree near the streambed, just south of the cabin's lone entrance. Ken Chichester's body, covered with a blanket that we'd pulled off a cot, was lying nearby.

"He's quiet for now," Petrone said. "Can't wait to get at him when this all plays out."

"Let's hope it's sooner rather than later," Kohlmeyer said. "Any good news?"

"We've got State Police and sheriff's officers coming in on ATVs, though it'll take them longer to get here," Petrone said. "We can put Ken's body on one of the choppers and get Corn out on the other one. Then we can figure out what to do next: join the search for Drake, figure out where Simmons went, or – well, whatever you decide to do, Bill. It's your show."

"You want to accompany Ken's body?" Kohlmeyer asked.

Petrone thought about it for a moment. "No," he eventually said. "I can't help Ken. I want to get the bastard who killed him, and he's still out there."

"All right, good. Let's put Corn on a chopper with Ken," Kohlmeyer said. "We can use the second chopper for aerial reconnaissance – maybe get a line on Drake, and Simmons, from up top. It could save us a lot of time."

I'd spotted another spy hole on the west wall and rapped my hand on the wood a couple of times, indicating where it was hidden, before asking, "You really think Simmons lit out with Drake?"

"If he didn't, Drake's likely to kill him and take the horses – or at least one of the horses. That's the logical thing, anyway," Petrone said.

I had my doubts but didn't offer an opinion. Discussing the what-ifs of the situation seemed to be a purely academic exercise anyway, and I had nothing but a gut feeling. But I didn't think that Simmons hooked up with Drake, or that Drake would let Simmons tag along, given their long-distance exchange just before Ken Chichester was shot. My guess was that Simmons left the camp because Drake scared him – with good reason.

Look what happened to Chichester. Look what happened to Bohn and Flowers. Look what's happened to who knows how many others before Raptor's Ridge? I thought.

"Drake is capable, determined, and he's not going to go down easy," Kohlmeyer said as he joined McDonough at the cabin's entrance. "There's nothing he wouldn't do to survive. We can't underestimate him. Not after last night."

McDonough asked the obvious question. "So what's our next move, Chief?"

"Wait for the choppers. We'll get a bird's-eye view and track him that way," Kohlmeyer said. "He's out there somewhere – maybe with Simmons …"

He let the thought trail off, and it suddenly struck me that we'd already made a number of assumptions about Drake, including his current whereabouts. It was becoming glaringly apparent that the serial killer had easily stayed a step ahead of us since we'd first placed him inside Raptor's Ridge – perhaps for reasons that we hadn't yet examined. I decided to kick a tire.

"Maybe not," I said.

"Maybe not what?" Petrone asked.

"Maybe he's not out there at all," I suggested. "Maybe Drake never left the mine. Maybe he's still in there, with plenty of supplies, waiting for us to hunt him down in the desert. Think about it: When we leave here, he just walks away."

The idea got Kohlmeyer's attention. He'd been staring out the cabin's entrance toward Chichester's body for the past couple of minutes, and he turned inside again, his face skeptical.

"Doesn't make sense," he said. "Given the chance, I'd've walked away last night – soon as it got too dark to see."

"That's just it," I said. "We'd expect him to put as much distance as he could between us and … wherever. I'm not sure he's wired that way."

The more I thought about it, the more convinced I became that we needed to eliminate the possibility that Drake was nearby before we abandoned the cabin for good.

"I don't know – sounds a bit crazy," Petrone said. "If it were me, and if I'd just killed a cop and had a chance to escape in the darkness, I'd do exactly that – get as far away as I could, as fast as I could. Hell, who wouldn't? You'd have to be nuts to stick around."

"Hard to make a case for sanity when it comes to this guy," Kohlmeyer said. "But I agree. I'd bolt."

"That's just it," I said. "It makes so much sense for him to do that, to cut and run, that it's unlikely he'd actually do it. This guy doesn't think the way we do – the way everybody does. He was trained by Army Rangers. Look what he's done so far without getting caught, or coming close to getting caught, or even being identified until now. Look at it from his view. We'd expect him to bolt because hanging around would be crazy, right? I think he's still here."

Petrone wasn't buying it.

"I don't know – no offense, Blake," he said. "Pulled up stakes and scramming is the smart move – the only move that makes sense."

"And that's exactly why I think he's still be here, right under our noses," I countered. "The very fact that he's not shooting at us tells us something. He's lulling us to sleep."

"He wouldn't shoot at us if he wasn't here, either," Petrone said.

"He does the unexpected. That's how he survives."

That last observation was met by silence, which prompted me to add: "It's at least worth checking before we blow town."

Kohlmeyer ran the whole thing through his head again, and it's a trait that I like about him. He's not one of those guys who believes that he's always right.

"We haven't checked the mine," he said a moment later. "We don't know where the tunnel leads, exactly." He looked around the room and offered a lopsided grin. "What do you think? Should we find out?"

McDonough and Petrone both indicated that it was Kohlmeyer's call, which was small comfort to the police chief.

"So how do we go about it?" he asked, as much to himself as to the rest of us. "If Drake's inside, poking our heads into that mine will be like jabbing a stick at a snake under a rock. It might be fun, but we're like to get bit."

"That's true," McDonough said. "The only change from last night is some daylight. It'll be tricky."

"Maybe not. Backup's coming within the hour," Petrone said. "That'll give us the manpower and the firepower we need to get it right – to make sure we don't miss anything and take him down for good."

"If he's still around," Kohlmeyer said.

I sensed that his instincts told him to simply charge into the mine, extracting an immediate measure of justice for Ken Chichester. But the more that I came to know Kohlmeyer during the AJ Bohn affair, the more I came to respect his judgment. That's why it didn't surprise me when he offered this:

"All right, settle in for a bit. We wait for the cavalry. Then we saddle up."

WEDNESDAY, 9:12 A.M.
FIFTH WEEK

Within two hours, the situation changed again, and for a final time.

An Air National Guard helicopter arrived from Bend and collected the body of Ken Chichester and a handcuffed and still-arrogant Little Cliff Corn, airlifting both back to Central Oregon's largest population center. A second ANG helicopter was scouring the countryside for any signs of Drake and Simmons. In addition, three State Police troopers and four Grant County deputies arrived on all-terrain vehicles, giving us a force of eleven men to determine whether Drake might've stayed behind to plot more mischief from inside the mine.

Given the serial killer's capacity for mayhem, I wasn't sure that eleven men would be enough.

Kohlmeyer, however, was determined to put an end to Drake's reign of madness, or at least to eliminate the mine as a potential hiding place. He was again directing traffic, having taken charge of the budding contingent of law enforcement officers, with help from Petrone.

"All right," Kohlmeyer said to the assembled troop, "here's the plan. We position four men on either side of the mine's entrance, starting with you two on the west side" – he pointed to two deputies – "and you two on the east side," this time pointing to two troopers. "I want you three" – more finger-pointing now – "to get up on top of the embankment over the mine and be ready to rope down after tying off on the junipers. The three of us" – referring to himself, Petrone, and McDonough – "will storm the front after we lay down some covering fire. Just don't move 'til you hear my signal. Trust me, you won't miss it. We clear?"

Everyone had been assigned a role but me, and I cleared my throat and asked the question that apparently only I was interested in the answer to:

"What do you want me to do, Chief?"

"Stay in the cabin or behind it, Blake. You can keep an eye out from here," he said, a half-grin tugging at the corners of his mouth, as though he were expecting an argument but had no intention of engaging in one. "I know you want in on this, and I get it. But I don't want you getting your ears or your ass shot off. I've got enough paperwork to do already."

"Look, Bill …"

"Just keep your head down and your eyes open when the shooting starts," he said, cutting me off. "And remember, Blake: The walls are paper-thin and won't provide much cover."

I wanted to argue the point. But the steely look in Kohlmeyer's eyes indicated that he was in no mood for debate and that he was running on some kind of internal clock, telling him, simply, that the time to move was now.

"All right then – let's get at it," he said to the group, dismissing me. "We do this by the numbers, we get our guy if he's in there – alive if we can – and we all go home to our families. That last part's damned important; keep it in mind. Questions?"

He waited for a tick and added, "OK, let's head out."

A single lingering note struck me like a sharp blow as Kohlmeyer, McDonough, and the rest of his party left the confines of Little Cliff's ramshackle cabin in the middle of nowhere:

We'd come a long way from Raptor's Ridge and the murders of AJ Bohn and Audrey Flowers, and from encounters with the Deeker brothers and Russell Vineyard and Ned McClinton and Floyd Strand and assorted other characters who were peripheral to the case in one sense and key components of it in another.

Caeli Brown, for instance.

If nothing else, the mess at Raptor's Ridge and its lingering aftermath had brought me imminently closer to Caeli.

I guess I'll have old AJ to thank for that, and I hope for a long time to come, I mused.

If ever I live so long.

The sudden sound of gunfire – rapid, staccato bursts from varying positions outside the cabin – halted my brief reverie. I pulled the P99 from its holster and quickly dropped to the floor. I then slithered toward the cabin's lone door, moving on my knees and elbows, placing as much plywood and framing timber as I could between my current position and the unseen entrance to the mine. Reaching the crude doorframe, I swung my body sideways, tucking into position along the south wall so that I could look outside toward Johnny Creek. My thinking was that I'd be in a position to act in the event that Drake somehow slipped the cordon of troopers and deputies and tried to escape the snare that we'd set for him by slipping over the embankment and into the streambed.

The initial burst of gunfire ended. I'd counted many dozens of shots from a variety of pistols and at least two sniper's rifles. This was followed by a loud whistle, the crack of a rifle, and the muffled boom of at least two flash grenades that were tossed into the mine's entrance by the officers on the west and east sides. I didn't know in advance that Kohlmeyer's crew equipped themselves with the non-lethal grenades before heading in, but it made sense. It allowed them a few precious seconds to enter the mine in relative safety.

I could hear Kohlmeyer's shouts and the ready replies of well-trained men running hard and fast on adrenalin and testosterone and righteous anger over the death of a fallen comrade.

I was expecting calls of "Hands high" and "Got him" and "Suspect secured" and "All clear" in the ensuing moments.

Instead, I heard the creak of the trap door at the northeast end of the cabin.

I'll admit now – and yes, it's long after the fact – that the prospect of Nick Drake emerging through the trap door had occurred to me at some point after Kohlmeyer ordered me to stay inside the cabin. But the thought of it actually coming about was so remote, so damned unlikely, that I'd readily dismissed it. I'd occupied my thoughts instead with the gunplay and the flash grenades and the whistled signals and the bustling activity that was taking place outside.

All I could manage now was a single whispered phrase:

"Aw, hell."

Maybe the chief overlooked the possibility in the excitement of the chase, once the helicopters and the ATVs arrived. Then again, maybe he secretly wanted me to be thrust into the heart of the action. I've thought long and hard, in the intervening months since the assault on the mine took place, that the idea might've occurred to him when he told me to stay inside the cabin.

I've never asked him about it, though, probably because, deep down, I don't want to know.

But who could say for sure, if asked, whether Kohlmeyer would even acknowledge the possibility that he just might have had it in mind? Or whether he might simply say that it was there all along but that he'd ignored it, just as I'd ignored it … because it was so damned unlikely?

At the time, though, none of that mattered.

The trap door was thrust violently upward, and the long, gleaming barrel of a rifle emerged, followed by a dusty red baseball hat and, an instant later, two dark eyes that quickly scanned the room.

Too quickly.

Because I was lying flat on my belly and tucked into an edge of the foundation near the door, the initial rapid pass that the serial killer's eyes made around the room failed to detect my presence.

As he set the sniper's rifle on the creaky wood floor and hoisted himself out of the tunnel and into a standing position, I trained my Walther on Nick Drake's chest, inhaled deeply, and said, as calmly as I could manage despite the jack-hammer beating of my heart, "Hands in the air, Drake. Now."

I was hoping that he would consider the possibilities, determine that his chances were not good, and give up on the spot. But I also knew, deep in the back of my brain, that a well-trained Ranger – and a wanted serial killer and a cop-killer besides – wouldn't go quietly, even though his chances of success were less than ideal.

But all of that consideration was wishful thinking anyway, and I knew it, too, even as it flashed through my head like electrical current streaking down a copper wire.

I thought that he'd reach for the sniper's rifle and bring it into play. But he fooled me and moved to his right, hard, grabbing at the same time for a holstered semi-automatic pistol that was strapped on his belt at the 6 o'clock position.

In my mind's eye, looking back, it all plays out in slow motion:

He has the pistol in his right hand and is swinging it toward me now. His body is falling at a steep angle of descent, making a counterstrike more difficult, and his face registers pure loathing and malevolence and penetrating evil. He's staring into my eyes, willing me to know who he is, what he is – to at last get a look inside his soul and to sense the pitiless darkness that's contained inside his wizened heart.

The Walther is set in its anti-stress trigger configuration, which shortens the pull considerably, and I fire four times in rapid succession, aiming for center-of-mass on the falling, fast-moving target. In truth, I'm hoping to hit anything – waiting at the same time for the gunfire from Drake's pistol that will snuff out my life and end any hopes of my ever seeing Caeli again.

But Drake's body hits the cabin floor with a resounding thud and skids into the east wall. The pistol he was holding clatters onto the dirty plywood and tumbles out of his hand, away from his outstretched arm. His eyes flicker once, and remain open, and he doesn't so much as twitch again.

I know that with certainty.

I kept the Walther trained on his prone body for a solid two minutes after he fell. I didn't move a single muscle, or utter a single phrase, or so much as blink my eyes a single time – not until Kohlmeyer and McDonough bolted into the cabin and cleared the room.

"Blake – you all right?" Kohlmeyer asked me.

"*Crepo il lupo*," I whispered in reply.

EPILOGUE

ALL THINGS IN THEIR PROPER PLACE

FOURTEEN MONTHS LATER

I wish that I could put a nice, tidy bow on the story and place it in a gift box under your Christmas tree, bringing everything to a logical close. But I can't. That only happens in the movies – like the ones that Audrey Flowers used to star in.

And while it's safe to say that we got most of the tale, Nick Drake's motives and movements, along with his exact number of victims, will probably never be known or fully understood.

I also can't say that I'm surprised at the way things turned out, now that it's over and the news trucks have headed north again and the TV people have gone back to covering marina fires and auto crashes – and all varieties of stabbings and shootings, of course.

If it bleeds, it leads … just as I tell my journalism students.

Here's what I can say for sure: Some of the people who were involved in the mess at Raptor's Ridge won, and others lost, and a few even lost their lives to gain their fifteen minutes of fame.

AJ Bohn already had his decades in the spotlight, but he was cashed out just the same, and for what? He would tell you, I suppose – if he were alive today – that the heart wants what the heart wants, even if it ultimately led directly to his death. At least we can say that his reputation was enhanced instead of sullied by what took place at his magnificent estate. Still, the locals were amazed when no contraband was found on the grounds; tongues around town didn't stop wagging for weeks. In the end, we can only hope that he went out with a smile on his face. The old boy deserved that much.

Audrey Flowers lost as well, although her star will continue to shine on for years to come. I caught one of her movies the other night on the late-late show. It was nice – for a brief moment, anyway – to remember what she looked like before the producers stopped calling, and age caught up with her, and AJ Bohn was the last leading man in her life. I choose to remember her that way and not as a dead body, in either a bathtub or a meat freezer.

Paul Deeker, AKA The Snarl, is buried in a shallow grave in the woods somewhere south of the estate. His brother won't give up the location, sad to say. His former minions, who told us about the violent argument the brothers had on the day that Paul disappeared, don't know, either. The State Police cadaver dogs have yet to roust the gruff, tough former Army operative from his eternal slumber. Maybe it's just as well.

Tom Deeker is serving a life term in the state pen, without the possibility of parole, for a variety of crimes, murder and accessory to murder included. He now writes letters to reporters from the local newspaper, demanding this and that, including a new trial, and sometimes a brief story will appear in print. It's generally always accompanied by a comment from the DA indicating that justice was served.

Lawrence Hultz Fuller, the aforementioned district attorney, remains as vain and as shameless as ever. I run into him from time to time, most often when I'm working in my private investigator capacity, and he usually reacts as though he's never set eyes on me before. I'll have to remind him one day that I vote regularly. One thing you can say about Larry the Loon, however: He did put a number of notches in his belt while prosecuting the various cases attached to the Bohn/Flowers case. He was re-elected in a landslide.

Nick Drake, the serial killer who murdered AJ Bohn, Audrey Flowers, and at least eighteen other women at last count, his mother included, is buried in a pauper's grave outside of Canyon City. No one attended the service. The funeral home handling burial arrangements for the state had to pay six men from Mitchell, sixty-eight miles to the west, to drive over for the day and serve as pallbearers. A non-denominational preacher was imported from faraway Bend, and I'm told that he kept his remarks both general and exceedingly short.

Little Cliff Corn, the former John Day chief of police who hauled me in for parading without a permit, was convicted of a host of crimes: kidnapping, attempted murder, accessory to murder, extortion. He was sentenced to a term of twenty-five years to life in the big house and began to sing shortly after it became apparent that no one from John Day, Canyon City, Mitchell, or anywhere else was going to rush to his aid. Much of what we learned about Drake came from Little Cliff as he pleaded for a better deal.

Monte Simmons, our guide to Little Cliff's cabin in the high desert, was spotted on horseback by a National Guard helicopter crew on the day that Drake popped out of a trap door and drew his last breath. Given the chance, Simmons didn't bother apologizing for deserting his comrades in the desert, me included. "Knowing that lunatic was on the loose was reason enough to hightail it out of there," he said. "If that means I don't get paid, well, then I don't get paid. Screw it."

Ken Chichester's wake in the rotunda of the State Capitol was a stirring public spectacle that brought a contingent of elected officials and representative law enforcement officers from almost every department in the state, and from a host of neighboring states as well. The commander of the State Police force in Oregon provided the elegant eulogy. Bill Kohlmeyer and Bob LeRoy, the county sheriff, spoke briefly at the service. Chichester's friend, Timothy Petrone, read a Robert Burns poem at the end, and a lone bagpiper provided a stirring sendoff on a Willamette Valley day that was fittingly rainy and dreary.

Betty Sours, the sweetheart in John Day whose telephone call saved my life, began courting an old high school flame she'd somehow reconnected with through the wonders of modern technology. Last I heard, she was moving to the western slopes of the Rockies, somewhere in Colorado. I figured that the town would miss her far more than she'd miss the people, or the memories, of John Day.

Timothy J. Petrone still rides herd on the State Police post in Grant County. He's been approached to become a candidate for the local district judgeship in an effort to displace the fool who'd released Little Cliff from captivity. It's my guess that Petrone would have a bright future on the bench, though I suspect he'd be happier wearing a Glock than a black robe.

Charles V. Downing was sentenced to twenty-five years to life for crimes ranging from extortion to arson, menacing to attempted murder. His lawyers have been trying to cut a deal to get him shipped to an out-of-state prison, where he'd be less likely to run into convicts he helped put away during his few years of legitimate time on the city's police force. I personally think that he should serve his time close to home, considering what he did and for how long he did it – but that's just me.

William "Buzzsaw" Stone and the other former cops who were involved in Downing's schemes all received lesser sentences. Each is doing time today in a prison at the far end of the state, where the smell of onions from nicely furrowed fields wafts daily into the air. Kohlmeyer testified at each of the trials, and in typical fashion, he didn't mince words. But why would he? The bad cops he'd inherited almost single-handedly pulled down the force that he's now charged with running.

Bill Kohlmeyer remains the capitol city's chief of police, although his political star is said to be on the ascendancy – a fact that has the current mayor nervous. Kohlmeyer continues to shake up and shape up the force, however, and I think that he's happiest there. I see him from time to time, and we acknowledge each other amiably. It's even safe to say that we respect one another, which is remarkable when you consider where we were when I first called him about the murders at Raptor's Ridge and the corruption in his ranks. I don't think that I'll get a Christmas card from him this year – but hell, who sends Christmas cards anymore?

Ron Clarin, the New York City-born officer who ratted out Downing and his cronies after briefly joining their merry band of thugs, left the state in the dead of night and headed east with the tacit blessing of the district attorney. Last I heard – through a snitch who hangs around City Hall – Clarin changed his name and is working as an ice fishing guide on the frozen lakes of Minnesota. At least it's honest work.

As to the former mayor, sitting judges, city councilmen, city inspectors, fire marshals, etc. and *ad nauseum* who were fingered by Clarin, cases are still being investigated, evidence is still being gathered, witnesses are still being debriefed, but only a few minor charges have been filed to date. One of the inspectors is suspected of taking the potshot at Kohlmeyer's house shortly after the Bohn/Flowers murders, but Larry the Loon has yet to make a case. At least two of the elected officials whose names surfaced publicly declared that they would not seek re-election. Another resigned abruptly and moved with his family to Texas, where such shenanigans are said to receive a warmer welcome.

Russell Vineyard took a hefty share of the inheritance he received from the Bohn estate and moved to Hawaii, where he bought a bungalow close to the beach and now spends his days with rum concoctions in his hands and flip-flops on his feet. I heard that he's keeping company with an exotic island beauty who's less than a third his age. Who can say which one of them is the real gold-digger?

Doctor Floyd Strand is even more of a man-about-town these days, and he was doing all right before the murders at Raptor's Ridge. He surprised me the other day when he said that he was thinking about using his inheritance to buy a sports bar; I suggested that he didn't have enough to do. The two of us play a weekly match at the local golf club, and my short game has improved because of it. Then again, he's now playing to scratch: It's best to keep your money in your wallet if you get an invite from the doc.

Edward L. "Ned" McClinton, AJ Bohn's resilient attorney, decided to expand his practice with his share of the inheritance. He re-hired his receptionist, imported a handful of top-notch Ivy League-schooled lawyers and a dozen promising and well-credentialed aides, and built a glass-and-brick showcase office on the river. He's now the new go-to guy among well-heeled jetsetters throughout the Pacific Northwest, including the software and sneakers tycoons. The career move surprised me, but hell – most everything lawyers do will take you by surprise if you pay attention.

Jim Maddaux, AKA Mad Dog, saw an uptick in his restaurant business while the news buzzards were still circling the bodies. He took full advantage for a time by introducing a handful of specials to his menu. Among them: AJ's Omelet (the inside joke was that it was stuffed with dead meat), Audrey's Salad (light and bright and tasty, with delicate greens and garnish – no inside joke at all), and Billy Boy's Big Burger (a half-pound of quality ground round with a jalapeño kick because, as the Dog has said more than once, "the chief of police in this town delivers the goods").

He also offered a special menu item for a time that he called The Biscuit's Special, in my honor. Don't ask; you won't get a logical answer anyway.

Todd Wright got his worn-out Volvo back, along with my old bucket of bolts. He sold the latter for 500 bucks, or so he said, and I applied that money to the cash purchase of a hot-off-the-line Cadillac CTS-V luxury coupe from what used to be called the Motor City Capital of the World. I had little choice in the matter. GM stopped making Pontiacs, which is what I would've bought, given the chance. The Caddy is a good substitute, though. It has a heads-up display and a bucketful of horsepower and a supercharger to boot, and it runs like a screaming breeze off the wild Pacific. It's also ridiculously fuel-hungry in an age of $4-plus-a-gallon gasoline prices. But it'll snap your neck back when you punch it off the line, and it'll do it again when you're traveling at eighty miles per hour or more through the mountain passes and decide that you want to get around that dog-slow logging truck. My guess is that it'll be a classic some day, and it's a hell of a lot of fun to drive in the meantime.

I got a few other tidbits out of the experience as well.

The most obvious item of note – the one that put me onto the front pages of the newspapers and on the TV screens for a couple of weeks – was brief title to Raptor's Ridge. My friend and attorney, *Michael Parker,* good man that he is and good to his word, wrote a contract that was solid enough, crafty enough, and pure genius enough to sail through the courts system without so much as a questioning look. Sure, it helped that McClinton was on the inside and not only supported the deal but actually was instrumental in adding a couple of clauses to the thing that put some much-appreciated cash into my pocket as well.

How much cash, you ask? That's between the IRS and me, though the new Caddy and a vacation home in Central Oregon should give you a hint.

Of course, few people wanted to see Raptor's Ridge demolished – AJ Bohn included, apparently – and the mansion's destruction was the only other true option available. Why he drafted his circuitous will the way that he did is something that he took with him to that other Raptor's Ridge. But I personally think that Parker warrants sainthood for figuring out a way to save the place. While I couldn't offer him the reward he deserved, I did send MG Mike, as I've now taken to calling him, a fully credentialed Walther MP 9mm submachine gun. It's a thing of rare beauty.

I actually held onto Raptor's Ridge for two weeks and a day – long enough to walk through every inch of the place, and to schedule a euchre marathon for the best players around – before I deeded the grounds, the mansion, and everything inside it to the state. The usual squabbles quickly ensued, and some of them linger to this day: park, museum, destination resort, corporate retreat home, a combination of all four, plus how to generate sufficient income for its upkeep. You can no doubt guess at the bedlam that ensued.

I suggested to the governor at the signing ceremony that he send a delegation to California to see how San Simeon, William Randolph Hearst's magnificent estate on the Pacific, is run. But he began squawking when the cameras stopped clicking and rattled on for a full two minutes about the financial drain that I'd personally saddled him with, as though he alone were responsible for paying the light bills. Ever the politician, he was soon spitting out phrases like "noose around my neck" and "pig in a poke," punctuated by the occasional well-timed epithet. I had to laugh at the look on his sanctimonious, jowly face when I pulled out my new cell phone and told him that I was recording his every word for that night's newscasts.

I don't think that I'm on his Christmas card list, either.

One other note: I proposed to *Caeli Brown* on the same day that I deeded Raptor's Ridge to the State of Oregon. I told her that I was hoping to trade one treasure for another –

one that was worth far more, one that was much closer to my heart. I'll never forget the look on her face. In fact, I used my very own, brand-new, slick-as-hell smartphone, the one that she'd forced into my hands a week earlier, to take her picture as she said yes.

There's no question that I came out way ahead on the deal.

You'll also find a new sign on the door leading into my recently renovated downtown PI's office. It reads, simply but eloquently:

Blake & Brown

Inside of a year, we hope to change it to Blake & Blake.

That's one change I'm eagerly anticipating.

ABOUT THE AUTHOR

William Florence is a former reporter and editor. He worked at newspapers in Michigan, Washington, D.C., South Dakota, Indiana, and Oregon for 25 years before heading the Chemeketa Community College journalism department beginning in 1993. He retired in 2015.

During his career, he was widely published in individual newspapers and wire services and in industry magazines such as *The Bulletin* for the American Society of Newspaper Editors and *APME News* for the Associated Press Managing Editors group, as well as noted travel publications such as *Arizona Highways* and *Michigan Living*.

He won writing awards in four states.

In addition to living in the West, he has traveled extensively throughout the region to gain an understanding of the land and its inhabitants. He studies Western lore, is knowledgeable about the customs and history of the Old West, and is especially well-versed in the firearms that were used during this colorful period. In his spare time, he writes the Max Blake Westerns series (available at www.amazon.com).

Mr. Florence attended colleges in Michigan and Ireland. He is a voracious reader (especially Western novels from all periods) and a movie buff (with Westerns again a favorite genre). He is married and has two adult children. His wife, Linda, a public schools administrator, is his toughest critic as well as his best friend.

*For More News About William Florence
Signup For Our Newsletter:*

http://wbp.bz/newsletter

Word-of-mouth is critical to an author's long-term success. If you appreciated this book please leave a review on the Amazon sales page:

http://wbp.bz/raptorsa

WILLIAM FLORENCE
EMERALD
RIDGE
A MAX BLAKE MYSTERY

ONE

STARDOM AND FAME

Maybe Andy Warhol was right, though there's debate that he even served up the famous everybody-gets-15-minutes quote.

Fame is a dangerous thing. It attracts, but it also repels.

I'm one of those guys who can do without it. I say that from experience; I've had my brushes with its seductive touch. My detective agency work has put my face on the front page and on TV a few times, but it's nothing that ever lasts. The news cycle keeps humming along, looking for the next big story, scandal, outrage, shiny object.

No thanks.

Here's one for you: I played in the old Tiger Stadium in downtown Detroit once, at second base, in a 10-inning game when I was in high school and our team of misfits somehow made it to the state championship. I was 17 and had no way of knowing that I'd never come as close to hitting the big time as I had on that crisp spring day, so long ago now that I don't easily recall the year.

"We just don't recognize the most significant moments in our lives while they are happening," old Archie "Moonlight" Graham told Kevin Costner's character in the baseball movie *Field of Dreams*.

Damned if he wasn't right.

No, hold on. I was on national TV ... *The Tonight Show Starring Johnny Carson.* My cousin Jerry, you see, is the fabled Dentist to the Stars, the man who keeps all of Hollywood smiling brightly, and he scored a couple of tickets when I was bumming around before finding meaningful work, long before I'd met Caeli. Hell of a deal, we all agreed, and were happy to head to Burbank and slog through the smog and the traffic and the general craziness of Southern California to experience a piece of television history.

My recollection of what took place is hazy at best – hell, it was a long time ago – but here's some of what I recall:

We had to be in our seats early, before 4 p.m., because the show was broadcast live on the East Coast and replayed later for the Left Coast crowd.

I remember that the theater was tiny, much smaller than it came across on TV.

I remember some of the general banter from the studio guy who came out before the cameras rolled and told us what was expected: watch the overhead flashing signs for instructions, applaud vigorously when prompted, no rushing the stage, no cat-calls … about what you'd imagine.

It was our luck that Johnny was off on the night we visited the City of Angels. His spot was filled by Sammy Davis Jr., even then an entertainment paragon. Robert Conrad, the star of a popular TV show of the day, was among the guests.

During his opening monologue, Sammy decided to take questions from the audience, and my arm shot up along with a hundred others, though I had no expectation that I'd be called or what I'd ask should the showbiz legend acknowledge my presence. But damned if he didn't point in my direction, and damned if I didn't figure it out a moment later, given that his glass eye was shining in the klieg lights and it was difficult to determine exactly where he was looking … or even pointing.

Still, I recovered and blurted out a question – something along the lines of, "We don't see enough of you on the big screen these days, Sammy; when are you going to make another movie?" He answered with what seemed to be a heartfelt rail at all of the sex and violence and nasty language that was readily prevalent in the movies of the day, adding that he'd consider another role only when Hollywood cleaned up its act. He was rewarded with modest applause, he took another question, and I remembered sitting there thinking, "Well, nuts. Now I've got to stay up past my bedtime and watch the same damn show that I'm watching right now."

Of course, I did exactly that.

For what it's worth, you needed a magnifying glass to spot my face in the audience, my voice (and question) was just barely audible, but Sammy seemed genuine regardless and I managed to make it through the entire TV showing before climbing into bed that night.

Somewhere, buried 650 feet in the earth in a former salt mine in Hutchinson, Kansas, a copy of that show is sitting in a metal storage tin, waiting for prying fingers that will never come to open it up again and take a look inside … a TV time capsule for eternity.

And now, thanks to the amusement of the internet, you can find the exact date of the show and even gaze at a photo of Sammy Davis Jr. behind the desk and Robert Conrad, immediately across from him, laughing uproariously, or at least appearing to do so.

Conrad is looking at the camera. It's hard to tell where Sammy is focused.

What? You were expecting the actual date? Use your own Google box.

I was at the laptop, searching for the meaning of life, or at least of my life now that I've retired. In time I started seeking out the lyrics to a Doobie Brothers song that I'd caught on satellite radio the day before and couldn't immediately fathom, even after years of hearing the tune … even after an hour of off-and-on consideration about the complexity of the lyrics, which go far beyond the typical June/Moon/Swoon that you get with mindless rock love songs.

At the time, I didn't get much past the idea that you had to hand it to a band that named itself after, well, a doobie.

What A Fool Believes, the song in question, soon morphed in my head into yet another Doobies tune, *Minute by Minute,* and I dialed up a YouTube version that ran in the background as I checked the latest stocks report, and I was about to click off the laptop and pass the day off as a total loss when I heard Caeli's Camaro pull into the garage. It took her a bit longer than usual to make it inside, and I figured that she must be bringing some work home and got up from the desk to give her a hand.

"Spotted this at the front door," she said, and she waved a folded sheet of paper in my general direction.

"What is it?"

"A flyer of some kind – from one of the area churches."

"And you know that because …"

I gave her a kiss as she slipped through the door, and she returned it with only moderate enthusiasm.

"It says so, right on the front," she said a moment later.

I'd lost track of the conversation by then and waved my hands to the side – a *What's that mean?* gesture.

"You asked how I knew the pamphlet came from a nearby church," she said.

"Yeah, right … I remember now."

"Look at the headline."

She unfolded it and pointed to the bold header: **Why Did Jesus Come to Earth?**

She handed it over at that point, and I'll confess that my answer was spontaneous, if not particularly well-considered, given my upbringing and mandatory viewings of *The Ten Commandments* during Easter week.

"I don't think it was to have me answer the front door," I said.

"Clearly. Otherwise, I wouldn't be fishing this off the porch when I get home from a hard day."

Yup. A zinger.

"Ouch. I had a hard day, too," I said.

"I can see that."

"At least I'm not in my bathrobe."

"Yes, quite the accomplishment – a lesson learned from yesterday, apparently. It's good to see that an old dog …"

She didn't finish the line – no need – and I grinned at her and tossed the flyer in the recycle bin with a nod to the heavens, trusting that an instant change in the weather and a sudden thunderclap wouldn't be my immediate reward.

"I was going to make dinner and even went to the store to buy some fresh goodies," I said, winding up for an apology of sorts.

"But …"

She flashed me the look when she said it, and every man on the planet knows exactly what look I'm referencing here.

"But the fish didn't look particularly good, and the romaine was a bit on the wilty side, and I even tried Albertson's after abandoning Safeway."

Now she appeared to be confused.

"Still no go. I figured that I'd treat you to the dinner of your dreams tonight in whatever restaurant you'd care to select: Salty's, the Riverview, Pompello's, Tapatio, Bumper's, Edgefield – you name it, and I'll wield the magic plastic when the time comes."

"Let me think about it," she said, and she looked momentarily distracted, as if she'd lost interest. "It's been a long day, and I can't shake the feeling …"

She hesitated, as though the prospect of talking about whatever she was sensing in that instant would somehow make it come true.

I was tempted to ask but didn't press, even when she brought it up again while we were waiting for our fish to arrive at Salty's, the spot Caeli eventually selected for dinner. We'd both ordered the special (rock fish with an extra helping of steamed veggies; hold the starch), and Caeli looked as serious as I'd seen her in weeks.

Or at least since it sunk in that my retirement did little more than keep me at home during the day, working two crosswords and mindlessly editing the local newspapers for grammatical miscues and researching Doobie Brothers lyrics on the side while she was overwhelmingly busy as the vice president for communications at a large area school district.

"You seem preoccupied," I said.

"Just tired. There's a lot going on."

The comment was innocent enough, but I was feeling guilty and scratched the urge to justify my existence.

"I sent an application to Mount Hood this morning."

Mount Hood is the local community college that sits within walking distance of our home in the trend-setting Troutdale community, east of Portland. I figured that Caeli would be relieved that I hadn't squandered yet another day away to nonsense.

"That's nice," she said, miles away.

"Yeah. They were looking for male models for the art classes in the fall, and I figured that I'd be a shoo-in."

"Good," she said, her mind still elsewhere. "Sounds great."

"I think I'll look particularly good, posing nude for nubile co-eds with a mind on more than their drawing skills," I added, piling on the fuel in an effort to shake her from whatever distraction occupied her attention. But it still didn't register.

"I'm wondering if I should go to the Hair Club for Men before I take my first assignment … in case the co-eds prefer a Patrick Dempsey 'do."

She didn't say anything for a moment and eventually checked her watch.

"They're slow tonight. I wonder if they rowed out there" – she waved at the Columbia River, visible through the windows – "to catch our dinner."

"I'll say it again, Caeli. You seem preoccupied."

"No. I'm OK," she said. "It's just that, well, I can't help thinking something bad is coming. Why or what, I don't know, but … something bad."

The words drifted away, and I concluded that not only was I an unlikely candidate to be hired as a male model for college art classes but that stand-up comedy wasn't going to work for me in retirement, either.

"Any idea what's prompting this?" I asked.

She shook her head from side to side – a gentle motion, slow and easy – but didn't say anything more. I knew better than to prompt her, and the fish arrived then and gave us something else to talk about. She was complimentary of the meal, as well as the wine, and she even mentioned that OPB's radio coverage of the big education story of the day included both her school district and superintendent in flattering terms.

The ride home along Marine Drive was pleasant, and the stereo, dialed into the ubiquitous satellite network, served up *What A Fool Believes* just as we pulled into the driveway.

"Hell of a coincidence," I said as I hit the garage door button and waited for the creaking mass of rickety aluminum to rise to the occasion. "I was thinking about this song earlier."

If she heard me, she didn't reply, and we were inside within minutes and Caeli was off to bed while it was still daylight, complaining of a slight headache and being overly tired.

I didn't give any additional thought to her off-hand comment that something bad was coming. Bad stuff always comes at you, regardless of your station in life or how much money you make or who your friends might be, or even who sits in the White House at any given moment. Bad stuff seems to be an equal opportunity caller.

It didn't dawn on me until much later that the Doobies tune became a No. 1 single in the same year that Sammy Davis Jr. and Robert Conrad shared a Burbank sound stage while Johnny Carson took the day off. I don't know what that says, exactly, but the essential lyric of the song, *"He came from somewhere back in her long ago,"* wouldn't truly resonate until the next day.

But resonate, it did.

Read More: **http://wbp.bz/era**

ONE

THE MILLS OF GOD
GRIND SLOWLY

Ever stop to contemplate how your life can turn on a dime?

A shift of the winds, an unexpected diagnosis, a glance in the rearview mirror (or a failure to glance behind you) – even the arrival of a single postcard in the mailbox: Snap your fingers and everything you know, everything you trusted or once took for granted, vanishes.

Bang.

Just like that.

Caeli's Uncle Jack, the former Archbishop of Armagh, was alive.

But who could tell in the initial rush of revelation whether this was good news or bad – a fact to celebrate or one to curse?

As I look back, contemplating the significance of the disclosure from the safety of time and physical distance and large bodies of water that even now help to separate the varied combatants who lined up to stake a claim, it was damned difficult to absorb and not much fun to speculate about when the news arrived.

I'll admit that I suspected the worst when the postcard showed up in the mailbox with a Vatican stamp attached.

That's likely because I'd previously seen an identical postcard, one with a British stamp, and recognized its significance.

Of course, learning that Caeli's uncle was alive was one thing – an inconvenient truth. Learning that he was under the protection of the Holy Roman Church, which historically has gone out of its way to shield legions of scoundrels and villains and other shady characters who've populated the hierarchy of the august institution for millennia, was another consideration entirely.

Jack a scoundrel?

You bet. That's exactly what he was – and he remains so in my mind.

Until a few weeks ago, I never would have placed those two words – Jack, as in Caeli's uncle, and scoundrel, as in miscreant and blackguard and scalawag – in the same sentence, paired with one another in the way that, say, Arm & Hammer or Simon & Garfunkel or Smith & Wesson are associated.

But that was before the events on Mutton Island, the 185-acre bird sanctuary off the western Irish coast, and Jack's efforts to overthrow the British government's rule in Ulster through force and violence and madcap adventure and misguided revolution. (You can read the fine details in *Emerald Ridge*, my accounting of the sordid tale, the background of which might help with what took place in its aftermath and even here, in this telling.)

The thing of it is, Caeli and I both were certain that Uncle Jack was dead, killed by steady, unrelenting machine gun fire on the island, along with his trusted right arm, Michael Corbin, and other like-minded revolutionaries who followed in the archbishop's terrorist-inspired footsteps and decided that the best way to unite the two Irelands would be to restart the historical mayhem of The Troubles.

Yeah. Exactly. What the hell was he thinking?

What the hell were any of them thinking?

We were there, Caeli and I, along with our two bodyguards-on-loan, Elmore and Leonard, planted on the barren, windswept island in a pelting rain, trying to rescue Uncle Jack from himself.

It turned out that Jack didn't want to be rescued.

Or at least, not then, he didn't.

But the situation took an enormous roundabout turn, unexpected and sure as hell unappreciated, when unnamed church officials stepped up to institute a capture of their off-the-reservation red-robed warrior, slamming him with a tranquilizer dart instead of a bullet and whisking him off Mutton Island and into waiting hands in Rome before any of us – or at least before Caeli and I – were able to see through the subterfuge.

I found this out weeks later when Jack sent Caeli a postcard depicting William Butler Yeats's tombstone in Drumcliff churchyard, County Sligo, with the final three lines of the great poet's 1933 masterwork *Under Ben Bulben* engraved on the stone monolith:

Cast a cold Eye
On Life, on Death,
Horseman pass by.

It was the same message that started the events leading to our arrival in Ireland and eventually on Mutton Island – the same message, delivered on an identical postcard, that resulted in, among other things, our ownership of a large estate on the Irish coast, near Limerick.

I eventually was able to confirm that church bigwigs, hoping to avoid the scandal that would accompany a rogue archbishop spraying gunfire across the land he so fondly called home, brought the once honorable and most reverend Sean "Jack" O'Lennox, the archbishop of Armagh, back into the fold, rather than allowing the Irish authorities and global media wolves to wail and gnash their collective incisors, along with their cameras and keyboards and flash drives and internet connections, on his sorry carcass.

Among other heinous deeds, Caeli's uncle was responsible for the murder of his longtime friend and church associate, the Rev. Monsignor Donald McBride. And yet, although church officials were cognizant of that horrendous crime and dozens more, they still took Uncle Jack in and placed him under their protective blanket in the notorious Secret Archives Building at the Vatican, where he was assigned to while away his days in peace and penance, doubtless told to account for his sins and misdeeds while sorting through mountains of paperwork that date back centuries.

Or so we initially were led to believe.

Somehow, at some point, all was not as it seemed and he slipped away just long enough to smuggle out the Yeats postcard, which he sent to Caeli. I retrieved it from the mailbox when it arrived days later and, rather than turning it immediately over to her, tried to determine whether Jack was, in fact, the miscreant of this latest endeavor, or whether it was all some sort of twisted joke, perpetrated on poor Caeli by a decidedly malevolent prankster … one other than her uncle, of course.

That question brought me to Roberto Fierro, the late Vinny Fierro's brother, a man we were previously unaware of despite our long association with Don Vincenzo and his son, Fredo.

I'd called Fredo when the postcard first arrived and asked if he could recommend anyone who understood the workings of the church in Rome. I was looking for an insider, someone privy to the Vatican's secrets. He told me to hang up, hang tight, and answer the phone when it rang again, which it did 20 minutes later.

Don Roberto, Freddy's uncle, and Vinny's younger brother as it turned out, was on the other end. I learned in time that he was a man who thoroughly understood the mysterious, secretive workings of the church … perhaps even better than the pope himself.

Yeah. It's who you know, all right.

So I laid it out for him during the phone call: the postcard, the context, the idea that the unsigned mailing may well have come from Caeli's uncle – even though Caeli's uncle, the one-time archbishop of Armagh, was supposedly dead, an event we'd witnessed as the guns were blasting away and the wind was howling and the birds, impervious and majestic, were soaring above the noise and chaos below.

"I can't prove it, but I suspect he's still alive and is being held at the Vatican – perhaps because he set this up as a fallback, or perhaps against his will," I told him. "I need to find out."

"Let me see what I can learn," he'd said and severed the connection.

The whole conversation didn't take but a couple of minutes, and most of that was me providing background … the same background I'm offering here.

He called again, long days later.

"He is under house arrest," Don Roberto said matter-of-factly.

"Son of a seagull," I muttered, and he laughed softly.

"This surprises you – even if you suspected it was true?"

"We saw him die," I said. "We were there. We watched it happen."

"Another reason, I think, to believe the *polizia* when they say even eyewitness accounts are notoriously … unreliable. Yes?"

"In this case, at least," I said.

He laughed again, heartily this time.

"I have been able to learn, through favors owed and others to be paid, this relative of your fiancée, Miss Caeli Brown, is restricted to the Vatican grounds, at least for now. But he is under constant … what is the word?"

He paused here, considering his options, and then said, "Yes, I have it. He is under constant surveillance from the pope's own *Guardia Svizzera,* along with that of another exceedingly powerful force at the Vatican, which has also taken an interest in your archbishop, it seems. At least two men are assigned permanently to watch over him, both in …"

I got the long pause again, and it dragged on for half a minute or more this time. I wasn't in a position to help or otherwise make a suggestion to allow him to move forward again because I wasn't certain where he was going.

"How good is your Italian, truly?" he asked at last.

"I can work my way around a menu all right," I said, choosing to be a bit more modest than was necessary.

"This is not my understanding, *Commendatore* Blake, but I appreciate your reluctance to … open up. Still, my command of your own language fails me this time. The Italian phrase is *poliziotto in borghese,*" he said.

"Yes. I understand," I said. "A plainclothes officer, sans the official uniform."

"Ah. *Si.* My English is mostly good, the product of a generally excellent education. But I sometimes pause over words that are not used often, or at least not by me," he said.

"I do the same in Italian," I said.

"So how did you know *borghese?*"

"That's me, more or less," I said, "although, to place a fine point on my current occupation, I'm actually a private detective in my spare time."

He mumbled in Italian.

"*Fin qui tutto bene, ma …*"

But he must have caught the language slip, so he tried again in English.

"Not to place too fine a point, to borrow your own phrase," he said, "but a private detective is a *investigatore privato* in Italian. It's not quite the same – you would agree?"

"*Si. Vero*. But it's also true that neither one, a plainclothes officer or me while I'm in my private detective job, wear a uniform, which was my point."

"*Molto bene*," he said. "*Capisco*. My brother spoke well of you, and often. I have heard of the arrangement he made with you and Miss Brown, to provide *consiglio* to young Fredo."

"Does that surprise you – or concern you, perhaps?" I asked.

At this stage, I knew precious little about the man, despite polite inquiries, and was fearful that close family ties might mean that bad blood would leak into Freddy's relationship with his uncle, who for all I knew had sought the role for himself.

Maybe Roberto already despises both Caeli and me, I thought. *Maybe I can't trust a thing he says.*

But he instantly put me at ease.

"Not worry," he said, adding quickly, "Did I say that correctly?"

"Almost," I said. "You either want 'Not to worry' or 'No worries.' Both forms are essentially the same thing. *Non c'e problema*."

"Yes, I see. *Molto interessante*. This is what happens when you grow old, as I have. My mind isn't what it once was, and my ..." – I got the pause again here – "... my aptitude for something new is also not what it once was."

He drew a deep breath before continuing.

"You have nothing to fear from me, my friend. Don Vincenzo and I were brothers, it's true. And although we were far different – or is it different by far? – with varying interests, we had much in common and remained generally close. But he was in Oregon, in exile, I like to think, and I was here, in *Roma*, tending to different parts of the same ship. From what I understand, Fredo is happy in America. I do not understand how or why that is so, but he assures me he is quite content, as did his father, many times through the years."

"Fredo is American through and through, Don Roberto," I said. "He doesn't think of himself as Italian, although I suspect he's proud of his heritage."

"Yes. I know," he said softly. "He even thinks in American … in English, I mean. But, as they say in your country, not to worry." He chuckled at that, an indication that his aptitude for learning wasn't so slow after all.

Then he added this:

"Just so you know, Professor Blake, I have spies everywhere, and I see everything – not just events inside the church."

"That's encouraging to know," I managed after a moment, wondering where he was going with the line … and why.

This time he laughed at my expense.

"Come now. It's not as bad as that." He mumbled some words in Italian that I didn't catch, despite the exceptional quality of the telephone connection, before adding, "Chief among my spies are two longtime *guardia del corpo* – men who protected Don Vincenzo and who now devote their lives to his son."

"Elmore and Leonard," I said.

"Yes, your adopted names for the pair, as I understand," he agreed. "I, of course, know them by their real names, along with their families and, in the case of Marcus, at least – Elmore to you – his place of worship and reading materials and a great deal more. His partner, the man you call Leonard, is a great deal harder to read, harder to know – especially from such a long distance. But I could tell you much about him as well, if you cared to know such things. I could even tell you his given name."

I was surprised at the admission and couldn't help myself from nudging him gently along.

"So you were snooping on Don Vincenzo through his bodyguards?" I said, striving for a lighthearted tone, although I'm sure that it sounded like a statement rather than a question to him.

But he laughed again, which came across as a soft tinkling on the line, seasoning added to a juicy steak.

"On my brother? Hardly, Professor Blake. You must watch too much American television or see too many of the British 007 spy movies. It was one of the kindnesses I paid to Vincenzo. There is a word in English explaining what I was doing, with my brother's consent, of course, but it escapes me. It means, let me see, in English …"

"Vetting," I suggested before he could get there.

"Yes. That is the precise word I was seeking. *Grazie*. It was one of the services I provided for my brother, and now for his son. I know all about you, of course … and about your fiancée, Miss Brown. Would you like me to take a moment and share? Your favorite wine, perhaps, or your fondness for fast American cars with far too much horsepower – you really should look more closely at Italian automobiles, you know – or your choice of German firearms, although why Americans insist on the use of firearms at all is a mystery to me, yes?"

"No need," I said, without bothering to provide an explanation to any of his observations. "But I am curious: Did you do this particular line of vetting for Don Vincenzo, or for Don Fredo?"

He laughed again, and I could visualize him waving the question off from thousands of miles away, even if I was unable at that point to attach a face to the voice.

"It is not important. Enough of this," he said easily. "You wanted to know about whether the man who sent Miss Brown the Irish postcard was in fact her late uncle. And I can tell you with full confidence, the man who was once the archbishop in the north of Ireland is as alive as either one of us. He mailed this most curious message to your home in Oregon precisely … would you care to know the exact date?"

I muttered another soft curse, and he again laughed gently.

"You have plans, no doubt, to … to do something with this knowledge, or perhaps about this knowledge," he said. "May I ask what it is?"

"Sure," I said. "Ask all you want. But at this stage, I have no idea what to do or even what say about it – not to Caeli, anyway, and especially not to you."

"You do not trust me?"

"I have no reason not to trust you," I said. "But your interests lie elsewhere. Beyond that, I don't know what to do with the information, if anything."

"Yes, I see. You are concerned your actions now could upset your Miss Brown. I share your unease, although … she also could find the truth by some other means and learn that you knew of the situation and chose not to share it. This would be another consideration for you … something to chew on, yes? But of course, I am overstepping my … what is the word?"

"Bounds, as a rule," I said, thinking to myself how much his voice and verbal intonations, and even his English lapses, reminded me of his brother. "Your assessment is correct. Still, I need time to process this, before I make a decision about what to do next."

"I understand," he said. "Should you need my assistance, on this matter or in anything I might do for you and your intended, or for the newly anointed heir, I would trust you to ask – no need to use Fredo as a broker."

Most excellent, I thought, though I'll confess here to not thoroughly thinking through the full ramifications of his offer.

As much as I'd enjoyed my friendship with Don Vincenzo, a man deemed by the FBI to be the *capo di tutti capi* of the entire western seaboard of the United States, I used to joke that it was good to have friends in low places.

But with Don Roberto, I figured, just the opposite was true –
or so I thought in that moment, anyway.

What I said to him was this:

"*Grazie mille, Don Roberto. Si è più gentile.*"

"*Non è niente,*" he said. "It is nothing."

We parted with an exchange of private telephone
numbers and a promise to remain in touch as needed. I knew
only, as I swiped the red button on my smart phone and the
clock started ticking as to what I'd decide to tell Caeli when
she got home, if anything at all, that I could take the matter
at hand in a dozen different directions, none of which would
be ideal.

Looking back, I simply wonder whether I should have
kept my big mouth shut entirely and destroyed the damn
postcard in the fires of hell itself.

Allow me to note one other point of interest before kicking
this portion of the story down the highway. During our
initial telephone conversation, Don Roberto mentioned that
in addition to the Swiss Guards, the elite force that protects
the pope, a second Vatican contingent, one he referred to as
powerful, had taken an interest in Caeli's uncle.

I only wish that I'd been paying greater attention at the
time.

Read More: **http://wbp.bz/wfmra**

MORE GREAT MYSTERY TITLES FROM WILDBLUE PRESS

Read more at: **http://wbp.bz/mystery**

NAKED ADDICTION by Caitlin Rother

"NAKED ADDICTION is a strong debut from a perceptive and unflinching writer. ... Detailed and tightly focused, the story unfolds on the sun-drenched but dangerous streets of San Diego."
–T. Jefferson Parker, NYT best-selling crime novelist.

wbp.bz/nakedaddictiona

HEADLOCK by Burl Barer

The updated edition of Burl Barer's classic mystery noir with a streak of insanity. A WildBlue Press Mystery Classic!
"Undeniable talent, pizazz and imagination"
— Jack Olsen, NYT best-selling author

wbp.bz/headlocka

PAPER WINGS by Les Abend

"Wow! ... Definitely an all-night pulse-pounder from a veteran airline captain who knows the ropes!" – John J. Nance, New York Times bestselling author of LOCKOUT

wbp.bz/paperwingsa

CREATED by Janice Boekhoff

"These weighty themes, which Boekhoff handles with skill, are much more than food for thought. They make for compelling reading." - Peter Eichstaedt, author of BORDERLAND and International Latino Book Award winner.

wbp.bz/createda

CREVICE by Janice Boekhoff

An intriguing and modern tale around the legend of the Lost Dutchman Mine. This debut novel has adventure, romance, and an insightful spiritual thread that readers will enjoy. - Marissa Shrock, author of THE FIRST PRINCIPLE and THE LIBERATION

wbp.bz/crevicea

www.ingramcontent.com/pod-product-compliance
Lightning Source LLC
Chambersburg PA
CBHW070813190726
48292CB00006B/1990